Colliers Cove

Also by the Author

Julie
A captivating novel with many twists and turns

With Rucksack and Bus Pass
Walking the Thames Path

Roots in Three Counties
Family history research

A Touch of Autumn Gold
A light-hearted insight into the older generation
and how they deal with life

The Golden Anklet
A love story set against family secrets and intrigue

Path of Injustice
The experiences of a young girl in the 18th century

Stranger from Berlin
A search behind the Iron Curtain

Colliers Cove

BEVERLEY HANSFORD

Copyright © 2023 Beverley Hansford

The moral right of the author has been asserted.

Apart from any fair dealing for the purposes of research or private study, or criticism or review, as permitted under the Copyright, Designs and Patents Act 1988, this publication may only be reproduced, stored or transmitted, in any form or by any means, with the prior permission in writing of the publishers, or in the case of reprographic reproduction in accordance with the terms of licences issued by the Copyright Licensing Agency. Enquiries concerning reproduction outside those terms should be sent to the publishers.

This is a work of fiction. Names, characters, businesses, places, events and incidents are either the products of the author's imagination or used in a fictitious manner. Any resemblance to actual persons, living or dead, or actual events is purely coincidental.

Matador
Unit E2 Airfield Business Park,
Harrison Road, Market Harborough,
Leicestershire. LE16 7UL
Tel: 0116 2792299
Email: books@troubador.co.uk
Web: www.troubador.co.uk/matador
Twitter: @matadorbooks

Edited by Helen Banks

ISBN 978 1805140 641

British Library Cataloguing in Publication Data.
A catalogue record for this book is available from the British Library.

Printed and bound in the UK by TJ Books Limited, Padstow, Cornwall
Typeset in 11pt Bembo by Troubador Publishing Ltd, Leicester, UK

Matador is an imprint of Troubador Publishing Ltd

MIX
Paper from
responsible sources
FSC FSC® C013056
www.fsc.org

To Rachel Barlow
For her enthusiasm and support

Chapter 1

Jacob MacGuff hesitated before turning into the driveway that led to the house. He had come this way quite often since the house had become unoccupied. It was a short cut to the beach where his dog Gyp loved to run wild.

This morning things were different. Usually he was the only person using the driveway, but today a car stood outside the house. It had passed him earlier on, with a man and a woman in it. He knew that, technically, walking on the property was trespassing, but after hesitating for a minute or so, he took comfort from the 'For Sale' notice that stood out boldly above one of the gate pillars. After all, he reasoned, he could be a potential buyer. On top of that, Gyp's tugging on the lead convinced him to continue on his walk.

It was strange, he thought. The house had been empty and for sale for the best part of two years. Nobody seemed to know what had happened to the two sisters who had previously owned it. Rumour had it that they had had to move away for some reason.

As he approached the house, he wondered who the car belonged to. Were the occupants the new owners of the property, or were they just prospective buyers? They were just emerging from the car as he drew near. He was surprised to see that they were not as old as he had thought from his first glimpse of them. Just youngsters, then, he thought. At his ripe old age of eighty-five, anyone under the age of thirty appeared to be a youngster to him. Scrutinising the couple, he guessed they were both still in their twenties. They glanced in his direction as they stood close to the open car doors, gazing at the house as if deciding where to proceed. He felt obliged to offer a greeting. He gave a cheerful 'Good morning.' Both of them replied, the woman even giving him a pleasant smile. At least they did not tell him off for trespassing, he thought.

As he and Gyp continued on their way, he wondered what business the two young people had with the house. Perhaps they were potential buyers after all.

His pondering became more complicated when he heard the man ask, 'Would you like me to come with you?'

The woman's answer was instantaneous. 'No, darling. Let me go on my own. I just want to look at everything again and then put things to bed and forget them.'

Jacob heard the man reply, 'OK, if you're sure. I'll wait in the car.'

The words set Jacob thinking again. What was it the woman wanted to do on her own, and what did she want to look at? It was an intriguing situation, but he guessed that was all he would ever learn about it. Led by Gyp, he hurried on his way down the track to the beach.

Jessica left the car and walked slowly towards the house. It looked lonely and forlorn now, but otherwise it was exactly as she remembered it. She stared through one of the now curtainless windows. This had been the sitting room, where she had often spent time in the evenings. The room was empty now, all the furniture removed, leaving in places patterns on the wall where it had stood. Satisfied with what she had seen, she wandered through a nearby wicket gate and along the path beside the house to another window. This had been the breakfast room. The sunlight was shining on the wall where the table had been, just as it had always done. She moved on and peered through another window. This had been the library, but now only empty shelves lined the walls. The room held unhappy memories, and she turned hurriedly away. She glanced at an upstairs window. This had been their bedroom. More unpleasant memories began to loom up and cloud her thinking. The recollections made her want to leave the house. She found her way to the broad track that eventually reached the beach. In the distance she could see the man with the dog whom she had greeted earlier.

It was a nice walk. It had been one of the pleasant surprises when she had first come to stay at the house, finding that there was a convenient and private access to the nearby beach. A few times she had walked along it wearing only her bikini and wrap – until life had changed for her.

She came upon the place suddenly. This was the spot where she had been discovered early one morning lying on the grass, almost naked, spots of rain falling on her body. She recalled the shock of waking up there, and the embarrassment of being found afterwards.

She hurried on, but it was not long before another painful memory came to her. A large oak tree spread its branches above the track. Here she had been found asleep beneath the tree, a rope noose around her neck. Another episode in her descent into hell. After that it had all been downhill for her. Nobody listened to her or believed her any more.

She was glad to leave the spot. It was something else to try and forget. She knew it was not going to be easy to put behind her what had happened. Coming here with Graham had been part of the process. As soon as she realised that their trip would bring them close to the area, she made up her mind to visit the house and its surroundings. Graham had not wanted her to come, but she had insisted. She wanted to see the place again and face her memories, unpleasant as they were.

She let the more recent recollection go and walked on, a little faster now, eager to finish her quest. In two minutes she had reached her destination. Here she paused again. Rough steps carved into the cliff face led down to the beach several hundred feet below. She could see the man down there, the dog now rushing madly back and forth barking.

Jessica had no inclination to join them. Or even walk along the path to her left. This would lead to the high point of the cliff, where the final dreadful incident had taken place. The beach also held painful memories. She had seen enough. She sat down on the rough seat that had been constructed close by. It was time to reflect, to put things in order and then do her best to forget.

How had it all begun? she pondered. Just over two years previously, when she was a bride of three months, Neil had proposed that they visit his sisters. He had described the house they lived in and its location close to the sea. She had looked forward to the visit with enthusiasm, eager to explore more of her new life. It was also an opportunity to get over losing her job so suddenly. Neil had suggested that she take some time off and have a rest before looking for another job, and the idea had appealed to her.

Laura and Sophie had welcomed her with open arms, almost as if she had been a long-lost sister. Even Mrs Benton, the housekeeper, had spoilt her. She and Neil had not been there long when Neil had had to leave on business. 'Stay here and relax and enjoy yourself,' he had said, and urged by his sisters she had willingly agreed.

It was after Neil left that life had changed for her. Strange things had started to happen that she could not explain. Everything had come to a head when she had been dragged screaming from the house in her nightgown by the man and woman in white. She had been labelled a violent patient.

Jessica did not need to test her memory any further. Everything after that was quite clear. It was now time to call it a day. Remembering that Graham was waiting patiently for her, she stood up, and with a last look at the beach she started to make her way back to the car – and to him.

Chapter 2

The day started much the same as every other working day. Jessica got up when the alarm announced seven-thirty, and then after that it was a quick shower and a leisurely breakfast listening to the news on the radio as she contemplated the day ahead of her. She had worked for the same company for the last five years, a finance house in the City. After leaving university she had had several odd jobs and she considered herself fortunate to secure her present position. She had continued working there even after her brief marriage to Graham had ended. The flat she now occupied had been the one she and Graham had shared. Situated in Ealing, it had been convenient for Graham's job in Westminster as well as hers.

It was close to half past eight when she left the flat. As she made her way to the front door, she encountered her neighbour Gwen, a middle-aged woman who lived in the flat below hers and was also leaving for work. When Jessica was looking for accommodation, she had worked briefly with Gwen, whose brother had been in the process of converting the semi-detached house where they both lived into two spacious flats. She had been over the moon when they offered her the upstairs one. Gwen was anxious to have somebody she knew occupying the top flat. Her own flat had access to the garden, which she tended in her spare time.

'Good morning, Jessica,' she said.

'Good morning, Gwen.'

'I hope it's not going to rain this morning. I got soaked yesterday,' Gwen commented.

'The forecast is that it will be fine today,' Jessica responded cheerfully.

'Thank goodness,' replied Gwen. 'Oh, we've got some post!' She was already bending down to retrieve the letters lying on the mat. 'One for you and two for me.' She handed one of them to Jessica.

Jessica glanced at the official-looking envelope and dropped it into her shoulder bag. She would read it later at work.

The two women left the house, and Gwen closed the door behind them. They shared the five-minute walk to the end of the road and then parted, Gwen heading for her local job, and Jessica to the tube station.

It was just after nine when Jessica walked into the offices of Larker Financial Services. Several other staff members were making for the lift and she joined them, returning their morning greetings. They took the lift to the fourth floor and separated to go to their various departments. The office where Jessica worked was a big one, with over twenty desks down each side. It was light and airy and it overlooked part of the City. Exchanging pleasantries with colleagues who were already at their desks, she made for her own, the last of a row, with windows on both sides, and turned on her computer. A glance at her diary confirmed that she had a meeting at ten-thirty. She sighed slightly. Meetings tended to go on a bit and delay her routine work.

It was not until her coffee break that her thoughts turned to the letter. She pulled it out of her bag and studied the envelope. It was a quality product and was addressed to Miss Jessica Walker. Intrigued, she carefully opened the flap with her nail file. The envelope contained a letter printed on heavy paper and had come from a firm of solicitors named Dinton, Walley & Dinton.

Dear Miss Walker,

I am writing to advise you that we are acting for the estate of the late Edward Walker.

I understand that you are a relative of the deceased, and I request that you contact our office at your earliest convenience to arrange a meeting.

Please note that it will be necessary for you to produce proof of your identity, such as a birth certificate or a current passport.

I look forward to hearing from you.

The letter was signed by Frank Dinton.

Jessica put the letter down. 'Gosh!' she exclaimed.

'What's the matter?' The question came from her colleague Mary, who was sitting in the canteen with her.

Mary's voice brought Jessica back to the present. 'I've had a letter from a solicitor. They want to see me,' she explained.

'Perhaps you've been left a fortune,' Mary joked.

Jessica laughed. 'Chance would be a fine thing,' she responded, making a face.

It was well after six in the evening when Jessica arrived home. She entered the house and quietly made her way upstairs. She could hear the sound of a radio emanating from Gwen's flat.

Once in her flat, she turned on the light and quietly closed the front door. As it was November, it was already quite dark both outside and in. Her first job was to kick off her shoes and enjoy the instant relief. She wandered into the tiny kitchen, wondering what to have to eat. She was not particularly hungry. Beans on toast seemed to be a quick solution. She turned on the radio to listen to some music while she prepared the food and ate it sitting at the kitchen table. It was a habit she had got into when dining alone.

After finishing her spartan meal, she made herself a mug of tea and carried it into the lounge, seeking the comfort of her settee. She liked her little flat. After she and Graham married, they had continued living there, planning one day to buy a house. Their marriage had lasted only just over two years. She had met him shortly after coming to work in London. They had been gloriously happy at first, but gradually they had drifted apart. Perhaps Graham's government job, which had taken him abroad quite often and away from her, had had something to do with it. They had divorced amicably and remained good friends. From time to time he would ring her up and ask how she was. She knew that if she ever needed advice about anything, he would always be there for her.

Sipping her tea, she read through the letter from the solicitor again. It was odd, because she had never heard of an Edward Walker. She wondered how they had managed to find out her address. And what was the letter all about? Was Mary right? Had she been left some money? No doubt she would find out soon enough. She had managed to telephone the solicitors that afternoon to make the required appointment. A pleasant receptionist had informed her that she could see Mr Dinton at 10'o clock the following day. Jessica had accepted the offer. She was on flexi time at work, had no meetings scheduled for that day and could come to the office late and work a bit later in the evening to make up her hours.

It was the muffled sound of her mobile phone, which was still in her work bag, that alerted her from her musing. She rushed to see who was calling before it stopped ringing. It was her best friend.

Quickly she clicked to answer. 'Hello, Babs.'
'Hello, Jessica. How are you?'
'I'm fine. How about you?'
'Great. How's work going now?'
'Fine. We've just been taken over by a bigger financial group, but there have been no drastic changes so far. How about you? What are you up to?'

'Terrific – I've just got a contract to write a new program for quite a big company, Grantham's. Do you know them?'

'I've heard of them. Good for you!' Babs was a freelance computer programmer who worked from home.

Babs changed the subject. 'What are you doing with yourself in your spare time these days?'

Jessica gave a little laugh. 'Not a lot. Come home in the evening, cook a meal and then perhaps listen to some music or read a book.'

'Sounds as if your social life is a bit dull. You need to get out more. Find yourself another man.'

Jessica smiled to herself. 'It'll happen one day,' she replied breezily.

'Do you still miss Graham?'

Jessica gave a quick answer, hoping that Babs would stop asking about him. 'Of course I miss him, but it was one of those things that just had to be.'

Even though some time had elapsed since the divorce, she still found it difficult to talk about it. Fortunately Babs appeared to get the message.

'OK, but don't leave it too late to get hitched again.'

Before Jessica could answer, Babs asked, 'What are you doing for Christmas?'

'Gosh. Christmas. I hadn't thought about it.'

'It's only four weeks away.' There was a slight pause. 'Look, if you've not got anything planned, why don't you come and stay with me? We would be just two girls together. We can cook a meal, go for a walk…'

It took a few seconds for Jessica to absorb her friend's offer. She hesitated. 'Well, if it would be all right, I'd love to.'

'Of course it'll be all right! That's settled, then. Come over on Christmas Eve.'

Jessica was beginning to feel enthusiastic. 'That would be great. I'm not working that day. What can I bring?'

'Just you… and perhaps a bottle of wine.'
'I'll do that, and I'll look forward to spending time with you.'
'Super. Same here. Must go now. I've suddenly remembered that I promised I'd ring a prospective client this evening. I just wanted to catch up with you and ask you about Christmas.'
'Yes, of course. Don't miss your client.'
'I won't, but bye for now.'
'Bye, Babs. Thanks for the call.'

Jessica put her mobile down beside her on the settee. Good old Babs, she thought, to think about her at Christmas. They had been at university together, and after they graduated they had gone their separate ways, only to find themselves later both working in London. Since then they had kept in touch with each other. Jessica picked up her tea. One sip told her it was cold. She made a face and put the mug down. Her attention turned again to the solicitor's letter, which she had abandoned on the floor when the phone rang. She picked it up and studied it again. It held more questions than answers. Musing over it suddenly made her remember that she had omitted to mention it to Babs. Still, she didn't know much at this stage. Hopefully tomorrow she would know more.

Chapter 3

It was a bright, sunny morning when Jessica with her trusty A to Z street map sought out the offices of Dinton, Walley & Dinton. She was surprised that they were housed in a modern office block. She had expected them to be in a large Victorian building.

It was just five minutes to ten when she pressed the security bell at the entrance to the block. A pleasant voice answered immediately. Jessica replied that she had an appointment with Frank Dinton and was given access to the building. The revolving door opened up into an airy entrance hall with a plush reception desk. A middle-aged woman sitting behind the desk asked if she could help. Jessica once again related her mission and was invited to take a seat. She had been waiting for no more than a few minutes when the receptionist called her over.

'Miss Walker, please take the lift to the third floor. Mr Dinton will see you in room 307.'

Jessica thanked her and made her way to the lift, which was close by. Arriving on the third floor, she found herself in a corridor with a number of doors opening off it. She walked along it, counting the numbers as she passed. When she reached number 307 she knocked gently on the door. After a few moments a voice bade her enter.

She found herself in a light-filled office. A large desk was the main feature, together with numerous chairs and several filing cabinets. A grey-haired man rose from the chair behind the desk. He held out his hand as he greeted her.

'Miss Walker, please sit down. I'm Frank Dinton.'

Jessica shook hands with him and selected one of the chairs in front of the desk.

Her host regarded her for a second. 'Thank you for coming in. You must be wondering what this is all about.'

'I'm quite intrigued. Can you tell me more?'

'Yes, of course.' He hesitated for an instant, glancing down at the papers on his desk, and then asked, 'Did you bring any form of identification?'

Jessica responded quickly. 'Yes. I've got my birth certificate and my passport. Oh, and my driving licence.' She retrieved them from her bag and placed them on the desk.

He smiled. 'I'm sure they'll do nicely. He picked up her birth certificate and studied it briefly, followed by her passport, and then replaced the two documents on the desk. 'That's fine. May I take copies of these for our records?'

'Yes, of course.'

He pressed a button on his desk and almost immediately a young woman entered the room.

'One copy of each, please,' he requested, holding up Jessica's birth certificate and passport.

The woman took the documents and disappeared. Mr Dinton turned his attention to Jessica. He smiled again. 'Now we can get down to the important agenda.' He glanced at the papers on his desk. 'How well did you know your uncle Edward Walker?'

'I'd never heard of him until I got your letter.'

'He was your father's younger brother,' Mr Dinton replied, looking at Jessica quizzically.

Jessica realised that she would have to explain. 'Our family was not particularly close. My parents divorced when I was eighteen and I think my father went to Canada. I never saw him again. My mother married again while I was at university. I never knew my paternal grandparents and I never heard any mention of my father having a brother.'

Mr Dinton nodded. 'It does happen. Actually, your uncle Edward went to Australia when he was a young man.'

Jessica was silent, absorbing the information she had just received.

Mr Dinton continued. 'He did quite well for himself in Australia, it seems. He must have known about you, because he appears to have left the proceeds of his entire estate to you.'

'Me?' Jessica was shocked.

'Do you have any brother or sisters?'

Jessica shook her head. 'I was an only child.'

Mr Dinton nodded. 'That is my understanding as well.'

Jessica wondered how he knew, but she made no comment. She was curious now to learn more about her uncle. 'You said my uncle did rather well for himself in Australia. In what way?' she asked.

Mr Dinton consulted the papers on his desk. 'It seems he made some very good investments. He even owned a gold mine.'

'A gold mine?' Jessica was aghast.

Mr Dinton smiled at her reaction. 'Your uncle's investments were quite extensive.'

Jessica was still struggling to comprehend what she had just heard. Her thoughts prompted another question. 'You say I'm the only person mentioned to receive a legacy?'

He nodded. 'That is so. You are the only beneficiary.'

'It's so odd,' she commented, almost to herself. 'I never knew him. I've never even met him. I didn't even know he existed.'

After another glance at the papers in front of him, the solicitor continued. 'From the information I have to hand, it would appear that your uncle never married and had no family to leave his wealth to.'

The word 'wealth' made Jessica ask another question. 'Would it be rude to ask how much my uncle left me?'

He responded immediately. 'Oh, I do apologise. Of course it wouldn't be. That's why you're here.' Yet again he consulted the documents. It was a couple of seconds before he answered Jessica's question. When he did it was with carefully chosen words. He cleared his throat and began. 'You must understand that we are liaising with legal authorities in Australia and a final figure has not been agreed. Assets will have to be disposed of and of course some tax will be involved.'

He paused for a second and looked at her, as if to ensure that he had her full attention. 'At the last calculation of your uncle's wealth a few years ago, it stood at about fourteen million pounds, using the exchange rate at that time.'

The information struck Jessica dumb for a few seconds. Surely she had misheard. The figure couldn't be millions. It must be thousands. She stammered a reply. 'I... I'm sorry, but did you say fourteen million?'

The solicitor smiled. 'Yes, I did.'

Jessica was still feeling overwhelmed. It was out of this world to comprehend so much money. She had never dreamed of owning such wealth. She would have considered herself fortunate if she had been left a couple of thousand. A sum of millions was too much to even think about at this stage.

Mr Dinton had been studying her intently. He seemed to guess what she was thinking. He voiced her thoughts. 'Of course, such a sum needs quite a lot of adjusting to. There are many issues to consider.'

Jessica nodded. She replied slowly, 'It's just that I've never envisaged being so wealthy. It's quite beyond my thinking.'

He smiled again. 'Of course. There is another factor to consider, though. The figure I quoted is now some years old, and the current one could be in excess of that – or it could be less. It would also be subject to inheritance tax, but you could still become a very wealthy woman. I will advise you in due course what the final amount will be. '

'Yes, I quite understand that.'

He nodded. 'Are there any questions you would like to ask at this stage?'

She shook her head. 'No, I don't think so. I'll wait until you know more.'

'Of course. Now that I have had this discussion with you, I will contact my Australian counterpart, and as soon as I have more details I will be in touch. May we have a telephone number where we can contact you?'

'Yes, of course.' Jessica dived into her bag for one of her cards. She handed it to him.

He studied it briefly, thanked her and then stood up. Clearly the interview was over. Jessica took the hint, rose from her seat and grasped the hand he offered.

'Thank you for coming in, Miss Walker. We will contact you again as soon as we have more information.'

'Thank you. I'll look forward to that.'

She quietly left the office and made her way down to the reception area. The receptionist glanced up and wished her goodbye. Jessica replied to the gesture and made her way through the revolving doors to the outside.

As she walked down the street, thoughts and questions flooded into her brain. Less than an hour ago she had entered the solicitor's office wondering why she had been called in. It had occurred to her that perhaps somehow she had been left some money. Perhaps a couple of hundred pounds – but now she had been told it could be millions. How did one deal with such an amount? Every day she handled money as part of her job, but it was always someone else's money. Now she would have to do the same for herself.

Logic gradually returned to her thinking. What to do with the money was something to consider when she had actually received it. Didn't the solicitor point out that the final figure was somewhat vague at this stage? No, the best thing was to just carry on with life and wait to hear from him. Thinking again of the solicitor made her recall that she had intended to ask him how he had found out her address. That was a bit of a mystery. During the interview she had completely forgotten. Now she kicked herself for not remembering. For the time being, it would have to remain an unanswered question.

Chapter 4

For the rest of the day, Jessica managed to dismiss from her thoughts her visit to Dinton, Walley & Dinton. The situation was greatly helped by the fact that when she arrived back at her desk around late morning several new jobs were awaiting her attention. It looked as if the extra hour she had decided to work that day would be a necessity. Only once was she reminded of the earlier events of the morning, and that was when she bumped into Mary during her lunch break.

'How did you get on?' Mary asked.

'Oh, well, I might be left a bit of money eventually.'

This appeared to satisfy Mary, much to Jessica's relief. At this stage she did not want to openly discuss her apparently new status.

It was well past her normal coming-home time when she eventually fitted her key into the lock and pushed the front door open. She was surprised to find Gwen standing in the hall, dressed to go out.

'Oh, Jessica, I'm glad I caught you. Your phone's been ringing quite a lot for the last hour.'

'Oh! Thank you for telling me. I can't think who that could be.'

'I expect they'll try again. Have a nice evening.' Gwen was about to go out through the door when she turned suddenly to Jessica. 'By the way, there's some post for you.'

With that, she departed, slamming the front door behind her. Jessica's reply of 'Thanks' was lost.

Jessica grabbed the small collection of envelopes Gwen had carefully arranged on the hall table and made her way upstairs to her flat. There was the usual routine of kicking off her shoes, and then she went into the kitchen. Dumping the envelopes on the table, she made her way to the bathroom. Five minutes later she was back in the kitchen considering what to eat. She looked in the food cupboard, but this gave her no inspiration. In the end she decided on the convenience of a boiled egg. She had just placed the egg in a saucepan when she heard the shrill ringing of the phone in the sitting room. She rushed in, grabbed the handset and collapsed on the settee.

'Oh, you're there. I've been ringing for ages. And your mobile was off.'

Jessica had turned off her mobile phone just before entering Mr Dinton's office, and she now realised that she had forgotten to turn it on again afterwards. She recognised the voice immediately. It was Natalie. Despite Jessica's divorce from her brother, she still kept in touch.

'Oh, Natalie, I'm sorry you had problems. I was working late today and I only just got back.'

'You must be keen!'

Jessica laughed. 'Not really. It's just that I took some time off this morning and decided to make it up this evening.'

This clearly stirred Natalie's curiosity. 'So, what exotic pleasure were you up to this morning?'

'Nothing very exciting. I had to go to a solicitor.'

'A solicitor? Why?'

Jessica hesitated. Should she tell Natalie? Maybe she should keep it to herself, at least for the time being. Then she relented. There was no real reason why Natalie should not know, provided that she kept everything confidential. She replied in a low-key way. 'Well, it appears that some uncle I never knew has died and left me some money. At present I don't know how much. It could be a lot, or it could be very little.'

'Why don't you know how much it is?'

'He lived in Australia,' Jessica replied simply.

Natalie said nothing, appearing to be satisfied with this answer.

It was Jessica who spoke again next. 'What puzzles me is how the solicitors here in London managed to locate me. Even the address was correct.'

There was a pause at the other end. Then Natalie spoke quietly. 'I think I know.'

'You know? How?'

'Graham told me.'

'Graham?' Jessica was astounded. How was Graham, her ex-husband, involved with her visit to Dinton, Walley & Dinton?

Natalie started to explain. 'Graham saw a solicitors' advert in one of the newspapers seeking the whereabouts of a Jessica Walker. Obviously he knew a Jessica Walker, so he contacted them. He told me about it just before he dashed off on holiday last week. I'm sorry. I should have told you. Graham asked me to, but I've been so busy recently.'

Jessica could sense that Natalie was a bit concerned. She hastened to rectify things. 'It's all right, really. It was very sweet of you both to act on my behalf.'

'Well, now you know.'

Before Jessica could respond, Natalie spoke again. 'You know, Graham is still very fond of you.'

'Perhaps. But he should move on. Things didn't really work out for us.' Jessica seemed to be thinking aloud.

'What was the real problem between you two? You appeared to have so much going for your marriage.'

Jessica found this a difficult question to answer. She took her time forming a reply. 'I'm not sure really. Perhaps we grew apart because he was away on business so much.' She lightened the tone. 'It's nice to have somebody to snuggle up to on a cold night.'

There was a chuckle at the other end of the phone. 'I guess you're right,' came from Natalie.

'Anyway,' she added, quite breezily, 'I wanted to ask you something. That's why I rang you.'

'I'm all ears.'

'What are you doing on Saturday evening?'

Jessica thought for a second. 'Nothing, really.'

'Good. You must come to my party.'

The invitation caught Jessica unprepared. She hesitated. Natalie had never invited her to a party before.

Before she could formulate a polite refusal Natalie spoke again. 'Do come. You'll love it. There will be lots of nice people there.'

'Where will it be?' Jessica asked, undecided.

'At my house, of course.' Natalie lived in Islington. Jessica had been there before with Graham.

Jessica struggled to make up her mind.

Natalie wasn't going to give up. 'Do say you'll come. We haven't seen each other for ages.'

It was the turning point. Jessica made up her mind. 'OK. What time?'

'About half past seven?'

'That'll be fine, but I won't stay late, and I'll have to get a mini-cab home.'

'That's super. See you then.'

They chatted for a bit longer, and then Natalie said she had to go. Jessica put the phone down, wondering vaguely if she had done the right thing, but it was too late now. Well, she had already made it clear that she would not stay very late.

She suddenly remembered that she had been in the middle of making something to eat when Natalie had phoned. Now her hunger was reminding her of the unfinished task. She wandered back into the kitchen. Setting the single egg to boil, she sat down at the table. Her attention focused on the post she had abandoned earlier. Two bills, and a postcard from a former colleague on holiday in America. The fourth item was a official-looking envelope addressed to Mr G. Scott. She studied it for a few seconds. It was unusual for her to receive any mail for Graham after all this time. The big problem for her was to redirect it, because she knew he was in the process of moving to a new apartment and she was not sure if he was still at his old address. Inspiration came while the egg cooked. Of course! It was simple: she would take it with her to Natalie's party. Natalie must know where her own brother was. It was a bit of luck that she had decided to accept the invitation after all.

Chapter 5

Saturday did not begin well for Jessica. She followed her usual routine of going to the hairdresser's early, followed by her weekly shop. As she was leaving the supermarket it started to rain. In desperation she took a taxi home, determined not to get wet.

Once back, she brewed up a coffee before starting the next weekly job of cleaning her flat, which she liked to do barefoot. While she was tidying the kitchen she dropped a sharp knife. She let out an 'Ow!' as it hit her foot. She stooped to pick it up and watched in horror as a spot of blood started to appear. She hopped to the first aid cabinet and dabbed some antiseptic on the wound. It still bled a little, though she was relieved to see that it was not a deep cut. She put a plaster on it, hoping that the bleeding would stop, and then carried on with her cleaning.

It was late afternoon when she turned her attention to the evening ahead. First was the question of what to wear. She opened her wardrobe and looked at one dress after another before deciding on a nice green long-sleeved, vee-neck number, but it badly needed the attention of an iron to make it acceptable to wear. Another job to do.

Completing her outfit presented another problem. It was now raining quite steadily, so some adjustments were required. First it meant wearing a raincoat and using an umbrella. The dress she had selected was knee length, so a raincoat would keep that dry, but the biggest problem was shoes. The sandals she wanted to wear with the dress were quite open. She did not want to arrive at Natalie's with wet feet, so she would have to wear her boots and change into the sandals when she got there. On top of everything else was the damage to her foot. When she took off the plaster the bleeding had stopped, but the tiny cut showed up quite well. The only solution was to cover it with another plaster.

When she left the house, she was pleased to find that the rain had eased off a little. She managed to make it to the station without getting too wet. It was the same at the other end. Though it was wet underfoot, the umbrella shielded her from the worst of the weather.

Arriving at Natalie's Victorian semi-detached house, she was surprised to see that nearly every window was completely lit up. She did not know a great deal about Natalie's working life, other than that she was a solicitor in a practice somewhere in London. She could remember her moving into the house three or four years previously.

She climbed the few steps to the front door and rang the bell. Nothing happened for several minutes, so she rang it again.

Almost immediately Natalie opened the door. 'Darling, I'm so glad you were able to come. Let me take your coat.'

Jessica gladly handed over her raincoat and sat down on a convenient chair to change her shoes.

Natalie immediately spotted the plaster on her foot. 'What have you done?'

Jessica made a face. 'A slight problem with a knife, but it's only a small cut.'

'Oh, poor you. Are you sure it's all right?'

'It'll be fine,' Jessica stressed.

Natalie was not convinced. 'Look, there's a doctor here amongst the guests. Would you like him to have a quick look at it?'

The suggestion alarmed Jessica. 'Heavens, no. It's all right, really.'

Natalie appeared to be satisfied, which was a relief for Jessica. The last thing she wanted was to be made the centre of attention over a minor cut.

As soon as Jessica had finished putting on her sandals, Natalie took over. Pushing a drink into Jessica's hand, she led her around and introduced her to many of the other guests. There must have been at least twenty-five people present, spread out into several rooms and the kitchen. Jessica found it quite exhausting meeting so many new people and soon forgot most of their names.

When at last the food was served she joined the crowd at the buffet table, put a few dainty morsels on a plate and retreated into one of the other rooms, which was quieter. A picture hanging on the wall attracted her attention. As she stood there looking at it she heard a voice behind her.

'It's rather nice, isn't it?'

She turned to see who had spoken. A rather pleasant-looking man was smiling at her.

'Yes, it is. I rather like it,' she replied.

'Are you into art?' he asked.

Jessica shook her head. 'Not at all, but I've been looking for a painting like this to hang on a blank wall in my flat.'

'A sort of modern Constable?'

Jessica grinned at the description. 'Yes, something like that.'

He glanced at her glass, which was now practically empty. 'Can I get you another drink?'

Jessica hesitated. She did not usually have more than one, but perhaps tonight…

She held out her glass. 'A gin and tonic would be nice, but lots of tonic.'

'Will do.' He took her glass. 'Oh, I'm Neil Atkins.'

Jessica smiled. 'I'm Jessica Walker.' Natalie had not introduced them.

Neil smiled again. 'Pleased to meet you, Jessica. I'll be back in a jiffy.'

He turned to leave the room and then stopped and faced her again. 'Can I get you something more to eat?'

'No, thank you.' She still had half a smoked salmon sandwich on her plate.

He nodded. 'OK.'

Jessica watched him disappear. He was quite handsome, she thought. On closer observation, she guessed he was slightly older than he had at first seemed. Certainly a few years older than her ripe old age of twenty-seven.

While she was waiting she sat down on a nearby settee. After a few minutes he reappeared holding two glasses.

He smiled at her. 'There's trifle on the menu now.'

Jessica didn't know whether it was a statement or a suggestion, but she shook her head. 'Not for me.'

Neil nodded. 'May I?' he asked, indicating the place next to her.

'Of course.' She moved over to make room for him.

He handed her the drink and sat down beside her. He took a sip from his own glass and looked at her. 'What do you do to earn a crust? I mean, what do you do for a living?' he asked.

'Oh, I work in the City for a financial house.'

'That's interesting. Which one?'

'Larker Financial. Do you know them?'

'I seem to have come across the name somewhere.'

'We're not very big, but we were taken over several months ago.' She was growing curious about her new companion. 'What about you? What do you do?'

'I'm a freelance adviser. My clients are companies that want to expand their business opportunities.'

'Does that involve a lot of travel?'

'Not really. I'm based in the UK, but I go to Paris quite frequently for one company.'

'It sounds very interesting.'

He suddenly asked, 'Are you married?'

She shook her head. 'I was married, but we divorced two years ago.' She added hurriedly, 'It was all quite amicable. We're still good friends.'

'It's nice when it's like that.'

'How about you?' she asked. 'Are you married?'

He laughed. 'Me? No. Thirty-four and still on the shelf.'

'Perhaps you don't try hard enough.'

He chuckled. 'You could be right.' He changed the subject. 'What do you do in your spare time?' he asked, adding with a smile, 'You look as if you might be quite sporty.'

Jessica laughed. 'I go walking or jogging now and then and occasionally visit the swimming pool, but that's about it. What about you?'

'I play squash and table tennis,' he replied. 'I also go to the gym regularly.'

They chatted on, asking each other questions, seemingly quite relaxed together. During a slight lull in their conversation, Neil came up with a suggestion. 'I've been thinking. You've been looking for a painting. I might be able to help. I know somebody who has a gallery. He deals in the type of painting you're interested in. I'd be happy to contact him on your behalf and make an enquiry.'

Jessica thought for a second or two. Neil's offer interested her, but she was a bit reluctant to become too enthusiastic until she had seen the gallery. She argued with herself and then common sense told her that the offer placed her under no obligation. She formulated a suitable reply. 'Well, I don't want to put you to a lot of trouble. I'd also want to see what's available before making a decision.'

'Yes, of course. That's quite understood. There's no obligation to buy if you don't see something that appeals to you.' Before Jessica could say anything, he spoke again. 'Why don't you give me your phone number, and as soon as I've spoken to Arnold, who runs the gallery, I'll give you a ring.'

'All right.' She took out her mobile phone and extracted a card from one of the pockets inside the wallet. She carried several copies of three cards with her. One was her business card, and another showed her full name, address and telephone number. The third just bore her telephone numbers, and it was one of these that she handed to Neil. 'It would be best if you gave me a ring in the evening. When I'm at work, you most likely won't get hold of me.'

'I'll do that. What time do you normally get home?'

She thought for a second. 'Around six usually, but it would be best if you made it after half past, just to be sure.'

'That's fine.'

They were interrupted by the sudden appearance of Natalie.

'So that's where you two are! What have you been up to?'

'We've been talking,' Jessica explained.

Natalie seemed exuberant. 'Well, I want you in the other room now. I've got some entertainment for you.'

They obediently followed her into the next room, which was crowded with people. The entertainment turned out to be a young woman with a guitar who sang popular songs, much to the delight of the audience, who applauded enthusiastically. This was followed by more food and drink.

It was almost eleven when Jessica decided to call it a day. She phoned for a mini-cab and when it arrived she said her goodbyes.

Neil's parting words were, 'I'll be in touch.'

It was close to midnight when Jessica arrived home, tired but glad she had gone to Natalie's party. It had been a rare evening out, and meeting Neil had been interesting. As she tucked herself up in bed, she wondered if he would keep his word.

Chapter 6

On the following Monday Jessica's telephone rang while she was preparing her evening meal. She rushed to answer it, expecting it to be Neil.

She was wrong. It was Natalie.

'Darling, you got home all right?'

'Yes, of course.'

'You disappeared early.'

'Not really. It was almost midnight when I got back.'

Jessica heard a giggle at the other end. 'Some people stayed until two in the morning. I didn't get to bed till four.'

'Who did the clearing up?'

'Don't ask. I spent all yesterday on it. I'm just about straight again now, and I'm exhausted.'

Jessica laughed. 'Well done.'

'You made quite an impression on Neil. What did you do to him? Charm him? He asked a lot of questions about you.'

Jessica chuckled. 'I hope you only told him the nice things.'

'Of course I did. If you're no longer interested in Graham, it's time you found yourself another man.'

'I'm quite happy as I am at the moment,' Jessica retorted. 'Anyway, what about you? You're someone to talk.'

She had never quite figured out Natalie's relationship to men. At one stage she had wondered if Natalie was more attracted to her own sex. That thought had taken a back seat when Natalie took up with several men one after the other. All had been notably younger than her. Jessica knew that Natalie was in her mid-thirties. Even Graham had been unable to throw any light on the subject.

On this occasion, Natalie was once again not giving anything away. 'Me? I have a very good sex life, thank you.'

'Good for you,' Jessica responded breezily.

It was Natalie who brought the conversation to a halt. 'Anyway, I just wanted to know that you got home all right and tell you about Neil.'

'Thank you very much,' Jessica replied with a laugh.

'Bye for now. Don't do anything I wouldn't do,' Natalie joked.

'That gives me plenty of scope,' Jessica quipped.

Natalie finished the call. 'Got to go now. I've got a few other people to ring.'

'Good luck.'

'Bye.'

With that the line went dead.

Jessica replaced the handset and wandered back into the kitchen. She was curious to know why, according to Natalie, Neil had been so interested in her. It brought her back to wondering if he would contact her again.

Later that evening, when she was relaxing with a mug of tea, the telephone rang again. She grabbed it from the nearby table. 'Hello.'

'Hello. Neil Atkins here. How are you?'

'I'm fine, and you?'

'Great. I'm ringing as promised. I've been in touch with Arnold at the art gallery. I think we're in luck. He's just taken into stock a few paintings he thinks might be of interest to you.'

Jessica could not help feeling a bit excited. 'When can I go and see them?' she asked.

'The gallery's in Windsor. I could take you there if it's of any help. I live in that direction.'

Jessica thought for a second. She did not want to travel in a car with a stranger, but reason told her that Neil was not exactly a stranger, and in any case Natalie knew him.

Before she could reply he asked, 'Whereabouts do you live?'

'Near Ealing tube station.'

'I know it. I could pick you up there.'

The suggestion appealed to Jessica. She responded eagerly. 'That would be fine. When, and what time?'

There was a slight pause before Neil answered. 'How about Saturday morning – say, ten o'clock?'

Jessica hesitated. She would have to alter her usual Saturday arrangements slightly, but it was an opportunity she could not miss. 'Yes, that would work for me,' she replied.

'Good. That's settled, then. I'll see you at ten on Saturday outside Ealing station. I'll phone Arnold and tell him we're coming. He doesn't normally open until midday in winter.'

'I'll look forward to it.'

'Me too. Bye for now.'

'Bye.' There was a click at the other end almost before Jessica had finished speaking.

She put the phone down, picked up her unfinished mug of tea and relaxed back onto the settee. She was pleased that Neil had rung. Somehow she felt that she wanted to see him again, and the thought that she might at last obtain the painting she had long planned to have was satisfying.

Saturday morning proved to be a bit of a rush around. Normally Jessica went to the hairdresser at nine o'clock, but Madge, who had been doing her hair for a long time, offered to come in at eight to accommodate her. After that it was a dash to the supermarket and back home. She had a quick cup of coffee while she put the shopping away, followed by a move to her bedroom to decide what to wear. After changing her mind several times, she eventually put on one of her work suits. After all, she decided, it was not a pleasure trip as such, but more a business excursion.

It was well past half past nine when at last she slipped on her everyday high heels, grabbed her bag and was off.

She reached the station a good five minutes early. She was pleased with her efforts so far and glad she had a few minutes to spare. The last thing she had wanted was to arrive at the station and find Neil waiting for her.

Her thinking had been correct. She had only been there for three or four minutes when a red car pulled up. She could see Neil waving to her. She walked smartly over to the car.

Neil had already opened the passenger door. 'Good morning,' he greeted her cheerfully.

'Good morning.' Jessica accompanied her greeting with a pleasant smile as she eased herself into the passenger seat.

'I hope you didn't have too much of a rush,' Neil said.

'Heavens, no. I'm always up early,' Jessica replied, fiddling with the seat belt. She thought there was no point into going into how she had had to change her normal Saturday arrangements.

'You look chic,' Neil remarked, as he put the car into gear.

Jessica gave a little laugh. 'Thank you. I wasn't quite sure what to wear. This is one of my business suits.' She realised with a bit of a start that Neil's remark was very similar to the sort of thing Graham would have said. On more than one occasion other women had been amazed at the interest her husband took in what she wore.

She could not help studying Neil's attire for a second. He was dressed in a sports jacket and open-necked shirt. She wished she had chosen something more casual as well, but it was too late now.

As they drove, Neil glanced at her. 'I hope we can get you fixed up with that painting. Arnold seemed to think he had something suitable.'

'It would be nice if he had,' replied Jessica. 'I've been looking for a long time.'

They chatted quite freely during the journey, each asking questions with the object of finding out more about the other.

Jessica asked Neil where he lived.

'I have a bachelor pad in Slough,' he replied. 'It's not much of a place, but it suits me. How about you?'

'I've been lucky. I have a very nice flat, quite near to everything, but also secluded and quiet.'

More trivial conversation took place between them, and in no time, it seemed to Jessica, they reached Windsor.

'I haven't been here for years,' she remarked. She refrained from adding that the last occasion had been with Graham.

'I come here quite often. It's not far from where I live.' As he spoke, Neil turned off the street into an alleyway. 'Parking can be difficult here during the week. There's a small car park behind Arnold's gallery that I can use today.'

'That's useful.'

Jessica liked the gallery on sight. She had envisaged that it would be quite small, but she was surprised that it covered two floors of what had once been a shop. Arnold turned out to be very friendly and extremely attentive. His first gesture was to offer Jessica and Neil a coffee. Jessica did not really want one, but she felt she had to accept, particularly as Arnold was opening up the gallery early especially for her visit.

Socialising over, and the coffee consumed, on Arnold's suggestion Jessica and Neil turned their attention to the artwork that adorned the walls. Paintings were crammed into every space, including the stairway leading to the upper floor. At first glance, Jessica could see that many of the works on view were not the type of thing she was looking for, but suddenly in a corner she discovered a beautiful landscape in watercolour. Shortly afterwards, she found a similar painting.

'Seen anything you fancy?' Neil asked.

'I've spotted two, but I'm not sure which to choose. Let me show you.'

They both took a few minutes to study the paintings in question.

'I like this one,' Neil remarked, indicating one of them.

'I think that's my favourite as well,' mused Jessica. Suddenly she changed her tone. Her mind was made up. 'I'm going to buy that one,' she announced.

Neil laughed. 'That's great. I thought you were going to get stuck for a second.'

Jessica shook her head. 'No, something tells me to take that one. I'm growing quite fond of it.'

'I'll call Arnold.' Neil shouted for the gallery owner, who appeared almost immediately.

'I'd like to buy this one,' Jessica said. 'How much is it?'

Arnold looked at the painting for a moment. 'That one is £250.'

'I'll have it.'

Arnold smiled at her. 'You've got good taste,' he replied. 'The artist is up and coming. I can see his paintings being sought after in a few years' time. 'And valuable,' he added.

'Can I take it now?'

'Of course you can. I'll get it packed up for you.'

'That would be super.'

'Do you want to go and have a coffee or something while I do that?' Arnold asked, looking at both of them.

'Yes, of course. We'll leave you to it. Half an hour sufficient?' asked Neil.

'Absolutely.' Arnold began the process of taking the picture down.

'Let's go,' Neil announced. He was already making a move to leave. 'See you in half an hour,' he said to Arnold.

Jessica followed him. Outside the gallery she made her point. 'I don't really want another coffee,' she said firmly.

Neil laughed. 'Nor do I. Let's go and have a look at the river.'

They wandered in the direction of the Thames and spent a good fifteen minutes watching the activity on the water.

This prompted Jessica to recall an event from her past. 'A

group of us girls from school spent a week on a boat on the river once. It was really good. I enjoyed every minute of it.'

'Really? I've got a boat on the river. It's laid up for winter at the moment.'

'Gosh, that's exciting!'

'I'll take you to see it one day if you like.'

'Will you really? That would be very nice.' She wondered if he meant what he said.

When they returned to the gallery they found that Arnold had the painting wrapped up protected for transport. Jessica quickly paid with her credit card, and Arnold carried the painting to the car for them. They left amid expressions of thanks. Arnold waved to them as they drove away.

On the way home Jessica was feeling pleased with the way things had gone. At long last, thanks to Neil, she had the painting she had always dreamed about.

'I really am grateful to you,' she said to him. 'You've been so helpful.'

Neil smiled at her. 'It was my pleasure.'

'The next thing will be to get it hung on the wall…' Jessica was thinking aloud.

'I could do that for you.'

Chapter 7

Jessica was pleased with Neil's offer to hang her picture, but at the same time she did not want to impose on his generosity.

'Are you really sure you want to?' she asked. 'You've done so much for me already.'

Neil grinned at her. 'It's no problem,' he answered. 'It's only a five-minute job, but I'll need a couple of tools.'

'What sort of tools?'

'A hammer mainly. Oh, and a measuring tape.'

Jessica thought for a second. 'I've got a hammer and I've got a tape measure.'

'That should be OK, but I'll also need a hanging bracket for the picture.' He paused. 'Perhaps I can buy one somewhere.'

'I'm not far from the shops.'

'Good. That's it, then. If it's OK with you, we'll do the job right away.'

'I feel I'm putting you to a lot of trouble…'

'I'd like to do it.'

For the rest of the journey they chatted together, finding out more about each other. In no time at all, following Jessica's directions, they pulled up outside her flat.

'You can park here,' Jessica explained, as she climbed out of the car.

Nell was surprised. 'That's unusual,' he remarked, already opening the boot.

Jessica made a face. 'You should see it during the week, when commuters park their cars.'

'Same everywhere,' Neil sighed. 'If you can manage the painting, I'll go straight to the shops.'

'Of course I can manage. I'm a strong girl,' she retorted with a laugh.

'Right. Where are the shops? Point me in the right direction.'

Jessica gave him instructions and then lifted out the painting. She was surprised to discover how light it was. After slamming the boot, Neil was off. 'See you later,' he said.

Jessica carefully carried the painting into the house. In the hall she encountered Gwen.

'That's an interesting-looking package,' remarked Gwen.

'It's a painting I've just bought,' Jessica responded as she made for the stairs.

'Oh, you must let me see it sometime.'

'When it's up on the wall,' Jessica called over her shoulder.

Once in her flat, she carefully removed the packaging. Looking at the painting anew, she was even more pleased with her purchase.

Now to find the hammer, she thought. She knew she had one somewhere. After several failed attempts, she suddenly remembered that it was in a small canvas bag with some other tools, left behind by Graham. She found the bag in the bottom of the cupboard in the spare bedroom. Eagerly she opened it. Ah, yes, there was the hammer and, wonder of wonders, there was also a measuring tape. She carried the little bag into the lounge and placed it on the floor below where the painting was to be hung. Hardly had she done that when the front door bell rang. She hurried to the intercom and answered it.

'It's me.'

She pressed the button to release the door catch. 'You're in.'

She went out onto the landing at the same time as Neil reached the top step. 'Gosh, you were quick!' she exclaimed.

Neil chuckled. 'The first shop I came to was an ironmonger's.' He produced a small brown paper bag.

'Come in. I've found the hammer and I've also got a measuring tape.'

'Great.'

Neil got to work straight away. Jessica held one end of the tape while they found the centre of the wall, and after that it was only a matter of hammering in the bracket. Neil fixed the painting in position, and then they stood back to view their handiwork.

'It looks good,' came from Neil.

Jessica was over the moon. 'It's really splendid. Better than I ever imagined.'

She hesitated and then voiced the idea she had formulated over the last hour or so. 'Neil, you've been so helpful. I don't know how to thank you enough. First, I owe you for the bracket, and second, can I take you out to lunch?'

'I never refuse a good offer,' he replied, grinning at her.

Jessica jumped into action immediately. 'Right. Do you want to wash your hands?'

Neil scrutinised his hands quickly. 'I guess I'd better,' he said, with a smile.

Jessica pointed him in the direction of the bathroom. While he was away, she stood admiring her new acquisition. The more she looked at it, the more she liked it.

When Neil reappeared, she moved quickly. 'Give me five minutes,' she called over her shoulder as she headed for the bathroom. 'Make yourself at home.'

Neil sat down on the settee. He cast his eyes around the room. He liked what he saw. It was pleasant, light and airy. Simply furnished, but practical. The settee and two armchairs took up the main area, but there was still plenty of room for a music centre, a bookcase and some more chairs. The carpet looked expensive and coordinated with the curtains. Everything was neat and tidy, unlike his room. The bookcase attracted him. You could very often discover what type of person someone was by the books they read.

He was just about to study the shelves when Jessica reappeared briefly on her way to the bedroom. 'With you in two minutes,' she called out.

The two minutes turned out to be five. When she returned, Jessica had changed into a blouse and skirt, together with a short jacket. The high-heeled shoes had gone, to be replaced by a pair of 'comfortables', albeit with a heel but more sensible for prolonged walking. Sheer tights completed her outfit. A trace of perfume was in the air.

Neil looked at her. He was beginning to like her. She had made an effort to be attractive, and he liked that in a woman.

It was after one o'clock when they arrived at the pub Jessica had in mind for lunch. It was quite busy, but they managed to find a table in a not too crowded area.

'Drinks are on me,' Neil announced. 'What will you have?'

Jessica thought for a second. 'It had better be a shandy, I think.'

'Leave it to me.' Neil headed for the bar and reappeared a few minutes later with Jessica's drink and a half-pint of beer for himself. He also carried a menu, which he handed to Jessica.

'Cheers.' Jessica sipped her drink as she studied the menu. It did not take long for her to decide. 'I'll have the fish pie,' she declared. 'I've had it before. It's very nice.'

Neil glanced at the menu briefly. 'I'll join you.' He headed off again to order.

They took their time over the meal, talking quietly, keen to learn more about each other. At one point Neil asked Jessica, 'Do you think you'll ever get married again?'

She smiled. 'Oh, I expect so. When Mr Right comes along. How about you? You've not even made it once.'

They both laughed.

Jessica suddenly became serious. 'It's not easy finding the right person to share your life. I thought I had once, but it turned out not to be so.'

'Would you like to tell me about it?'

Jessica did not reply immediately. She was quiet, thinking. 'I suppose I got married quite early. I was only 22, and then Graham was away a lot because of his job. It felt as if I was married and not married, if you know what I mean.' She paused for a second. 'At the start it all seemed good. We liked the same things and we had the same interests, but somehow it went wrong.'

'That must have been tough for you.'

Jessica suddenly perked up. 'Anyway, it's all in the past now.'

Neil nodded. He felt a wave of sympathy for her. Clearly the divorce had affected her more than she cared to admit. He decided to change the subject. 'I'm really pleased you found the painting you wanted,' he said.

'Thanks to your help.'

They chatted on for a little while longer until they noticed that the pub was gradually emptying. Eventually there were only a few people remaining after the lunchtime increase in business. Jessica suggested that they leave.

They made their way back to her flat. Now the sun was out and despite it being late November the day had become warm. It was a pleasant walk.

As they reached their destination, Jessica felt she had to offer some form of hospitality. 'Would you like to come in for a coffee?' she asked.

Neil shook his head. 'Not this time. I must get back to get some things before the shops close.'

'Well, thank you again for helping me.'

He smiled at her. 'My pleasure,' he replied. 'Thanks for lunch.'

He opened the car door. He hesitated, and then suddenly he took hold of her hand and kissed it, accompanied with a hurried 'Thanks again' as he climbed into the driving seat and closed the door. He rolled down the window. 'I'll be on my way, then,' he said, starting the engine.

'Goodbye, Neil.'

The car started to move off.

'I'll be in touch,' he called out.

'Please do,' she called back, but she was not sure if he heard. She saw him wave just before the car disappeared from view.

Jessica walked slowly back into the house. Their parting had been a bit rushed and she wondered if she should have offered her cheek instead of letting him kiss her hand, but it was too late now.

'I'll be in touch,' he had said. She hoped he would, but she would now have to wait and see.

Chapter 8

She did not hear from Neil immediately. One week passed, and then another. She began to think that she had seen the last of him. Just ships that pass, she thought. She had hoped upon hope that he would telephone, but as the days went by she began to accept the fact that she would most likely not hear from him again. Yet every time she looked at the painting on her wall she was reminded of him and the assistance he had given her. She was aware that she had felt attracted to him in rather the same way as she had first been attracted to Graham.

One evening in the middle of the third week after their visit to the gallery, the phone rang. She picked it up, thinking it would most likely be Babs or Natalie.

'Hello. It's Neil.'

Jessica's heart missed a beat.

Before she could answer properly, Neil spoke again. 'Sorry I've not been in touch. I had to go to Paris urgently.' He paused, and then continued almost as if he were thinking aloud. 'I suppose I could have given you a ring from there, but work took up all my time and there didn't seem to be a moment to spare…'

'It's all right, really.'

'Good. I'm glad of that. Anyway, how are you?'

'Oh, I'm fine. Working hard. How about you?'

'I'm good.'

There was a bit of a pause. It was Neil who spoke first. 'I was wondering if I could take you out to dinner one evening.'

The suggestion immediately appealed to Jessica. 'I'd love to. When and where?'

'There's not much left of this week. How about Saturday?'

Jessica liked the idea. She could carry out her usual Saturday routine, and her hair would be newly fixed. 'That'll be fine for me,' she replied.

'Great. I know a little place down on the river. It's really nice.'

'I'm looking forward to it.' She meant it. 'What time?'

'How about...' Neil was clearly thinking the arrangements out. 'How about if I pick you up about half past six? That should give us plenty of time. I'll book a table for eight o'clock.'

'I'll be all ready.'

'It's fixed, then.'

'Super,' Jessica replied breezily. Suddenly she thought of something. 'Hey. Give me your number, just in case I need it.'

'Of course. I'll give you my mobile.' He reeled off the number.

Jessica took up a handy biro and scribbled the number down. 'Got it.'

'OK. Any problems, give me a ring.'

'Will do.'

They chatted for several minutes more, until Neil said he had other calls to make. It was the signal to end their conversation.

As she replaced the telephone on its stand, Jessica could not help feeling joyful. Not only had Neil contacted her again, but she now had a dinner date. She started thinking about what she would wear. That necessitated a peek into her wardrobe. She had not been taken out for dinner for ages, and some of her dresses had been worn many times. She pulled dress after dress out of the wardrobe, but soon came to the conclusion that she would have to buy a new one. Shoes were another problem. She had her gold sandals, but they were now showing distinct signs of wear. She would take an hour off work, she decided, and do some shopping.

Things did not go exactly as she had planned. The next day she took the promised hour off to look for a dress. It did not take her long to realise that she would need more time. She remembered that it was late night shopping in the West End. She would go straight from work and have more time to spend. Even this turned out to take longer than she had anticipated. By the time she had completed the task, the shops were almost closing. On top of that, she was now beginning to feel decidedly hungry and tired. The good thing was that she was now satisfied with her purchases. She had looked at a lot of dresses and had tried on a few but had almost given up when she spotted something that took her fancy. It was a green knee-length dress with a vee neckline. As soon as she tried it on, she could see that it suited her slim figure and fair hair. Next she spent some time in the shoe department. After much deliberation and trying on she selected a high-heeled strappy sandal in silver. The heel was higher than she normally wore, but she figured that she would not have to do too much walking if Neil picked her up in his car. She had spent far more than she had intended to, but she consoled herself with the thought that since her divorce she had been frugal in her spending on clothes.

It was well after nine by the time she returned home. She was tired and hungry, but she was pleased with her new outfit. She now looked forward more than ever to her dinner date with Neil.

On the Saturday, she followed her usual routine of visiting the hairdresser. This time she had also made an appointment to have a pedicure. If she was going to show more of her feet, she was going to make sure that she looked smart in that area. She had her nails painted a delicate shade of pink.

Late in the afternoon, she was horrified to see a few flakes of snow falling, but she was relieved to observe that by the time she needed to get ready, all traces of it had disappeared.

She was ready well before the appointed time for Neil to pick her up. She tried to do one or two small jobs at her desk but found it difficult to concentrate. A few minutes before half past six her doorbell rang. She answered it.

'Hello. It's Neil.'

'I'm ready. I'm coming down.'

As she was walking down the stairs, taking careful steps in her new shoes, Gwen appeared.

'Going somewhere nice?' she enquired.

'I'm going out for dinner,' Jessica responded gaily.

'Have a lovely time,' Gwen called out, as she disappeared into her own flat.

Jessica always felt that her neighbour led rather a quiet life. She was probably a good thirty years older than Jessica, and her main entertainment seemed to be having friends round to play cards.

Neil was standing close to the front door. He greeted her cheerfully.

'Hello again,' she replied. This time she offered her cheek for a kiss.

They made their way to the car. There was still the odd flake of snow in the air and it had turned colder. Jessica felt the chill in her dress and sandals. She was pleased to find that it was comfortably warm in the car.

'I had a horrible thought that we were going to be snowed up,' she remarked, as she clicked home the seat belt.

Neil smiled at her as he started the car. 'Me too,' he replied.

It took longer to reach their destination than Jessica had envisaged. A good forty-five minutes had passed before they pulled into a pub car park, which was already quite full.

'It looks like a really nice place,' she exclaimed as the car drew to a halt. She could glimpse the river Thames behind the pub. Twinkling lights decorated the façade of the building.

Neil grinned at her. 'I had a bit of a job to get a booking. They're very busy at this time of year. Good job I know the owner.'

'I'm glad you do.'

'Hope we get a decent table,' he remarked, as they walked into the pub.

They did not need to have worried. Neil's friend and host met them in the entrance. After hand-shaking and cordial dialogue, he ushered them to a table overlooking the river.

'It's one of the best tables in the house,' Neil whispered to Jessica.

'It's fantastic,' she replied.

They took some time to study the extensive menu.

'I don't really want the Christmas dinner,' Jessica said in a whisper so that the couple on the next table who were enjoying the festive meal could not hear her.

'Likewise,' returned Neil quietly. 'It's best on Christmas Day. I'm going to have a steak.'

Jessica gave the menu a final glance. 'I'll have the salmon with a salad, please.'

'What about wine?' Neil asked, picking up the wine list.

'I don't really know much about wine.'

Neil laughed. 'I'm the same.'

'Let's go for the house wine.'

'Good idea. White or red?'

Jessica thought for a second. 'Could we have white?'

'White it is.'

Later in the meal Jessica posed the question she had been wanting to ask ever since first meeting Neil. During a pause in the conversation she brought up the subject. 'Can you tell me a bit about your family?'

Neil swallowed a mouthful of food. 'There's not much to tell.'

'I'd love to hear about your early life.'

'Of course.' He paused for a few seconds. 'I was really brought up by my two sisters. They're much older than me.' He smiled. 'I guess I must have been an afterthought – or an accident.'

'What about your parents?'

'Mum died when I was only seven. That's why my sisters stepped in and looked after me. Then later on I was sent to boarding school.'

'Is your father still alive?'

Neil shook his head. 'Dad died a few years ago.'

'I'm sorry,' Jessica replied. 'Your background is a bit like mine. My parents divorced at about the time I went to university. Mum got married again, but she died five years ago. I think my father's in Canada.' She added ruefully, 'That is, if he's still alive. I never heard from him after he left.'

'And you've no other relatives?' Neil asked.

Jessica thought for a few seconds. It was on the tip of her tongue to tell him about her latest discovery, her uncle Edward. In the end she decided not to. Not yet, she thought. She simply replied, 'None that I'm in contact with.'

Neil nodded, apparently satisfied with her reply.

They chatted on, continuing to learn more about each other. By the time their coffee had been served and drunk, almost two hours had passed.

It was Jessica who at length glanced at her watch and exclaimed, 'Gosh! It's nearly ten. Where did the time go?'

It was the signal for them to leave. Neil settled the bill and they made their departure. It was a shock to discover as they stepped outside that the ground was now covered with a blanket of snow. Fine flakes were still falling as they drove back to Jessica's flat. Fortunately the main roads were clear.

As they drew up outside the house, Jessica wondered if she should show hospitality and offer Neil another coffee. The situation was resolved for her.

He kept the engine running. Jessica undid her seat belt and made a move to get out of the car. 'Can I offer you another coffee?' she asked.

Neil shook his head. 'It's tempting, but I feel that with this weather the best thing is to go straight home.'

She nodded. 'I understand.' She leaned towards him. 'Thank you for a lovely evening.' She allowed their lips to meet.

'See you again soon,' he replied, as they drew apart.

Jessica smiled. 'Of course, and now I will let you get home safely.'

She got out of the car and started to walk towards the house. 'Good night,' she called softly, blowing him a kiss.

He waved and the car started to move off. She watched it go for as long as she could and then walked carefully up the path to the front door, conscious that her skimpy footwear did little to protect her feet from the cold, wet snow.

Quietly she entered the house. It was in darkness. Gwen was no doubt in bed. As she climbed the stairs Jessica wondered when she would next see Neil. She hoped it would be soon.

Chapter 9

When she woke up the next morning, Jessica was surprised to see that all traces of snow had disappeared. After a while the sun came out and brought the appearance of a pleasant winter's day.

She kept thinking about the previous evening. Despite her initial reservations, she had enjoyed herself immensely. Neil had been both attentive and good company. She felt eager to see him again. Since her divorce she had not had a very active social life, more or less avoiding dates with the opposite sex. On the one occasion that she had accepted an invitation to go out with a man, she had been dismayed when he tried to undress her in the taxi on the way home. It had made her aware that being divorced made her a target for men who seemed to think that divorcees were available for one-night stands, which had never been her thing. She preferred to get to know a person before any intimacy took place. She had had an unfortunate experience when she was at university. She had gone to a party, had too much to drink and ended up in bed with an almost complete stranger. Afterwards, the fear that she might be pregnant had affected her for days and she had vowed never to get into that situation again.

It was during the afternoon, while she was relaxing with the Sunday newspaper and a mug of tea, that her telephone rang. She grabbed the handset.

'Hello. It's me – Neil.'

'Neil! It's great to hear from you. Are you well? Did you get home OK?' Jessica was more than pleased. There was almost excitement in her voice.

She heard a bit of a laugh at the other end of the phone, and then Neil replied, 'Affirmative to both.'

It was Jessica's turn to giggle. 'Sorry to bombard you with questions.'

'It's fine. I meant to ask you something last night.'

'That sounds intriguing.'

'Not really, but I meant to ask you what you were doing for Christmas.'

Jessica thought hurriedly. Was he about to suggest meeting up? She was looking forward to spending a few days with Babs then, something she had not done for years. Christmas was only a few days away, and she knew she could not disappoint her friend at this late stage. She formulated a simple answer for Neil. 'I'm spending it with an old friend, a woman I was at university with. You know, a girlie weekend.'

She heard him chuckle. 'Ah,' he replied. 'If you'd been free, I'd have suggested we get together and do something.'

'Oh, what a shame… That would have been nice. I'm sorry.'

'It's OK.'

'What will you do all on your own?'

There was another bit of a laugh. 'Oh, I'll go to the nearest pub and see if I can scrounge a meal.'

'Oh, poor you.'

'Not at all. On Boxing Day I'm going to Paris. Some friends have invited me over for a few days.'

'That'll be nice. Do you like Paris?'

'It's a great city. Have you ever been there?'

'Once, a long time ago.'

'Tu parles français?'

Jessica gave a bit of a laugh. 'Schoolgirl French,' she replied. 'How about you?'

'Pretty fluent now.'

They chatted on for almost half an hour, mainly about trivial things. It was Jessica who brought an end to the call, saying she had to go out, which was quite true because she wanted to get a walk in while it was still light and sunny.

The next few days at work were busy ones for Jessica as she desperately tried to complete a number of jobs before the looming Christmas break. By working a few hours' overtime she managed to get them all done.

On the last day at work, the day before Christmas Eve, was the office party. Jessica was not particularly enthusiastic. She knew from past experience that it was a time when some members of the workforce, male and female, tended to have too much to drink and then act rather silly, particularly some of the males who seemed to consider it an opportunity to have sex if possible with female members of staff who had had too much to drink and had abandoned all inhibitions. On this occasion, she let the party get going and then slipped away unnoticed. She still had one or two bits of shopping to do before Christmas.

On Christmas Eve she enjoyed getting up a bit later than normal and taking her time getting ready to go to Babs's house. Knowing that her friend's cooking skills were not good, she had taken the opportunity of arriving in good time. Babs lived in a small Victorian house near Greenwich. Jessica had been there on several occasions and liked its quiet location. She arrived just before three in the afternoon.

She had hardly rang the bell when the front door was thrown open. Babs stood there dressed in jeans and barefoot.

'Darling, you're nice and early! Come in.'

Jessica followed her into the tiny lounge. Babs's cat Pedro viewed her from the comfort of an armchair, at the same time stretching and yawning.

'Come into the kitchen and I'll make us a coffee,' said Babs.

Jessica followed her into the tiny kitchen. It gave her the opportunity to view the catering arrangements.

Babs busied herself producing two mugs of coffee while she

kept up a constant flow of chatter. At one point she opened the fridge door and exclaimed, 'Oh, no… We're a bit low on milk.'

It was the opportunity Jessica had been waiting for. 'I can nip out and get some,' she offered eagerly.

'Oh, would you? You're an angel.' Suddenly, with a quick glance into the fridge, Babs asked, 'Can you also get a tin of food for Pedro? I'll show you the one he likes. She reached into the fridge and produced a can.

Jessica made a mental note of the one to buy. 'Are we all right for food?' she asked. 'Can I get anything else?'

Babs thought for a second or two. 'I've got a chicken and some potatoes… Oh, and a Christmas pudding.'

'What about veg?'

It seemed that in that direction all Babs could produce was a bag of carrots well past their sell-by date. Jessica made a further mental note.

She dived off to the nearest supermarket. It was packed with last-minute shoppers, and some of the shelves were already empty, but she managed to get what she wanted and returned to Babs's house with two heavily laden bags.

Jessica stayed with Babs for three days and enjoyed every minute. The two friends went for walks and spent hours just chatting about a whole range of subjects. Jessica mentioned her possible legacy, which intrigued Babs, who asked a lot of questions she was unable to answer, such as when she would receive the proceeds of her uncle's will. The only recent contact from Dinton, Walley & Dinton had been a letter signed by Frank Dinton in which he had apologised for the time everything was taking and explained that he was still waiting for more details from Australia and would contact her again as soon as he had more information. Jessica was content to wait.

During her stay with Babs, she did most of the cooking. After observing her friend's initial attempts to cook the Christmas dinner, she had politely suggested that she take over, an offer that was gratefully accepted by Babs, whose cooking skills did not seem to have improved. Jessica had the impression that she existed mainly on take-aways.

Babs wanted to know about Jessica's private life since she had got divorced, particularly regarding boyfriends. In the end Jessica told her about Neil and how she felt about him. She had not heard from him since he had asked her about Christmas, but she was eagerly anticipating his next contact with her.

Chapter 10

Jessica did not hear from Neil between Christmas and New Year. Somehow she had thought she probably would not receive a telephone call during that time, but when nothing happened she felt disappointed. She consoled herself with the thought that Neil had made no promise to phone her, and in any case, she reasoned, he might still be in Paris.

She had no plans to celebrate New Year's Eve, but she received an invitation the day before from Natalie, who told her she was hosting an evening with a few friends. The invitation also included the suggestion that Jessica stay over until the following day. Jessica accepted and made her way to Natalie's in the early evening.

She was the first to arrive, and over coffee Natalie quizzed her quite a lot, in particular about Neil. She asked if Jessica had seen him recently and how she felt about him, whether he had taken her out and what he was like. Jessica was surprised at all the questions and wondered vaguely if Natalie still cherished the hope that she and Graham would get back together. When they had told her that they were getting a divorce, Natalie had been quite concerned and had done her best to try and reconcile them. However, they had thought things through carefully before announcing their decision. Just in case Natalie's thinking was heading in that direction, Jessica took the opportunity to emphasise that a reconciliation was not on the cards.

Natalie's few friends turned out to be six people, none of whom Jessica knew. Nevertheless, she enjoyed the evening, which did not finish until one in the morning. The rest of the night she spent in Natalie's spare bedroom, being kept awake by the traffic outside and the noise from revellers on their way home. She got up and opened the bedroom door when she heard a noise downstairs. It turned out that a couple were also spending the night there. When she eventually went down she discovered Natalie and her two other guests already in the kitchen having breakfast.

It was a leisurely meal. Eventually the couple said they had to go. Jessica helped Natalie tidy up, mainly washing up glasses from the night before. It was late morning when she at last made her way home. As it was a bank holiday, the journey took longer than normal. Public transport seemed to be either non-existent or on a go-slow. She at last reached her flat in the early afternoon. She did not fancy preparing any food. Instead she made a mug of tea and sat down to enjoy it. Afterwards she stretched out on the settee and relaxed.

She woke up with a shock. It was already dark. She glanced at her watch. It was almost five. The previous short and disturbed night had caught up with her. She was about to get up and draw the curtains when her mobile rang. She had to remember where she had left it, eventually recalling that it was in the overnight bag she had taken with her to Natalie's. Panic-stricken in case she missed the call, she desperately retrieved the mobile and clicked the answer button.

'Hello. You are there. I thought you must be out.' It was Babs.

'Sorry. I was out seeing the New Year in so I had a late night last night, and I fell asleep when I got back. For a minute I couldn't remember where I'd left my mobile.'

'There's a story in there somewhere. Come on. What have you been up to?'

Jessica knew that Babs would insist on hearing all the details. She related where she had been the previous night.

After that they chatted for a long time. Babs wanted to know if she Jessica seen Neil over the holiday. Jessica had to admit that she had not heard from him. It made her wonder when he would contact her again.

It was to be nearly a week later, when she was back from work. She had just finished her evening meal and was starting to wash up the dishes, when her telephone rang. She picked it up, thinking it might be Babs or Natalie.

'Hello.'

A now familiar voice answered. 'Hello. It's Neil. How are you?'

'Neil! It's great to hear from you. How are YOU?'

'Oh, I've had a bit of a cold. Laid me up for a few days, but I'm all right now.'

'Oh, poor you. Was that in Paris?'

'Yes, worse luck.'

'Such a shame when you're on holiday.'

'I know. Anyway, what have you been up to?

'Not a lot. Living a quiet life.'

'We'll have to change that. Guess what? I've got two tickets for *Honolulu* this Saturday.'

'What?' Jessica was astounded. 'I thought it was virtually impossible to get tickets for that for the next six months or so.'

She heard a slight laugh at the other end of the phone. 'I know somebody in a ticket office. Anyway, would you like to come?'

'I'd love to.' She was already excited.

'Right, then. It's a date. It's a matinee performance – that's all I could get.'

'That would be fine.' She was already planning how she would organise her day to accommodate everything. 'Where shall we meet, and what time?'

'I've been thinking about that. Do you know Angelo's coffee bar in Soho?'

'I can find it.'

'I'll give you directions. Suppose we meet there about half past one? That'll give us a nice bit of time.'

'I'll be there.' Jessica had not been to a West End show for years, and to be able to see *Honolulu* was fantastic.

Neil spoke again. 'I thought after the show we could have a meal out, make an evening of it.'

'That would be super. I can't wait.'

'Great. That's fixed, then.'

They chatted for a long time after that, Jessica asking about Paris, and Neil asking a lot of questions about her background and her interests. By the time they had finished, almost half an hour had passed.

Jessica put the phone down, pleased with the start to her New Year. Neil had contacted her again and seemed keen to continue seeing her. On top of that, to be able to go and see the current West End hit was something she had only dreamed about. Life was certainly good, she decided.

Chapter 11

Jessica was looking forward to seeing *Honolulu*. The weather had been cold all week, with lots of rain, but when Saturday arrived it turned out to be bright and sunny, albeit a little chilly. She was out and about early, and by mid-morning, after a hurried visit to the hairdresser and the supermarket, she was back home savouring a well-deserved mug of tea.

She set out early to meet Neil. He had given her full instructions about where to meet, but she had a horror of being late. She was well on time when she found Angelo's, but she was surprised to find Neil already there, occupying a window table from which he could see her arrive. She waved to him as soon as she spotted him. He rose to greet her as she approached the table.

'Hi. I'm not late, am I?' She offered a cheek for his greeting kiss.

'Not at all. I was here early.'

He hesitated before sitting down again. A half-finished cup of coffee was already on the table. 'Can I get you a cup of tea or coffee?' he asked.

'A cup of coffee would be great. Black, please. No milk or sugar.'

'Shall be done. What about something to eat? Have you had any lunch?'

Jessica smiled and shook her head. 'No. I was a bit concerned about being late.'

Neil gave an understanding nod. 'They do a marvellous toasted teacake here. I'm going to have one. What about you?' he asked.

'Sounds lovely. Yes, please.'

'I'll be back,' he called over his shoulder as he made his way to the counter. He liked Angelo's bar. He used it whenever he was in central London. The Italian couple who ran it were used to seeing him, and as he spoke a little Italian they would chat to him half in English and half in Italian.

He stood waiting for the coffee to be brewed. From where he was standing, he had a clear view of Jessica. She was an attractive woman, he thought. He wondered what had happened to her marriage. He had touched upon the subject several times, but he had found her reluctant to go into details. Still, she would tell him one day perhaps. He had watched her approach Angelo's, striding out in her high heels, pausing now and then to study the street, anxiously seeking her destination.

He returned with the two coffees.

Jessica smiled. 'Just what I need,' she remarked gaily.

'They'll bring the rest over when it's ready.'

He had hardly finished speaking when the waitress approached carrying two plates.

They lingered over their snack until Neil said it was time to go. It was only a five-minute walk to the theatre, and as they slowly made their way there he slipped his hand around Jessica's.

Jessica enjoyed the show very much. She was surprised to find that their seats were the most expensive ones, in the circle. At one point, when she whispered to Neil, 'These seats must have cost a fortune,' he just grinned at her. The tickets had been expensive, but he was sure it was going to be worth it. Jessica was worth making an effort for.

After the show, Neil took her to a small Italian restaurant he knew. He had clearly made a booking, because they were taken straight to a table when he mentioned his name.

For Jessica the restaurant was a good choice. She had always enjoyed Italian food. On this occasion she knew at once what she wanted. After a brief glance at the menu, she asked, 'Can I have minestrone soup? I really like it.'

'Of course. It's great for a cold evening. I think I'll join you.' Neil was still engrossed in the menu. 'What about the main course?' he asked.

Jessica looked at the menu again. 'I think I'll have a veal cutlet with salad.'

'Same here.'

'And house wine?' she queried.

He laughed. 'Why not?'

They took a long time over dinner, chatting away freely. It was getting on for nine when they eventually left the restaurant. Remembering the expensive seats they had occupied at the theatre, Jessica wanted to pay for their meal. Neil flatly refused, but in the end they agreed that the next time they went out to eat, she would pay.

Neil wanted to escort her all the way home, but knowing that he had not brought his car, Jessica insisted that she make her own way. It seemed grossly unfair for him to accompany her to Ealing and then make his way back to Slough by public transport late at night. He reluctantly agreed. They parted at the station, this time lingering longer over a kiss.

It was the start of a more intense relationship. After that evening in London, Neil kept in constant touch. They now saw each other at least once a week. They went to shows and concerts in the West End and dined out regularly. Neil strove to take Jessica to events he knew she would like, and in turn she tried to suggest things that would make him happy.

As time passed, Jessica realised that her relationship with him was not just a passing phase. When he was not with her, she felt that something was missing. She was gradually falling in love with him and she suspected that he felt the same way about her. So far their relationship had not become physical, but she knew that a change would come and she had to be prepared. For the first time since her divorce, she visited a family planning clinic and made sure she was protected. She had no objection to the next stage of their relationship when it happened, but she was determined to be ready for it.

It happened sooner than she expected. They had been to a cinema in Ealing to watch a film Jessica was interested in. She invited Neil back to her flat for a coffee before he went home. He had been there several times before, usually for a brief visit when he came to pick her up. This time was different. Once in the flat, Jessica directed him to the settee while she made two mugs of coffee.

When she came back into the lounge, Neil was standing in front of the bookcase, browsing the shelves. 'You have some interesting reading matter,' he observed, glancing up as she entered the room.

Jessica gave a little laugh. 'I'm always buying books,' she admitted. 'One of these days I'll have no room left to put them.'

Seeing her set the mugs down on a side table, Neil returned to his position on the settee. Jessica went over to the music centre. She selected a CD and placed it in the tray. Soft music filtered into the room as she sat down next to him.

Neil picked up his mug of coffee and looked around the room. 'You have a really nice flat,' he remarked.

Jessica nodded. 'I love it. I'm really very lucky to have it.' There was a pause, and then she asked, 'What's your place like?'

Neil grinned. 'A bit of a mess, really. It's very small. Just somewhere to sleep and eat.'

'Oh, that's a shame. You should get something better.'

He smiled again. 'One day, perhaps.'

They drank their coffee slowly. An hour passed, and at last Neil got up from the settee. 'I guess I'd better go,' he said.

Jessica hesitated, and then moved to kiss him. Their lips touched, but this time it was not a brief kiss. Their lips lingered without any thought of parting, and their kissing became more intense. They started to caress each other's bodies and then suddenly Neil's hand was on her breast. She made no move to stop him. The next minute, he was opening the buttons of her blouse. Jessica knew that the point of no return was being reached. She slowly drew Neil's jacket off his shoulders and tossed it onto the settee. She stepped out of her shoes. Without heels, she was just a little shorter than him. Neil was now caressing a bare breast, and Jessica was running her hands over his naked chest and back. Suddenly she grabbed his hand and gently led him into the bedroom.

She woke up several hours later. It was still completely dark. Neil was sleeping quietly beside her. Their clothes were scattered over the bedroom floor, abandoned in the midst of their passion. She glanced at the bedside clock. Its hands showed that it was still several hours to her usual getting-up time. Contented, she snuggled up to Neil's naked body and slept once more.

'Room service.'

Neil stirred in his sleep. For a second or two he was disorientated. This was not his bedroom. His memory came flooding back as his eyes focused on Jessica, who was standing smiling beside the bed, in her dressing gown, holding two mugs of tea.

'Good morning, lover,' she piped up.

Neil took the mug she offered. 'Good morning, beautiful,' he replied.

She sat on the edge of the bed, carefully adjusting her dressing gown, and sipped her tea.

It was Neil who spoke next. 'Sorry I took advantage of you last night.' There was a hint of a smile on his face.

'You didn't, and I enjoyed it.'

'I enjoyed it too.'

Jessica was quiet for a couple of seconds, but she was the first to speak again. 'That was the first time since my divorce.' She turned to humour. 'I was afraid I'd forgotten how!'

'You were fantastic.'

She smiled.

Neil suddenly looked at the clock. Its hands showed seven. 'Goodness! Is that the time? I'd better make a move.'

'I'll get us some breakfast,' Jessica announced, falling in line with his concern.

He shook his head. 'No time. I've got a dental appointment at half past eight.'

Jessica acted quickly. 'OK. I'll leave the bathroom free for you.' She thought for a moment. 'I have to be at work on time as well. I've got a meeting at half past nine.'

Neil drained the last of his tea and handed the empty mug to Jessica, who, with 'I'll leave you to it,' disappeared into the kitchen. Ten minutes later Neil appeared, fully dressed.

'I'm sorry you've got to go,' Jessica remarked. She added breezily. 'We'll arrange it better next time.'

'I'll make sure we do,' Neil said, grinning.

'Can you creep out?' Jessica asked. 'I won't come down...' She glanced at her apparel and smiled. She wondered if Neil had guessed that she was practically naked under her dressing gown. On top of that, she expected Gwen to be up and about. She knew her neighbour was quite broadminded, but just for a while she did not want to share Neil with anybody, even those asking polite questions.

They exchanged a lingering kiss, and then Neil was off. Jessica watched him descend the stairs and open the front door quietly. She blew him a kiss, and he was gone.

She went back into her flat. In the space of a few hours, things had changed between her and Neil. She was glad it had happened the way it did. She was still thinking about the previous night as she scuttled round the flat, having a quick breakfast and then getting ready for work.

As she walked to the station, she felt alive, full of exhilaration. It was a feeling she had not had for a long time. She now had a focus in life and she was enjoying every moment of it. Even the dull work meeting she had to participate in could not dampen her new outlook on life.

She couldn't wait to see Neil again. She hoped it would be soon.

Chapter 12

Jessica did not have long to wait. Neil phoned her the following evening.

Polite preliminaries over, she asked, 'Did you get to the dentist on time?'

She heard a chuckle at the other end of the phone. 'Just about,' Neil replied.

'That reminds me. I'm due for a checkup,' she remarked.

She was about to add something, but Neil chipped in first. 'Would you like to do something this weekend?'

'I'd love to.' Jessica could hardly keep the excitement out of her voice.

'Great. I'll have a think.'

'I've got an idea,' she said.

'I'm all ears.'

'Well,' she began, 'the local amateur dramatic group I belong to is putting on a play in the church hall this week. I'm pretty sure I can get tickets for Saturday evening.'

'I didn't know you were an aspiring actress. Tell me more about this hidden talent.'

Jessica laughed. 'I'm not. I have no talent whatsoever in that direction. I'm just one of the helpers. What do you think of my idea?'

'What's the play?'

'Oh, I'm sorry. It's one of Alan Ayckbourn's. *Table Manners.*'

'That sounds great. What time does it start?'

'Half past seven. We can walk from here.'

'I'll look forward to that. I haven't been to a play for ages. What time shall I come over?'

Jessica brought in the next part of her plan. 'How about a meal beforehand?'

'I think that's a very good idea. Where shall we go? The place we went to last time, or would you like to suggest somewhere else?'

'Why don't I make us something to eat? I can cook, you know.' She laughed.

'I'll be happy to sample your cooking. What time would you like me to get to you?'

Jessica thought for a second, formulating her plan. 'I'll prepare a meal for half past five. Come a bit before that, and then we'll have plenty of time.'

'Will do. Can I bring anything?'

'No, just you.' Jessica replied. Suddenly she thought of something. 'Oh. You could bring a bottle of wine.'

'I'll do that.'

Jessica hesitated over her next question. She had to pluck up courage to voice it. 'Oh, and Neil, would you like to stop over?' Now I've said it, she thought. She waited anxiously for his answer.

'I must remember to pack a toothbrush,' he responded quickly.

'No dental appointment this time?' Jessica chipped in. There was humour in her voice.

'I'll cancel it,' Neil joked, following her lead.

They chatted for a short while longer, until Neil mentioned that he had to go out.

Jessica put the phone down and relaxed on the settee, thinking about what she had said. It was a bit out of character for her to be so forward, inviting a member of the opposite sex to spend the night in her flat. She knew that the invitation was an offer to share her bed, but somehow she had felt propelled to do it. Anyway, she reasoned, I've done it now, so I can't do anything about it. She turned her attention to planning for Saturday and what sort of meal she would prepare for Neil. Already she had something in mind. It only needed the final touches.

Saturday turned out to be fine and sunny, if a trifle cold. Jessica carried out her usual Saturday routine. After visiting the hairdresser she popped into the beauty salon next door and had some work done on her finger and toe nails, changing them into a deeper shade of pink. Next it was the butcher's, where she purchased two juicy steaks. A quick visit to the supermarket completed her mission.

It was already mid-morning when she arrived back home. As she entered the hall, she encountered her neighbour. She greeted her with a pleasant 'Good morning, Gwen.'

Gwen gave her a beaming smile. 'Gosh, you've been out already. You are an early bird. I always try to lie in a bit at the weekend.'

'I've got quite a lot to do today,' Jessica replied with a smile. Suddenly it occurred to her that perhaps she ought to tell Gwen Neil would be staying over. Before Gwen could say anything else, she took the opportunity. 'Oh, Gwen. I must tell you. Neil – you remember you met him? He'll be staying with me tonight.'

She waited a little anxiously for Gwen's reaction. She was pleasantly surprised. Gwen beamed again.

'Oh, yes. Of course I remember him. That's nice for you. He looked like such a nice young man. I'm happy for you. I hope you get on well together.'

Jessica was pleased with Gwen's reaction. Back in her own flat, she gave a sigh of relief. It was rare for her to entertain men in her flat, and she had been a bit concerned about how Gwen might react. Vaguely she wondered if Gwen was aware that Neil had already spent the night with her. She quickly dismissed the thought. It was no longer relevant. Gwen seemed quite happy with the situation and that was all that mattered.

After a quick cup of coffee and a glance through the newspaper, she threw herself into cleaning her flat from top to bottom. She dismissed any form of lunch except for a mug of tea, which she drank as she worked. It was early afternoon by the time she had finished. Next she attended to her catering arrangements. It was a long time since she had prepared a meal for a guest, and she took careful pains to see that everything was as nearly perfect as she could get it. By mid-afternoon she had made a salad, the potatoes were prepared for roasting, and the steaks were ready to cook. She dug out a tablecloth and carefully laid the table for two.

Satisfied with her efforts, she turned her attention to what to wear. She already had a few ideas, but even then she removed several dresses from her clothes cupboard for inspection before making her final choice. As there was still a chill in the air outside, she chose a woollen long-sleeved dress in a pleasant shade of blue. She had a bright brooch to go with it. Footwear was not a problem inside the house. She had a neat pair of court shoes that matched the dress perfectly, though she knew that the higher heels would mean a change of footwear later to go to the evening event.

She was completely ready and relaxing with the newspaper when the front doorbell rang. She went to the window and looked out. Neil's car was parked outside. She hurried to the intercom. She knew it must be him, but habit made her say, 'Hello.'

'Hello. It's Neil.'

Jessica pressed the button and called out, 'You're in.'

She hurried to where she had abandoned her shoes. She did not normally wear heels in the house. She sped as quickly as she could to greet Neil. By the time she reached the landing he was already well up the stairs. She smiled and called out, 'Hi!'

Neil was carrying several bags and had a leather weekend case over his shoulder. Jessica greeted him with a kiss. She could smell his aftershave.

'Mmm. You smell nice,' she remarked.

Neil grinned at her. 'Specially for you,' he replied, adding, 'I've brought you these.' He handed her a bouquet of flowers and kissed her.

'They're lovely. Thank you.' She turned to enter the flat. 'Come in,' she said.

'I've brought two bottles of wine,' Neil explained, handing her one of the bags. 'I didn't know if I should get white or red, so I bought one of each.'

Jessica laughed. 'Well, we don't need to drink both at the same time.' She became serious again. 'You can put your bag in the spare bedroom,' she said, indicating the door, 'and then just relax in the living room while I put these flowers in some water.' As an afterthought she said, 'There's today's newspaper on the settee. Would you like some tea or coffee?'

'Tea, please,' Neil responded with enthusiasm, smiling at her as he headed for the spare bedroom.

'Give me five minutes,' she replied, as she made for the kitchen.

She returned a few minutes later carrying a vase with the flowers arranged in it. 'They really are beautiful,' she said, placing the vase on the table.

'Like the recipient,' came from Neil. He was sitting on the settee reading the newspaper and looked up as Jessica spoke.

She went over to him and kissed him. 'Now for the tea,' she declared, returning to the kitchen.

Three minutes later she came back with two mugs of tea. 'Milk and one teaspoon of sugar,' she remarked as she placed one in front of Neil.

Neil politely put the newspaper down and picked up his tea. 'Have you read all the news?' he asked.

Jessica laughed. 'That'll be the day, when I manage to read a newspaper right through.'

Neil grinned. 'Me too.'

They chatted as they drank their tea. After a while Jessica looked at her watch. 'Time to start cooking,' she announced.

'Shall I help?'

Jessica shook her head. 'No. You're the guest. Sit back and enjoy the newspaper. How do you like your steak?'

'Medium, please.'

'One medium,' Jessica confirmed, 'and one well done.'

Back in the kitchen she donned an apron and busied herself finishing their meal. At one point Neil popped his head around the door and commented, 'Nice smell.'

'Wait till you've tasted it.'

They took their time over the meal, which, to Jessica's satisfaction, Neil appeared to enjoy.

At last Jessica looked at her watch and announced that she would do the washing up before they left for the show. Neil insisted on helping.

'You can dry the dishes,' she suggested.

When they had finished, she whispered, 'Give me five minutes,' and disappeared into the bathroom and then the bedroom. The comfortable shoes she had picked out were already lying on the floor. She just needed her warm overcoat to complete the outfit.

When she returned to the lounge, Neil had changed into a jacket and tie. A light raincoat was lying nearby.

It was a fine starlit evening as they made the ten-minute walk to the church hall. Jessica had managed to purchase the last two tickets available. As they arrived at the venue, Neil could see that quite a lot of people there knew her. She whispered to him that most of the people greeting them were members of the amateur dramatic group.

They both enjoyed the performance, which had quite high-quality acting. In the interval Jessica talked a little about the cast, what their jobs were and what other parts they had performed in the past. Neil listened intently, asking a question here and there.

They walked back to the flat hand in hand. The moon appeared briefly until it was hidden behind clouds. At one point, Neil stopped and gently kissed Jessica's lips. She responded with enthusiasm, but then pulled away, whispering, 'Keep it till later.'

They quietly entered the house and crept up the stairs.

Once in the flat, Jessica took off her coat and put it in the bedroom. She returned a second later to find that Neil had removed his jacket and tie and was sitting in one of the armchairs.

Aware of her role as host, Jessica asked, 'What would you like for a nightcap?'

Neil smiled at her. 'Just you.'

'I come as an extra,' she quipped.

She did not wait for a reply, but walked over to the sideboard and took out a bottle. She held it up. 'How about this? It's a liqueur. I've had it ages.'

'It won't have gone off,' Neil replied, smiling and nodding his acceptance.

Jessica filled two liqueur glasses with the amber liquid, handed one to Neil and sat down opposite him.

They spent a good half hour sipping the liqueur and chatting. It was Jessica who made the first move. Draining the last few drops of liquid from her glass, she stood up.

'I'm going to change into something more comfortable,' she announced, making a move towards the bedroom. As she left Neil she scolded herself for using such a time-worn statement, but it was too late to do anything about it.

Once in her bedroom, she set about carrying out her plan. She opened one of the drawers, pulled out a nightdress and held it up briefly. It was a 'shortie' and, to say the least, brief. Natalie had given it to her for Christmas at around the time she and Graham were deciding to separate. Perhaps Natalie had envisaged that it might re-ignite the marriage. If that had been the object, it had had no opportunity to do so. Jessica had never worn it and it had lain in the drawer ever since. Now at last she had a use for it.

Disrobing completely, she quickly donned the nightdress and put on her dressing gown over it. A dab or two of perfume, and she was ready.

When she returned to the lounge, she was surprised to see that Neil had also changed his clothes and seemed to be wearing pyjamas and a dressing gown. Like her, he had dispensed with shoes or slippers.

Rising from his chair, he watched her approach. The next moment they were in each other's arms, gently kissing.

'You smell delicious,' he murmured.

'So do you,' she whispered.

Suddenly she grabbed his hand and led him into the bedroom. They kissed passionately, and he gently slipped the dressing gown from her shoulders. His hands found her breasts under their flimsy covering. Jessica drew off his dressing gown and discovered that he was naked to the waist. They moved onto the bed, where they continued to kiss and caress each other.

Chapter 13

The relationship continued with dedication from both parties. Few weekends passed when they did not meet. At times, if there was an event that attracted them, they also met during the week. They indulged in a variety of pleasures, visiting West End shows, concerts and on one occasion the Ideal Home Show. They would frequently dine out somewhere.

Jessica found herself becoming increasingly attracted to Neil. He was always attentive and caring. Their sexual encounters were regular and became a normal part of their relationship. Neither had discussed taking a step further and making things more permanent, but deep down Jessica felt that in time this would happen. In the meantime she was happy to enjoy his company.

It was getting close to Easter when one week Neil announced that he would not be seeing her as usual at the weekend because he was going to inspect his boat and get it ready for the coming season. Jessica felt disappointed. He had talked about this before and she had hoped that she would be included. However, she consoled herself with the thought that perhaps she would be in the way and maybe he preferred to work on the boat without a second person involved. Instead, she threw herself into spring cleaning her flat, working from dawn to dusk. When Sunday evening came, she was exhausted, but pleased with her efforts.

She had expected Neil to contact her the following week, but there was no word from him. It was not until the Monday before Easter that he phoned her. He was full of apologies, explaining that he had had to dash to Paris at short notice. Jessica expected more details, but none came and she was too polite to ask. Instead she just remarked, 'You like your Paris, don't you?'

Neil laughed. 'Well, you could say that it earns a crust of bread.'

She was just about to ask how his work on the boat had gone, when he asked her, 'What have you got planned for Easter?'

'Nothing really. I'm free.'

'Good. That's what I hoped. How about spending the weekend on my boat? The weather forecast is good.'

Jessica did not hesitate. 'I'd love to.'

'Fine. That's settled, then. Can you be free on Thursday?'

'Yes, of course. I'll take a day's leave.'

'That would be great. In that case we can drive down on Thursday morning. Suppose I pick you up about half past ten?'

Jessica thought for a second. Yes, of course she could make it. 'That's fine with me.'

'That's good, because that way we'll miss a bit of the Good Friday traffic.'

Neil's comment prompted Jessica to ask, 'Where is your boat?'

'At present it's at Marlow.'

'Oh, I've been there!'

'I know somewhere there where I can leave the car for a couple of days,' he added, explaining that parking near the river was not always easy to come by.

Jessica was thinking out the practical aspects of the weekend. 'What shall I bring?' she asked.

'Yourself,' Neil joked.

She laughed. 'Yes, I know. But what else?'

He became more serious. 'Some food would be useful. There's tea, coffee and sugar there, but we'll need some milk and some eats.'

Jessica grabbed a piece of paper and a pen. 'What food would you like me to bring?'

There was a pause before Neil answered. 'Fairly easy things to cook,' he suggested.

Jessica could see that she would have to take control. 'Right. What sort of cooking arrangements are there on the boat?' she asked.

'We can fry things, boil things and there's a kettle to make tea – and we can eat out some evenings. There are some nice pubs along the way.'

Jessica had scribbled down a few things. She studied the scrap of paper. 'That gives me a good idea. What about breakfast?'

'How about muesli? That's easy.'

'Muesli it is.' Jessica was writing as she spoke. 'OK. I'll look after the eats side of things.'

They continued to chat for almost half an hour.

It was Jessica who finally ended the call. 'I'll see you on Thursday, then. I'm really looking forward to it.'

'Me too.'

After she put the phone down, Jessica spent some time deciding what food to buy and then turned her attention to the clothes she would take. It was quite late when she retreated to bed.

She could hardly wait until the Thursday. When it arrived, she was up early, conscious that she had to buy food before Neil arrived.

She was at the supermarket when it opened at seven. A quick tour around its shelves provided enough inspiration to fill two bags. Carrying them was quite difficult, as they were heavy. She was glad when she reached home.

Back in her flat, she put the finishing touches to her wardrobe for the weekend. She received some influence from the weather. It had been warm and sunny all week, and fine weather was promised for the Easter weekend. She had already laid out some items. She retrieved her rucksack from a cupboard and started to pack, putting in underwear, a spare pair of jeans, evening slacks and blouse, a woolly just in case of colder weather, and her waterproof anorak. By the time she had finished, the rucksack was full and she wondered how items like the blouse would fare, but there was nothing she could do about it. One last thought was a pair of shoes with heels. She was thinking of the dining-out evenings. She just about found room in the rucksack for them.

It was well after ten by the time she was ready. The doorbell rang just before half past. She hurried to the intercom.

'It's me, Neil.'

She pressed the button. 'Come on up. I'm all ready.'

Half a minute later Neil was in the flat. She kissed him and gave what was now her usual greeting. 'Hello, darling.'

He responded with his own usual 'Hi, poppet,' and gave her a kiss in return.

She turned to the bags containing the food. A little anxiously she said, 'I've got some eggs, some sausages, bread rolls, butter and milk, two pasties and some bits of salad.'

Neil grinned. 'We won't starve with that! I've brought some things as well.'

Jessica suddenly thought of something. 'Oh dear. I should have bought a bottle of wine.' Inwardly she scolded herself for not remembering.

Neil smiled. 'Don't worry. I topped up the bar when I was there last week.'

Together they carried everything downstairs to his car. The boot was already half full, but they managed to put the food bags in. Jessica's rucksack went on the back seat.

Jessica dashed back to her flat to collect her short jacket. In spite of the sunshine promising another warm day, it was still cool at this time in the morning.

They stopped on the way at a service station for a cup of coffee. Jessica thought perhaps she should have offered Neil a hot drink when he arrived at the flat, but it was a passing thought and they both enjoyed the break in their journey.

It was close to midday when they arrived in Marlow. They left the car in a car park and carried their luggage to the boat. They had to walk further beside a busy road than Jessica had anticipated and she was glad when they came to the river and were on the quiet towpath.

Eventually Neil announced, 'Here it is,' and stopped alongside one of the moored boats.

Jessica was surprised when she saw it. 'Gosh! It's much bigger than I expected!' she exclaimed.

'It can sleep four people, five at a pinch.' Neil had already put his bag down and hopped on board. He undid the cover to allow access to the interior. Two minutes later Jessica was handing him their bags and her rucksack.

He held out his hand. 'Welcome aboard.'

Once inside, Jessica looked around keenly, interested in everything. Neil was eager to show her all the features.

The cockpit, or steering well, divided the boat in two. In the rear, or stern, there was a small cabin with a double bunk. Forward of the steering well, several steps led down into the main cabin, which had a bunk on either side and a folding table in the centre. Jessica had already taken note of the cooking stove. When Neil pulled back the curtains that covered the tiny windows, the cabin was bathed in sunlight, making everything look cosy.

Bags were passed down into the cabin, and then Neil asked, 'Will it be all right if I leave you to put things away while I go and move the car? As I said the other day, I have the use of a safe parking place, but it involves a bit more of a walk.'

'Of course it will. I'll find my way about. Leave it to me.'

'See you soon, then.'

In a way, Jessica was glad to be on her own, because she could take her time and explore everything. The first task was to put away the food. She found the food cupboard and carefully stowed all the items they had brought with them, and even discovered a cool box for the milk. She was relieved to find a small compartment with a toilet and washing facilities, having wondered what kind of arrangements there would be on board. She went into the rear cabin to deposit her rucksack on the bunk, and discovered a hanging cupboard for clothes, and best of all some drawers beneath the bunk. This led to her unpacking her rucksack and putting her clothes away. She was pleased to see that they had survived her packing and the journey without too many creases.

She was sitting on one of the bunks in the main cabin reviewing her activities when she felt movement on the boat.

The next moment Neil appeared at the top of the steps. 'Everything OK?'

'I've put everything away,' she replied.

Neil grinned. 'How about a cup of tea?' he asked.

'I'll make it.' Jessica jumped to her feet. 'But you'll have to show me how the stove works.'

'It's quite easy,' he assured her.

Jessica helped fill the kettle and, under Neil's watchful eye, turned on the gas and lit the ring. She placed the kettle over the flame, watched it for a second and then turned to him. 'Why don't we have the pasties I bought this morning?'

'Good idea.'

In less than five minutes, Jessica had produced two mugs of tea and set out two plates with the pasties and some tomatoes. They sat in the cabin enjoying their simple meal and listening to the sounds of the river.

While Neil checked the engine to make sure everything was in order, Jessica did the washing up and tidied the mugs and plates away. She was just finishing when the noise of the engine sounded, with an accompanying vibration throughout the boat. It stopped as suddenly as it had begun, and Neil reappeared in the cabin.

'It's a bit late to start going anywhere now,' he said. 'I suggest we stay here tonight. We can look around Marlow this afternoon. What do you think?'

Jessica was all for it. She was keen to explore the town.

They spent the afternoon there, stopping at one point to have coffee in one of the cafés. It was early evening by the time they returned to the boat. While they were relaxing in the main cabin, Neil suggested that they go back into Marlow a little later for their evening meal.

Jessica was in agreement, but first she had another question. 'Where are we going to sleep?'

Neil looked at her. 'The other cabin is the best one.' He paused. 'Nice and cosy.' There was humour in his voice as he added, 'Of course, we can have a cabin each if you prefer.'

Jessica gave him a reproachful look. 'We will use the rear one.'

'You mean the aft one.'

'Same thing,' she retorted. She disappeared into the other cabin. 'Give me two minutes.'

It was five minutes before she reappeared. Neil was sitting in the main cabin. He too had changed his clothes. Jessica had retrieved her blouse and slacks and was taking careful steps in her high heels.

They dined in a restaurant Neil had pointed out earlier. It was quite quiet when they arrived, but the room filled up quickly. They took time over their meal, which was accompanied by a carafe of house wine.

They walked slowly back to the boat, hand in hand. The evening was quite chilly and Jessica was glad she had brought her trusty jacket. Neil had carried a pullover and now appreciated its warmth.

Once back on board, they lost little time in retreating to bed. Jessica fell asleep snuggled up to Neil and listening to the water lapping at the boat.

She was up early the next morning. She had already washed and dressed and was well on with preparing breakfast when she heard the sound of Neil's electric razor. Several minutes later he appeared, stifling a yawn.

They kissed briefly. Neil looked out of the window. 'It's going to be another fine sunny day.'

'Oh, good,' Jessica replied, as she poured hot water into two mugs.

'I've got the hang of the stove quite quickly,' she announced, setting the mugs on the table next to the bowls of muesli she had already prepared.

They had a leisurely breakfast and then Jessica got up to clear away the dishes while Neil disappeared to check something on deck.

She had just finished her domestic tasks when Neil poked his head down into the cabin. 'Ready to go?' he asked.

'Yes. I must see this!' she called up.

She made her way up the steps to the cockpit. As she did so her shoe slipped, the leather sole failing to get a grip. She realised that her choice of footwear was not suitable for boat life. Neil had observed her dilemma. He glanced down at her feet as she joined him. After hesitating for an instant, she slipped off one shoe and then the other.

'Can I go barefoot?' she asked, looking anxiously at him.

He smiled. 'No problem. But you should put on some shoes if you go ashore.'

'Of course.'

She watched as he started the engine and undid the mooring ropes. Soon they were moving slowly along the river. She took everything in with interest: the houses on the banks of the river, and the joggers on the towpath. She was fascinated by the waterbirds, who continued doing their own thing, seemingly oblivious of them passing.

Neil concentrated on steering, and at one stage he asked Jessica if she would like to have a go. With a little bit of apprehension she agreed and found that once she had got used to the sensation, she quite enjoyed it. Neil took over again when she suggested that she make some coffee. Breakfast seemed a long way off now.

Around midday, they stopped and tied up. Jessica fried the sausages and some eggs. She was quite happy playing with the stove now.

The day passed quickly. Jessica was very contented with life on the river. In a short time she had learnt to steer the boat and control the engine, and whenever they came to a lock she knew the routine and passed the rope to the lock keeper. In spite of it being Good Friday, there were not many boats on the river until the afternoon.

When they tied up for the night, they decided to eat in, and Jessica prepared another meal, which they enjoyed with a bottle of wine. It was dark before they at last retreated to their sleeping quarters.

The weekend seemed to fly by. The weather was kind to them and only on one day did it rain. Undaunted, they continued with their travels. Neil donned his oilskin, and Jessica sought refuge in her waterproof anorak.

On the last day, they returned to their starting point and were relieved to find the mooring still free. Once again they decided to eat onshore, this time in one of the hotels.

They had reached the coffee stage of their meal when, during a lull in the conversation, Neil took the opportunity he had been waiting for. Studying Jessica intently, he asked, 'Happy, poppet?'

Jessica nodded enthusiastically. 'Absolutely. It's been fabulous.' She grinned ruefully. 'Even having to go barefoot.'

Neil laughed. 'You were great. Count yourself a fully fledged able seaman now.'

'I've really enjoyed it,' she murmured.

Suddenly Neil leaned across the table. He took one of her hands. 'We get on very well, we two, don't we?'

She nodded. 'First class. I've no complaints.'

There was a slight pause, and then Neil spoke again.

'I was wondering... That is... I was wondering if you would consider marrying me.'

Chapter 14

There was another brief moment of silence between them. It was broken by Neil. 'Of course, I understand if I've been too hasty. If you want some time to think about it, I can wait.' He looked anxiously at Jessica, waiting for her response.

Jessica said nothing for a few seconds. Thoughts were racing through her mind. Over the past few weeks she had been aware that their relationship was becoming more intense. Somehow she had expected that something like this might happen that weekend. She knew she had to formulate a reply carefully.

She continued to hold Neil's hand as she spoke. 'I'd love to marry you. You have so many of the qualities I look for in a partner.' She paused for a few seconds. 'You're kind and considerate, and I think you would be loyal, but I can foresee two problems.'

'What are they? Tell me. I'm sure we can overcome them.'

Jessica again chose her words carefully. 'One of them would be your job. You seem to go abroad quite a lot.' She waited for a reaction from him. When none came, she continued. 'My first marriage failed because my husband frequently went away for his work. At times it was as if I wasn't married. I wouldn't want to experience that all over again.'

Neil had been listening intently. Now he was quick to respond. 'Jessica, that's not a problem. I can easily switch to doing more work in the UK. I can concentrate on my clients here.'

Jessica nodded as she absorbed his words. What he was saying seemed very reasonable.

'What's the other problem?' he asked.

She thought for a second. She had never told him about her alleged legacy. It seemed unfair at this stage to keep it to herself, but she was limited in what she could relate. To date she had had no confirmation from Frank Dinton of how much she was going to inherit, but she felt that she had to say something.

She smiled. 'Well, actually you might be marrying an heiress.'

'What?' For a moment he seemed dumbfounded. 'Tell me more.'

Jessica explained about her visit to Dinton, Walley & Dinton and the subsequent letters she had received informing her that things were still being sorted out in Australia.

'At this stage I don't know how much I'm going to receive. It could be millions...' She laughed. 'Or it could be nothing.'

'Either way, it's not a problem,' Neil remarked thoughtfully. He chuckled. 'You might be able to buy me that Porsche I always wanted.'

'Or a bicycle,' Jessica chipped in.

They both laughed.

Neil became serious again. 'I'll try to be a good husband and live up to all the qualities you like.'

'And I will try to be a good wife.'

After another moment of silence Neil reached into his pocket and produced a small package. He handed it to Jessica. 'Then perhaps we can seal our agreement with this.'

Jessica undid the wrapping on the package. She carefully opened the tiny box it concealed. A ring nestled in its interior.

'May I?' Neil whispered.

Jessica allowed him to take the ring and place it on her finger. She held it up to the light.

'It's beautiful,' she murmured. She looked at Neil quizzically. 'It's my birthstone,' she said. 'How did you know?'

Neil grinned at her. 'Secret,' he replied.

She continued to look at him, perplexed.

'You left a birthday card in the bedroom. It had the date on it.'

Jessica made a face. 'A girl can have no secrets!' she exclaimed, but there was a twinkle in her eye.

Neil responded quickly. 'I really am sorry,' he stressed, clearly concerned.

'Darling, it's quite all right. Really it is.' She leaned towards him for a kiss.

Their lips met, much to the amusement of the couple at the next table, who perhaps had overheard too much of the last few minutes' proceedings.

Jessica and Neil left the restaurant soon afterwards and walked slowly back to the boat. At one point Neil halted and embraced Jessica. They kissed and remained hugging each other until they heard someone approaching. It was the end of a glorious day.

They drove back to London on the Monday morning, happy and contented. Neil stayed with Jessica that night, after an afternoon and evening making their future plans. They were both in favour of a quick and quiet wedding. When it came to discussing a honeymoon, their opinions differed. Jessica wanted to go to Paris, but Neil had other ideas. They ended up agreeing to go to the Algarve.

When Jessica returned to work the following day, things felt different. She had left work the previous Wednesday as a single businesswoman, and now she was a bride-to-be. She only told two colleagues of her plans. The relationship with most of her co-workers was purely a business one.

One of the first people she told about her new status was Babs. As soon as she had finished her evening meal she phoned her.

'Jessica,' Babs said in response to her greeting, 'I've been thinking about you. What have you been up to? What did you do for Easter?'

'I was on a boat on the Thames.'

'Oh, wonderful! Who were you with?'

'Neil Atkins. It was his boat.'

Babs was about to reply, but Jessica beat her to it. 'I've got some news for you. We're going to get married.'

'Gosh! Good for you, but that was rather quick. You've only known him a short while.'

Jessica laughed. 'About three months. Long enough to get to know each other.'

Babs began to grow more curious. 'Has he been married before?'

'No. I'm the only one who's second-hand.'

The statement amused Babs, but she was concerned for her friend. 'You'll have to watch your step.'

'I will,' Jessica retorted.

'Anyway, I'm really pleased for you. I was beginning to think you'd be left on the shelf.'

'Look who's talking!'

Babs hastily changed the subject. 'When's the wedding?'

'It's not fixed yet, but it'll be soon.'

'A big one like last time?'

'Heavens, no! That was a once-in-a-lifetime event. This time it will be very quiet.'

'Let me know when and where.'

'Of course. Can I put you down as one of the witnesses?'

'Happy to be of service.'

After a slight pause Jessica asked, 'So, what have you been doing since we last spoke?'

Babs immediately launched into elaborate details about her work, all the successes she had had and all the problems she had encountered, plus an account of her Easter weekend, which she had spent with friends in Devon. In the end the two friends were on the phone for over an hour.

Jessica had a somewhat different response when she

telephoned Natalie. After the preliminaries were over, she announced her news.

'I'm going to get married again.'

'Congratulations! Who to?'

'Neil Atkins. I met him at your party before Christmas.'

'Oh, yes, I remember. But you haven't known him very long.'

'Long enough,' Jessica assured her.

There was a pause, and then Natalie spoke again. 'You know, it's funny, but I always thought you and Graham would get back together.'

Jessica knew how Natalie felt about the divorce, so she chose her reply carefully. 'Well, we gave marriage a good go. It didn't seem to work for either of us and in the end we decided to go our separate ways.'

'I always thought you were made for each other.'

'Perhaps that was one of the problems. Maybe we were too much alike.'

She wished Natalie would stop talking about her marriage to Graham. She tried to move the conversation on. 'Anyway, I've found somebody else now.'

After another pause Natalie responded, voicing her words as if deep in thought. 'Jessica, I'm speaking as a friend now. Are you quite sure about this? After all, you've only known Neil a few months.'

Jessica sighed to herself. 'Quite sure.'

'Then I wish you both all the very best.'

'Thank you.'

'Have you told Graham?'

'No. I suppose I'd better.'

'Would you like me to?'

'Would you? I would appreciate that.'

'OK. I'll tell him.' Natalie paused again. 'When is the wedding?'

'We haven't decided on a date yet, but it'll be quite soon. Perhaps the end of the month. You'll come?'

'Gosh, I might be in America then.'

'Well, I hope you can make it. I'll let you know as soon as we've made the arrangements.'

'Thank you. Oh! I'll have to go now. There's somebody at the door.'

Jessica said her goodbye and put the phone down. It had not been an easy call. The response from Natalie had not been quite what she had expected. Jessica knew that she and Graham were very close, and during their marriage Natalie had been a very good friend to her. She had been very shocked when their divorce was announced, and had done her best to prevent it from happening. Still, Jessica mused, you cannot please all the people all the time. She turned her attention to preparing a list of all the things she needed to buy in time for her wedding.

She was interrupted by the sound of the doorbell. She went over to the intercom, but Gwen had beaten her to it. Jessica went out onto the landing and saw her standing in the hall.

'Problem?' Jessica enquired. It was unusual to hear the doorbell at night.

'No. Wrong house.' Gwen sighed. 'Some people can't read these days.'

Jessica laughed. 'I know what you mean.'

Gwen appeared to want to linger. The two occupants of the house did not see a great deal of each other. This was the opportunity, Jessica thought, to tell Gwen about her new status.

'I've got some news for you,' she announced quite breezily.

'Oh, do tell me!'

'I'm going to get married again.'

'Oh, how splendid! Anybody I know?'

'It's Neil Atkins. You've met him.'

'Is that the nice young man who's been visiting you?'

'Yes, that's right.'

'And will you both be living here after the wedding?'

Jessica assured her that they would, and could see the sense of relief on her face.

'It will be so nice to have a man in the house again,' Gwen enthused.

Back in her flat, Jessica settled down again to her list. At least this time round, she thought, things were simpler. Her thoughts turned again to her wedding to Graham. Natalie had been the prime instigator in arranging things. Their parents lived in a beautiful manor house in Oxfordshire and they had gone up there for the wedding. The night before the ceremony, Jessica had stayed with an aunt of Graham's who lived close by. Natalie had arrived early on the morning of the wedding to help her get ready. This was perhaps help Jessica could have managed without, but she had gone along with everything.

After the wedding ceremony they had left the church in a white Rolls-Royce, a surprise that Graham had arranged for her. The reception, with over sixty guests, had been held in a local hotel. A friend of Graham's family had acted as MC for the event.

Neither Jessica nor Graham had been quite prepared for the mischievous antics of Natalie and the best man, a friend of Graham's. After the meal and champagne, it was announced that Graham would remove Jessica's garter, which Natalie had provided and insisted she wear. When the ritual had been performed to Natalie's satisfaction, there was another surprise for the happy couple. While standing close together talking to some of their guests, they had suddenly found themselves handcuffed together, a situation they had had to endure until the reception broke up.

The vintage car had returned in the early evening to convey Graham and Jessica to the hotel where they would spend the night prior to departing for their honeymoon in Rome.

Reflecting on her first wedding made Jessica realise how different this one would be. She was rather pleased that it would be a quiet affair. The nature of this event was indicated by the small number of items she had down on her list. Last time there had been an expensive white dress. This time she planned to buy a simple suit. Neil had insisted that he make the arrangements at the register office as well as booking the honeymoon. While Jessica was glad to be relieved of the task, she hoped he would not be too long in doing so. She would have to apply for leave as soon as the date had been fixed.

She did not have to wait long. Neil phoned her a few nights later. Instinctively she knew it would be him as she picked up the handset.

'Hi, poppet.'

'Darling, it's good to hear from you. How are you?'

'I'm fine, and I've got some news for you.'

'Super! I'm all ears.'

'First, the wedding will be on the day we said – the Saturday. I've booked that. Half past eleven in the morning. I've managed to get us on the 8am flight to Faro the next day. I've still got to book the hotel.'

'That's fantastic! You've been busy.'

'We're coming back on the…' There was a pause as Neil looked up something. 'Yes. We're coming back on the following Saturday.'

Jessica was going to reply when Neil beat her to it. 'We've still got to sort out a meal for the guests after the wedding.'

'I'll do that,' Jessica chipped in quickly. 'I think it will be just us and the two witnesses. My friend Babs will be one of them. Natalie might not be able to make it, because she's likely to be in America, and Gwen won't be able to come.'

'Why's that?'

'I don't know. I think she's got something else on.'

'You get on quite well together, don't you?'

'Absolutely. I couldn't have a better neighbour. Oh, and she told me it would be nice to have a man in the house again.'

'Gosh, that gives me something to live up to!'

'I'll book some leave tomorrow,' Jessica announced. She was thinking of all the things she would have to do. She suddenly thought of something else. 'We need a second witness.'

'No problem. I've already got someone in mind. Greg Patton. You haven't met him yet,' Neil replied quite casually.

'Oh, that's good.' Jessica was relieved that something else was settled.

They chatted on, each of them thinking of more things to say. In the end it was Jessica who broke up the party.

'Well, I'd better sign off now and get my beauty sleep.'

'Me too,' Neil replied. 'I've got to go to Birmingham early tomorrow. I'll give you a call when I get back.'

'I'll look forward to that. Safe journey, darling,' Jessica responded cheerfully.

'I'll be thinking about you,' he replied.

'Bye then. All my love.' She meant it.

'Bye for now. Love you.'

With that the call ended.

Jessica put the phone down. Now it was all arranged, except for booking a restaurant. Talking to Neil had been another major step. Now things were arranged. It was only a matter of days before she would be a married woman again, with a loving husband.

Chapter 15

The next few days flew past very quickly for Jessica.

The day after her evening chat with Neil, the first thing she did on arrival at work was to fill in a chit for the necessary leave and take it to the personnel department.

It was comparatively easy to book a table at a restaurant. The next and biggest task ahead of her was to buy a costume for her wedding, and a trousseau for her honeymoon. She quickly abandoned any thoughts of doing it at the weekend or in the evening. Instead she took another day off out of the several weeks' leave she had accumulated.

On the day she had chosen for her shopping trip, she went up to the West End early and focused on Oxford Street. She was in the John Lewis store as soon as it was open. A quick coffee in The Place to Eat, and then she set about her search. She tried on numerous outfits until at last she found her ideal solution, a neat velvet figure-hugging two-piece costume in a pleasant shade of dark blue. At first she thought the skirt was too short, but assurance from an assistant convinced her that it was the one to buy. Another department provided a white silk blouse. Shoes were a difficult search. She thought she had found the solution when she spied a pair of classic high-heeled court shoes in a near-matching shade, but the department did not have her size. In the end the assistant located a pair in another branch and offered to have them despatched to her, which was a relief. Sheer tights to go with the outfit were an easy purchase.

After a bite to eat, she spent some time in the lingerie department. Two sets of underwear and a nightdress were added to her packages. The nightdress was almost transparent and could make no claims to keep her warm, but she was determined to please Neil on her wedding night. It was late in the afternoon by the time she had finished making her purchases. She had so much to carry that she decided to get a taxi home. The thought of struggling on the underground at rush hour was too much to contemplate. On an impulse, she made a last-minute purchase in a sexy underwear shop. With memories of her first marriage, she indulged in two red silk garters, though she had no definite plans at this stage about when she would wear them. This was going to be a surprise for Neil.

Back at the house, just as she was entering the hall, Gwen spied her and, seeing her loaded with parcels, wanted to know what she had been up to. In spite of being tired, Jessica showed her the outfit she had bought.

Gwen approved immediately. 'That suit is absolutely made for you,' she announced.

In the end Jessica showed Gwen practically all of her purchases. It was a tired bride-to-be who finally made it to her flat. Kicking off her shoes, she relaxed on the settee for ten minutes before making herself something to eat. It had been a tiring day, but she knew that in the end the time she had spent looking for an outfit would have been worthwhile. After all, Neil was worth making a big effort for, she pondered. She wouldn't be getting married again.

That was not the end of Jessica's shopping. Next it was new clothes for her honeymoon. She spent several lunch breaks looking around the shops and acquired a range of items, including several summer dresses, shorts, a new bikini and underwear. Last of all she bought a new suitcase to replace her existing one, which had broken wheels. Returning to the office with this caused some mirth and comments from her colleagues.

One evening she had an unexpected phone call. She answered, thinking it would be Neil.

'Hi. It's Natalie.'

'Natalie, how are you? This is a surprise. I thought you were going to America.'

'I am, but I just wanted to tell you that I spoke to Graham yesterday evening.'

This was not really information Jessica wanted to hear. Why did Natalie keep bringing up the subject? She did her best to hide her feelings. 'Oh, that's nice. How is he?'

'He was pretty sick when I told him you were getting married again.'

Again this was something Jessica did not want to know. She took a deep breath before replying. 'I don't know why. We've been divorced for over two years. What does he think? That I'm going to remain unmarried for the rest of my life?'

'I understand what you're saying. It's just that I think Graham always thought divorce would be an interlude, and that you would get back together.'

This is ridiculous, Jessica thought. Here I am, a few days away from getting married again and my ex-husband still thinks he has some sort of possession of me. I've got to stop it once and for all, particularly with Natalie.

She took a deep breath. 'Look, Natalie, you don't seem to understand. It's true that Graham and I were very much in love at first, but after a while things began to go wrong. I just became a thing, an object, second to Graham's job. He used to disappear, sometimes for weeks at a time, and then return expecting me to be there ready to wash his underwear and have sex with him. And then after a few days it would all start over again. I even spent Christmas on my own once.'

There was a bit of a pause, and then Natalie said, 'OK. I get the point. I guess I'm a bit of a busybody. Tell me to shut up next time.'

Jessica could see the way things were heading. She liked Natalie and did not want to fall out with her. 'I'm sorry if I was a bit blunt. I didn't mean to upset you. I know how close you and Graham are.'

She heard a bit of laughter from the other end of the phone line.

'Look,' Natalie said, 'you didn't upset me, and I hope you and Neil are very happy together. You deserve somebody like him. I'm sorry I can't get to the wedding.'

'I'll miss you,' Jessica replied, and she meant it.

'I know. I'll see you soon.'

Before Jessica could respond, Natalie spoke again. 'Sorry, Jessica. I've got to go. Bye for now.'

With that, she was gone.

Jessica replaced the telephone on its hook and sat down again. It had been an odd call. She hoped Natalie wasn't upset after all. Graham and Natalie were very close together in age, and perhaps this had made them very protective of each other. But as far as she was concerned, her time with Graham was finished and she saw no point in Natalie trying to keep bringing up the subject. In a few days' time she would be married to Neil Atkins, and that was all there was to it.

The morning of the wedding turned out to be bright and sunny, and this pleased Jessica completely. The last thing she wanted was to have rain on her suit, or to have to appear under an umbrella. She was up early and took her time to pack her new suitcase for her honeymoon.

After eating a small breakfast she changed into her wedding outfit. Neil had said he would pick her up at half past ten and she didn't want to keep him waiting. She was ready except for shoes, which lay beside her suitcase ready to put on by ten. In the meantime she decided to have a cup of coffee. She was just sitting enjoying this when the front doorbell went. She went to the intercom.

'Hello.'

'It's Sir Galahad in person,' came the reply.

'Enter, Sir Galahad,' Jessica answered breezily.

Two minutes later Neil was in the doorway. He was carrying a small suitcase, and a bouquet of flowers and a buttonhole for her. He immediately kissed her.

'Hey, don't spoil my makeup!' she exclaimed, but she was laughing as she spoke.

'Nothing will spoil you today, poppet.'

Jessica took control. 'I'm all ready.' She glanced at her watch. 'Have you got time for a coffee?'

'Absolutely.'

'Right. Sit down, and I'll make you one.' She disappeared into the kitchen.

After enjoying their coffee, it was time to go. Neil had arranged a taxi, which arrived as they were leaving the flat.

It was only a ten-minute drive to the register office. Babs was already waiting. She greeted both of them with a hug, and gave Jessica a kiss. There was another wedding in progress, so they had to wait a quarter of an hour, during which Babs did most of the talking. While they were waiting, Greg, the second witness, turned up. Aged about thirty, Jessica guessed, and quite affable. She was surprised that Neil had never spoken of him until they came to discuss the wedding arrangements.

The registrar greeted them in a friendly manner. Jessica was surprised how quick the ceremony was. One minute she was Jessica Walker, and the next she was Jessica Atkins. It was a thrill when Neil slipped the wedding ring on her finger. He had instructed Greg to take some photographs, something Jessica had forgotten to ask him about.

It was another ten-minute taxi ride to the restaurant Jessica had booked for the meal. She had indicated to the owners that it would be a wedding celebration lunch, and she was surprised on arriving that they had taken full notice of her comment. The party were led to a secluded corner where a table had been beautifully prepared and decorated. There was even a small wedding cake on a side table.

The meal itself was a jolly event. The champagne flowed freely and everybody became relaxed, including Greg, who turned out to be quite entertaining. In the end, it was over two hours before the party came to an end. Neil wanted to pay the bill, but Jessica insisted and used her credit card.

Outside, the party finally broke up. There were parting congratulations from Babs and Greg and then each went their own way. Neil and Jessica returned to the flat by taxi, arriving there in the middle of the afternoon. They took their time over a cup of tea, going over the events of the day so far. Eventually Jessica disappeared to freshen up and change. She had purchased a second costume for going away, light green with a white open-necked blouse. She was glad to have a change of footwear. The wedding shoes had done their job but had proved to be a bit uncomfortable to wear.

She took the flowers down to Gwen, remarking, 'They'll be dead by the time we come back.' She also gave her a piece of the wedding cake, which the restaurant had carefully wrapped up for them.

Then it was time to leave. Neil picked up his suitcase from the hall and carried it to the front steps, together with Jessica's. The taxi arrived on time, and they were off to Gatwick and the hotel Neil had booked for the night.

During their evening meal, Neil raised his glass of wine and gazed at Jessica.

'To us, darling,' he said. 'Many happy years together.'
'Many,' she agreed. Their glasses clinked together.
'Happy, poppet?'
'Unspeakably,' Jessica murmured.
They kissed across the table.

Chapter 16

Two months had gone by since Jessica and Neil returned from their honeymoon. They had enjoyed to the full their break in Portugal. The weather had been perfect, and each day they had spent hours on beautiful beaches. Jessica would sometimes swim in the sea while Neil relaxed on the sand. Neil had admired Jessica's bikini and remarked on what a nice figure she had, which had pleased her. It had been a long time since anybody had paid her such a compliment.

Jessica had become accustomed to having Neil around and sharing space with him. She had worked out a daily routine, rising a little earlier than him and spending time in the bathroom. By the time he got up, she was in the kitchen preparing breakfast for the two of them. Breakfast was always a quick affair on the days when she had to leave for work. Sometimes Neil worked from home, spreading paperwork over the dining table and stretching the telephone to the full length of its cable. She had already discovered that he was not the tidiest of people, and this often made a little extra work for her.

They were contented in each other's company and it seemed as if nothing could spoil their happiness. But Jessica was unprepared for the events that were about to unfold.

One morning, just as she was leaving for work, the postman delivered a letter from Dinton, Walley & Dinton. The letter asked her to contact Frank Dinton at her earliest convenience. Jessica had several meetings lined up, so three days had passed before she once again entered the solicitors' premises. A quick check-in at reception, and within five minutes she was entering Frank Dinton's office. He stood up as she entered, and held out his hand.

'Good morning, Miss Walker. Please sit down.'

Jessica shook his hand, returned his greeting and sat down. Smiling, she said, 'I got married since we last met. I am now Mrs Atkins.'

He smiled. 'Congratulations. Thank you for letting me know. I shall update your details.'

There was a brief pause as he referred to the papers in front of him. He cleared his throat and began to speak. 'I asked you to come and see me because there has been a change since we last spoke.' He paused again and looked at her.

'What sort of change?'

The solicitor cleared his throat again. 'The last time we met I indicated the estimated value of your late uncle's estate.'

'Yes. You told me it was worth about fourteen million pounds.'

He glanced at his papers again. He studied her as he continued. 'Miss Walker... I'm sorry, Mrs Atkins – I also told you that that figure was several years old and would probably change.'

Jessica was silent, trying to relate to what the solicitor was saying. Questions were racing through her mind. 'How much is it now?' she asked.

Frank Dinton studied her closely as he replied. 'According to the latest information we have received from Australia, it now stands at between twelve and thirteen million pounds. However, as I explained to you at our last meeting, most of that figure is subject to inheritance tax, which is currently forty per cent, and there will also be expenses to be deducted. You will probably receive about seven million pounds.'

The news struck Jessica like a thunderbolt. 'Phew,' she managed to gasp. She was trying to relate to what she had just heard, but the solicitor was speaking again.

'Of course, the final amount will be determined by the rate of exchange on the day of transfer.'

Jessica nodded. A question popped into her thoughts. 'Mr Dinton, I am curious to know why the amount of money is so much less than it was the last time we spoke. Do you know the reason?'

He answered quickly. 'We have to remember that the original figure was only provisional, but in answer to your question, from the information I currently have it would seem that the problem has been with the gold mine your uncle owned. It has run out of gold.' He added quickly, 'In addition, it would appear that some of the investments your uncle made have not performed as well as they might have done.'

'Oh, I see. That explains everything.'

It seemed as if the solicitor read her thoughts. 'You will still receive a considerable sum of money,' he pointed out with a smile.

Jessica laughed. 'It's more than enough for me to handle.' She was about to add a further comment, but he spoke again. 'Such a large sum of money can be quite life changing. Have you considered what you will do with it?'

She smiled briefly. 'I haven't had much time to think about it, but I think initially I'll put it somewhere safe and carry on as normal for a while. There will be plenty of time later to decide what to do with it.'

He nodded in agreement. 'Very wise, if I may say so.' He looked at her thoughtfully. 'Do you have a financial adviser?'

'Not at this stage, but I deal with large sums of money every day in my job.' She hoped her reply would satisfy him.

It seemed to work, because he immediately said, 'Yes, yes, of course,' and changed the subject. 'Mrs Atkins, we will of course require your bank details for the transfer. Perhaps you should advise your bank that this sum of money will be arriving. Some special arrangements might be required.'

'Yes, I'll do that,' Jessica replied.

After she had provided the required details, it was clear that the interview was coming to a close.

Frank Dinton shuffled his papers. 'Do you have any other questions?'

Jessica shook her head. 'I don't think so. I'll wait to hear from you again.'

'Yes, of course. If there are any questions you have overlooked, please contact us.'

With that and the usual pleasantries, they shook hands again and Jessica left his office.

Once outside the building, she walked slowly in the direction of her workplace. In the past few weeks, she had been vaguely wondering what it would be like to receive such a large sum of money. Now that it seemed to be happening, she felt that she had to have time to adjust to her new situation. She had never dreamed of having so much money at her disposal.

As she was passing a coffee bar she knew, she glanced at her watch. She would have missed her coffee break at work. On the spur of the moment, she decided to go in. She ordered a coffee and retreated to a table in a corner. She needed time to think, but first she had to tell Neil the latest news. She took out her mobile and dialled his number.

He answered straight away. 'Hello, poppet.'

'Hi. I've just left the solicitor's office.'

'What's the news?'

Jessica paused for a second. 'The solicitor says I'll probably get about seven million pounds.'

'What?' Neil sounded aghast. 'I thought it was supposed to be more than that.'

Jessica smiled to herself. 'It was, but it seems that the mine ran out of gold.'

'Oh, so we won't be able to buy that villa in Monte Carlo?'

Jessica laughed. 'No, but seven million will come in useful when we eventually buy a house.'

'Yes, of course it will.'

Jessica glanced at her watch again. 'Anyway, darling, I've got to get back to work now. We can talk about it again tonight.'

During the next few weeks, Jessica did her best to come to terms with her new situation. This entailed several extra jobs. Following Frank Dinton's advice, she made an appointment and visited her bank. She explained her mission to an uninterested but polite member of staff, who made several suggestions to her for the smooth transfer of the money and offered to put her in touch with the bank's investment team. Jessica politely declined. She had already made up her mind to split up the money and deposit it in several safe outlets until the dust had settled. Frank Dinton had asked her whether she had made a will. Neil had already suggested that they each do so. Jessica left all her worldly goods to her new husband.

After that she settled back to enjoying life with him. On the home front, there had been one or two minor problems to sort out. One had been the parking of Neil's car. Often during the week he would return in the evening to find nowhere close to the house to leave it. A solution came from Gwen, who knew of somebody local who had a garage for rent.

The availability of a car made another positive change for Jessica, who started to drive again. She had taken lessons and passed her test while she was married to Graham, but she had not driven since. Now if she and Neil went out at the weekend she would drive, renewing her confidence and enjoying being behind the wheel again.

The next problem was a massive shock. The day started like many of the previous ones. After saying goodbye to Neil, Jessica started out for work. There was the usual packed train and the walk from the tube station to her office. She arrived early and only a few of her colleagues were at their desks. She settled back in her chair and reviewed the day's schedule. She had a meeting in the afternoon, but that was her only commitment for the day. She was busying herself sorting out the paperwork she would need, when her internal telephone rang. This was unusual so early in the morning. She picked up the handset.

'Ah, Jessica. Can I see you right away?'

'Yes, of course.' She recognised the voice. It was Marion Phelps, her line manager.

'I'll be in the personnel office. Join me there.'

'Yes, of course,' Jessica repeated. She wondered why the meeting was in the personnel office. Perhaps they're going to give me promotion, she thought vaguely.

'As soon as you can.'

'I'll be there in two or three minutes.'

Jessica put the phone down. She thought Marion sounded a bit abrupt.

She climbed the two flights of stairs to the personnel office and halted before the door marked Grant Stone, Personnel Manager. She gave a loud knock on the door.

Immediately a voice bade her enter.

Grant Stone and Marion Phelps were sitting behind the large desk.

'Good morning, Jessica. Please take a seat,' said Mr Stone.

Jessica sat down on one of the chairs facing her two colleagues.

There was a moment's silence. The personnel manager was perusing the papers on his desk. At last he looked directly at Jessica. 'I see you've been with the company for five and a half years.'

'Yes, that's right.'

He glanced down at his papers briefly and then directed his gaze at her again. 'As you are aware, the company was taken over recently and this has meant some important changes here. These changes will affect our employees. I regret that I have to tell you that your job is no longer available.'

The news hit Jessica head-on. She struggled to quite comprehend. 'You mean… You mean my job has ceased to exist?'

He nodded. 'That's correct. Unfortunately, there is no further employment available to you here.'

Jessica was stunned by this further news. At first she had assumed that she might be offered another job within the company. Now she was being dismissed, thrown away like a piece of litter. She attempted some sort of reply. 'You mean I'm being made redundant?'

'That's exactly it, Jessica,' Marion Phelps cut in.

'You will receive three months' salary as a redundancy payment,' added the personnel manager.

Jessica barely heard the statement. She was already thinking ahead. 'When will I be leaving? Will it be the end of the month?' she asked softly.

Mr Stone shook his head. 'No. We feel that it is in the best interests of everybody if you leave immediately – today.'

It was the final blow. Jessica hardly heard his next words. 'Of course, the company would like to thank you for the contribution you have made to its success over the time you have been with us.'

Jessica could think of nothing more to say.

It was Marion who spoke next. 'If you have no further questions, Jessica, I'll give you a hand to collect your things.'

Jessica hardly noticed as she was handed an envelope and allowed herself to be led from the room. As she stood up to leave, Mr Stone briefly looked up from his papers and uttered a curt 'Good morning'. Automatically Jessica replied with a barely audible 'Good morning. Thank you.'

Marion escorted her down to her own office. Some of their colleagues glanced up with enquiring looks. From her own desk she produced two plastic carrier bags. 'You need to clear your desk of personal items,' she announced.

Almost like a zombie, Jessica commenced the task. As she went through the desk drawers, a variety of items were displayed briefly before being grabbed by Marion and placed in the bags.

Marion picked up Jessica's notebook and moved it to one side of the desk. Clearly Jessica was to be denied any access to it. Jessica removed the last items from her bottom drawer, a spare pair of shoes she kept there in case she got wet travelling to work.

When the task was clearly coming to an end, Marion asked, 'Is that everything?'

'Yes,' Jessica whispered. She was close to tears.

'I need your security pass,' Marion demanded.

Jessica removed it from around her neck and handed it over.

Marion gestured towards the door. 'I'll show you out.'

Jessica could hardly believe what was happening as she followed her to the exit. She was being escorted out of the building as if she was a criminal. They passed her puzzled colleagues. Jessica could not bring herself to meet their gaze.

When they reached the front entrance, Marion held out her hand. 'Goodbye, Jessica. Thank you for all your hard work.'

'Goodbye,' Jessica whispered. Marion watched her walk away and then turned to re-enter the building.

Jessica walked slowly, almost aimlessly. She constantly choked back the tears that threatened to overwhelm her. She still could not believe what had happened in the space of less than an hour. She had come to work happily planning the day ahead. Now she was walking away without a job. She spied a snack bar and entered it. She had to think. She bought a coffee and took it to a table.

She sat there, sipping the coffee and going over the events of the last hour again and again. It was the harshness of how things had been carried out that affected her the most. To be dismissed just like that, as if she had committed some crime! The indifferent attitude of both Marion Phelps and Grant Stone was almost unbelievable, and hard to understand. She had always thought that she got on quite well with her line manager. Marion's treatment of her in the last hour was a complete transformation.

She sat there for a long time. Eventually she felt a little calmer and more in control. She could get another job, she knew that, and at least she hadn't been left destitute. She could take her time to sort herself out. First she had to phone Neil and tell him what had happened. Her first attempt failed, but when she tried again five minutes later he answered.

'Hello, poppet. What are you up to?'

Now for it, Jessica thought. There was a tremor in her voice as she spoke. 'I've been sacked.'

'What? How did that happen?'

She took a deep breath. 'Well, I went into the office as usual and was immediately called to personnel. It's all to do with this recent take-over. My job no longer exists.'

'And they didn't offer you anything else?'

'No.'

'That's awful. That sort of thing seems to be happening too often.'

Jessica was silent for a few seconds. 'I think it was the manner in which it happened more than anything else. I was discarded like a bit of dirt on the floor. Marion, my boss, who I always got on quite well with, was so cold and formal.'

'I've heard about that happening to other people,' Neil commented. 'I guess it's just the way things are done these days.'

Jessica would have continued, because she needed to talk to someone, but Neil took up the conversation. 'Look, poppet, I've got a meeting with someone in five minutes. Make your way home and I'll join you as soon as I can.'

This made her feel even more sad, but she understood that he had to go. She simply said, 'OK. See you soon.'

'Love you. Bye.' He rang off.

Jessica drained the last of the coffee from her mug and slowly made her way home. It was late morning when she arrived. She had no inclination to do anything. She sat down on the settee and waited. She glanced at the two plastic carrier bags that contained her possessions. Looking at them brought painful memories. She took them into the bedroom and placed them out of site. She remembered the envelope Grant Stone had given her. She took it out and looked at the documents it contained. The most important item was her P45. She looked at it and wondered when she would be able to give it to a new employer. She returned to the living room and stretched out on the settee, waiting for Neil to return home. Perhaps he would have some ideas for her future.

Chapter 17

The next few weeks were quite stressful for Jessica. She was constantly reminded of her unemployed situation. Neil was very supportive, but it was during the day that she felt her new status most. She continued to get up early and make breakfast for Neil and herself, but then she watched him depart for work. After that, the long day dragged. If he decided to work from home, she usually went out to the shops, but after she had done that a few times it lost its appeal.

Neil had been quite pragmatic about her redundancy. After all, he had pointed out, she was being paid for the next few months, so why not sit back, enjoy the freedom, and use the time to find another job?

Jessica knew this was sound advice, and she did her best to carry out his suggested plan. She searched the newspaper every day for likely positions and contacted several agencies. She had two interviews, but one company felt she was over-qualified for their vacancy, and for the other one she had insufficient experience. She weighed up the possibility of working locally. If she did so, she could afford to take a lower salary because she would be saving on travel costs. Unfortunately, nothing nearby came her way.

She was saddened when Neil announced that he would have to go to Paris again. 'It will be one of the last times,' he assured her.

While he was away, she continued her efforts to find a job. At first she thought he would only be gone for two or three days, but then he phoned her, most apologetic that he would have to stay longer. In the end he was away for the best part of a week.

When he came back he suggested that they spend a couple of weeks with his sisters in the West Country. 'Laura and Sophie are longing to see you,' he added.

The thought of being away from her immediate environment was appealing. When Neil explained that his sisters lived in a large house near the sea, that clinched the matter for her.

Their departure arrangements were quickly settled. Once a decision had been made, they were both eager to get going. Neil was looking forward to spending some time with his sisters, and Jessica was keen to meet them and see where they lived.

It was a bright sunny day when they left the city. They took turns with the driving, Jessica renewing her acquaintance with the motorway. They took their time over the journey, at one point exiting the motorway and having lunch in a pub Neil knew of.

It was mid-afternoon when they left the busy main roads and ambled along a country lane with farmland on each side. Eventually they came upon a settlement.

'This is the nearest village to the house. It's only about three miles now,' commented Neil.

'It's lovely!' exclaimed Jessica, taking in the picturesque church nestling amongst trees, and the pub next to the village shop.

'The shop is also the post office,' Neil explained.

'That's very convenient,' Jessica remarked.

They were already leaving the village behind and winding up a hill towards the coast, and it seemed like no time at all before Neil was turning the car onto a gravel drive between two impressive gateposts. A large house came into view.

'This is it,' he announced.

'It's huge!' Jessica exclaimed.

He nodded. 'Dad inherited this place from my grandfather before I was born and then left it to my sisters when he died. They love it and won't even think of moving to a smaller place.'

'But it must cost a fortune to keep it going.'

Neil smiled. 'Dad was pretty wealthy. He left us three children well provided for.'

Jessica would have liked to ask how his father came by so much money, but by then the car had arrived at the house. The next instant the front door opened and two older women emerged full of smiles. Clearly these were Neil's sisters.

Jessica and Neil got out of the car and were immediately welcomed. Neil greeted his sisters with a hug and introduced them to Jessica, who immediately found herself at the centre of attention.

After a brief hug Laura stood back, took Jessica's hand and looked at her. 'Jessica, it's so lovely to see you. Welcome! We were afraid Neil was going to keep you all to himself.'

Jessica smiled in return. 'It's lovely to be here,' she replied.

It was Sophie's turn next. She too hugged Jessica. 'Yes, indeed. Welcome to the family, Jessica.'

Jessica had only just time to thank her before Laura took charge of the proceedings. 'Now, come along into the house, Jessica. And Neil, you bring your luggage up to the Primrose Room.'

To add action to her words, she took Jessica's hand again and led her up the steps to the front door, followed closely by Sophie. Neil was busy taking the suitcases out of the car.

The front door opened up into a spacious hall with a large fireplace. A staircase wound its way upwards, hugging two walls. Laura immediately led the way to the upper floor, where a wide corridor appeared to stretch the length of the house. They walked along it to the end. Jessica looked at the oil paintings decorating the walls, while Laura and Sophie chatted nonstop about the weather and how nice it was to have her and Neil staying with them.

Eventually a door was thrown open and the three of them entered a large bedroom that had windows on two different walls. The enormous double bed seemed to be almost lost in the room.

'We thought you'd like this room. It was always our parents' favourite,' Laura explained. 'The bathroom is next door.'

'It's really lovely,' Jessica replied.

Just at that moment Neil appeared with the two suitcases.

'We'll leave you to settle in now. Supper at six.' It was Laura again. 'Neil, show Jessica everything.'

'Will do,' he replied.

'See you later,' Sophie said. The two sisters moved to the doorway.

'Thank you very much,' Jessica called after them.

As soon as the door was closed, Jessica rushed to each window in turn. They looked down on different parts of a large garden. When she had satisfied her curiosity she turned to Neil, who was standing smiling at her.

'Darling, the house is so huge, and this room… I've never slept in a room as big as this.'

Neil grinned. 'The house is two hundred years old. It used to be a base for smuggling, with the sea not far away.'

How many bedrooms are there? It seems enormous.'

'Six on this level, plus a nursery.'

'And you grew up here?'

'Yes, but I was only here for the first few years of my life. I went to boarding school when I was ten, and then on to university. After that I didn't visit the place very much.'

'Oh, what a shame! But your father lived here?'

'Yes, he did.'

Jessica wondered if there had been some sort of friction between Neil and his father. Perhaps he didn't want to tell her for now. Maybe another time, she thought.

For the next ten minutes or so they were busy unpacking the suitcases, and their conversation was mainly about the holiday that lay ahead of them, though at one point Jessica did volunteer another question. 'What did your sisters do for a living?' she asked.

'Laura was a nurse, and Sophie was a teacher,' he replied, 'but when Dad died and they inherited this place, they gave up work and came back to live here permanently.'

'And neither of them ever married?'

Neil shook his head. 'No. I guess they never found the right guy.'

Jessica was intrigued by the two sisters. On first seeing them she had been struck by their clothes. Both wore long dresses, almost as if they were from a bygone age, and she guessed that neither was as old as she looked. In time, she assumed, she would learn more, but for now she was content to let her questions wait. It seemed as if the family must have been very well off financially if the two sisters could afford to give up work and come to live in this rambling house.

She was in for another surprise when she visited the bathroom, which was also large and was dominated by a sizeable bath and sink. Huge brass taps gurgled forth streams of water. Everything about the room had the appearance of being from a different age. The lavatory was much the same. A massive Victorian toilet pan stood in the long, narrow room. Pulling the chain produced a torrent of water, making enough noise to waken the soundest sleeper.

Jessica was full of humour when she returned to the bedroom, where Neil was still sorting out the things he had brought, including his laptop and some papers. He intended to do some work while he was there.

Jessica could not help talking about what she had just seen. 'Darling, the fittings in the bathroom and toilet are so ancient. They must date from Victorian times.'

Neil laughed. 'They do.'

Jessica wanted to see the rest of the house and the garden, so with Neil as guide, they set off on a tour. Jessica was amazed at the number of rooms on the ground floor. A large sitting room full of shabby furniture, a dining room with a table big enough to seat ten people, a breakfast room next to the huge kitchen, and a library. It was this last room that attracted Jessica. There were bookshelves crammed with dusty books from floor to ceiling on every wall, barely leaving space for the window and the door. A quick look satisfied her. All the books were old and there did not seem to be anything of interest to her amongst them.

'These all belonged to my father and my grandfather,' Neil remarked.

The outside of the house was as interesting as the inside. As well as a large garden, there was an orchard with fruit trees.

Neil took Jessica to a secluded part of the garden where there were the remains of a cottage. 'I used to play here as a child,' he remarked. He regarded the ruins intently. 'It was in much better shape then. It had a roof.' He laughed.

Jessica tried to imagine him as a small boy using the grounds as a play area. It must have been a fascinating place for a child, she thought. This prompted another question from her. 'Did you have lots of friends around to play?' she asked, looking at him.

Neil smiled at her. 'Not really,' he replied. 'I didn't really make any friends until I went away to school.'

'It must have been quite lonely for you.'

Neil nodded but said nothing. Jessica guessed that she had hit an area of his past that he would rather not remember.

She quickly changed the subject. 'What did your father actually do? I mean, what was his job?'

Neil reacted as if surprised by the question. 'Dad? He was a stockbroker, but he also had business interests.'

'It looks as if he was successful,' Jessica remarked, glancing in the direction of the house.

Neil chuckled. 'He was. Very successful.'

That, thought Jessica, answers quite a lot of my other

questions. She now understood how Neil's sisters were able to live in the huge house without any apparent income.

After they had made an extensive tour of the garden and surrounding area, Neil took Jessica along a path that led away from the house. It was almost as if the drive continued, only now they were walking on a rough track. There were trees on both sides in places.

'Where does this go?' she asked.

Neil grinned. 'You'll soon see.'

Almost immediately the track ended on a strip of grass surrounded by bushes. Jessica could hear the sea not far away. Neil led her to the edge of the strip. A flight of rough steps led down to a tiny cove with a sandy beach.

'Gosh! A private beach!' she exclaimed.

'Not exactly private. There is another access at the end of the cove.'

'It's super.'

They wandered back to the house and got ready for supper.

This brought another surprise for Jessica. Neil's sisters turned up wearing a change of clothes and specially groomed for the event. They looked almost as if they had stepped out of a Dickens novel. Jessica was glad that she had taken trouble with her own appearance and put on a long skirt and a pretty blouse. Neil was now wearing a jacket and tie.

Laura appeared to almost reprimand him. 'Neil, we have a guest. We need some wine.' She turned to Jessica. 'Jessica, we'll be having fish. Would you prefer red or white wine?'

'I'm quite happy with either, but perhaps white would be nice,' Jessica answered.

'Oh, good. That would be my choice as well,' Laura remarked. She addressed another instruction to her brother. 'Neil, there's a bottle of white wine being chilled in the kitchen. We'll have that.'

Neil promptly disappeared and returned a couple of minutes later with the prescribed wine.

Conversation during the meal tended to centre on Jessica. Laura and Sophie asked question after question, until at one point Neil butted in, 'You two will tire her out with all your questioning.'

'But she's part of the family and we want to know all about her,' Sophie piped up.

Neil's words seemed to have some effect, because the tone of the conversation changed slightly.

Towards the end of the meal, Sophie asked, 'Do you swim, Jessica?'

Jessica nodded. 'Yes, I do. I love swimming.'

'Oh, then that's splendid. Colliers Cove is excellent for bathing.'

'Neil showed it to me earlier. I'm looking forward to swimming there.'

'It's so much nicer in the sea than in a swimming pool, don't you think?' Laura asked.

'Absolutely,' Jessica replied.

Laura continued with the subject. 'It's such a pity Neil can't join you, but he's never learnt to swim.' She sighed. 'We did try to teach him, but he hated it.'

'Well, it's never too late to learn,' Jessica replied.

Neil jokingly joined in. 'I leave swimming to the fish.'

The subject was dropped at that point, as Laura insisted that they all leave the table and go into the lounge for coffee.

Much later, Jessica lay contentedly beside Neil in the giant bed. She was happy with how the day had gone, and those to come promised more pleasures. She could not have known what the days ahead would bring, events that would be markedly different from the ones she envisaged.

Chapter 18

The next morning Jessica woke up to see the sun streaming through one of the windows. Neil was still asleep, so she crept out of the bedroom and into the bathroom. When she returned fifteen minutes later, he was sitting up in bed yawning.

'Wake up, sleepyhead,' she teased him.

'What time is it?' he asked, picking up his watch. 'It's only half past seven!' There was an air of indignation in his voice.

Jessica planted a kiss on his lips. 'I know, darling, but it's such a nice day that I thought maybe we could do something, perhaps go sightseeing.'

Neil's face took on a worried look. 'That would be lovely, poppet, but I have to do some work this morning.'

Jessica was disappointed, but she quickly resigned herself to the situation. Neil had already explained that there would be some days when he would need to work. Her next remark was quite cheerful. 'In that case I'll go for a swim. I can't waste a good beach like that.'

'I'm awfully sorry, poppet.'

She smiled. 'Don't worry. I can amuse myself. What time's breakfast?'

'Laura and Sophie never have breakfast. Ours will be when we get there.'

'Great. Then hurry up and get washed and dressed. I'm hungry.'

Neil laughed. 'Right, boss,' he replied, jumping out of bed and preparing to leave the room.

It was a good twenty minutes before he reappeared. During his absence Jessica had been thinking. She decided to alter her plans.

'Darling, I need to keep an eye on getting another job. I'll have to buy a newspaper. I think I'll take a walk to the village after breakfast. I should be able to get one there.'

'It's quite a long way. Take the car.'

'Well… If I can that will be useful.'

'No problem, poppet.' He rummaged in his jacket pocket and handed her the car keys.

Jessica accepted them gladly. Using the car would mean that she could check the newspaper quickly for any likely jobs and still go for a swim.

It was well after half past eight when they made their way downstairs for breakfast.

Laura greeted them from the lounge. 'Good morning. Did you sleep well?'

'Like a log,' Jessica replied.

'Good. Now, come into the breakfast room. Mrs Benson will get you something to eat.' She turned to Jessica. 'Sophie and I don't eat breakfast, but we'll have a snack later with our coffee.'

The breakfast room was rather shabby. It contained several tables, chairs and other items of furniture that looked as if they had been put there because there was nowhere else for them to go. An old, faded screen was placed in front of a door that appeared to be no longer in use.

One of the tables was against a wall and was illuminated by the morning sun. Jessica made a beeline for it. She and Neil had barely sat down when a plump, middle-aged woman appeared.

'Good morning. I'm Mrs Benson,' she announced for Jessica's benefit. 'Now, what would you like for breakfast?'

Jessica decided to have a change from her normal muesli. She asked, 'Can I have some scrambled eggs?'

'Of course you can,' Mrs Benson replied. 'I got some lovely ones from Rick's farm yesterday.' She turned to Neil. 'And I guess you would like your usual.'

Neil grinned. 'Of course.'

'One sausage, or two?'

'One if they're large, please, two if they're small.'

'Tea or coffee?'

They both settled on tea. With the words 'Give me five minutes,' Mrs Benson disappeared in the direction of the kitchen.

'She's been around since I was a kid,' Neil remarked dryly.

'She seems very efficient.'

Five minutes later, it was not Mrs Benson who brought in their breakfast, but a slim, dark-haired young woman.

'This is Marie,' Neil announced.

Jessica responded with 'Hello, Marie' to the young woman's rather formal 'Good morning.'

Seeing Mrs Benson and Marie made Jessica think that Neil's sisters' overheads must be quite high. She whispered to Neil. 'How do your sisters manage to keep this house going and also employ staff?'

Neil laughed. 'With difficulty,' he replied.

Jessica was left pondering. As the day progressed, she came to understand that Mrs Benson had the role of cook/housekeeper, while Marie was a kind of maid. The two of them lived in the neighbouring village. Mrs Benson was always bright and cheerful, a deep contrast to Marie, who seemed quiet and withdrawn as if she hated her job.

Immediately after breakfast Jessica took the car to the village. It was a pleasant drive, but at one point the road started to descend steeply. A sign alerted drivers to select a low gear. Jessica followed the advice and went slowly down the hill. She soon discovered the reason for the warning: at the bottom of the hill was a rather nasty bend. After that it was only a matter of a couple of minutes before she was in the village.

She was surprised to discover how big it was. Her initial impression had been that it was quite small and sleepy, but as she stood in the centre she could tell that it was a thriving community. She was pleased to see that there were some newspapers on a stand outside the post office. She selected one and went inside to pay for it, remembering at the same time to buy some stamps.

The woman behind the counter was friendly and inclined to chat. 'I've not seen you before. Are you living locally?'

'I'm staying with Laura and Sophie Atkins.'

'Goodness! I've never known them to have any visitors!'

'I'm married to their brother, Neil.'

'I didn't know he was married. Congratulations!'

The woman seemed to want to chat further, but after a few minutes Jessica managed to extricate herself from more questioning when another customer came into the shop.

Back at the house, she discovered that Neil had set himself up in the library, on a table in front of the window. He was drinking a cup of coffee. A little later Sophie, on passing the open door and observing Jessica sitting in the corner reading the newspaper, brought her a coffee, before slipping away again to join Laura in the lounge.

Jessica scanned the vacancies column. Having discovered that there was nothing suitable, she decided to resume her original intention for the morning and go for a swim. Neil was clearly too busy to accompany her. She told him where she was going and departed for their bedroom, where she changed into her bikini. Anticipating before they came away that she might have a bit of a walk to the sea, she had remembered to pack her beach robe, which covered most of her and concealed the bikini.

Wearing her flip-flops and carrying a large towel, she set off for the beach. It was not easy walking, because the track was very stony in places, but she managed quite well and soon reached the point where she could look down at the cove. She quickly realised that it was not as big as she remembered it from the previous day. It was quite secluded, with a rocky outcrop at each end of a sandy beach. Not far away was what looked like a small island. She thought it would be interesting to swim across and explore it, but for now she would be content to swim close to the shore. She carefully made her way down the steep steps.

After spending some time in the sea, enjoying the feel of the salt water on her skin, she lay down on a convenient rock to sunbathe. A little later she wandered around the beach and in the process discovered the second entrance to it via steps like the ones she had descended earlier. Eventually her watch told her that it was time to return to the house for lunch.

She walked back in her bikini, which was now almost dry. As she neared the house she decided that modesty should prevail and donned her beach robe again.

She let herself into the house and retreated to the bedroom unseen. She quickly changed into a summer frock, tidied her appearance and made her way downstairs.

Following the sound of voices, she found Neil, Laura and Sophie chatting in the lounge. It was Neil who greeted her first.

'Ah, there you are.' He laughed. 'I've been getting a telling-off for neglecting you.'

'Oh, I've been swimming and sunbathing and exploring the beach,' Jessica replied breezily.

'Did you enjoy yourself, dear?' Laura asked, looking at her with apparent concern.

'It was lovely,' Jessica assured her.

'It is a lovely beach,' Sophie observed.

'Do you ever spend time there?' Jessica asked. She found it hard to imagine the two prim and proper sisters in swimming costumes.

The answer to her question was immediate and final.

'Oh, no. Not any more,' Laura replied firmly.

And that, thought Jessica, appeared to be it.

It was Neil who changed the subject. 'I'm going to show Jessica the house secret,' he announced.

'A secret?' Jessica was intrigued.

Sophie cut in almost reproachfully. 'Neil, you're not going to take Jessica down that horrible place.'

'Why not? There's no reason why she shouldn't know about it,' he replied indignantly.

'It's so horrid and dark down there,' Sophie complained.

Neil laughed. 'You've just got a thing about it,' he retorted.

Sophie turned up her nose and shook her head, but did not pursue the matter further.

By this time Jessica was enthralled and could barely wait to find out what the house secret was and why Sophie had such a strong negative opinion about it.

Neil disappeared, muttering something about finding some torches.

By the time he returned, Laura and Sophie had disappeared, leaving Jessica sitting in the lounge.

'Ready, poppet?'

She stood up immediately. 'Absolutely,' she replied. 'I'm intrigued to know what I'm going to see.'

Neil just laughed. 'Let's go,' he said. He pushed a large torch into her hand. 'We'll need these,' he explained, holding up a second one.

Jessica followed him back into the hall. He opened a door and switched on a light just inside to reveal a flight of stone steps, at the bottom of which was a stout wooden door. There was a key in the lock, which he turned. He pushed open the door and fumbled for the light switch within.

They were in a large cellar with a vaulted brick roof. It appeared to serve as a storage area for cleaning materials. Mops, buckets and brushes were there. There were also some items of food stored on the shelves. Jessica could see trays of vegetables.

'This cellar extends under the whole house,' Neil explained.

'It's huge,' she remarked.

Neil was already examining another door. A key was hanging

on the wall beside it. He fumbled with the lock. 'Not used very often.' He grinned at Jessica.

The key suddenly turned and the door swung open with a grinding sound. It was dark on the other side, and this time there was no light switch.

'We need our torches now,' Neil advised, switching his on.

Jessica followed suit. The light from their torches revealed more steps leading downward.

Neil turned to her. 'Watch your step,' he said.

She could see why he issued the warning. The steps appeared to be cut out of rock and were rough and uneven.

After descending a few steps, Jessica could see that they were now in a slightly sloping tunnel, seemingly also carved out of the rock. Neil was already starting to walk down it.

'Where are we going?' Jessica asked.

'You'll see soon,' Neil called out over his shoulder.

She followed him along the tunnel. The floor was hard sand, the walls were solid rock, and the ceiling was barely a foot above her head. A very tall person would have had to duck. She could smell the sea, and a kind of breeze brushed her cheeks. The tunnel began to get narrower. They turned a bend, and daylight appeared ahead of them.

Suddenly they could walk no further. A metal grille barred their way. It reached from floor to ceiling but had an inbuilt door of the same material, secured by a huge padlock. A key hung on the wall nearby. Neil took it and fitted it into the lock.

'It could be rusted up. I guess it hasn't been opened for years,' he remarked, almost to himself.

He was wrong. After a bit of a struggle the padlock clicked apart, and the metal door swung open with a horrible creaking noise.

Jessica followed him through the door. 'Where are we?' she asked.

'You'll see in a minute.'

They made their way between high rocks, and suddenly everything opened up. Jessica gasped. 'It's the beach where I was this morning!' she exclaimed.

Neil grinned at her. 'Exactly.'

'But what's the reason for the tunnel? It's like a private entrance to the beach from the house.'

Neil shook his head. 'It's more than that. At one stage, perhaps two hundred years ago, the house was a hub for smuggling. They landed the contraband in the cove, and then carried it up through the tunnel to the cellar of the house.'

'Phew. That was pretty clever.'

'It was. It went on for many years and apparently the authorities never found out.'

'Were the smugglers your ancestors?' Jessica ventured.

Neil laughed. 'No way. This happened a long time before my grandfather bought the house.'

The story intrigued Jessica. She would have lingered and asked more questions, but Neil was already making a move to return to the house.

They entered the tunnel and he secured the padlock and replaced the key on its nail. As they walked back towards the steps, he remarked, 'This gets flooded at high tide.'

'How did the smugglers manage, then?'

'They had to choose a night when it was low tide and the tunnel was clear.'

Jessica was trying to imagine what it was like in the days of the smugglers, when Neil volunteered some more information.

'It was my grandfather who closed off the tunnel with the iron gate. Somebody had once got caught by the tide and drowned in there.'

'Oh, how awful!'

The story saddened Jessica. She was relieved when they had climbed the steps and were back in the house. She took the opportunity to go upstairs and clean up.

When she returned downstairs, she found that lunch was ready and Neil and his sisters were already sitting around the dining table. Ham, cheese and a salad were laid out, together with a large pot of tea.

Jessica ate lightly. She never took much at midday.

This was noticed by Laura, who remarked, 'Jessica, you eat so little. You're much too thin. Have some more.'

Jessica shook her head and smiled. 'I never eat a lot in the middle of the day, but really I've had quite a nice meal.'

Laura seemed intent on continuing the discussion. 'You don't want to be too thin, Jessica. Men like to feel flesh on the bones of a woman.'

'Neil likes me just as I am,' Jessica protested.

Laura shook her head and tutted, but said no more on the subject, which was a relief for Jessica. She wondered how Laura's opinion fitted in with the size of the two sisters, both of whom were quite thin.

After lunch Neil returned to the library to work, and Jessica wandered out into the garden with the newspaper. She found a pleasant seat by the lily pond.

She spent some time going through the rest of the newspaper. Eventually she lost interest and placed it on the seat beside her, and watched the goldfish darting here and there for a while. She found her thoughts returning to the tunnel under the house. She was glad she had seen it, but somehow she felt it was a place she did not want to have any contact with again.

Chapter 19

Jessica woke from a muddled sleep. She struggled to work out where she was. It was still dark. She sat up in bed and listened. The sound of whispering was quite loud now. She wondered if it was coming from the corridor outside. Perhaps it was Laura and Sophie talking. Sometimes it seemed to be just muttering or whispering, and from time to time there was a soft laugh.

Eventually she got up and went to the door, carefully opening it and looking out into the corridor. There was nobody to be seen. She returned to bed. Neil still slumbered beside her.

She waited another five minutes and then could stand it no longer. She shook Neil. He struggled to wake up.

'What's the matter?'

Jessica grabbed him. 'Listen. Can you hear it?'

'Hear what?' He was still half asleep.

'The whispering and muttering.'

Neil sat up and listened for a few seconds. 'I can't hear anything.' He stifled a yawn.

'But you must be able to hear something,' Jessica insisted.

'I'm afraid not, poppet.'

'But I can hear it all the time.'

Neil listened again. 'Can't hear a thing,' he remarked quite flippantly.

'But I can hear it,' Jessica pleaded. 'I've been listening to it for quite a while.'

Neil gave a bit of a laugh. 'You're dreaming,' he retorted. He lay down again, turned over and went back to sleep.

'But—' Jessica stopped short. What was the use? He wasn't going to take any interest. In a tiny way she felt neglected, but there was nothing she could do about it. The sound was still in her ears. She depressed the switch on her watch to display the time. It was just after midnight. She settled back down, trying to ignore the constant whispering and occasional laugh that reached her ears, but sleep would not come.

How long she remained like that she had no idea. Neil slept soundly beside her, oblivious to her discomfort. Suddenly she was aware that the noise had stopped. She sat up again. At first she wondered if her ears were playing tricks on her, but when she was confident that she could no longer hear the whispering, she settled back in bed and tried to go back to sleep. She tossed and turned, constantly thinking about the mysterious sound, puzzled that only she had heard it, and irritated that Neil had not been more supportive.

It was well on into the night when sleep did at last overtake her. Even then it was disturbed, full of disjointed dreams and brief periods of wakefulness. When she woke up, it was daylight. She glanced at her watch. It was still quite early, hours and hours until breakfast. She jumped out of bed and tiptoed to one of the windows. It was a bright morning and it had the appearance of becoming a fine sunny day.

She glanced towards the bed. Neil was still asleep. Suddenly an idea came to her. Why not go for an early morning swim? The next instant she was changing into her bikini and flip-flops. Slipping on her beach robe, grabbing a towel and her mobile, she was ready. A glance at Neil prompted her to find a scrap of paper and scribble on it 'Gone to the beach for a swim'. She left it on the table next to the bed, where she knew Neil would see it. A final look, and she was on her way, after carefully and quietly closing the bedroom door.

She crept downstairs. The house was peaceful and quiet. She was surprised to discover the outside door unlocked. It made her wonder if somebody was already out and about.

She enjoyed the walk to the cove. The birds were singing and there was freshness in the air. It was pleasant to be out so early.

When she reached the steps leading to the beach, she made a rapid change of plan. Her original intention had been just to swim, perhaps sit down and enjoy the early morning for a bit and then return to the house. Now another idea took hold. The small island looked inviting. A strip of water separated it from the shore, but the distance did not hold any fears for her. She was a strong swimmer and had swum longer distances.

She hurried down the steps to the beach, removed her robe, placed her watch and mobile in the pockets, took off her flip-flops and made her way to the water.

She set out with steady swimming strokes towards the island. She had reached about half way when suddenly she felt as if an invisible force was pulling her in a different direction. Realising that she was caught in a current, she tried desperately to turn back to the beach. The more she struggled, the more it seemed she was making no headway. Somehow she managed to escape the pull and make for the safety of the beach. It seemed to take a long time and completely sapped all her energy. Arriving eventually on the shore, she flopped down exhausted on the sand close to the water, trying to regain her breath and strength.

'Are you all right?'

Jessica looked up. A middle-aged woman was standing looking down at her, holding a lead at the end of which was an inquisitive dog. Jessica hurriedly adopted a sitting position.

She smiled to reassure the woman. 'I'm fine, thank you.'

'I was worried for you when I saw you struggling in the water,' the woman said.

'I was trying to swim to the island,' Jessica replied.

'It's dangerous in that strip of water. There's a strong current there.'

'I didn't know that before I went in.'

'There used to be a notice about it,' the woman remarked, nodding in the direction of the steps.

'Well, I know now,' Jessica replied. 'Thank you for your concern.'

'As long as no harm has been done.' The woman turned to go. Then she hesitated and turned to Jessica again. 'Are you staying locally?' she asked.

Jessica nodded. 'Yes. I'm staying with Laura and Sophie Atkins. I'm Jessica. I'm married to their brother, Neil.'

'I haven't seen Laura or Sophie Atkins for years. They never seem to go out anywhere. Lily Benson works for them. She seems to get on with them OK.'

'They're quite nice really,' Jessica remarked.

The woman's dog started to tug on the lead.

Jessica stood up and glanced towards the spot where she had left her clothes

'Well, cheerio,' the woman said, as she started off up the beach. 'I might see you again sometime.'

'Yes, of course. Goodbye, and thanks again,' Jessica called after her.

The woman waved her hand and went on her way, her dog leading.

Jessica made her way back to where she had left her robe and flip-flops. She retrieved her watch from the pocket of the robe. The hands showed her it was time to return to the house.

She made her way up the steps and set off at a good pace along the track. She had hardly gone more than a few yards when one of her flip-flops broke.

'Oh, no!' burst from her lips. A quick inspection of the offending item established that it was not immediately repairable and, worse still, it was unwearable. She tried walking wearing just one, doing a sort of hop. It did not work. In desperation she removed the other flip-flop. She would have to walk back to the house barefoot.

She made her way gingerly up the path, doing her best to avoid the sharp stones. Her thoughts were now occupied with a different subject. The experience hung over her. She knew that she had been lucky. Only her strong swimming had saved her from disaster. She could easily have been swept out to sea and drowned. One thing stuck in her mind. Why had nobody warned her? Why had neither Laura nor Sophie told her of the danger? Even Neil, for that matter? He must have been aware of the situation.

As she approached the house, she saw him coming towards her.

'I came to look for you. I was getting worried,' he exclaimed as he drew close. He glanced at her bare feet. 'What happened?'

'My flip-flop broke,' she replied simply. Suddenly the ordeal of the morning welled up inside her. 'I nearly got caught in the current,' she burst out.

Neil looked puzzled. 'How?'

'Why did nobody tell me how dangerous it was to swim there?' She was almost in tears.

Neil put his arm around her. 'We did,' he said softly.

'When?'

'Yesterday, when we were talking,' he replied quietly.

Before Jessica could say anything, he urged her forward. 'Let's get back indoors,' he said.

Jessica said little on the way back into the house. She was still stressed about her experience, together with the fact that she was puzzled when Neil indicated that she already knew about the danger. She had no recollection of receiving any warning. She was hoping that once they were back in the house she could slip quietly up to the bedroom and get changed.

It was not to be. Just as they reached the bottom of the stairs,

Laura appeared. She scrutinised Jessica for a second and then exclaimed, 'What's happened? You look upset, Jessica.'

Before Jessica could reply, Neil butted in. 'She got caught in the current at Colliers Cove.'

A look of concern swept over Laura's face. 'Oh, no. How awful. Are you all right?'

'I'm fine. Just a bit shocked.'

'It's so dangerous, that strip of water between the beach and the island,' Laura continued. 'Someone drowned there once.'

This was the last thing Jessica wanted to hear, but it seemed that Laura was not inclined to let the matter drop. She turned to Jessica and said softly, 'But we did warn you.'

This was too much for Jessica. Her reply was swift. 'That's what Neil tells me, but I don't remember that at all.'

Laura looked at her in amazement. 'It was the first evening you were here. Don't you remember? We asked you if you liked swimming.'

'I remember that, but I don't remember anybody saying anything about any danger in the cove.'

'Perhaps you've forgotten,' Laura suggested soothingly.

That's preposterous, Jessica thought. She would never have forgotten something like that.

She was about to reply when Laura noticed that she was carrying her flip-flops. 'Are you having problems with your flip-flops?' she asked.

'One of them has broken,' Jessica replied simply.

'I think I've got a pair like that I don't use. What size do you take?'

'Five,' Jessica replied.

Laura nodded. 'That's it, then. I'll find them for you.'

Jessica thanked her, without a great deal of enthusiasm. She just wanted all the attention to end so that she could retreat to their room. It was Neil who came to her rescue. Placing his arm around her, he gently led her upstairs.

Once in their bedroom, Jessica flopped into a chair. She felt physically and mentally drained.

Neil knelt down beside her and took her hands in his. 'Look, poppet. Forget about everything. It was just an accident. Nothing happened. Just put it behind you.'

Jessica nodded slowly. 'I suppose you're right.'

He reached forward and kissed her. 'That's the most sensible thing,' he said.

Chapter 20

In spite of Neil's reassuring words, Jessica still felt troubled about what had happened to her that morning.

For a short while she sat in the chair and did her best to sort out her thinking. Perhaps putting the incident behind her was indeed the most sensible thing. There was no point in hanging on to something that caused so much stress. After all, she reasoned, no harm had been done and she was still in one piece. She was still puzzled why both Neil and Laura had insisted that she had been told about the danger, but perhaps there was a logical explanation. Perhaps she really hadn't heard or taken in their warning.

Neil snapped her out of her pondering. 'I'm going downstairs for some breakfast. I'll see you there.'

Jessica jumped up. 'Give me five minutes, and I'll join you.'

In the end it was a good half an hour by the time she had showered and dressed. She realised that she had probably missed breakfast. Neil would have already eaten his. She would just have to go without, she decided. It didn't matter.

As she made her way downstairs, she could hear voices coming from one of the rooms. She followed the sound, and discovered Neil and his two sisters talking in the lounge. All three of them were standing up just inside the room.

It was Laura who spotted her first. 'Ah, there you are, Jessica. We were getting worried about you.'

'I'm sorry. I'm sorry I'm so late.'

Laura held up her hand as if to stop her speaking. 'Not at all. No need to apologise. You've had a bad experience.' She looked quite concerned.

'How are you feeling now, poppet?' Neil asked.

Jessica managed to raise a smile. 'I'm fine, darling. Just a bit tired.'

'You've had a nasty time,' Sophie remarked, as if to offer support to her.

'You need some breakfast,' Laura announced.

Jessica protested. 'No, no, it's all right. Really it is. I can go without.'

The two sisters were horrified at this suggestion.

'Oh, you can't do that,' Sophie insisted.

Laura took a firmer line. She grabbed hold of Jessica's hand. 'You need something to eat. Come along.'

Jessica allowed herself to be led to a table in the breakfast room where a place was still laid for breakfast. Neil followed.

'Now, sit there, Jessica. I'll go and tell Mrs Benson you're here.'

With that Laura disappeared. Neil sat down opposite Jessica, clearly quite concerned.

'Are you sure you're all right?' he asked.

'Yes, I'm OK. Just a bit tired, that's all.'

Neil continued looking at her. 'I'm sorry if you thought I was a bit off in the night. Just going back to sleep again, I mean.'

Jessica forced a smile. 'It's all right. Really it is.' She hesitated for a second. 'I just can't understand why you weren't able to hear anything.'

'Hmm. It's odd, isn't it?'

They were interrupted by the arrival of Mrs Benson. 'Good morning, Jessica,' she said. 'What would you like for breakfast?'

Jessica did not feel like eating. She shook her head. 'I'm so late that I don't feel like breakfast. Perhaps just a cup of coffee.'

Mrs Benson was aghast. 'But you must eat something,' she insisted.

Jessica could see that she was on a losing tack. She thought quickly. 'I'll just have a slice of toast, then.'

This satisfied Mrs Benson. 'I'll get that for you straight away. Toast and coffee.' She returned to the kitchen.

'I need to go into the village to get a newspaper,' Jessica announced. 'I'm unemployed. I have to find a job.'

'There's no hurry,' Neil urged. 'If you're going to the village, though, I'll come with you. I could do with getting out of the house.'

After eating, Jessica felt a little better, and she was quite happy when Neil handed her the car keys and said, 'You can drive, poppet.'

Once in the village, Jessica bought a newspaper and then she and Neil did a bit of exploring. Tucked away behind the main street was a small supermarket. Jessica went in and bought some fruit and a few necessities. Neil suggested buying a couple of bottles of wine to supplement his sisters' stock.

Next they had a quick look at the village church. A notice outside informed them that the building dated back to the fourteenth century. Jessica would have liked to see inside, but when they tried the door it was locked. After that they went to the village green, which still had some ancient stocks. Neil took a photograph with his phone of Jessica sitting in them but refused to pose for her to do likewise.

When they returned to the house, Laura and Sophie were drinking coffee in the lounge. They invited Jessica and Neil to join them, but Neil said he had some work to do and Jessica wanted to read the newspaper. Neil retreated to the library.

Jessica had a longing to sit outside in the sunshine. She wandered out into the garden and found a seat where she could sit and enjoy the sun filtering through the trees behind her. She scrutinised the situations vacant column, but found only one possible job. Perhaps she would write a letter of application later on.

It was pleasant sitting there in the peace and quiet. She leaned against the back of the seat and closed her eyes for a few minutes.

She woke with a start, realising that the hours of lost sleep had caught up with her. A glance at her watch showed that the best part of an hour had slipped by.

'Jessica, my girl, this won't do. Pull yourself together,' she said to herself.

She was about to get up and return to the house when Neil appeared. He greeted her.

'There you are. Lunch is about ready.'

They returned to the house. Jessica dashed quickly upstairs to wash her hands and freshen up. When she came downstairs again, Neil and his sisters were already in the dining room.

During the meal, much to Jessica's dismay, Laura and Sophie brought up the subject of her disturbed night.

'I always find that a cup of cocoa is an excellent way of dropping off to sleep when I go to bed,' Laura remarked. 'Why don't you try it, Jessica?'

'Perhaps,' Jessica replied vaguely.

'What you need is one of my sleeping tablets,' Sophie piped up.

Jessica said nothing. She just wished the two sisters would not keep referring to the incident. It was Neil who came to her aid and quickly changed the subject.

She was relieved when lunch was over. Once again she had been subjected to Laura's comments that she ate too little and what she should do about it. She was quite happy the way she was and was not going to indulge in eating more just to please somebody. Graham had quite often praised her neat, trim figure, although Neil had only commented on it a few times.

Immediately after lunch Neil returned to the library, explaining that he had more work to do. Again Jessica was a bit disappointed. She had been hoping that they could do something together, perhaps some sightseeing in the wider area. She kept her feelings to herself and instead wrote an application for the job she had seen advertised. Fortunately she had brought her laptop and mini-printer with her.

After that, she tried reading in the library but felt that she was in Neil's way. On top of that he was constantly on his mobile phone, which was distracting for her. In the end she decided to return to the garden to read. She sat down again on the seat she had occupied earlier. After a while she decided that the book she had found in the library did not hold her interest as much as she had hoped it would. On top of that the seat was now in the shade. In the end she decided to explore a bit more of the garden.

She spied an almost hidden footpath and decided to see where it led. It was narrow and was flanked on both sides by tall bushes. It twisted here and there, so it was almost impossible to see where it finally went.

She had been walking for several minutes and was on the point of turning back when she suddenly came face to face with a man. He stared at her as if she were a ghost. It took her a second or two to overcome her own surprise and shock. She was the first to venture any form of communication, and voiced a cheerful 'Hello.'

The man continued to stare at her and then mumbled something inaudible. She tried to communicate again. 'I'm Jessica,' she announced. 'I'm staying with Laura and Sophie with my husband Neil.'

Again the man made some sort of reply, but it was unintelligible. It suddenly dawned on Jessica that he could not speak. She was wondering what to do next when he spun around and hurried off in the direction he had come from, leaving her standing there puzzled. From their brief encounter she judged that he was perhaps a few years older than her. He had a mop of ginger hair and he looked like some sort of workman, as he was dressed in overalls.

Jessica decided to return to the main garden. She had just reached the seat by the pond when Neil appeared.

'Hi. I've been looking for you,' he said.

'Sorry. I've been doing some more exploring.'

'Where did you go?'

'Oh, I followed a path just over there.' She pointed in the direction she had just come from.

'I know that one. It actually leads to a large wood. I used to go there as a kid.'

'I didn't get that far. But I had a most odd experience,' Jessica said.

'What happened?'

'Well, I was walking along and I met this strange man. He looked as if he was a workman, but he didn't appear to be able to speak properly.'

Neil chuckled. 'You've met Mags.'

'Mags?'

'He does the garden and is a sort of odd-job man.'

'Now I know,' she replied with a little laugh.

'He lives in a caravan just off that path you walked along. He's a bit shy with strangers.'

'I'll know the next time I meet him.'

Returning to the house, Neil said he had some more work to do and Jessica went up to their bedroom. Once there she spent a leisurely time washing her hair and doing her nails. She was relaxing in a chair when Neil arrived to get ready for dinner. He glanced at her and then came over.

'You're not still thinking about this morning?' he asked, concern in his voice.

Jessica did her best to smile. 'I'll be better tomorrow.'

'Of course you will.' He bent over her and placed a kiss on her lips. Then he stood up and smiled at her. 'Get ready for dinner. What you need is a stiff brandy. That'll drive away all your anxieties!'

Jessica laughed for the first time that day. 'I might even get drunk,' she quipped.

For the next ten minutes she busied herself getting ready. She had bought a new blouse for their break and this was the time to wear it. It would go well with her long skirt. She also had a new pair of high heels to wear. She guessed they might be a bit uncomfortable at first, but she would endure it.

They went downstairs together. The smell of dinner in the air made Jessica feel hungry. Following the sound of conversation, they found Laura and Sophie in the lounge.

To Jessica's dismay, Sophie immediately raised the subject of her ordeal at the beach.

'It's so awful you had a bad time in Colliers Cove this morning.'

Jessica's heart sank. Just when she had decided to try to forget the whole incident, here it was being brought up again in public. All she answered was one word: 'Yes.'

That did not deter Sophie. 'It really is dangerous there at times,' she remarked.

Fortunately for Jessica, nobody made any further comment.

Laura and Sophie were already sipping what looked like sherry. Neil, who had been busy at the drinks cabinet, brought Jessica a glass of amber liquid. It was the promised brandy.

As she sat there sipping the warming, calming drink and listening to the conversation between Neil and his sisters, the events of the morning seemed to fade into insignificance.

Conversation over dinner was quite congenial, though it took place mainly between the other three. Laura insisted on having some wine with the meal. Jessica made it clear that she only wanted half a glass. Wine on top of the brandy made her feel quite light-headed. She was not used to drinking so much alcohol at one time.

After their meal and coffee, Sophie suggested a game of Canasta. It was years since Jessica had played. She had almost forgotten how. In the end, it turned out that Laura was the best player, and Jessica the worst.

As they all parted at the end of the evening, Laura jokingly said to Jessica, 'After all that drink, you WILL sleep tonight.'

Jessica sincerely hoped that she would.

Chapter 21

Jessica came to her senses slowly. Reality crept in. She had been woken by the same sound as on the previous night. She lay there now, completely aware of it, the whispering interspersed with the occasional smothered laugh.

Suddenly there was something new. 'Jessica... Jessica... Come and join us...'

The change made her sit up. Who was calling her name, and why? The sound reverted to whispering. I can't have imagined it, she thought. Then suddenly it was there again, calling her name.

She lay back down and did her best to block out the sound, first putting her fingers into her ears and then, when that did not work, putting her head under the bedclothes. In the end she sat up again, exasperated. Neil was still sleeping soundly beside her. After his reaction the night before, there seemed to be no point in waking him. She looked at her watch. It was just after midnight.

Then an idea came to her. Slipping quietly out of bed, she grabbed a spare blanket from the cupboard and crept quietly out of the room. As she opened the door, Neil stirred and she was afraid she had woken him. For an instant she froze in her tracks, but then he appeared to settle again. With a sigh of relief, she stepped into the corridor and silently closed the bedroom door.

She made her way down the stairs, silent on bare feet. The house was quiet. She went into the lounge and headed for the sofa. Stretching out on its generous proportions, she at once felt relaxed and content. She covered herself with the blanket and nestled her head into one of the cushions. She would stay here until first light and then creep back to the bedroom.

Suddenly she woke up with the realisation that somebody was close to her. When she opened her eyes, a half-scream burst from her lips. Mags was looking down at her. At the same time Jessica realised that the blanket had slipped almost off her. She was only wearing her nightdress. She was never quite sure what happened next. Mags mumbled something inaudible and appeared to reach out a hand towards her. She raised herself to a defensive position, at the same time uttering a shout. Mags turned and hurried from the room.

Jessica tried to collect herself together. It was now daylight, and she had slept past the hour when she had intended to go back upstairs.

The next instant Laura appeared in her dressing gown. 'Goodness!' she exclaimed. 'What's happening? What are you doing here?'

Jessica tried to overcome her emotions. 'I came down here to try and get some sleep. That noise started again.' She hesitated. 'I woke up. Mags was standing over me. He frightened me.'

Laura stared at her accusingly. 'What did you make such a noise for? Mags comes into the house every day at this time. I get him some breakfast.'

'I'm sorry. I didn't realise that, but he did frighten me.'

Laura's response was to shake her head slowly, still looking at Jessica. Suddenly she spoke again, this time quite sternly. 'Go and get ready for breakfast.'

Her words and tone made Jessica jump up. She grabbed the blanket and made to leave the room. As she did so Laura spoke again. 'And cover yourself up,' she commanded.

Her words drew Jessica's attention to her flimsy clothing. She wrapped herself in the blanket and fled from the room, embarrassed.

Back in the bedroom she found Neil up and about. He looked surprised when she entered.

'You're up early,' he said.

'I'm not. It's half past seven,' she retorted.

Neil immediately knew something was wrong. He came over to her, put his arms around her and kissed her gently. 'What's wrong, poppet?' he asked.

Slowly she related her experience. When she had finished, he was quiet for a few seconds. 'Gosh,' he began. 'I can understand how you feel. Laura can be very protective of Mags at times.'

'I really thought he was going to attack me or something. I let out quite a yell.'

Neil smiled. 'I guess he was as surprised as you were.'

Jessica made no reply.

'Look, poppet, leave things with me. I'll have a chat with Laura.'

Jessica was feeling miserable. 'I didn't mean to cause such trouble.'

'You haven't,' Neil replied, smiling at her. He glanced at his watch. 'You'd better get ready for breakfast.'

Jessica took his suggestion on board and disappeared in the direction of the bathroom.

When she came back, Neil was no longer there. She was dressed and ready when he reappeared.

'Everything's sorted out,' he announced cheerfully. 'I've had a word with Laura.'

Jessica just acknowledged his words with a nod and a quiet 'Thank you.' She felt slightly put out that Neil was sorting out her problems, but she reminded herself that Laura was his sister.

When the two of them went down to breakfast, Laura acted as if nothing had happened, which was a relief to Jessica.

Neil tucked in to his fried breakfast. Jessica toyed with some toast. The kitchen did not appear to have muesli. She wondered if she should buy some in the village, but on second thoughts worried that that might upset Laura again. Perhaps best to stick with toast.

She pondered the relationship between the two sisters. Laura appeared to be the leader, with her younger sister falling in line with what she wanted.

After breakfast Jessica decided to go to the village to buy a newspaper. Neil did not seem to be inclined to go with her, handing her the car keys with a grin and the words 'Enjoy yourself.'

As she was leaving the breakfast room, she encountered Laura, who was full of smiles, a pair of flip-flops in her hand.

'I've got these for you,' she announced. 'I don't want them back.'

'Oh, thank you!' Jessica exclaimed, as she accepted the gift.

'Don't want to see you wandering around with bare feet again.'

'I'll try not to.'

Laura disappeared into the kitchen.

Jessica decided to return to the bedroom and leave the flip-flops there before driving to the village. As she reached the top of the stairs, she came upon Marie. She greeted her cheerfully.

Marie replied with a soft 'Good morning' and then looked as if she wanted to say something else. Her response made Jessica hesitate, but then Marie seemed to change her mind and hastened on her way. Jessica hurried to the bedroom.

It was bright and sunny when Jessica set off for the village. She turned on the radio for company. She was quite used to Neil's car now and enjoyed driving it.

It was pleasant along the country road. Approaching the steep hill, Jessica changed to a lower gear. As the gradient began to increase, she started to brake. At first she did not quite comprehend why the car was not slowing down. Then the reality struck her. The brakes were not working. She tried desperately to keep pushing down on the brake pedal. The car was gathering speed fast. She changed to a lower gear still and the engine noise increased. What made her think of the handbrake she would never know, but suddenly she grabbed it and pulled hard. It slowed the car a little, but she was terrified as the bend at the foot of the hill loomed up. Desperately she swung the steering wheel over to try and avoid a collision with the tall hedge bordering the road. What happened next was beyond her control. The vehicle lurched to the left and came to rest at an alarming angle against the hedge.

She struggled to get out of the car. Shaking all over, she leaned cautiously against it and remained there for a while, trying to recover from the shock of what had just happened. At one point she remembered that the ignition would still be switched on, although the engine was no longer running. Somehow she managed to reach in and retrieve the keys.

'Are you all right?'

Jessica turned to face the sound. A man was approaching looking concerned.

She did her best to reassure him. 'Yes, I'm fine.' She tried to muster a smile. 'Still in one piece,' she added.

The man looked at her and then at the car. 'What happened?'

'The brakes failed when I was coming down the hill.'

'Gosh. Good job you managed to stop the car.' As he spoke the man glanced at the car again and then at the hedge.

Jessica followed his gaze. She could see now how lucky she had been. Just at the point where the car had left the road was a deep ditch. It was this that had finally brought the vehicle to a halt. A few yards further on there was a low fence. If the car had hit that it would not have stopped it. Jessica walked over to the fenced area. On the other side the land dropped away to the sea, a long way below. The sight made her feel sick. She knew that she had had a narrow escape from disaster.

Her thoughts were interrupted by the man speaking again. 'Are you staying locally?'

His words brought Jessica back to reality. 'Yes. I'm staying with Laura and Sophie Atkins. I'm Jessica Atkins. I'm married to Neil.'

The man's face broke into a smile. 'I know Laura and Sophie quite well. I also know Neil.' He held out his hand. 'I'm Jim Foster, the local GP.'

Jessica shook his hand. 'I'm pleased to meet you – and rather glad you came along.'

'You had a lucky escape.'

Jessica was about to answer when he asked, 'Can I give you a lift somewhere?'

She forced a smile. 'I'd better go back to the house and let Neil know what I've done to the car.'

'I'll run you back,' he replied. He looked more closely at the car. 'Fortunately, the ditch seems to have prevented any major damage, but the car will have to be towed out. I know somebody who could do that.'

Jessica allowed him to lead her to his car. She settled herself into the passenger seat.

Jim broke the brief silence between them. 'You say you're Neil's wife. I didn't know he was married.'

'We got married quite recently.'

It did not take long for them to reach the house. Jessica prepared to get out of the car. 'Thank you for all your help,' she said.

Jim smiled. 'Pleased I was around.'

As Jessica climbed out of the car, her saviour did likewise. 'I must say hello to Neil,' he explained. 'I haven't seen him for ages.'

As they entered the house, the first person they encountered was Neil.

'Jim!' Neil exclaimed, with a look of surprise.

The two men shook hands. After the pleasantries were over, it was down to Jessica to explain what had happened. She looked at Neil. 'The brakes failed on the car.'

'On Hangman's Hill,' Jim added.

Neil was aghast. 'What? The car is only two years old and it was serviced last month.'

Jessica said nothing. She was still feeling unsteady.

'But what about you, poppet?' Neil asked. 'Are you OK?'

Jessica did her best to conjure up a smile. 'I'm fine,' she replied. 'I'm just a bit shaky still.'

'I think I can help you there.' It was Jim who spoke. 'Just give me a minute. I'll get you something from the car.'

When Jim had disappeared, Neil put his arm around Jessica. 'Tell me what happened,' he said quietly.

As best she could, Jessica gave an account of her experience. 'Well, everything was fine until I came to that steep hill on the way to the village. I put my foot on the brake and nothing happened.'

She thought for a moment before continuing. 'Like an idiot, it took me a couple of seconds to think of using the handbrake.' She looked up at Neil. 'The car is in a ditch.'

'Blow the car. As long as you're safe. That's the important bit.'

The doctor returned carrying a small box. He extracted two tablets and handed them to Jessica. 'Take these. They'll settle things down right away.'

Jessica accepted them graciously.

'I'd better get going and attend to my patients,' remarked Jim. He shook hands with Neil again and then turned to Jessica. 'Don't hesitate to contact me if you need anything,' he remarked as he shook her hand.

'I will. Thank you for all your help,' Jessica replied, with a little smile.

Just as he was about to drive off, Jim spoke again. 'Neil, I'd get Judd to collect the car if I were you. He's very good.'

'That's who I was going to contact,' Neil called out.

With a wave of the hand, the doctor disappeared.

Suddenly Laura and Sophie appeared.

Neil said, 'Jessica's had an accident. The car brakes failed on Hangman's Hill.'

'But that's awful!' Laura exclaimed. She studied her sister-in-law. 'Are you OK, Jessica?'

Jessica nodded. 'I'm fine.'

It was Sophie who piped up next. 'You should lie down for a bit, Jessica. You can get delayed shock, you know.'

Jessica nodded in partial agreement, but said nothing.

Laura took up the suggestion. 'Sophie's right. You really should rest for a while.'

'I'm all right. Really I am,' Jessica protested.

Neil was insistent. 'No. You've had a bit of a shock. Listen to the advice. Come and sit down and take the tablets Jim gave you.'

Rather than protest further, Jessica allowed herself to be conducted into the lounge and made to sit on the settee. Neil and his sisters looked down at her with a mixture of sympathy and concern. She was beginning to become embarrassed by all the attention.

'Take the tablets Jim gave you,' Neil urged.

'I'll get you some water,' Sophie offered.

Jessica protested that she did not want the tablets, but in the end she agreed reluctantly to comply with the wishes of Neil and his sisters.

After more suggestions about what she should do, they left her alone.

Jessica settled into the quiet of the lounge. Neil had disappeared into the library to work. From time to time she could hear the voices of Laura and Mrs Benson in the kitchen. It was peaceful sitting there by herself. She started to go over the events of the morning. Neil would have phoned the garage by now. When the car had been repaired and he went to collect it, she would go with him, she decided. It would be good to have it back, because it was a way of getting to the village for a daily newspaper. She still had to find a job.

She woke suddenly, unclear for a second or two where she was. Then her memory came flooding back. She had dozed off on the settee. A glance at her watch told her that she had been asleep for almost an hour. The sun was now streaming into the room. It encouraged her to go out into the garden and get some fresh air.

She found a seat in the shade and sat there admiring the flowers and listening to the bees. Neil found her there close to lunchtime.

'Hi!' he called out as he approached. 'How are you feeling now?'

'I'm fine. I fell asleep in the lounge. I came out here to get some fresh air.'

'Most likely did you good.' Neil had some news for her. 'The car's ready. I'm going to pick it up this afternoon.'

'Oh, good. Gosh, that was quick! What was the problem?'

'There was no problem. They found nothing wrong with the brakes.'

Chapter 22

For a full five seconds Jessica stared at Neil. 'But that's impossible,' she said. 'The brakes failed and I ended up in a ditch. It was only by sheer luck that I didn't go over the cliff and be killed.'

Neil looked a bit uncomfortable. 'Well, that's what the garage said,' he replied. 'There's nothing wrong with the brakes.'

'I want to come with you when you go to pick up the car.'

'Oh, there's no need for that.'

'I'm coming,' Jessica replied firmly, making it clear that there was to be no further discussion on the subject.

Neil nodded as if in agreement. Then he spoke as if he had remembered something. 'I've got to make a phone call. I'll be back in a minute.' With that he disappeared to the library.

Left on her own, Jessica tried to make some sense of what he had said. To be told that there was nothing wrong with the brakes seemed unbelievable. She could even now feel the shock of pressing on the brake pedal and realising that nothing was happening. Perhaps the garage hadn't found the fault.

Neil returned and announced that lunch was ready. The meal was largely dominated by Laura and Sophie talking about various accidents that had happened on Hangman's Hill.

'It's such a dangerous road, and that hill in particular,' said Laura. 'You were extremely lucky, Jessica.'

'People keep telling me that,' Jessica remarked, wishing that the conversation would move on to something else.

Neil must have guessed how she felt, because when Sophie was about to pipe up with yet another anecdote, he waved his hand and butted in. 'That's enough about Hangman's Hill, Sophie. It's upsetting for Jessica.'

Sophie stopped talking and appeared to be sulking.

Jessica was glad when the meal was over. After lunch she went to sit in the garden. She went to her favourite spot and sat quietly looking at the scenery around her. She had been there for about ten minutes when Mags appeared and started doing some gardening close by. He was within hailing distance, so she called out a greeting.

Mags looked up and mumbled a reply. From then on, every so often he would look up from his work and stare at her intently. Whenever she attempted any form of communication, all she received in return was grunts or mumbled speech. Eventually, feeling uncomfortable under his gaze, she stood up and started to walk away. She called out 'Goodbye,' but Mags did not reply.

Back in the house, she found Neil waiting in the hall.

'I've ordered a taxi to go to the village,' he announced.

'Good. I'm ready.'

'Are you sure you want to come?'

'Darling, of course I do.'

A few minutes later the taxi arrived.

Jessica was intrigued to know where the garage was. She had not come across it on her previous trips to the village. She was surprised to find out that it was tucked away behind the small supermarket. The first thing she noticed was Neil's car parked outside. While Neil paid the taxi driver, she walked towards it. A man in overalls emerged from the workshop and greeted her.

'Good afternoon,' she replied. 'We've come to collect our car.' She nodded in the direction of the vehicle.

'Yours, is it?' the man asked.

Just at that moment Neil joined them. 'Good afternoon, Mr Judd,' he said.

'Nice to see you again,' the man replied. 'Your car's all ready for you to take away.'

'You said on the phone that you hadn't found any problem with the brakes,' Neil said.

'No problem with them at all. We've checked everything and we've road tested the car as well,' Judd replied confidently.

'But something was wrong with them,' Jessica butted in. 'They failed on Hangman's Hill this morning.'

A younger man came out of the workshop and joined the discussion. 'Nothing wrong with those brakes,' he remarked.

'But that's not possible. I could have had a fatal accident,' Jessica insisted.

The young man looked at her. 'Were you driving?' he asked.

'Yes, I was driving.'

The young man smirked. 'Sure you didn't put your foot on the clutch pedal instead of the brake?'

The suggestion irritated her. The mechanic's remark implied that she was a silly little girl who should not be driving.

'I'm sorry,' she retorted, 'but I do know the difference between the clutch pedal and the brake pedal. The brakes failed on this car, and that's all there is to it.'

The young man shrugged and walked back into the garage.

Neil quickly defused the situation by suggesting that he now pay for the work. Handing Jessica the car keys, he disappeared into the office with Judd. Jessica went over to the car and sat in the passenger seat.

A few minutes later Neil was back beside her. As they started off he remarked, 'Well, that's that.'

'I don't care what they say,' Jessica declared. 'The brakes definitely failed.'

'Yes, it is odd, isn't it?' he replied.

Jessica said very little for the rest of the journey. She found it hard to relate to the current situation. This morning she had tried to slow the car down on a steep hill, only to find that the brakes were not working. Somehow she had stopped the car and had narrowly missed having a serious accident. Yet now she was being told that there was nothing wrong with the brakes. Had she accidentally placed her foot on the clutch pedal? she wondered, and then quickly dismissed the notion. If she had done that, she would have realised straight away.

Back at the house Neil said he had some telephone calls to make and went off to the library. Jessica decided to go for a walk.

For some reason she found herself going towards the cove. Once there, she took off her shoes and wandered slowly along the beach, happy to feel the sand beneath her feet and listen to the cries of the seabirds. A fresh breeze blew in from the sea and she enjoyed breathing in the fresh salty air.

It was the sound of a voice behind her that stirred her from her solitude.

'Hello again.'

Jessica turned round to see the woman she had encountered the previous day. She greeted her with a smile.

'Not swimming today?' the woman asked.

Jessica shook her head and smiled again. 'Not today.'

'I was so worried when I saw you yesterday struggling to get back to the beach. You must be a very strong swimmer.'

'Fairly good,' Jessica acknowledged. 'I was top of the class at school for swimming.'

'Good for you!'

Jessica's new acquaintance hesitated for a second, and then spoke again. 'You know, a woman was drowned here a few years ago. It really is very dangerous in places.'

'Well, I certainly don't intend to repeat the experience,' Jessica commented, hoping that her remark might change the subject from what was still a rather painful one for her.

The woman seemed to take the hint. Looking up at the cloudless sky, she remarked, 'It's a lovely day, isn't it?'

'Super,' Jessica replied.

The woman gave a bit of a sigh. 'My husband was going to take me out for the day.' She sighed again. 'But we couldn't go after all.'

'Oh. Why was that?' Jessica asked sympathetically.

The woman seemed eager to explain. 'He runs the car repair garage in the village. There was an accident near here this morning. A car went out of control on Hangman's Hill and ended up in a ditch. The owner asked my husband to go and retrieve it, so we had to cancel our plans.'

The woman had not quite finished. 'The driver had a very lucky escape. Just past where the car stopped, there's over a hundred-foot drop to the sea below.'

'You must be Mrs Judd!' Jessica cut in. 'I met your husband earlier this afternoon.'

The woman looked enquiringly at her.

'I was the driver of the car.'

'Goodness, you were lucky. How are you feeling now?'

'I'm fine. I was just a bit shaken at the time.'

'I should think so.'

A thought struck Jessica. 'Did the garage have to do a lot of work on the car?' she asked.

'Well, not a lot, but they had to fix the brakes.'

Jessica was aghast. She was silent for a few seconds, trying to take in what she had just heard.

Mrs Judd spoke again, as if to emphasise what she had just said. 'The car had no brakes.'

'I understand,' Jessica replied, still in thought.

Mrs Judd had confirmed what she knew already. The brakes were not working. But why was everybody insisting that there was nothing wrong with them? It did not make sense.

It was Mrs Judd's dog who broke up the conversation. He looked up and started to whine.

'Jojo wants to go now,' Mrs Judd remarked. 'I'll say goodbye.' She started to move off.

'Bye,' Jessica called out. She watched the pair make their way along the beach. She glanced at her watch. It was time for her to go too.

As she started up the steps, she spied Neil coming down to meet her. They met halfway up.

'I guessed where you were,' he announced, planting a kiss on her cheek.

'I've just met Mrs Judd.'

'Mrs Judd?' he queried, a bit puzzled.

'The wife of the garage owner.'

'Oh, yes. I know,' he replied.

'Neil, she told me her husband had to fix the brakes. Yet the garage staff told me there was nothing wrong with them.'

She waited for an explanation.

Neil grinned. 'The word "fix" is bit vague. Of course they would have had to fix the car to establish what was wrong with it.'

Jessica stared at him. His explanation just did not seem to make sense.

'But that's crazy,' she blurted out.

'I can see it might be a bit difficult to understand.'

'I still say the brakes weren't working,' Jessica insisted quietly. There did not seem to be anything more she could add.

They were mostly silent as they made their way back up the path. Jessica kept thinking about her terrifying experience on Hangman's Hill and what had transpired that afternoon. It all seemed so odd and it did not add up.

As they approached the house, Neil stopped and looked up at a tree. Some of the giant oak's branches grew over the track. 'I used to climb that when I was a boy,' he said.

'How old were you?'

He thought for a second or two. 'Eleven or twelve, I guess. I used to lie along that branch, the one overlooking the track. When people came looking for me, quite often they would pass underneath and not see me.'

'It must have been quite a lot of fun for you.'

Neil grinned at her. 'It was.'

Back at the house, Jessica went up to their room to get ready for dinner. Neil joined her a few minutes later.

'I thought we might go out somewhere tomorrow,' he suggested. 'Spend the day seeing the sights.'

Jessica was immediately alert. 'That would be great,' she said enthusiastically.

'That's settled, then. We'll leave after breakfast and make a full day of it.'

Jessica was looking forward to doing something different. So far their visit to Neil's sisters had been rather dull, except for the disturbing incidents that had affected her.

Over dinner, the subject of their day out was brought into the conversation by Neil. From then on, it seemed to Jessica that Laura and Sophie took over the planning, suggesting this or that place that she and Neil could visit. Once again she was glad when the meal was over.

After they had finished, Sophie retired early, stating that she had a headache, and Laura said she had something to attend to. Neil and Jessica were left on their own in the lounge. Neil produced a map and they discussed what they would do the following day. It was late when at last they went to bed.

Upstairs Jessica began to get ready for the night. Neil was already in bed, apparently asleep, when she emerged from the bathroom and returned to their bedroom. He had complained of being tired earlier. Jessica was also tired after her experience of the previous night and the shock of the accident, but she had a plan for the night and she was determined to stay awake for a bit longer.

She lay there waiting until she was sure Neil was fast asleep, and then she slipped out of bed. Picking up a blanket and her pillow, she grabbed her mobile phone and crept silently out of the room, closing the door behind her. On the opposite side of the corridor was a bedroom she had investigated earlier in their visit. She quietly opened the door, entered the room and closed the door behind her. The room was small and was empty except for a chest of drawers, a wardrobe and a single bed with a mattress. It was the bed that was Jessica's objective. She would spend the night here and hopefully not hear any whispering. She carefully set her phone's alarm for half past five. That would give her plenty of time to creep back to bed before Neil woke up. Having made all her preparations, she covered herself with the blanket and settled down to sleep.

The alarm woke her from a dream. She groped around for the mobile. Switching it off, she felt pleased with the night. She had not been disturbed. It was time to return to her proper bed. Phone in hand and the blanket over her arm, she went to open the door. It resisted her efforts. Try as she might, it would not open. She came to a shock conclusion. The door had been locked from the other side. She was a prisoner in the room until somebody came to let her out.

Chapter 23

Jessica tried to analyse the situation. Who could have locked her in? It did not make any sense. She tried the door again, in the faint hope that she had been mistaken. Perhaps it was stuck. She tried with all her might to open it, but it was clear that it was locked.

She went back to the bed. There did not seem to be anything else she could do at this stage. Everybody else would still be asleep. She would have to wait until Neil woke up and then shout at the top of her voice for attention.

She sat there on the bed, the blanket around her shoulders to ward off the chill in the room. Time seemed to pass very slowly. The hands on her watch were just coming up to seven when she made a move. She went over to the door and was about to shout for help when something made her try the handle again. She almost overbalanced as it responded to her efforts and the door opened freely.

Grabbing the blanket, she prepared for a dash to the safety of their bedroom. As she was crossing the corridor, she heard a slight sound and glimpsed a figure disappearing down the stairs. She recognised the person immediately. It was Mags.

The sight of him started to make her think. Had he locked her in and then come and unlocked the door? She almost dismissed the idea immediately. Why would Mags want to do such a thing? On the other hand, why would anybody want to do such a thing?

She entered the bedroom to find Neil already up. He looked at her in surprise.

'I wondered where you were,' he remarked with a grin.

'I went into the bedroom across the corridor to get a decent night's sleep.' She hesitated. 'But somebody locked me in.' She looked at Neil as she waited for his reaction.

'Locked you in? Who would do that?'

'I don't know, but it happened.'

Neil thought for a moment. 'You're sure the door wasn't just stuck?'

Jessica shook her head. 'No, it wasn't stuck. Somebody deliberately locked me in, and then unlocked the door a few minutes ago.'

'But the whole household would have been asleep.'

Jessica shook her head again. 'No,' she said firmly. 'Not everybody. Just before I came back in here, I saw Mags disappearing down the stairs.'

'Mags?'

'Yes, Mags.' She paused. 'You know, Neil, I don't understand him. He never seems to reply if I speak to him. He just mumbles something unintelligible. On top of that he continuously stares at me.'

Neil laughed. 'Mags is quite harmless,' he replied.

Jessica was silent for a few seconds. Neil came over to her and put his arms around her. 'Look, poppet. Forget the incident. There is most likely a plausible explanation.' He kissed her on the lips.

When they parted, Jessica smiled, but it was a forced smile.

Neil tactfully suggested that she get ready for breakfast. Jessica nodded in agreement and made her way to the bathroom. She took her time having a shower and then went back to the bedroom. Neil was no longer there.

When she went downstairs, she found him in the lounge talking to Laura. They both looked up as she entered the room.

'Ah, there you are, Jessica,' Laura said. 'Good morning.'

Jessica smiled and returned the greeting.

She was unprepared for Laura's next remark.

'I hear you've had some problems this morning.'

Jessica's heart sank. Why had Neil told Laura about her ordeal? She summoned up a response. 'Yes. That's correct.'

Laura looked at her. Her eyes were steely grey, searching. She continued to stare at her as she spoke again. 'You went into another bedroom to sleep.' It was both statement and question.

'Yes, I did. I wanted to have an uninterrupted night's sleep,' Jessica replied simply.

'But you had difficulty getting out of the room this morning.'

Jessica was a bit taken aback. It was clear that Neil had discussed her experience with Laura in detail. It made her feel helpless and vulnerable. Her answer was brief and to the point. 'Yes. For some reason I found the door locked when I wanted to leave.'

Laura's reaction was immediate. 'That's not possible. The door must have just been stuck.'

Jessica shook her head. 'I don't think so,' she replied.

'It couldn't have been locked,' Laura retorted firmly. She turned to leave. It seemed that as far as she was concerned that was the end of the matter.

Neil and Jessica made their way into the breakfast room. Jessica was silent. Why did everybody deny everything that had happened to her? It did not make sense.

Once they had sat down, Neil looked at her. 'Feeling better now?' he asked.

'I'm fine, Neil. But I still insist that the bedroom door was locked.' She paused for a second. 'And I think I know who did it.'

Neil was startled. 'Who?'

'Mags.'

'Mags?' Neil appeared aghast at the suggestion. 'What makes you think that?' he demanded.

Jessica was quick to reply. 'What was he doing wandering around the house at seven this morning?' she asked.

Neil smiled at her. 'Sorry, poppet, that won't do. Mags still has a room in the house. He only spends the summer in the caravan. He most likely came into the house early to get something and not meet anybody. He's very shy.'

Once again Jessica was left with an unsolved mystery. She was quite sure the door had been locked, but everybody was trying to tell her she was wrong. Before she could make any further comment, Mrs Benson came into the room and asked them what they would like to eat. Neil tucked into a large cooked breakfast, but Jessica stuck to her scrambled eggs. Once again it was Marie who served the meal. Neil appeared to communicate with her quite well, but Jessica had found that, try as she might, Marie did not seem inclined to open up to any sort of conversation with her. It was odd.

While they were having breakfast Sophie came in. She too had heard about Jessica's early-morning problem.

'Oh, poor you,' she said, looking sympathetically at her.

Jessica was becoming a bit tired of being the centre of conversation because of events beyond her control. She was glad when Sophie partially changed the subject and made her an offer.

'Jessica, would you like to take one of my sleeping tablets tonight? They really are good and I can guarantee you will get a good night's sleep. I take one every night.'

Jessica did not think it was a good idea, but she did not want to appear ungrateful. She thanked Sophie and said she would see how she felt towards the evening.

Sophie had not quite finished. 'What about a mug of cocoa?' she asked. 'I always find that helps as well.'

Jessica was lukewarm to the suggestion, but she replied graciously, 'I might try it.'

After a bit more casual conversation, Sophie left the room.

As soon as she had disappeared, Neil asked, 'Why don't you accept Sophie's offer of a sleeping tablet? Nothing ventured, nothing gained, I say.'

Jessica was surprised at his words. 'Darling, you know I don't like taking things like that.'

Neil smiled at her. The next second he leaned across the table, and their lips met.

'Do it for me, poppet,' he whispered.

No more was said on the matter, as Jessica changed the subject to where they were going that day.

After breakfast Neil said he had a couple of telephone calls to make and Jessica disappeared back to their room. It did not take her long to get ready. After a quick dash to the bathroom to freshen up, she changed into the new 'summery' blouse she had purchased prior to the holiday. That, together with her slacks, was the outfit for the day. She shoved her feet into her sandals, grabbed her mobile, bag and sunglasses, and went back downstairs.

On the way she met Neil climbing the stairs two at a time. 'Give me five minutes,' he called out as he passed her.

The five minutes turned out to be ten, but Jessica did not mind. She waited in the garden, enjoying the pleasant morning sunshine. While she was there, Mags passed by, pushing a wheelbarrow. Once again she was subjected to his unwavering stare. This time when she greeted him, he replied with something that resembled 'Morning.' Jessica would have liked to say more to him, but he hurried on his way. A few minutes later she observed him watching her from the other side of the garden.

Neil reappeared, holding the car keys. 'If you're ready we can go,' he suggested.

'I'm ready,' Jessica replied enthusiastically.

She enjoyed their day out. They had mid-morning coffee in an 'olde worlde' café Neil knew about. It was in a picturesque village, and Jessica took a lot of photographs with her smartphone.

They visited a beach and spent some time walking along the sand hand in hand. Lunch was in a country pub.

The day was only marred for Jessica by a statement Neil made as they were driving back to the house. 'Poppet, I know you won't like this, but I have to return to London for a meeting. It's tomorrow, so I'll drive there and back in one day.'

'Oh, I'll come as well, then!' Jessica exclaimed.

Neil shook his head. 'I'll be quicker on my own, and I won't have time to go to Ealing,' he replied hurriedly.

Jessica still pursued her idea of going with him. 'Perhaps you can drop me off somewhere and collect me later,' she suggested.

'It won't work that way,' he insisted. 'I don't know where I'll be at any given time.'

Jessica was not going to give up. She completely failed to see the obstacles Neil was raising. 'But I won't be any trouble. Really. You can drop me off somewhere and I can get public transport.'

'You would most likely have to wait hours somewhere for me. Let me go on my own. I'll be quick.'

Jessica could see that his mind was made up. Clearly he did not want her to accompany him. She felt a bit upset, but she realised there was nothing she could do about it. If Neil did not want to take her, that was that. Anyway, she was not going to let it spoil their day out.

No more was said about the matter, and Jessica resigned herself to the fact that she would have to spend the next day on her own. Perhaps she would go swimming, she thought, or just sit in the garden and read.

It was late in the afternoon when they returned from their outing. The sun had now retreated behind clouds, and there was the feel of rain in the air. As they entered the house, they encountered Sophie.

'Did you have a nice day?' she asked.

'It was lovely,' Jessica replied.

Neil told Sophie where they had been and what they had seen.

After a while Sophie changed the subject. Turning to Jessica, she remarked, 'Dr Foster was here today and he was asking about you.'

'Asking about me?'

'Yes. He wanted to know how you were after your accident on Hangman's Hill.'

'Oh, I see,' Jessica replied, puzzled that the doctor should show such concern. The thought made her add, 'He's a very dedicated doctor.'

Sophie's face broke into a smile. 'Oh, he's like that. He calls in every week to check on my asthma and arthritis. He's more of a friend than a doctor. He often has a cup of coffee with us. Sometimes he stays for dinner.'

'Gosh, what a doctor!' Jessica exclaimed. Curiosity made her ask, 'Is he married?'

Sophie shook her head. 'He was. He got divorced several years ago. He lives on his own, but he has a housekeeper.'

At that moment Laura joined the group. For a couple of minutes the talk centred again on Jessica and Neil and where they had been that day.

Suddenly Neil addressed Laura. 'I have to drive up to London tomorrow. I'll leave early and be back in the evening.'

Laura looked surprised. 'All in one day?'

'It's no problem as long as I leave early.'

'What time will that be?' Laura asked.

'Around six.'

'Is Jessica going with you?' Sophie asked.

Neil shook his head. 'No. Make sure you look after her while I'm gone.'

'Of course we will,' Laura and Sophie replied in unison.

Jessica and Neil began to ease themselves away from the two sisters, who seemed inclined to want to continue to stand in the hall and chat.

Jessica was still intrigued about the doctor. Back in their bedroom, she remarked, 'Jim Foster seems to be a very unusual doctor.'

Neil laughed. 'He's really a family friend. He's always here looking after my two sisters.'

Lucky them, Jessica thought, to have a doctor like that.

During dinner Laura referred to Neil's proposed early departure. 'Neil, I'll get some breakfast for you tomorrow so that you'll have something to eat before you go.'

'I'll get up early as well,' Jessica chipped in.

'Darling, there's no need for you to do that,' Neil stressed.

'I want to see you off,' she insisted with a smile.

No more was said on the subject, but Jessica made a mental note of the time Neil set his phone alarm.

She was anxious about spending the night in the room. At first she lay awake listening to Neil sleeping soundly beside her. In the end her anxiety overcame her. She slipped out of bed quietly, grabbed her mobile and a blanket, and crept as quietly as she could out of the room.

Entering the bedroom opposite, she checked to see if there was a key in the lock. There was none. Sitting on the bed, she set her mobile alarm for half an hour before Neil's. Having accomplished that task, she settled down for the night. It didn't matter if somebody locked her in. Neil would be up early and she would raise a din to be let out. With that thought, she dropped off to sleep.

Chapter 24

Jessica woke up with a start. For several seconds she tried to work out what was happening. Then the reality sank in. The whispering was in the room with her. She sat bolt upright listening.

'Jessica... Jessica... Come and join us.' The sound of the voice was intermingled with muffled whispering and soft laughter.

She jumped out of bed and tried to locate where the sound came from, but it was difficult to establish the exact position. It seemed to flow from the ceiling.

She crept back to bed and pulled the blanket over her head to try and block out the sound, but with limited success. How long she lay listening she was not sure. At one point she glanced at her watch and the hands indicated that it was half past midnight.

Suddenly she was aware that the noise had stopped. She waited, expecting it to start again, but it did not. She tried to go back to sleep, but sleep would not come. The hours passed slowly. Towards dawn, she dropped off. She was woken by the sound of her mobile alarm. Her fingers fumbled to turn it off.

Her watch showed that it was almost five o'clock. She dragged herself up and made her way to the bedroom door. Would it be locked? To her relief it opened freely. She spent some time in the bathroom and was back in the bedroom before she heard Neil stir and make his way to the bathroom. It was her opportunity to return to their room and start to dress.

When Neil returned she was fully dressed and ready to see him off.

'You're up early,' he greeted her.

'I slept in the other room, but the whispering followed me,' she said quietly.

Neil put his arms round her and kissed her. 'I'm sorry about that,' he said softly.

'I've not had a lot of sleep,' she whispered.

'Why not go back to bed, then? You'd feel better.'

She shook her head. 'No.'

He kissed her again. 'We'll have to do something about your broken nights,' he said firmly.

Jessica did not reply. Instead she broke free and looked at her watch. 'You need to get going,' she stressed.

Ten minutes later they made their way downstairs. Laura was already in the kitchen in her dressing gown. She greeted them in a low voice as they entered, and they both replied in kind.

Jessica was not expecting what came next.

'Did you have a good night, Jessica?' Laura asked.

Jessica hated having to answer. 'Not really.'

Neil enlightened Laura further. 'She's not had much sleep.'

Laura was immediately concerned. 'Oh, no, Jessica. Not again. We're getting quite concerned about you.'

Jessica tried to smile. 'I'll be all right,' she replied.

Laura looked at her, seemingly full of concern, but did not make any further comment.

It was Neil glancing at his watch that changed the course of the conversation. Laura immediately asked them what they would like to eat. Neil wanted a full cooked breakfast, but Jessica only wanted a cup of tea. Even that decision brought forth a remark from Laura.

'You really should eat something, Jessica. You're very thin. You need to eat more.'

'I eat enough. Really,' Jessica insisted.

Her reply did not appear to convince Laura, who straight away shook her head, before turning to the cooker to start preparing Neil's breakfast.

While Neil was eating and Laura and Jessica were sipping cups of tea, Neil suddenly made an announcement. He turned to Jessica. 'I forgot to tell you. I know you like to look at the newspaper, so I asked Mrs Benson to bring one with her when she comes to work.'

It was a surprise for Jessica. 'Oh, thank you, darling. That's really very thoughtful of you.'

Neil grinned at her. 'It's a long walk to the village,' he replied.

Breakfast over, he hurriedly collected his briefcase and laptop, and then he and Jessica went out to the car.

Neil got into the driving seat and lowered the window. He switched on the ignition and peered at the dashboard. 'I should have filled up with petrol yesterday. I hope they'll be open in the village.'

'Will you be all right?' Jessica asked anxiously.

'There's enough.' He leaned forward to give her a kiss.

'Have a good trip,' she called, as he started the engine and the car began to move off slowly.

A wave of hands, and Jessica stood and watched the car disappear. Neil gave a toot on the horn as he turned the car out of the drive and onto the road.

Jessica walked slowly back into the house. She would have loved to go with Neil. She wondered why he had been so adamant that she should not accompany him. It was, she reflected, the first time that he had ever refused her anything. It was very odd. Men are all so different, she thought. She had already discovered that in many ways Neil was not as caring as Graham had been.

As she entered the hall, she was confronted by Laura, who looked at her quite sternly.

'Now, Jessica. You look very tired. You must go back to bed for a few hours.'

Jessica shook her head. 'I'll be fine.'

Laura would have none of it. The next instant she took hold of Jessica's arm and started to lead her up the stairs. Jessica had no option other than to comply. I'm being treated like a child, she thought.

When they reached the bedroom, Laura threw open the door. She released Jessica's arm.

'Now, Jessica, get undressed and into bed,' she ordered.

Jessica obeyed silently. She was tired and she did not feel like protesting or arguing. She kicked off her shoes and slipped out of her blouse and slacks. Laura was already standing by the bed, the covers turned back.

Obediently Jessica allowed herself to be tucked up in the bed.

Laura drew the curtains over the windows. 'Sleep well,' she said. She slipped out of the room and quietly closed the door.

At first sleep would not come. Jessica kept going over things in her mind: Neil refusing to let her go to London with him, the accident on Hangman's Hill, almost drowning in the tide, and her sleep being disturbed by laughter and muffled voices – and she repeatedly asked herself why all these things were happening to her.

She woke up suddenly from a muddled dream. She did her best to force her brain into action. When she realised what was happening, she cried out, 'Oh, no...' The voices were there again. For a few seconds she lay listening. It was the same all over again. Desperation overtook her. She jumped out of bed, struggled into her slacks and blouse, and made for the door, in her haste forgetting her shoes. One thought was on her mind: she had to escape from the voices. She hurried along the corridor and down the stairs. She could hear activity in the kitchen. It made her slip into the library. She headed for the comfortable high-backed swivel chair in front of the window, sank into its depths and managed to put her feet on the windowsill. Facing the window, she knew she could not be seen by anybody looking into the room.

She glanced at her watch. It was not yet half past seven. She could only have been asleep for a very short time. Why, oh why, she asked herself, did she keep hearing these voices? It seemed as if she was the only person who did. But why just her? She hated the idea, but was it all her imagination? She dismissed the thought right away. No, she told herself, she could not be imagining it. She fell into a doze.

Something made her wake up. At first, she struggled to work out where she was. Then her memory came flooding back. Suddenly she felt a sense of shock. Somebody was peering at her through the window. A moment later she realised who it was. Mags. Aware now that she had seen him, he turned and hurried away, quickly disappearing from view.

Jessica looked at her watch again. It was almost half past ten. She had been asleep for nearly three hours. She lay back in the chair. It was pleasant just sitting there looking at the garden, which was now bathed in sunlight. A thrush searching for food took up her attention. She watched with mild amusement as it strove to pull a worm out of the lawn. Suddenly it took off, as if disturbed by something. The next moment Mags appeared pushing a wheelbarrow. He passed by and never looked in her direction.

A sound behind her made her aware of someone entering the room. She looked round to see Marie standing there, a newspaper in her hand.

'Good morning, madam,' she said. 'I've been looking for you. Mrs Benson brought this in for you.' She handed the newspaper to Jessica.

'Good morning, Marie. That's kind of you. I must see Mrs Benson and thank her.'

'Would you like a cup of coffee?'

Jessica smiled at her. 'I'd love one.'

'I'll go and get it for you.'

Jessica hardly had time to thank her again before Marie spun around and hurried from the room.

Jessica pondered the brief incident. She had hardly had any contact with Marie previously and had almost come to the conclusion that Marie did not like her job and wanted to have as little contact as possible with her employers and their guests. Now suddenly she had displayed a totally different attitude. It was odd, Jessica thought.

She settled back down and was just beginning to look through the newspaper when she heard somebody entering the room again. She assumed it was Marie, but she was wrong. The next instant Laura stood looking down at her, a mug of coffee in each hand.

'Marie told me you were here. I'd been wondering where you were.' She handed Jessica one of the mugs.

Jessica took it and thanked her.

She thought Laura would leave, but Laura drew up a chair close by and sat down. She scrutinised Jessica for a few seconds and her eyes took in Jessica's bare feet, which were still propped up on the windowsill. Jessica felt embarrassed, remembering Laura's previous comments about her state of undress. She did not need to have worried. Laura's focus was on other matters.

Taking a sip of her coffee, Laura said, 'You didn't stay in the bedroom.' It was part question, part statement.

Jessica shook her head. She gave a simple 'No' by way of an answer.

'Did you hear noises again?'

'Yes. That's why I came down.'

Laura took another sip. Still studying Jessica, she spoke again. 'You know, you really need to do something about this sleep of yours.'

'I'll be fine soon,' Jessica replied, hoping that Laura would either leave or change the subject.

Laura shook her head. 'You're not being fair to yourself or Neil.'

Jessica did not appreciate her sister-in-law's concern. 'I'll be all right,' she said. She sipped her coffee.

Laura was not going to give up. 'Neil is very worried about you.'

Jessica was surprised by this remark. 'He's never said anything to me,' she replied.

'Of course not. He wouldn't want to upset you further,' Laura said quickly.

For a few seconds there was silence between them, each quietly drinking her coffee. It was Laura who spoke again first.

'Why don't you have a chat with Dr Foster? He'll be able to give you something to help you sleep.'

Jessica was aghast at the suggestion. 'But I'm not ill,' she protested. She paused. 'Besides, I never go to a doctor.'

Laura said nothing for a moment, as if thinking of a suitable reply. When she did speak, it was in a soft, caring voice. 'Jessica, you know Neil, Sophie and I only want the best for you.'

Oh dear, Jessica thought. I hope I haven't upset her. It was time to choose her words carefully. 'I do appreciate your concern for me, but I promise I'll be better soon.'

Laura stood up and picked up Jessica's empty mug. She made one last comment as she turned to leave. 'Well, think about my suggestion.'

'I will.'

Jessica heard Laura close the door quietly behind her. She remained sitting in the chair. It was pleasant just being there, but the newspaper lying on her lap prompted her to return to more practical matters. She scrutinised the situations vacant column, but did not find anything that might be even remotely suitable.

After scanning through the rest of the newspaper, she decided to go back upstairs and freshen up. Her watch told her it was just after eleven. There was plenty of time left before lunch. Perhaps she would go for a swim or take a walk and explore a bit more of the surrounding area. She popped into the kitchen to give Mrs Benson some money for the newspaper, but was informed that Neil had already paid for it.

In the end she had a quick swim before lunch, taking care to avoid the stretch of water between the beach and the island, and in the afternoon she went out into the garden to sit in what was now her favourite seat, under a giant oak tree. She spent most of the time reading a book she had discovered in the library that had taken her interest.

During the afternoon, Sophie stopped by for a chat. 'How are you feeling now?' she asked.

Clearly she had been the subject of conversation between the two sisters, Jessica concluded. 'I'm fine,' she replied, hoping that the answer would deter Sophie from pursuing the subject of her health. It was not to be, as Sophie's next comment was to prove.

'But you haven't been sleeping,' Sophie insisted.

'I have had some sleep.'

Jessica was not expecting Sophie's next suggestion.

'You need to see Dr Foster. He really has done wonders for me. He would give you something to help you sleep.'

Here we go again, Jessica thought. She hoped her reply might close the subject. 'I'm thinking about it.'

It seemed to work, because Sophie moved on to another topic. 'When's Neil coming back?' she asked.

'He said he'd return this evening, but I've not heard from him yet.'

As it was now late afternoon, Jessica was beginning to wonder why Neil had not phoned her. Supper loomed up and still there was no word from him. She was now quite worried.

It was later in the evening, while she was sitting in the lounge watching television with Laura and Sophie, that her mobile phone rang. She answered it quickly.

'Neil, where are you?' She was already on her way out of the room to avoid disturbing the others.

'In London.'

'London? But I thought you'd be on your way back now.'

There was a slight pause at the other end, and then Neil spoke again.

'I'm sorry, poppet, but something's come up. I can't get back tonight. It'll have to be tomorrow. I'm dreadfully sorry.'

Chapter 25

Jessica was silent for a few seconds. It was a blow. She had really expected Neil to return that evening as he had assured her he would. She struggled to give a positive reply. 'I'm sorry you can't get back today after all. I miss you.'

'I'll be back tomorrow. I promise.'

Jessica made a big effort. 'OK. I'll see you tomorrow, then.'

'I'll be back by lunchtime.'

'I'll be waiting.'

'Bye for now. Sleep well.'

'Of course. Bye.'

Jessica clicked to end the call. She fought back her disappointment. Neil not coming back as he had promised reminded her of Graham's behaviour. How many times during that marriage had she experienced something similar? Now it seemed to be happening all over again.

It took a few minutes for logic to alter her thinking. Neil had his work to do and she had no idea what had prevented his immediate return. It was unreasonable of her to compare her marriage to Neil to her previous one. No, she asserted, she had to be fair and not jump to conclusions. It was also unreasonable of her to be so curt with Neil on the telephone.

Her thoughts were interrupted by the sudden appearance of Laura.

'Was that Neil on the phone?' Laura asked.

'Yes, it was.'

'When can we expect him back?'

'Not until tomorrow.'

Laura's reaction was immediate. She shook her head. 'He works too hard.'

Jessica did not reply.

At that moment, hearing them talking, Sophie joined them from the lounge. 'When's Neil coming back?' she asked.

Laura beat Jessica to a reply. 'Tomorrow.'

Laura's statement produced almost a wail from Sophie, who at once complained, 'But he promised we would play canasta this evening.'

'We can find a game three people can play,' her sister replied.

This suggestion seemed to pacify Sophie, who immediately made a move to the lounge. 'Let's go, then.'

Laura and Jessica followed her. Jessica was half-hearted about playing cards. She felt tired and would have preferred an early night. However, rather than telling the two sisters how she felt, she decided that it was better to go along with their idea of a card game. On top of that the thought of going to bed raised the memory of the horrible whispering noise.

It was after eleven before Laura and Sophie, much to Jessica's relief, decided to call it a day. The two sisters both decided to have some cocoa and more or less insisted that Jessica join them. Reluctantly she agreed and Sophie disappeared to the kitchen, reappearing five minutes later carrying a tray with three mugs of cocoa, and warning that the drink was very hot. Jessica took the opportunity to say that in that case she would take hers up to the bedroom. Laura and Sophie raised no objection and Jessica wished them good night and left them in the lounge.

Up in the bedroom, Jessica made her plan. She sipped her cocoa and took her time getting ready for bed. Finally she sat propped up in bed, her mobile phone handy. It was now getting on for midnight. She would sit and wait for the whispering to start.

She woke up in a panic, wondering if tiredness had spoilt her plan, but a glance at her watch reassured her. She had only dropped off to sleep for a short time. It was five minutes to twelve.

She sat waiting, mobile in hand. The minutes ticked away and then suddenly the noise started. She glanced at her watch. She remained there listening, struggling to make any sense of the whispering, but as before it was incoherent and too muffled. Only when she heard her name did it make any sense. 'Jessica… Jessica… Come and join us.' Then the sound changed again to whispering and faint laughter.

She continued to listen, and then without warning the noise stopped. She checked the time again. Exactly ten minutes. Well, she thought, if that's a ghost, its timing is perfect. She felt pleased that she had carried out her experiment. If it occurs at the same time on other nights, that will prove something, she thought.

She sat there for a few minutes more, but all was quiet. She settled back in bed and fell asleep.

In the morning, she woke to rain beating on the windows. She hopped out of bed and went to have a look out. It was a miserable scene. Dark grey clouds covered the sky, and heavy rain was falling. She went to the bathroom to shower, taking her time, conscious that it was still early. It was not quite half past seven when she went downstairs.

The house was quiet. Jessica went into the library and sat in her favourite chair overlooking the garden. It was pleasant just sitting there, watching the rain falling and the birds busy searching for food in spite of the weather. A thrush, perhaps the one she had seen before, was busy on the lawn searching for worms. The sight occupied her attention for several minutes.

A sudden noise behind her alerted her that someone was close by. She swung around to see who it was. Mags was standing in the doorway, his eyes wandering aimlessly around the library. As soon as he realised Jessica was there, his eyes fixed on her.

For a full two seconds they gazed at each other in surprise. It was Jessica who broke the silence. She offered a greeting. 'Good morning, Mags.'

Mags said something she could not understand and then turned around and left before she could say anything else.

Jessica called after him, 'Mags, please don't go,' and hurried to the door. When she looked out into the corridor, he had disappeared. She returned to her chair.

It was perhaps half an hour later that a further sound behind her stirred Jessica. She turned around to find Sophie standing in the room.

'Oh, that's where you are,' Sophie said. 'We wondered if you were up.'

'Good morning, Sophie. Yes, I've been up a little while now,' Jessica replied cheerfully.

'But how did you sleep?' Sophie appeared quite concerned.

'I had a lovely sleep, thank you.'

At that moment Laura appeared. 'Good morning, Jessica. Did I hear you had a good night?' It was clear that she had heard part of their conversation.

Jessica gave a simple answer. 'Yes, you did.' She was determined to introduce the topic that concerned her. Before Laura could say anything else, she spoke again.

'I timed the whispering sounds last night. They occur exactly between twelve and ten past.'

Laura looked at her questioningly. 'I don't understand what you mean,' she said.

Jessica was ready with an answer. 'Well, if it happens at the same time tonight, either the ghosts are pretty good at timekeeping or there's another reason for the punctuality.'

The two sisters stared at her. It was Sophie who broke the silence.

'It's time for your breakfast, Jessica.'

Jessica took the hint and made her move into the breakfast room. She was surprised that Sophie followed her. When she sat down, Sophie hovered close by and was the first to speak.

'Did you see Mags this morning?'

'Yes, I did. He came into the library earlier on.'

She was not expecting Sophie's next remark.

'He likes you.'

Jessica was aghast. 'Likes me? He never even speaks to me.'

'That's because he's very shy.'

'I see.' It was the only reply Jessica could muster up. The way Mags acted and responded to her seemed a gigantic contradiction to what Sophie was saying. She was glad when Mrs Benson appeared and asked her what she wanted for breakfast. Sophie left the room.

Jessica tucked into the scrambled eggs she had requested. Nobody interrupted her, though she could hear Laura and Mrs Benson talking in the kitchen. Sophie was nowhere to be seen. Jessica had been puzzling out the relationship between the two sisters. Laura appeared to be making most of the decisions, and Sophie appeared to be quite happy to accept the more passive role. She had already made a mental note to bring up the subject again with Neil. Thinking of him made her wonder what time he would return. Hopefully it would be soon. Spending so much time on her own, she had developed a kind of boredom.

It was still raining heavily. This curtailed any hope of doing anything outside the house. In the end Jessica returned to the library and started to explore some more of the books. The majority of them, she had discovered, were travel books, some of them very early editions. She chose one that looked interesting and once again settled in the chair. She was interrupted by Marie with the newspaper Mrs Benson had brought. She quickly scanned the situations vacant column, but nothing in it appealed to her.

She had been in the library for about an hour when once again she heard the sound of the door opening. She turned around, expecting it to be Sophie or Laura, but she was wrong.

Jim Foster entered the room. He carefully closed the door behind him and walked over to her. He greeted her with a smile. 'Good morning, Jessica.'

Jessica had already risen from her chair. She was unsure how she should address him. She played safe and greeted him formally. 'Good morning, Dr Foster.'

He grinned at her. 'Call me Jim. I'm on first-name terms with the rest of the family.'

Jessica thanked him politely. She wondered what he wanted with her, and she was soon to find out.

He drew up a chair opposite her and looked at her closely. 'How are you now, after your car accident the other day?'

Jessica was surprised at the question, but she answered with, 'Oh, I'm fine. No problems.'

Again he scrutinised her. 'But you have had some problems sleeping?'

The question caught her unawares. She wondered how he knew. The information could only have been related to him by Laura or Sophie. Or even perhaps Neil. She hesitated before answering. When she did it was with a simple 'Yes.'

'Would you like to tell me about it?'

Again she hesitated. Normally she would have been reluctant to confide in a stranger, but perhaps because she felt alone with the problem, she was more willing to share it. She thought out her answer carefully, taking her time.

'Well, it's this laughter and whispering I hear at night. It wakes me up. I also hear my name being called.'

'Can you make out what the whispering is about?'

'No. It's quite indistinct.'

'And it happens every night?'

'Yes.'

'Does anyone else hear it?'

'No. Only me.'

Jim looked at her searchingly. 'Has anything else been troubling you?'

Jessica began to shake her head but then hesitated. Somehow she had to confide in somebody.

She began. 'Well, it's a bit odd, really.' She paused. 'But when the car was taken to the garage, they said there was nothing wrong with the brakes.'

'And what did you think about that?'

Jessica gave a little laugh. 'Well, it was quite ridiculous. I'm going down a hill and the brakes fail completely, and there's nothing wrong with them?' She thought for a second, and then added, 'You saw what happened.'

He nodded. 'Yes, I did. Anything else you want to tell me?'

Jessica responded quickly. 'There is one other thing.' She stopped for a second, gathering her thoughts. 'I went swimming and nearly got caught by the tide in Colliers Cove. Laura and Sophie told me they'd warned me of the danger, but I know they didn't.'

'You've had a lot of problems lately, haven't you?'

'Not really.'

'I understand that you lost your job recently.'

'Yes, that's true, but it was just one of those things that happens in my profession.'

There was a pause, and then Jim responded, 'Sometimes these things take some time to register and take effect on our health.'

Jessica smiled at him. 'I'm really quite fit and healthy,' she replied.

He quickly agreed. 'Yes, of course, but you need to think about your sleep. That's most important.' After a brief silence, he spoke again. 'I think we need to ensure that you get a good night's sleep. Let me prescribe something for you.'

Jessica was not in favour. 'I never really need anything. It would be wasted on me. But thank you for the offer.'

Jim was not deterred. 'Let me prescribe them anyway. You might find them useful at some point.'

Jessica could see that there was no point in arguing. If he wanted to waste drugs, that was up to him. Her reply was a bit blunt. 'OK. But I'm not promising I'll take them.'

He glanced at his watch. 'I have to go now, but I'll be calling at the pharmacy sometime today. I can drop something in for you later.'

Jessica smiled and thanked him. He left almost immediately, saying something about having to see Sophie.

By lunchtime, Jessica was becoming increasingly concerned that Neil had not returned. She had fully expected him to arrive by late morning. Now it was almost midday and still he had not appeared.

Lunch was dominated by Sophie extolling the caring qualities of Jim Foster. Both she and Laura knew that he had prescribed something for Jessica.

'I do hope you're going to take the medicine,' Laura said. 'We need to get on top of your sleepless nights.'

'Yes, you must take the tablets,' Sophie echoed.

'I'll see how I feel,' Jessica replied.

'Oh, but you must take them.' Sophie seemed quite alarmed at her words.

Jessica was glad when the meal was over and she could escape the attentions of the two sisters, who seemed intent on persuading her to take the drugs.

After lunch the rain stopped and the sun came out. Jessica decided to go to the beach. As she walked down the path, there was a pleasant freshness in the air.

When she arrived at the cove, she had a brief swim and then found a secluded place out of the wind and enjoyed sitting there in the sunshine.

At one point she dozed off. It was the ringing of her mobile phone that woke her up. The display told her it was Neil. Perhaps he had already arrived at the house and was calling to let her know.

She clicked to answer.

'Hi, Neil. Where are you?'

'In London.'

'Still in London? When are you coming back?'

'Not today, poppet, I'm afraid.'

Chapter 26

Jessica was alarmed at the tone of Neil's voice. 'What's wrong? You sound worried.'

She heard laughter at the other end of the phone. Neil spoke again. 'Sorry about that. Everything's fine. It's just that the car's broken down.'

'Broken down? What happened?'

'Oh, I started back, but it seems the clutch has gone.'

'Where were you when it happened?'

'Fortunately, still in London.'

'So, what's going to happen now?'

'It's being repaired.'

'How long will that take?'

'It should be ready today.'

'Gosh, that's quick.' Jessica thought for a second or two. 'So, when will you be back?'

'All being well, tomorrow. I'll try and make it in the morning.'

'Please. I'm missing you.'

'I'm missing you too, poppet.' Suddenly he asked, 'Where are you now?'

'I'm on the beach. It was raining here until about an hour ago, but now it's nice and sunny.'

'Same here.' Neil suddenly sounded concerned. 'Poppet, please be careful about when you go swimming there. I don't want to lose you.'

Jessica gave a little laugh. 'Don't worry, darling. I will. Once is quite enough in that current.'

'Good.' He spoke again immediately. 'Look, I'm going to have to ring off. My phone battery's right down. I forgot to charge it last night.'

'OK. I'll say goodbye then. Remember, I'm missing you, darling.'

'Me too. See you tomorrow. Bye for now.'

'Bye, darling.' Jessica just had time to get her reply in before Neil ended the call.

So that was it. He wouldn't be back today. Jessica felt rather upset, but there was nothing she could do about it. It was, she thought, part of married life, for her at least, though in fairness she acknowledged that in the current circumstances it was not Neil's fault, and of course he had promised that his trips away from her would diminish over time. Taking her thinking further, she scolded herself for not being more understanding. I'm just a selfish, silly little wife, she concluded.

The brief sunshine of the afternoon had now gone. Clouds had gathered in the sky and a fresh breeze had sprung up. In her bikini, Jessica felt cold. There was even a hint of rain in the air. She got up, slipped into her beach robe and started back to the house.

As she walked along the track, she suddenly saw Mags appear from the bushes. He was perhaps fifty yards in front of her. He glanced in her direction and then walked quickly ahead of her. Jessica quickened her pace, but in her flip-flops she was unable to catch him up. The incident reminded her that she had intended to talk to Laura or Sophie about their strange gardener.

When she entered the house, she met Laura in the hall.

'Ah, you're back, Jessica. You missed Jim Foster. He left these for you.'

Laura went over to a nearby table, picked up a box and handed it to her. 'I hope you're going to take them,' she said.

Jessica shook her head. 'I already told him I don't need any medication.'

'But what about your lack of sleep?'

'I don't need sleeping tablets,' Jessica insisted.

'Oh, well. You know what you're doing.'

Jessica could see that Laura did not take kindly to her decision to refrain from taking the tablets, but she had given in graciously, she thought.

Laura quickly departed and Jessica made her way to the bedroom. Once there, she examined the box Laura had given her. It contained a small quantity of white tablets. The label on the lid gave instructions to take two tablets on retiring for sleep. There was also a warning not to exceed the stated dose. Jessica put the box on the dressing table and turned her attention to dinner. She had not envisaged that she and Neil would be spending so long with his sisters, and now she was running a bit short of outfits to wear. While contemplating the problem, she went to the cupboard to select something different to put on. She was busy selecting a suitable garment when one of Neil's jackets dropped off its hanger. It hit the floor with a metallic clunk. She picked it up to hang it up again and discovered a key lying on the floor of the cupboard, having presumably dropped out of the pocket.

She picked it up and stared at it for a few seconds. A sudden thought came to her. She left the room and crossed the corridor to the room she had found herself locked in. She paused for a second and then fitted the key into the lock and turned it. It operated perfectly. She unlocked the door again, withdrew the key and went back into the bedroom. The action she had just performed raised a bombardment of questions in her brain. Why did Neil have the key? What possible reason could he have had for locking her in the room? After pondering the questions for a full five minutes, she gave up. The only solution would be to present them to Neil when he returned. She replaced the key in his jacket pocket and concentrated on getting ready for the evening.

At dinner the conversation was dominated at first by Sophie, who continued to heap praises on Jim Foster, saying how good he was and how he had helped her with her sleep problems. Jessica could tell that this was all for her benefit, and she refrained from getting deeply involved in the conversation.

Suddenly Laura spoke directly to her. 'What are you going to do with your inheritance?'

Jessica was taken aback. She was not aware that Laura and Sophie even knew about her changed circumstances. She guessed Neil must have told them.

She gave a little smile. 'I didn't know you knew about my windfall.'

Laura looked at her with an expression of surprise on her face. 'But you told us about it.'

Jessica felt a bit embarrassed at the statement. 'Oh, I'm sorry. I must have forgotten,' she managed to get out.

'You told us all about it the first evening you were here, at dinner. Don't you remember?' Laura insisted.

Jessica shook her head. 'No, I don't.'

Sophie piped up. 'Yes, you did tell us. I remember quite clearly.'

'Well, I must have forgotten,' Jessica repeated, hoping the subject would now be dropped.

It was not to be.

Laura returned to her original question. 'So, what are you going to do with all that money?'

Jessica smiled. 'I haven't actually received it yet, but to answer your question, it's all happened so quickly that I haven't had time to digest the situation or think about what I'll do with the money.'

'Had you considered sharing it with your family?'

It was an odd question, Jessica thought.

Before she could answer, Laura spoke again. 'You know, Neil has always wanted to set up a hospitality or retail business

– something where he has direct control and employs other people.'

Jessica did not know. 'Oh. He's never mentioned that to me,' she replied.

'He'd be really good at it.' This was from Sophie.

Jessica said nothing.

Sophie changed the subject. 'And poor Neil, his car broke down. Do you know where?'

'I'm not sure, but it was after he started back, somewhere still in London,' Jessica answered.

'When will he be back?' Laura asked.

'Hopefully tomorrow morning,' Jessica replied.

'He works much too hard,' Sophie remarked.

The conversation was broken up by the appearance of Mags in the doorway. He did not speak, but simply looked at the three of them.

Laura immediately jumped up. 'OK, Mags. I'm coming,' she called out.

She and Mags headed in the direction of the kitchen.

'Mags has come for his evening meal. Mrs Benson is off today,' Sophie explained.

'I see,' Jessica replied.

The position Mags held in the household had always puzzled her. He might have been the gardener, but he appeared to have a number of privileges, including having access to the house whenever he wanted it. He seemed to have all his meals provided. Jessica had asked Neil about it, but he had been unable to enlighten her any further. It was an odd situation, she thought.

Laura returned and Sophie immediately suggested a card game. Jessica did not really want to take part, but felt obliged to do so.

It was half past ten before Sophie decided that she had had enough of playing cards, much to Jessica's relief. She was just about to retire to her room when Sophie reminded her that she should wait for her cocoa and again brought up the subject of the sleeping tablets.

'Can I bring you a glass of water for your tablets?' she asked.

Jessica shook her head. 'I'm not taking any,' she replied quickly.

Sophie shrugged and went into the kitchen. Laura had already disappeared somewhere.

Left on her own, Jessica remained sitting in the lounge. She recalled their earlier conversation. In a way it troubled her. Why had Laura and Sophie insisted that she tell them what she planned to do with her pending legacy? They had assured her that she had told them about it, yet she was certain she had not done so. Now some doubts were creeping into her thinking. There was also the case of the swimming to consider. All the family had insisted that they had told her of the dangers, yet at the time she had been sure that this had not happened. Was she losing her short-term memory? No. That was too ridiculous to contemplate. Even so, tinges of doubt lingered on. How the accident with the car happened was also a mystery. Surely she hadn't put her foot on the clutch instead of the brake, as the man at the garage had suggested. She had never experienced anything like these events before. Strange things were happening, and she was troubled by this.

Her pondering was broken by the return of the two sisters. Sophie was carrying a tray with two mugs of cocoa on it, one for Jessica and one for herself. Laura did not indulge in the cocoa ritual. Jessica guessed that she drank her usual tot of whisky.

Jessica picked up her mug and announced that she would drink it in her bedroom. Neither of the sisters objected, and with good nights tendered, she departed.

She took her time getting ready for bed in spite of feeling tired. Because she was sleeping alone, she resorted to her pre-marriage mode of dress, a thin sleeveless nightshirt that reached to just above her knees. For some unknown reason she had put it into her luggage for this trip. Since her marriage she had intentionally worn more erotic clothing in bed, to stimulate intimacy between Neil and herself. She had already discovered that Neil was not as amorous in bed as her previous husband had been. She had accepted the situation. After all, she considered, she had made her bed and must now lie in it, regardless of how things were.

Once in bed, she drank the cocoa and prepared to set the alarm on her mobile phone, once again intending to time the whispering she felt sure would happen.

It was a task she did not complete. Suddenly she felt unusually tired. She lay back on the pillow for a second, and then sleep overtook her.

Being fully awake came slowly to her. She was lying somewhere, but it did not seem to be her comfortable bed. She felt something hit her face, quickly followed by something else. She opened her eyes and tried to focus on her surroundings.

Suddenly, the reality of her situation struck her. She was not in her bed.

Chapter 27

The shock of her situation hit Jessica like a battering ram. She had been correct in her assumption. She was not in her bed. Instead she was lying on the ground. Spots of rain were beginning to fall. She struggled to a sitting position, trying to assess where she was. As she gazed around, she realised that she was beside the track that led to the beach. As she sat there, questions began to cloud her thinking. How did she come to be there? Had she got there by herself? She could recall a muddled dream in which she had seemed to be carried somewhere. Was it just a dream, or had it been real? She wondered what time it was. It was quite light. She made to look at her watch, but she had taken it off as she got into bed, as she always did.

A cool breeze fanned her and made her shiver. To her horror, she realised that she was still wearing her flimsy nightshirt – and it was raining. She stood up unsteadily and gazed around. The house was not far away. She had to get back to its comfort without delay. Questions bombarded her brain as she stumbled along the track, but all she could think about was getting back to her bedroom without being seen.

As she neared the house, another problem arose. The front of the house leading to the entrance door was surrounded by a gravel path that was even more painful than the stony track to walk over with bare feet. She was relieved when she reached the front door. For a brief moment she had the awful thought that it might be locked and she would have to wait until somebody was around to open it and let her in. She had no idea what the time was, except that it was early morning.

Luck was on her side. When she tried to open the door it responded easily and allowed her to enter the house. Now to quickly get back to the safety of the bedroom, she thought.

It was not to be. As she crossed the hall, heading for the stairs, Laura appeared in her dressing gown. For a full second she stared at Jessica, and then harsh words burst from her.

'Jessica! What are you doing, wandering about outside half-naked?'

The words stung Jessica. All she could stammer was, 'I don't know… I… I… woke up outside.'

'Go and get some clothes on!' Laura snapped, though slightly less sternly.

At that moment Mags appeared in the kitchen doorway. He stared at Jessica with a grin on his face.

Jessica took one look and sped up the stairs as fast as she could. She was conscious of both Laura and Mags watching her retreat.

She hastened to the bedroom and entered its security, slamming the door behind her. She stumbled across the room. The duvet was pulled back as if someone had just got up. She tore off her damp nightgown, wrapped her dressing gown around her and sank down on the bed, exhausted and stressed.

She was not sure how long she sat there regaining her breath, her brain trying to analyse what had happened to her. She glanced at her wrist to ascertain the time, and then remembered that her watch was on the bedside table. She picked it up. It was only seven o'clock. She had a sudden urge to visit the toilet and carefully crept out of the bedroom. She encountered nobody either going or coming. The house was silent. She guessed that only Laura was up, making Mags some breakfast.

Once back in the bedroom, she lay down on the bed, adopting a foetal position.

She remained there for a while, going over the events of the last hour or so. What had happened to her? How had she ended up outside? And that odd dream she could vaguely recall. Had somebody actually carried her from her bed? It was all so strange, so complicated. Then there had been Laura's harshness to contend with – and Mags grinning at her. It was all too much to bear. She wanted to go home, far away from Laura and Sophie – and Mags. When Neil returned, she would insist that they go back to London. That was all she wanted, the comfort and security of her own home.

She woke up slowly. Then came the realisation that she must have fallen deeply asleep. For some reason she had a headache. Still half asleep, she fumbled for her watch and peered at the small dial. The hands showed that it was close to ten. Gosh! she thought. I've been asleep for hours.

She made her way to the bathroom and indulged in a long shower. A good half-hour had elapsed before she eventually made her way downstairs. She could hear voices in the kitchen, certainly that of Mrs Benson and perhaps of Laura. She slipped into the library and sat in her favourite seat, looking out onto the garden. The rain had eased off and the sun had reappeared. For now she just wanted to be alone.

She had been sitting there for about half an hour when she heard the door open. She turned to see Laura standing there holding a mug.

'Ah, there you are, Jessica. I've been looking for you. I've brought you some coffee.'

'Thank you,' Jessica responded. Now that she set her eyes on it, coffee was very welcome.

Laura set the mug down on the side table close to Jessica. She pulled up a chair and sat down, looking at her closely. She spoke softly, with a hint of concern. 'You had a bad time last night?'

Jessica nodded. 'Yes,' she replied in a quiet voice.

'Do you know what happened to you?'

Jessica shook her head. 'No. I went to bed and the next thing

I knew I woke up outside.'

'Has it ever happened to you before?'

'No. Never.'

Laura was silent for a second, continuing to study Jessica intently. She spoke again. 'You were sleepwalking.'

'Sleepwalking?' Jessica was stunned by the suggestion.

'Yes. It happens to some people. Sophie used to sleepwalk.'

'But why should it happen to me suddenly like this?'

Laura smiled at her. 'Perhaps you're worrying about something.'

'I can't think of anything.'

'Well, you lost your job.'

Jessica smiled briefly. 'Oh, that. That doesn't bother me. I was due for a change anyway.'

There was a period of silence between them. The mention of jobs reminded Jessica that in the last few days she had been a bit relaxed about looking for employment. She needed to get back home and make a proper effort.

Laura interrupted her thoughts. 'Mrs Benson tells me you haven't had any breakfast,' she said softly.

'I was so late,' Jessica explained.

'Would you like her to get you something to eat?'

At first Jessica was going to decline. She hesitated, and then Laura repeated her offer in a slightly different form.

'What about some muesli? You like that, don't you?'

That idea appealed to Jessica. She suddenly realised that she was a bit hungry. She guessed the muesli must have been bought specially for her. 'That would be nice,' she replied.

'Leave it to me.' With that, Laura disappeared to the kitchen.

Five minutes later Marie appeared, carrying a bowl of muesli and a newspaper.

'I've brought you some breakfast and Mrs Benson got you a newspaper,' she announced, setting the bowl down on the table beside Jessica. She gave her a pleasant smile.

'Oh, thank you, Marie,' Jessica responded.

'Would you like some more coffee?'

Jessica glanced into her mug. 'No, thank you. I'm fine. I've almost half left.'

Marie turned to leave and then hesitated as if she had something to say.

Jessica helped her out. 'Did you want to say something?' she asked.

Marie glanced briefly at the door, almost to check if anybody was around, and then she turned to Jessica. 'You had a bad night?' she asked.

Jessica guessed it was now common knowledge, distributed by Laura. She answered briefly. 'Yes. That's correct.'

She was surprised by Marie's next question.

'Could you tell me about it?'

Marie sounded so sympathetic that Jessica felt obliged to comply with her request. As briefly as she could, she related her experience.

Marie listened intently. When Jessica had finished, she appeared to think for a second and then she spoke. 'I had an aunt once who used to suffer from sleepwalking, but I never remember her lying down outside and sleeping.'

Jessica was about to answer when Laura reappeared. Marie quickly left the room.

'Neil's been on the phone,' Laura announced. 'He's on his way back. He'll be here soon.'

Jessica wondered vaguely why Neil hadn't phoned her, but quickly dismissed the thought. After all, Laura was his sister. What was more intriguing to her was Marie's sudden interest in her night's experience. Marie had always appeared to be remote and disinterested. Now it seemed she wanted to speak with her. It was odd, Jessica thought.

She responded cheerfully to Laura. 'Oh, it's nice he's coming back so early. I thought he'd be much later.'

'I'll go and organise some coffee for him. I think he'll need it after that long drive.'

With that remark, Laura disappeared. Shortly afterwards, Neil appeared in the room. Jessica jumped up to meet him.

'Darling, you're back lovely and early!' she exclaimed. She smiled at him. 'You must have started out at the crack of dawn.'

Neil laughed. 'Nearly,' he replied. He embraced Jessica, holding her tight, and kissed her. 'Sorry for the delay, poppet.'

'I missed you so much,' she breathed, kissing him frantically.

They held each other for a long time, and then Neil fumbled in his pocket and produced a small package. He pressed it into her hand.

She broke away and sat down to examine it. It was beautifully wrapped in gold paper and had a matching ribbon.

'What is it?' she asked excitedly.

Neil grinned as he went to sit down on the other side of the table. 'Open it and see.'

Jessica carefully removed the paper wrapping to reveal a small box.

'Open it,' he urged.

Jessica lifted the lid of the box. Inside nestled a bottle of perfume. 'Darling, what a fantastic present! Thank you.' She stood up and went over to kiss him again.

Eventually he broke free. He looked at her. 'Forgive me for being late,' he said.

'Of course, darling.' Jessica moved back to her chair. 'Can I open it?' she asked.

'Please do.'

She took up the tiny bottle and opened the cap. She sniffed the contents.

'Darling, it's fantastic. Thank you again.'

She held her wrist to the bottle. She took another sniff and then offered her wrist to Neil.

'It's great,' he responded.

She regarded the label on the bottle. 'It's French, isn't it?' she asked.

They were interrupted at that point by Laura bringing Neil a mug of coffee. Laura eyed the tiny bottle.

'Ah, somebody's had a present,' she remarked.

'Yes. Smell this.' Jessica held up her wrist to Laura.

Laura obliged. 'Mmm. Beautiful,' she said. She went out of the room, muttering that she would leave them alone to catch up on each other's news.

Jessica was anxious to talk to Neil about the things that were bothering her. She waited until he started drinking his coffee, and then she began. 'Neil, I had another awful experience last night.'

He nodded. 'I heard a bit about it from Laura. Tell me what happened.'

For a second a sense of irritation swept through her. Once again she felt she was being treated as if she were a small child. So Laura had already told Neil about last night's events. Well, now she would give her version. Slowly she related what had happened as she remembered it.

Neil listened intently, waiting until she had finished before making any comment. When he did speak, he was sympathetic. 'Poppet, I'm really sorry about what happened to you.'

Jessica hesitated, and then spoke again. 'Darling, something's happening to me here. Strange things I've never experienced before.'

'Go on.'

'Well, there was the business about swimming, and then all the problems with the car, and now apparently I'm sleepwalking.' She suddenly thought of something else. 'Oh, and there's another thing. Laura and Sophie insist that I told them about my legacy on the first evening we were here. I know I didn't. You are the only person in the family I've told.'

Neil stood up and came over to her. She rose to meet him,

and he took her in his arms. He lifted her chin and spoke to her softly. 'Poppet, you did tell them.'

Jessica was aghast. It was the last thing she had expected. She broke free of Neil and sat down again, crouching over, her head in her hands. 'I am not losing my memory,' she almost shouted.

'Of course you're not. You're just stressed.'

She shook her head. Suddenly she sat up and raised her voice again. 'I am not stressed.' She looked directly at him. 'Neil, I want to go home. It's not good for me here.' Her voice was firm, demanding.

He responded hurriedly. 'Yes, of course. But we can't yet.'

He stopped short as Jessica looked at him questioningly. He continued. 'It's Laura's birthday next week, and Sophie's is only a few days after that. We'll have to stay for that.'

Jessica was deeply disappointed. Her cherished idea was not going to happen. She quickly came up with an alternative. 'Why can't we go home now and come back for their birthdays? I can do some of the driving.' She looked expectantly at him.

He was quick to answer. 'No. We must stay here,' he replied firmly.

Jessica felt neglected. Once again, Neil was refusing to accede to her request. She wondered if his current behaviour was influenced by his sisters. Whatever the reason, it was clear that her desire was not going to be met.

Neil could see that she was unhappy. He held her again. 'Poppet, it'll be all right. You'll see,' he whispered.

'I expect so. I guess I'm just being silly.'

There was a silence, and then Neil announced, 'I've brought the post from the flat. Five letters for you.' He handed them to her.

Jessica just gave a quiet 'Thank you.' She was still thinking about his refusal to return to London. It was almost unthinkable, but she wondered if she could go back on her own by public transport.

Neil remained silent. It was obvious that his decision not to return to London had not gone down well with Jessica, but it had to be. Eventually he stood up, sensing that she wanted to be alone. 'I'll go and get the rest of my stuff from the car,' he announced.

Jessica forced a smile. 'All right, darling.'

Once he had gone, she glanced through the newspaper. There were a couple of jobs she could have applied for, but what was the point? If she received an invitation to an interview, she wasn't in London anyway. She was on the other side of the country. In the end she lost interest and put the newspaper down. She turned to the letters Neil had brought. One envelope in particular caught her attention. It was a letter from Dinton, Walley & Dinton.

Chapter 28

Jessica opened the envelope carefully. The letter was printed on the stiff parchment paper that she was now familiar with. She hurriedly read it.

> Dear Mrs Atkins,
>
> We are pleased to advise you that the financial affairs of the late Edward Walker have now been settled.
>
> The amount due to you after all taxes and expenses have been paid is £7,228,153 (seven million, two hundred and twenty-eight thousand, one hundred and fifty-three pounds). A detailed statement is enclosed with this letter.
>
> This sum has now been deposited as per your recent instructions and we trust that this is in order.
>
> Should you have any questions or require further assistance, please do not hesitate to contact us.
>
> Yours sincerely,
> Frank Dinton

Jessica glanced briefly at the statement accompanying the letter and then sat back thinking. So it had happened at last. She was now a rich woman, or rather she and Neil were a well-off couple. She knew it was going to take time to adjust to her new situation. Together, she and Graham had been quite comfortably off, and as a single woman she had always managed, but now things were completely different. She and Neil would be able to buy a nice house somewhere and afford other luxuries. It occurred to her that she had no idea what his income was. She knew that before they met his lifestyle had been simple, to say the least. She had seen where he lived before their marriage, and it had surprised her. His accommodation had consisted of a small, dingy room in a large house occupied by five or six tenants, all sharing spartan facilities.

The return of Neil jerked her out of her thinking. He sat down and smiled at her. 'Good news?' he asked. 'I guessed one of the letters was from the solicitor.'

Jessica smiled at him. 'You are now married to a very rich woman,' she remarked quite casually.

'Dare one enquire how much?'

'Just over seven million pounds, so slightly more than I expected.'

Neil whistled. 'Gosh! We'll be able to afford a Rolls-Royce now,' he replied with a grin.

'Two. One for each of us,' Jessica joked. She became serious again. 'It's money beyond my dreams. It will certainly take a bit of time to get used to.'

'Where is it now?'

'It's split up and in a number of deposit accounts.' She paused. 'I think it would perhaps be best if we left it there and let the dust settle a bit. What do you think?'

Neil nodded. 'Absolutely. Don't do anything in a hurry.'

Jessica suddenly changed the subject. 'Oh, I wanted to ask you something,' she began.

'Fire away,' he responded with one of his grins.

'I was getting something out of the wardrobe in the bedroom, when I picked up a key. I think it must have fallen out of your pocket.'

'A key?'

'Yes. I tried it in the door of the bedroom opposite ours, the one I was locked in, and it worked.'

She looked at him closely as she waited for him to answer.

He showed no sign of emotion. 'Really?' he asked. 'Well, sometimes keys are designed to fit more than one lock.'

Jessica shook her head. 'No, it wasn't that kind of key, and it fitted perfectly,' she insisted. She turned to the most important question she had to ask. 'How did you come to have it?'

Neil looked at her for a second and then laughed. 'Ah, I can see where you're leading. You think I locked you in the room.'

'But how did you come to have the key?'

Neil was quick to answer. 'I found it,' he explained simply. Then, seeing Jessica's questioning face, he elaborated. 'It was lying in the corridor. I meant to give it to Laura, but I forgot.'

Jessica stared at him. She had been wrong. There was a simple explanation. But somebody had locked her in that room. If it wasn't Neil, then it must have been…

'It must have been Mags,' she announced.

'Mags?'

She was quick to answer. 'Yes. Mags must have locked me in the room. He was in the corridor when I eventually got out.'

Neil made no reply at first, as if thinking things out. Jessica waited.

Eventually he said, 'I'll have a word with Laura about it.' It seemed that Jessica would have to be satisfied with that. She became aware that he was smiling at her. Suddenly he moved across to her. He took her in his arms and gently kissed her.

'If you're locked in a room, I want to be in there with you,' he whispered.

I'm just being a silly little girl, imagining things, Jessica thought. She responded to Neil's kiss, and they embraced for several minutes.

It was Neil who eventually broke away. 'I need to make a few phone calls,' he whispered.

'And I want some fresh air,' Jessica announced.

She left him in the library and, the newspaper tucked under her arm, she collected the two mugs with the intention of returning them to the kitchen. Halfway there she met Marie, who relieved her of them.

Jessica wandered out into the garden. It was now a pleasant sunny day. She headed for her favourite seat in the sunshine and scanned through the rest of the newspaper. Eventually she lost interest in it and just sat there for a long time enjoying the peace and solitude. From time to time the experiences of the past few days came into her thoughts. Things were beginning to worry her. A few days ago, the suggestion that she was losing her memory would have sounded ridiculous. Now, again and again she was being told she had not remembered something quite recent. Her logic tried to remind her that these events had only happened in the last few days. Was she so stressed that she did not recognise the fact? It all seemed to be so complicated to comprehend.

She suddenly became aware of someone watching her. Mags was standing on the path opposite looking at her intently. She felt uncomfortable under his gaze. Usually as soon as she made eye contact he would quickly walk away, but this time he continued to stare at her.

She called across to him. 'Good morning, Mags.'

He mumbled something inaudible and then turned and walked away.

And that's that, she thought.

A little later, Neil arrived to tell her that lunch was coming up. As they walked back towards the house, Jessica could not help bringing up the subject of Mags again.

'Mags is a very strange person,' she began. 'He never speaks. Just stares at me. Even if I say something to him, he never properly answers me.'

Neil laughed. 'It takes him a bit of time to get used to people. And then of course his speech isn't very good.'

'Has he had any treatment for the problem?'

Neil shook his head. 'I don't believe so.'

They reached the house, and the subject of Mags was dropped.

Jessica went upstairs to freshen up. When she came back, the other three were already gathered in the dining room. Sophie immediately brought up the subject of Jessica's sleepwalking.

'I hear you had another bad night, Jessica.'

'Something like that,' Jessica replied.

'I used to sleepwalk regularly,' Sophie declared.

Jessica said nothing, and this prompted her to continue.

'I sometimes did it every night.'

'That must have been awful.'

Jessica did not anticipate Sophie's next comment.

'You need to talk to Jim Foster about it. He helped me a lot.'

Jessica made no reply, and the conversation was changed by Neil asking Laura something.

After lunch, Neil announced that he had some work to do. Yet again Jessica felt disappointed. She had anticipated at the start of the trip that they would be spending time together exploring the area and relaxing, but now it seemed that Neil viewed their stay with his sisters as a working holiday. So far they had had just one proper day out.

Jessica raised an objection. 'Must you work now?' she asked, adding jokingly, 'After all, you've neglected me for two days.'

Neil had a ready answer. 'Yes, I know, poppet. It will get better, I promise. It's just that things have piled up a bit.'

Jessica knew that there was nothing else she could do. Reluctantly, she would have to amuse herself again. 'I think I'll go to the beach, then,' she announced.

'Enjoy yourself,' Neil replied. 'And take care.' He planted a kiss on her lips.

Jessica hurried up to the bedroom. Ten minutes later she reappeared, dressed in her bikini and flip-flops, her beach robe draped casually over her shoulders.

She was a bit sad to be alone, but she knew that, unlike Graham, Neil did not swim and had no enthusiasm for lying on a beach. She and Graham had often gone swimming together and on one occasion they had swum naked in a deserted cove. Thinking of the incident made her scold herself. Why do I keep thinking of Graham? she asked herself. That episode of my life is over. I'm married to Neil now. I have to make that work.

When she reached the beach, as usual there was no one in sight. She had a swim and then relaxed on the sand. The sun had retreated behind clouds, but it was still pleasant and warm there.

She had been there a little while when the sound of somebody close by made her open her eyes and sit up. Mrs Judd, the woman she had met on the beach previously, was out with her dog.

The dog, setting his eyes on Jessica, ran over to investigate and sniff her. Mrs Judd rushed up to her.

'I'm so sorry to disturb you,' she said breathlessly. 'Jojo just wants to be friendly.'

'It's all right,' Jessica replied with a smile. 'It's nice to see you again.'

'I was wondering whether I might see you today.'

'I thought I'd take the opportunity to spend a bit of time here, since it's such a nice afternoon.'

Mrs Judd looked around. 'Are you on your own again?' she asked.

'Yes. Neil doesn't like the beach or swimming very much.'

'What a pity! But that's like my husband. All he thinks about is work, though.'

'Oh, that's a shame.'

'Are you staying long with Laura and Sophie?'

'I'm not sure. Perhaps a few more days.'

Mrs Judd was silent for a second or two, and then she said, 'I worked for Laura at the house once.'

'That's interesting,' Jessica replied. Somehow she felt that Mrs Judd wanted to say more. She was correct. Mrs Judd spoke again.

'Sophie's quite nice, but she's dominated by her sister. Laura's a bit bossy.'

I know that, thought Jessica, but she refrained from voicing her opinion. She felt that was the correct stance on her part.

Mrs Judd continued. 'As to that son of hers, he'd be better off being looked after in a home.'

'Her son?'

Mrs Judd looked at her in surprise. 'Yes. Mags.'

'Mags is Laura's son?'

'Yes, of course. Didn't you know?'

'No, I didn't,' Jessica replied. Another family secret I've not been told, she thought. She was puzzled that Neil had not enlightened her.

Mrs Judd had more to relate. 'Of course, it was all a long time ago, but Laura was never married. Mags must be about thirty by now.'

'He does the gardening,' Jessica remarked.

Mrs Judd sniffed. 'That's to save Laura money.'

Jessica made no reply, but Mrs Judd still seemed inclined to want to talk.

'I only worked there for about six months,' she continued. She looked at Jessica. 'Then I got accused of stealing money.'

'Oh, no!' Jessica exclaimed.

Mrs Judd nodded. 'Turned out in the end that Mags had taken it. But I left anyway. I'd had enough.'

'I should think so!' Jessica replied.

There was silence between them for a few seconds, Mrs Judd scrutinising Jessica. 'I wish I had your slim figure,' she said.

Jessica smiled. 'I have to work at it.'

'Well, at least you can wear a bikini,' Mrs Judd responded, a hint of regret in her voice.

'You'll have to go on a diet,' Jessica answered cheerfully.

'Fat chance of that, with my old man around,' Mrs Judd muttered.

At that moment, the dog started to whine.

'Jojo's tired,' announced Mrs Judd. 'I'll have to go.'

Goodbyes were exchanged, and Jessica watched the pair walk to the end of the beach and start to climb the steps. She stayed a little longer and then, as a chill wind started to sweep in from the sea, she decided to call it a day.

When she returned to the house, Neil was in the hall talking to Laura. They both greeted her, but Jessica felt embarrassed about being in her bikini and quickly went upstairs to get ready for dinner. Looking through the clothes she had brought, she realised that she had grossly underestimated the amount of time she and Neil would be spending with Laura and Sophie. In the end she chose a pretty blouse she thought would do another turn, and the long skirt to go with it. Her high heels completed the outfit.

When she went downstairs, Neil was in the library. He did not appear to be working.

Jessica decided to join him. 'Finished work for the day, darling?' she greeted him.

Neil nodded. 'Absolutely. Enough is enough. Did you have a nice time at the beach?'

'I did. I saw Mrs Judd again.'

'Mrs Judd?'

'Yes. The wife of the man who repaired the car.'

'Oh, yes, of course.'

'She told me she used to work here.' Jessica came to the part she wanted confirmation about. 'She also told me that Mags is Laura's son.'

'What?' Neil was aghast.

'Is it true?'

Neil responded quickly. 'Yes, it is. But it's not general knowledge. Laura is a bit sensitive about it.'

'You could have told me.'

Neil was silent for a few seconds. When he replied, his voice was hushed. 'I'm sorry, poppet. I could have told you, but I was a bit afraid you might let something slip. Even I don't know the details and most people in the village have no idea. I guess Mrs Judd must have found out when she worked here.'

Jessica had to be satisfied with that.

Their conversation was interrupted at that point by Sophie informing them that dinner was about to be served.

During the meal, Neil and his sisters did most of the talking. At one point Sophie remarked that Jessica was being very quiet, and the conversation centred on her for a few minutes, after which it reverted back to the other three.

After dinner, Sophie wanted to watch a television programme, Laura immediately expressed an interest, and as it looked as if Neil was going to stay for it too, Jessica felt obliged to join the party.

It was getting late when the programme finished. Sophie immediately went into the kitchen to prepare cocoa for Jessica and herself. When she brought it in, Jessica excused herself, saying that she was rather tired and would take her drink upstairs. Neil said he would follow shortly.

Once in the bedroom, Jessica lost no time in putting a plan into action. Ten minutes in the bathroom, and she was back. She desperately wanted to be ready for bed before Neil appeared. She retrieved the sexy nightdress she had brought with her and put it on. A glance in the mirror told her all she wanted to know. One word described the garment – revealing. If that didn't turn Neil on, nothing would. A dab or two of the perfume he had given her was the finishing touch. She gulped down the cocoa and dived into bed. Now to wait and surprise him.

Chapter 29

It seemed to take hours for Jessica to wake up. There was the smell of the sea in her nostrils, accompanied by a feeling of dampness. She struggled to open her eyes. She began to feel cold water rising around her. The shock forced her to full consciousness. She looked about her. Where was she? What had happened to her? She was lying on a bare stone floor, with water creeping up. She pulled herself up to a sitting position. The surroundings she was in were strange, yet somehow familiar. For a good five minutes she sat there trying to establish where she was. She could remember going to bed. She had put on a sexy nightdress and was waiting for Neil. Now she was in a cavern-like space with water covering the floor.

She managed to stand up, and then the reality of her situation struck her. She knew where she was. She was in the tunnel under the house, the one that led to the sea, the tunnel that Neil had shown her. But how did she get here?

At first the rising water puzzled her. Then she realised what it was. It was the tide coming in. She knew that the amount of water in the tunnel might increase enough to fill it. She had to get out as fast as she could.

She hurried to the steps that led up to where she knew the heavy door to the cellar was. One look at the door told her all she wanted to know. There was no handle or any other means of opening it. She tried desperately to prise it open with her fingers, but it was clearly secured from the other side.

She beat on the door with both hands and shouted as loudly as she could, but there was no response. She kept trying to attract attention for several minutes, but it seemed that nobody could hear her. She wondered what time it was. It felt like early morning, but she could not be sure. Was everybody in the house still asleep? With no watch, it was impossible to tell.

Suddenly she had an idea. Of course! The tunnel led to the beach. Perhaps she could get out that way. Swiftly she sped along, splashing through water that was already above her ankles. The tunnel began to get lighter as she neared the beach. She reached the iron grille at the end. The door in its centre was securely closed with the huge padlock. She remembered that when she had been with Neil he had unfastened the padlock with a key that hung on a nail on the wall. She found the nail, but there was no key. She could have wept with disappointment and frustration. It was clear that there was no getting out that way.

Desperately she made her way back to the steps. The door to the house was the only way out. If only someone would hear her cries for help. She beat upon the door again, yelling at the top of her voice. Nobody opened the door and no sound came from the other side.

She waited, hammering on the door and continuing to shout for help at intervals. If she climbed down from the steps onto the floor of the tunnel, the water would already be almost up to her knees. Eventually it would reach the roof. If she was not rescued, she would drown when the tide was at its highest.

How long she continued her efforts, she had no idea. She was about to give up when she heard a noise on the other side of the door. Again she shouted. Slowly the door opened. A familiar figure stood there, gazing at her in amazement.

'Marie!' Jessica gasped. 'Thank you. Thank you. You've saved my life.'

'I was in the cellar and I heard something,' Marie explained. She continued to look at Jessica, who was standing there in her wet and revealing nightdress. 'But you're soaked! How did you get in here?'

Jessica was close to tears. The reality of what she had just experienced was beginning to sink in. 'I don't know,' she replied miserably. 'I went to bed and I woke up here. It's filling up with water.' She began to shiver.

Marie took control. She put her arm around Jessica and spoke softly. 'Come along. You need to get out of those wet things. You need a hot bath to warm you up, and you need a hot drink.'

Jessica allowed Marie to lead her up the steps to the cellar and then up into the house. 'What time is it?' she murmured.

'It's half past nine,' Marie whispered. 'They've been looking for you everywhere.'

Jessica did not reply. At that moment they reached the hall. Sophie was standing there. She looked at Jessica in amazement and then shouted in the direction of the kitchen. 'Jessica's here!'

A second later Laura appeared, a look of both surprise and shock on her face. 'Jessica, where have you been?' she exclaimed.

'I… I don't know,' Jessica stammered. It was all she could say.

'We've been searching everywhere for you. Neil is still outside somewhere.' Laura seemed to be almost blaming Jessica for the problem. She stared at her for an instant and then barked out, 'Look at you, Jessica! You're all but naked!'

Embarrassed, Jessica instinctively used her hands to cover herself. She was now almost in tears.

Laura had not quite finished. She issued another instruction. 'Marie, take Jessica upstairs and see to her.'

Jessica made no response as Marie gently helped her upstairs, her arm still around her. When they arrived at the bedroom, Marie opened the door and led her in. Exhausted and bewildered, Jessica slumped into the nearest chair.

Marie took control again. 'Come along,' she said. 'Get out of that wet nightdress and I'll run you a nice hot bath.' She made for the door. 'I'm going to get you a hot drink.'

Left on her own, Jessica tried to work out what had happened to her, but there were no answers to her questions. How had she got into the tunnel? How had the door been closed, locking her in?

The knowledge that Marie would soon return prompted her to make a move. She stripped off the wet nightdress and dropped it on the floor, and put on her dressing gown.

Wearing that made her feel just that little bit better. She had just resumed her seat when Marie returned, carrying a tray with a mug of tea and a plate of toast.

'I've brought you something to eat as well,' Marie announced.

Jessica thanked her as cheerfully as she could.

Marie scrutinised her for a second. 'Your bath's ready. Come along before it gets cold.'

Jessica found herself been led along the corridor to the bathroom. Once there, she found that modesty was a low priority. Marie helped her out of her dressing gown and into the warm water, and then dashed off and appeared a minute later with the tray, which she placed on a stool next to the bath.

'Will you be all right now?' she asked.

'I'm fine,' Jessica replied. 'This is lovely. Thank you very much for your help.'

Marie smiled. 'I'd better go and do some work now,' she said. With that, she made for the door.

'Thank you again,' Jessica called after her.

Once Marie had gone, she lay back in the bath, enjoying its soothing warmth. From time to time she sipped the tea and munched the toast. She was surprised at Marie's kindness towards her, almost like a mother caring for her daughter. It was a long time since anyone had treated her like that. She knew it was the sort of thing Graham would have done. When she broke her leg once, he had looked after her and pampered her. Neil was different. Suddenly she thought, there I go again, making comparisons. She quickly dismissed that thinking.

She took her time in the bath. Eventually, when she could feel the water growing cooler, she emerged and went back to the bedroom. It did not take her very long to slip into a pair of slacks and a blouse from the limited selection of clothes available to her.

She was just about ready to go downstairs when Neil appeared.

'I've been looking for you, poppet,' he announced, as he gave her a kiss.

'Yes, Laura told me.'

'I looked around the garden and then went along the path down to the beach, thinking you might be there,' he went on, with a look of concern.

'I was here, in the house.'

'Where?'

Jessica hesitated for a second. She formulated her reply carefully, taking a deep breath before speaking. 'I went to bed last night, waiting for you to come up, and then I must have fallen asleep.' She paused for a moment. 'I woke up this morning lying in a pool of water in the tunnel leading to the beach. The door to the cellar was shut tight, the water was rising, and I couldn't get out.'

Neil stared at her. 'But how—'

She interrupted him. 'Marie heard me banging on the door and shouting for help and rescued me.'

Before he could say anything else, Jessica spoke again. 'Neil, do you realise that if Marie hadn't come along in time I would have drowned?'

Neil took her in his arms. 'Thank goodness she heard you,' he murmured.

'But how did I get there?' Jessica demanded.

Neil stepped back and looked at her, slightly astonished. 'You must have been sleepwalking again.'

'Sleepwalking?' Jessica retorted. 'Sleepwalking, and I managed to close a heavy door behind myself?'

'It can happen.' He grabbed her arms. 'You're not suggesting that somebody did it on purpose? Surely not.'

'I don't know,' Jessica replied. 'It's all very odd. All sorts of strange things have been happening to me since I came here.'

'You're just under a bit of stress, that's all.'

Jessica suddenly pleaded, 'Darling, can't we return to London? I'll be better then, you'll see.'

Neil shook his head. 'I'd love to say yes, poppet, but you know how it is. We just have to stay until after my sisters' birthdays.'

Defeated, Jessica made no reply.

Neil broke the silence. 'If you're ready, let's go downstairs. Laura and Sophie are really worried about you.'

Hand in hand they went down to the hall.

Just as they arrived there, Laura emerged from the lounge. She looked at Jessica. 'How are you feeling now?' she asked.

'I'm OK,' Jessica replied.

Laura gave her a questioning look. She made a move towards the lounge. 'Come and sit down,' she commanded.

Jessica and Neil followed her obediently in silence.

Jessica wondered to herself what would happen now.

Sophie was already in the lounge doing a jigsaw puzzle. 'You've had another bad night, Jessica?' she asked.

'Yes.' Jessica did not elaborate.

Once they were all seated, it was Laura who commenced the proceedings. She turned to Jessica. Her voice was soft, and not unkind. 'Jessica, you really do need to do something about these incidents you're having at night.'

'What?' Jessica asked. It was the only thing she could think of on the spur of the moment.

Laura was silent for a second or two before she replied, as if she wanted to ensure full attention to what she had to say. 'You need to talk to Dr Foster about them.'

The suggestion puzzled Jessica. How Jim Foster was going

to rectify the situation she had no idea. 'I don't know how he's going to be able to help,' she replied.

'Of course he can help,' Laura retorted.

'He's helped me such a lot,' Sophie piped up.

'You really should see him,' Laura insisted.

It was Neil who spoke next. 'Laura's right, poppet. You must do something. Let's face it: nothing ventured, nothing gained.'

Jessica almost smiled at Neil's turn of phrase, but she was determined not to be pressured into seeing the doctor. 'I'll think about it,' she responded, an element of firmness in her voice.

Her decision seemed to have the desired effect. Laura did not pursue the subject further.

Thankfully the meeting broke up almost immediately. Neil wanted to make a telephone call, Laura was wanted by Mrs Benson, and Sophie clearly wanted to concentrate on her jigsaw puzzle. Jessica took the opportunity to go out into the garden.

She was sitting on her favourite seat watching a bumblebee busy at a flower when Mags passed by. She greeted him. He did not reply, but grinned at her with a knowing kind of look and continued on his way. A thought came to Jessica. This in turn produced more questions. Was Mags indeed involved in what was happening to her? Had he locked her in the bedroom? Had he taken her down to the tunnel below the cellar in the night? The more she thought about it, the more it seemed like a possibility. Laura and Sophie couldn't have carried her from the bedroom, and it wouldn't have been Neil, so who else could it be except Mags? Somehow she could not accept the idea that she had been sleepwalking.

She was stirred from her pondering by Neil, who came to announce that lunch was ready. She walked back to the house with him. She was beginning to tire of the routine of midday lunch. For one thing it was a bit boring, and for another she disliked and had no need of two sit-down meals a day. She wondered what the extra food was doing for her weight and figure. She had searched in vain for a pair of scales to weigh herself.

After lunch, Neil hurried off to do something important that he said was work-related, and Jessica returned to the garden. Life was beginning to get tedious, she thought. She resumed her pre-lunch seat. It was not unpleasant sitting there partly in the shade. She had been there only a few minutes when Mags came by again. Once again she received that grin. This convinced her more than ever that he had had something to do with her night-time escapades. That led to an uncomfortable realisation. If Mags was the culprit, then he must have seen her almost naked. That thought was not a pleasant one.

She was roused from her thinking by the sudden appearance of Sophie, who waved to her as she approached. As soon as they were within talking distance, Sophie made an announcement.

'Ah, there you are, Jessica. Jim Foster wants to see you.'

Chapter 30

'Jim Foster wants to see me?' Jessica asked.

'Yes. I expect it's a follow-up from the other day,' Sophie explained, with a bit of shrug of her shoulders.

Or for something else, Jessica thought, remembering Laura's suggestion that she see the doctor. Puzzled, she allowed Sophie to escort her back into the house.

Once indoors, Sophie made for the library. As soon as they arrived there, Sophie disappeared with a hurried apology.

Jessica entered the room and was surprised to find Neil sitting in there with Jim Foster, who had a cup of coffee in front of him.

'Hello, Jessica. Come and sit down,' Jim said.

Jessica took a seat beside Neil, who smiled at her.

Jim sipped his coffee. 'How are you now?' he asked Jessica.

'I'm fine… That is, except for certain things.'

'I understand you're still having disturbed nights.'

Jessica nodded.

'Can you tell me about it?'

Jessica was a bit reluctant at first, but then she thought, why not? She related her experience in the tunnel.

Jim listened intently.

When she had finished there were a few seconds of silence between them, and then he asked quietly, 'How do you think you got there?'

Jessica considered the question for a few seconds. Should she tell him what she thought, or say nothing? In the end she decided to speak out. 'I think I was taken there,' she replied firmly.

'You don't think you were sleepwalking?'

'No.'

'What makes you think you were taken there?'

'I can't see how I could have walked all the way down into that tunnel and then closed a heavy door behind me,' Jessica asserted. 'A door that could only be opened from one side,' she added.

Jim was clearly considering her comments for several seconds. He asked a more searching question. 'Who do you think might have taken you there?'

Jessica had been put on the spot. What should she say? She had no evidence that it was Mags. For several seconds she struggled to formulate a reply. In the end she simply said, 'It could have been Mags.'

Jim's face gave no indication of how he felt about her remark. All he said in reply was, 'I see.'

Jessica began to worry whether she had said the wrong thing. Jim's next remark once again did not reveal his thinking. He paused, as if working out what to say. When he spoke, it was almost as if he were thinking aloud.

'I think in these cases there is very often deep-seated stress.'

'But I'm not stressed!' Jessica butted in.

'I would like to make a suggestion.' He looked directly at her.

'Please do.' It was Neil who spoke.

Jim continued. 'I have a colleague who runs a private clinic not far from here. I believe it would be good for you to go there for a few days and completely relax.'

'But I'm all right. Really, I am,' Jessica insisted.

'I think you should go, poppet,' Neil remarked.

'Darling, I don't think I am ready for that yet.'

'Well—' Neil started to say something else, but Jim interrupted him.

'I'll leave the thought with you. If you change your mind, give me a ring and I'll arrange everything. Dr Jackman is a good friend of mine.'

With that he stood up to leave. 'I must just have a word with Sophie before I go,' he remarked casually.

After he had left the room, there was a brief silence, which was broken by Neil. 'Poppet, I do think you should have taken up Jim's offer. What have you got to lose?'

Once again Jessica felt she had to defend her decision. 'Darling, I am not ill. I don't need to go to a rest home.'

'But you do have these problems with sleepwalking,' Neil pointed out.

'That's what everybody tells me,' she retorted.

'But you do agree that something is happening.'

'Yes, something IS happening.'

'But you can't go around blaming someone like you did just now, trying to say that Mags has something to do with your problem.'

Jessica blushed slightly. 'Yes, I know, and I'm sorry I mentioned his name, but I do believe he is involved somehow.'

'Why?'

Jessica thought for a second before answering. It was a tricky question, but she felt she had to justify her opinion. 'I don't think I have been sleepwalking. I believe somebody locked me in that bedroom and somebody took me to the tunnel leading to the beach. I must have been carried there. Laura and Sophie couldn't have done that. You wouldn't have done it, so that only leaves Mags. I don't like the way he looks at me, almost leering. I know for a fact that he wanders around the house at night. I've seen him.'

'You can hardly accuse somebody just because they look at you.'

Jessica said nothing. Now she was bitterly regretting mentioning Mags, but there was nothing she could do about it.

She still thought she was correct in her assumption, but it was quite clear that nobody else agreed with her.

Neil spoke again. 'Even if Mags was involved as you say, what about the whispering you say you heard? How do you account for that?'

He looked at her intently, waiting for an answer.

Jessica shook her head. 'Darling, I don't know. I just know that it happens.'

'It's all very strange,' Neil remarked, almost casually.

Jessica felt angry and unsupported. Her next remark was tinged with the frustration she felt. 'Darling, I want to go home. Can't we just go?'

'Laura and Sophie would be very offended and upset if we did.'

Jessica was about to answer, but he returned to his argument. 'Anyway, why do you want to leave? We're welcome here. The weather is good and we need to relax and enjoy everything.'

'I just want to go home. I don't like it here,' she replied, almost in a whisper.

'That's hardly fair to Laura and Sophie. They've enjoyed having us here and they've gone out of their way to make us feel welcome.'

Jessica reacted quickly. 'I'm sorry, darling,' she replied. 'I know they mean well and they've done their best to welcome me, but there are other reasons. I'm a woman. I need to have my own things around me. I didn't think we would be here for so long. I've run out of clothes completely. I could go back to London on the train by myself and then come back in a couple of days' time.'

'No, don't do that. Leave it a few more days and then we'll both go. We can do it in a day, there and back.'

It was a breakthrough of a kind, Jessica thought. At least I've made some progress from the previous outright refusal. Even with that, she felt she needed some confirmation. 'Do you really mean it?' she asked.

Neil suddenly stood up and bent over her. He placed a kiss on her cheek. 'Of course I mean it, poppet.' He looked at his watch. 'Look, it's still quite early. Hours and hours until dinner. I need to get a couple of things. I could do with going to the village. Want to come with me?'

'Ooh, yes, please.'

'OK. I'll just get one or two things, and then we'll go.'

'I'll go and get ready.' She was already up and making for the door. 'See you in a few minutes.'

She dashed upstairs. A quick freshen-up, and she was back down in five minutes flat.

Neil was already waiting for her and together they made for the car. Several minutes later they were in the village. Neil wanted to go to the village store to buy a few items of stationery. The shop had a small stock of essentials. Jessica browsed the shelves while he made his choice. She settled on a packet of ginger biscuits, a favourite of hers.

Outside the shop again, they decided to explore a bit more of the village. Jessica was once again attracted to the quaint old church, which stood surrounded by an ancient churchyard.

'Some of the graves are quite old,' Neil observed.

'I wonder if the church is open today. I'd love to see inside.'

Though he had seen it before, Neil was as keen as Jessica to go in. As luck would have it, when he tried the door, it opened readily.

Once inside, they had to adjust to the darkness. As they grew used to it, Jessica was quite impressed. 'Just look at that stained glass window,' she whispered to Neil.

'Good afternoon,' came a voice.

They had been so absorbed in the interesting interior that they had not heard anybody approaching. They both turned to see a tubby individual, clearly the vicar, standing nearby.

'Good afternoon,' they uttered in chorus.

'Do you like our church?' the vicar asked.

'It's really beautiful. It must be very old,' Jessica remarked.

The vicar nodded. 'It dates back to the fourteenth century, but the bit you see now is much newer. It was built in the seventeenth century.' He chuckled.

'Have you been vicar here a long time?' Jessica asked.

The vicar beamed at them over ancient spectacles. 'I shall have been here thirty years next year,' he announced.

Jessica was going to say something, but before she could he asked, 'Are you staying locally?'

'We're staying with my sisters, Laura and Sophie Atkins. I'm Neil, and this is my wife, Jessica,' Neil explained.

The vicar's face lit up. 'Ah, young Neil!'

'Reverend Thomas!' Neil exclaimed in sudden recognition.

'It is indeed.' The vicar smiled at them again. He looked at his watch. 'You must excuse me. I'm due at a meeting of the WI in a few minutes' time. Do please have a look at everything and enjoy your visit.'

'Thank you. We will,' Neil replied.

'And please remember to close the door securely when you leave.'

'We'll do that,' Jessica assured him.

He wished them goodbye and hurried away.

As he disappeared, Neil whispered to Jessica, 'I remember him from when I was a boy.'

They spent a further ten minutes in the church and then left, carefully closing the door behind them as the vicar had requested. After the dark interior of the church it was pleasant to be out in the sunshine again.

They explored a bit more of the village. Despite her previous visits, every corner they turned seemed to reveal something new for Jessica. The biggest surprise of all was a café with a sign outside saying 'The Old Coffee Shop'.

'Gosh! It's still there,' remarked Neil. 'I used to buy ice cream here when I was a kid.'

Jessica was more interested in something else. 'How about a coffee?' she asked.

'Good idea.'

A bell jingled as Neil pushed open the door. The café was not busy. Two elderly ladies occupied one of the tables. Both scrutinised the newcomers.

Jessica greeted them with a cheerful 'Good afternoon' as she made her way to a table in a corner. They had hardly sat down before a young woman appeared and greeting them, order pad in hand.

'We'll have a coffee each, and...' Neil looked at Jessica enquiringly.

'I think I'd like a piece of cake,' Jessica responded, looking across at the display behind the glass at the counter.

'Fruit cake or cream cake?' the waitress asked.

Jessica thought for a second. 'I think it had better be fruit cake,' she remarked, making a face.

'I'll have cream cake,' Neil announced.

The waitress repeated the order back to them and then disappeared into the kitchen.

'Well, this is rather nice,' Neil remarked, looking round the room.

'It's lovely to come across something like this,' Jessica replied. 'So many places like this have just disappeared and been replaced by coffee shop chains.'

At that moment the waitress reappeared with their order.

There was a bit of a silence between them, as they sipped their coffee and sampled the cake.

'Mmm, this is delicious!' Jessica exclaimed.

Neil nodded in agreement, his mouth full of cream cake.

During the conversation that followed, Neil brought up Jim Foster's suggestion again. 'Have you had any more thoughts about it?' he asked.

Jessica was adamant. 'Darling, I'm not ill. I've told you, I don't need to go to a rest home.'

'But you have to admit that you're having these problems at night.' Neil's voice had a caring tone about it.

'I've only had them since I've been here,' she retorted. She had not meant to be so blunt, but she was beginning to be fed up with the subject.

Neil was not about to give up. 'Poppet, I'm worried about you. Laura and Sophie are too.'

'I am NOT ill,' Jessica insisted.

Before he could respond she spoke again. She chose her words carefully. 'Darling, I know you care about me, and Laura and Sophie are both very sweet, but I really need to return home to an environment I'm used to. I'll be fine then. I really mean it.'

Neil nodded. 'I understand. Just give it a few days more, and then we'll go back to London, but I still feel there's no harm in taking up Jim's offer.'

Jessica did not reply and Neil did not pursue the subject, much to her relief. Instead they talked about the paintings that hung on the walls of the café.

It was a good hour later that they finally left, prompted by the waitress reversing the sign hanging on the door.

As they drove back to the house, Jessica felt satisfied that it was on the cards that they would soon be returning to London. She would just have to stick things out and hope that there were no other unpleasant incidents.

As they entered the house, they encountered Laura, who was carrying a coil of light rope. 'Did you have a nice afternoon?' she asked.

It was Jessica who replied. 'Yes. Super. We explored the village and had a cup of coffee in a delightful café.'

'It was the Old Coffee Shop. The old place is still there,' Neil added.

Laura nodded. 'Yes, it's still there, but new people are running it now.'

She saw Jessica looking at the rope. She gave a little laugh. 'I'm not going to hang myself. It's for a new washing line. Mags is going to fix it up for me.'

Neil grinned. 'It does look dangerous,' he quipped.

'I'm going upstairs to get changed for supper,' Jessica announced, making a move towards the stairs. She left Neil and Laura talking in the hall.

She took her time getting ready. She lamented having yet again to wear the blouse and skirt she had already worn on several other evenings, but there was nothing she could do about it. She was glad their stay would only be a few days more and then she could get back to normality.

When she returned downstairs, she was surprised to see Jim Foster sitting in the lounge with Laura and Sophie. Neil whispered to her, 'Jim's been invited to dinner.'

Despite Jessica's initial apprehension, dinner and the follow-up in the lounge turned out to be quite pleasant. Jim Foster proved to be quite an entertaining guest. It was late in the evening when at last he declared that he had better return to duty.

It was at this point that Sophie announced that she would make some cocoa for Jessica and herself.

Jessica had other ideas. 'I think I'll give the cocoa a miss tonight,' she said.

Sophie looked horrified. 'But you can't, Jessica,' she insisted.

Laura butted in. 'You really must have it, Jessica. You need a good night's sleep.'

Jessica shook her head. 'No, really, I don't want any. I've had a glass of wine. That'll help me sleep.'

Laura looked as if she was going to say something else, but Neil butted in.

'Darling, let me get you a hot whisky. It'll work wonders.'

'Well, not really…' Jessica began hesitantly.

Neil was already heading off to the kitchen, followed by Sophie.

Meanwhile there was another lecture for Jessica from Laura on the need to have a good night's sleep.

Sophie returned, a mug of cocoa in her hand, followed by Neil, who was carrying a glass of amber liquid, which he handed to Jessica with a smile.

'Drink that, darling. It's a good old-fashioned remedy.'

'I think I'll take it upstairs,' Jessica replied.

'I'll come up as well,' he remarked.

They said goodnight to Laura and Sophie and retreated to their room.

Once there, Jessica went into the bathroom. Five minutes later she was back. Neil was taking his time getting undressed. Jessica slipped into her nightdress and got into bed.

'You haven't had your nightcap, poppet,' Neil pointed out.

Jessica made a face. 'Must I? I don't really like whisky.'

'Yes, you must. I prepared it specially for you.'

Jessica screwed up her face again. She picked up the glass and downed the contents in several gulps. She made another face as she put the glass down on the side table. As she did so she thought she noticed some sediment in the bottom. Before she could take another look, sleep overtook her.

Chapter 31

Jessica slowly came to consciousness. There seemed to be a draught blowing on her. A drop of water fell onto her face. She struggled to comprehend what was happening. She was lying on something hard and uncomfortable. Things were digging into her back. Another drop of water landed on her face and trickled down. She forced herself to open her eyes and saw a grey sky above her.

Realisation came suddenly. She was not in her bed. She was lying on the stony ground, gazing up at the sky and the branch of a tree. It was starting to rain. She was conscious of a chill wind blowing. Her flimsy nightdress was of little protection.

The stark awareness of her predicament made her sit up. She suddenly recognised where she was. She was on the track leading to the beach. She was conscious of something around her neck. She put her hand up to feel it. It was a rope noose…

Suddenly she heard voices approaching.

'She's here.' It was Neil. He rushed up to her. 'Jessica, are you all right?'

Jessica's distress came through. 'What's happened? Why am I here?'

He bent down and put his arm around her. Carefully he removed the noose from around her neck.

An out-of-breath Laura arrived at the scene. She looked at Jessica with disdain.

'Jessica, what on earth are you about?'

Jessica could not bring herself to reply.

'Let me help you up,' Neil said. With his strong arm around her, Jessica managed to stand.

'It's raining. You're going to catch your death of cold,' Laura declared, an element of reproach in her voice. Her eyes fixed on the rope noose that was now lying on the ground. 'That's my new washing line,' she announced with disgust as she picked it up.

Neil began to lead Jessica back to the house in silence, followed by Laura.

All of a sudden Mags appeared. He scrutinised Jessica from head to foot. She became even more distressed and was embarrassed to be seen by him, scantily dressed as she was. She did her best to cover herself, but with little success. Fortunately, Laura issued an instruction to him.

'Mags, go and finish your breakfast, and take this with you.' She handed him the rope.

With a grin in Jessica's direction, Mags took the rope, turned and hurried off, much to her relief.

No further words were spoken between the three of them as they returned to the house. Neil still had his arm around Jessica, who was full of a mixture of disbelief and misery. The rain was now falling steadily and beginning to soak her as she stumbled along, her bare feet ill-equipped to deal with the rough terrain. She was glad when they at last reached the house.

As they entered the hall, Sophie appeared. 'Goodness gracious, Jessica, what happened to you?' she exclaimed.

Jessica was too distressed to answer. Neither Laura nor Neil replied or made any comment.

Neil led Jessica upstairs to the bedroom, where she collapsed into a chair. Tears flowed down her face as she buried it in her hands.

'I don't know what's happening to me,' she whimpered.

Neil had his hand on her back. 'You're just under a bit of stress, that's all,' he replied softly.

'I'm not stressed,' she sobbed. 'Things are happening to me that I've never experienced before.'

Before Neil could respond, she sat up. Tears were still running down her face. She spoke slowly and quietly almost to herself. 'I must be going mad. That's what it is. I'm going mad.'

Neil put his hands on her shoulders and forced her to look at him. His voice was firm and positive. 'Nonsense. Get that idea out of your head. You're just going through a bad patch. Things will get better. You'll see.'

She made no reply.

'Look, poppet,' he continued. 'Get out of that wet nightdress and go and have a hot shower.'

It sounded like a good idea. Jessica made an effort and stood up. Grabbing her dressing gown, she made her way to the bathroom. Neil said nothing as he watched her leave the room.

She took a long time over her shower. The water was warm and comforting. It was a good twenty minutes before she returned to the bedroom. Neil was no longer there.

Wrapping her dressing gown tightly around her, she lay down on the bed. Thoughts and questions raced through her head. What she had been experiencing was unreal. Was she going crazy? Was she imagining everything? But what about the incident in the tunnel and the one this morning? She hadn't imagined those. They were certainly real, but why had they happened?

She was unaware of how long she lay there. Time seemed to have little meaning. A knock at the door stirred her from her thoughts.

The door opened and Marie entered. She was carrying a tray. 'Good morning, Jessica. I've brought you some breakfast,' she announced.

Jessica raised herself up and greeted her.

Marie placed the tray on the bedside table. On it was some toast and a mug of tea.

Jessica suddenly realised she was hungry. 'Oh, you're an angel! Thank you.'

She expected Marie to leave, but Marie lingered, looking at her with concern.

'You had another bad night?'

Jessica replied with a simple 'Yes.'

She thought that would be the end of the conversation, but Marie pulled up a chair and sat down.

'Would you like to tell me about it?' Marie's voice was soft and encouraging.

Something in the tone of her voice prompted Jessica to relate what had happened. Marie listened intently.

'Everybody thinks I'm sleepwalking,' Jessica concluded.

Marie was silent for a few seconds, as if digesting what Jessica had said. 'And what do you think?' she asked, her voice still soft.

Jessica thought for a moment before answering. 'Sometimes I think I must be going mad, but I don't think I am. It's just that these awful things keep happening to me.'

'Just since you've been here?'

'Yes.'

Marie made no immediate reply. Jessica spoke again.

'This morning I had a noose around my neck.'

'What? You mean you intended to hang yourself?' Marie was aghast.

'It looks like it,' Jessica replied miserably.

'If you weren't sleepwalking, how do you think you got to where you were found?'

Jessica pondered the question. When she did reply, it was slowly, as if she were reliving the experience. 'I think I was carried somehow… Perhaps I was dreaming… I seem to recall being carried.'

'Who would do that?'

'I don't know.' Somehow Jessica did not want to suggest that it was Mags. She was trying to decide whether to bring him into the conversation, when she suddenly thought of something else.

'There's another thing…' she began.

Marie looked at her expectantly.

Jessica continued. 'I was barefoot. If I'd been sleepwalking, I'm pretty sure the sharp stones on the path would have woken me up. Walking back was quite an ordeal without shoes.'

'I'd have thought so too,' Marie remarked.

At that instant the door opened and Neil entered. Marie jumped up at once and made a move to leave. Neil glanced in her direction as she closed the door behind her.

'What's she doing here?'

It seemed an odd question to ask. Jessica simply replied, 'She brought me some breakfast.'

'Oh, I see.'

Jessica sipped her tea and started to eat the toast.

Neil looked at her for a second. 'I'll leave you to enjoy it, then. I'll see you later downstairs.' With that, he departed.

Jessica ate her breakfast slowly. The toast and the tea were getting a bit cold, but it did not matter. She needed time to think. The events of the last few days were beginning to affect her. She had felt surprised and comforted by Marie's interest and obvious sympathy. It was hard for her to comprehend how she had misjudged her. When she had first met her, she had thought her disgruntled and disinterested, but now she seemed to have changed.

Jessica did not know why, but she knew that she had to get away. If Neil wouldn't come with her, she would go home on her own by public transport. Marie would know the best way to do that. She would ask her at the earliest opportunity.

Even her relationship with Neil seemed to have changed. Since they had been with his sisters, he had appeared to be influenced by them. No intimacy had taken place between them since they had arrived at the house. He almost treated her as a stranger. She comforted herself with the thought that once they got home things would go back to how they were before.

She took her time getting ready to go downstairs. It was close to ten when she eventually emerged from the bedroom with the breakfast tray. She descended the stairs carefully and went straight to the kitchen. Only Mrs Benson was there, on her mobile phone. She smiled and nodded to Jessica in acknowledgement for returning the tray.

As Jessica left the kitchen, she could hear voices in the lounge. She entered the room to discover Neil, Laura and Sophie deep in discussion.

Laura saw her come in. 'Ah, there you are, Jessica. We were just talking about you.'

This was the last thing Jessica wanted to hear, but she sat down on the settee beside Neil.

Laura took up the conversation again. 'Jessica, we have to do something about this sleepwalking of yours. We can't have you wandering about the countryside half-naked. One of these days you'll catch your death of cold.'

Jessica was irritated by the remark. 'If it is sleepwalking,' she replied.

'What do you mean?'

Jessica took a deep breath. I've got to say it, she thought. She spoke slowly and positively.

'I fail to see how I was able to walk barefoot over the stony surface of that track without waking up. On top of that, sleepwalkers don't usually lock themselves in a room from the outside.'

Laura was clearly surprised by her reply. 'I don't know what you mean,' she responded almost angrily. She paused for a second. 'The fact is that we have to do something about you.'

'And what are you suggesting?' Jessica asked.

Laura had a ready reply. 'You'll have to be locked in the bedroom at night.'

Jessica was both horrified and alarmed. 'You must be joking,' she retorted.

'It's the only solution,' Laura snapped back.

Neil suddenly entered the conversation. 'I think I know what can be done.'

Three pairs of eyes were immediately on him.

'I'll lock our bedroom door from the inside and keep the key. That way Jessica won't be able to get out without waking me.'

'That's a good idea,' responded Laura. 'I'll find the key for you.'

Neil turned to Jessica. 'Would you be happy with that?' he asked.

Jessica shrugged her shoulders. 'It doesn't look as if I have any say in the matter,' she replied coldly.

Laura changed her approach. 'Jessica, we do mean well. It's for your own safety. You must admit that it can't be very nice to wake up outside somewhere in your nightie.'

Jessica forced a bit of a smile. 'No,' she replied.

Sophie, who until this time had been silent, suddenly piped up, 'We do want the very best for you, Jessica.'

'Yes, I'm sure,' Jessica replied.

The group broke up when Laura announced, 'I'm going to get the key to your bedroom door. I think I know where it is.'

'I know where it is,' Sophie said. 'You put it in the drawer in the hall.'

Laura shook her head. 'I don't think so.'

The two sisters went off to look for the key, disputing its location.

Jessica and Neil were left alone. It was Neil who spoke first.

'I'm sorry about these new arrangements, poppet, but Laura is really worried about you. You can't keep wandering about at night. You might hurt yourself somewhere.'

'You mean sleepwalking?' There was an icy tone in Jessica's voice.

'Don't take it the wrong way. My sisters really do want the best for you.'

Jessica did not reply immediately. She was thinking and she knew what she had to say. She spoke in a clear, firm voice. 'Neil, I have to go home. Something has happened to me here. I am not myself. I just have to go home and sort myself out.'

'You can't go. We've discussed all this before. You agreed that we would stay until after my sisters' birthdays. They would be so disappointed if we left now, and perhaps even offended.'

'Darling, I know we talked about it before, but I have to go. You stay here. I can find my own way home. I'm a big girl.'

Neil was adamant. 'You can't go.'

Jessica took a deep breath. 'I'm going. If you wish, I'll try and explain to your sisters.'

'No, poppet. Sleep on it, and we'll talk about this tomorrow.'

'The situation will still be the same tomorrow,' she insisted.

For the first time he grinned at her. 'You never know. You might change your mind.'

He stood up. 'I've got to go and earn my keep,' he said, laughing. He bent over and kissed her on the cheek. 'See you later.' With that, he was gone.

Jessica remained where she was. She could not understand why Neil was not on her side. He seemed to be eager to please his sisters and not concerned about her. He had always been so eager to please her, to bend to her wishes, and now, since they came away, he seemed to have changed.

It was almost as if she didn't matter to him any more. She felt neglected.

She sat there for a long time. Thoughts came and went. There were so many questions for which there did not seem to be any answers. What had happened to her in the last few days worried her deeply. She was determined to return home. It was the only solution she could come up with.

The sound of her mobile phone ringing jolted her out of her

thinking. Only this morning she had slipped it into her pocket, conscious that for the past few days she had virtually ignored it, which was not like her.

She tapped the screen to answer.

'You're still alive, then,' came a familiar voice.

'Natalie! It's so good to hear you.'

'Likewise. I've been trying to contact you, but your phone was switched off.'

'I'm dreadfully sorry. I keep forgetting to switch it on. But it's lovely that you called.'

'Well, I'm glad you answered. There's something I want to talk to you about.'

Chapter 32

Jessica was delighted to hear from Natalie. It was almost like a breath of fresh air. She was also intrigued to know what she wanted to talk to her about. She glanced at the battery charge on her phone. It was very low. She hoped it would last out the call. Inwardly, she scolded herself for not keeping the phone switched on during the day and checking the battery level, which was her normal routine.

'So, where are you?' Natalie asked.

'Oh, we're staying with Neil's sisters in the West Country. We've been here over a week now. It's nice and quiet here.'

'What have you been up to?'

'Not a lot really. A little swimming, sunbathing, exploring.'

'How do you get on with Neil's sisters?'

'OK. They're a bit old-fashioned. The whole house has an air of a past age about it.'

'How's Neil coping with it all?'

'OK, I think. They still seem to dominate him a bit. You see, they more or less brought him up.'

'And how are you?'

'Me?'

'Yes.'

'Oh, I'm OK.'

'Hmm. I sense you're holding something back. You're not your usual chirpy self.'

'I'm fine.'

'No, you're not. I can tell. Come on. Tell it all to Auntie Natalie.'

'Well, there's not really much—' Suddenly Jessica stopped. She had to talk to somebody. Natalie was always understanding. She made up her mind. She had to convey to her friend what was happening to her. She started again. 'Well, it's just that I don't know if I'm going crazy or not. Some of the things that have been happening to me lately make me think that way.'

'What sort of things?'

Jessica knew that she had to go into detail. Slowly and carefully, she related everything that had happened to her. Natalie listened, not saying a word, until Jessica told her about the events of that morning. When she came to the bit about waking up with a noose around her neck, Natalie reacted rapidly.

'What? Do you mean to say you were going to hang yourself?'

'It looked that way.'

'What did Neil say?'

'He was horrified. He found me and took me back to the house.'

'What about his sisters?'

'Only Laura, the older one, was there. I think she was a bit cross because it was a new washing line she'd bought that was around my neck.'

'Is that all?'

'Well, there was Mags.'

'Who's Mags?'

'He's a sort of handyman. He lives nearby. Laura seems to look after him.' She hesitated. 'He saw me practically naked. It was awful.'

'How was that?'

'I had one of those almost transparent nighties on when I was found this morning, and he saw me.'

There was a bit of a laugh at the other end of the phone.

'Be sure your sins will find you out,' Natalie said flippantly.

'It was awful. He just looked at me and grinned.'

'Didn't he say anything?'

'No, he never does. He just stares and grins.'

'Sounds a bit weird. Anyway, what's happening now? What are you going to do about it?'

Jessica hesitated about telling Natalie her decision. She had not yet formulated any travel plans. Before she could make up her mind, Natalie prompted her again.

'You're holding something back. What's the problem?'

'It's not a problem really. It's just that I've decided to come back to London on my own.'

'What about Neil?'

'He's staying here for his sisters' birthdays. They're both close together, I think next week sometime.'

'And he wanted you to stay as well?'

Jessica had deliberately left that bit out. 'Yes.'

'I see.'

'I don't know what you see.'

Natalie was silent for a few seconds. Then she asked something that puzzled Jessica. 'Tell me, has Neil ever said anything to you about his life before he met you?'

'Not a lot. I know his sisters more or less brought him up until he went to boarding school and then university. Why do you ask?'

'Oh, just curious.'

Jessica changed the subject. 'Hey. That's enough about me. How about you? What are you doing?'

She heard a kind of groan at the other end of the phone.

'Oh, the usual dull stuff. Conveyancing. I handled a house that had been sold for three million the other day.'

'Gosh! Who's going to live in that?'

'Someone from abroad, I think.'

Jessica was about to ask another question, but Natalie chipped in first.

'Anyway, with your new-found wealth you could buy a house like that.' Jessica heard her giggle.

'No, thanks. Not for me,' she replied.

'I want to ask you…' Natalie paused. 'Jessica, you're not worried about the money you've been left, are you?'

The question made Jessica chuckle. She was still grinning as she answered. 'Heavens, no. I've not really thought a great deal about it. It's in several banks for safety and that's about as much as I've done.'

'What does Neil think about it all? I mean, marrying an heiress.'

'He's not said very much about it. He's left it all up to me.'

Natalie changed the subject again, curious to learn more about where Jessica and Neil were staying and what plans they had for the future. Suddenly she asked, 'How soon are you planning to come back to London?'

'I'm not sure at this stage. I'll have to find out where the nearest railway station is. Anyway, as soon as possible.'

'Look, forget about coming by train. I'm coming to pick you up.'

'Do you really mean it? It's over three hours' drive.'

'Don't worry about that. Just give me a day or so to clear a couple of things off my desk.'

'That is so kind of you. It really is an offer I can't refuse. Thank you.' Jessica felt a sense of relief. She had not been relishing the idea of a long train journey.

'It's settled, then. I'll give you a ring when I'm coming. Leave your mobile on.'

'I will – and I'm sorry you couldn't get hold of me before.'

'No problem.' Natalie sighed. 'Well, I suppose I'd better get back to doing some work. I'll speak to you soon.'

'I'll look forward to that.'

Natalie's tone changed slightly. 'And, Jessica…'

'Yes.'

'Do take care.'

'I will. Thank you.'

'Bye for now, then. I'll be in touch.'

Jessica suddenly remembered Natalie's opening statement. 'Natalie, you said you wanted to talk to me about something.'

'Oh, yes. I need to get on now, though. I'll tell you when I see you.'

'OK, then. Bye for now.'

'Bye.'

There was a click as Natalie ended the call.

Jessica leaned back and went over their conversation. She wondered what it was that Natalie wanted to talk to her about. No doubt she would find out in due course. Natalie had been so positive and was an important part of the life she wanted to get back to. Good old Natalie, she thought, offering to come and pick her up. It had solved a lot of her problems.

At that instant Neil reappeared.

'Who were you talking to?' he asked.

'Natalie.'

'Natalie? What did she want?'

Jessica was a bit puzzled by Neil's question. In reply she just remarked, 'She's going to come and pick me up and take me back to London.'

Neil looked surprised. 'When?' he asked.

'Oh, in a day or so. She has some work to finish first. She's going to let me know.'

Neil nodded but said nothing.

There were a few moments of silence between them.

Jessica stood up from the settee and went over to the window. She looked out at the garden, which was now bathed in sunshine. 'I think I'll go outside and sit somewhere in the fresh air until lunchtime,' she announced.

'Good idea,' Neil replied. 'While you're doing that, I'll make a couple of phone calls.'

'Fine. See you later.' She was already heading for the door.

She wandered out into the garden and selected her favourite seat. She had only been there a minute or so when she regretted not taking something to read. Mrs Benson no longer brought her a newspaper, and looking for a new job seemed remote. She would concentrate on that when she got back to London. In the meantime there was not much she could do about it. Her thoughts came round again to her relationship with Neil. She had felt neglected on this trip. He seemed to spend most of the time working, leaving her to amuse herself. Things would be better when they returned home, she reasoned.

The sound of footsteps nearby roused her from her pondering. Mags was walking on the path opposite. He was carrying a coil of rope that looked similar to the one she had had the traumatic experience with earlier in the day. She felt she should greet him.

'Good morning, Mags.'

The sound of her voice appeared to alert him from his own thoughts. He glanced in her direction. Then he held up the rope and mumbled something inaudible accompanied by his usual grin.

Jessica did not reply and he went on his way. His manner and action were disconcerting. She wondered if he was able to talk at all. She had never heard him speak, though he and Laura seemed to be able to communicate. It was odd, she thought.

Mags had barely gone out of sight when Sophie appeared from the direction of the house.

'Jessica,' she called out, 'Jim Foster is here. He wants to see you.'

Jessica breathed an inward sigh of despair. Her immediate reaction was one of 'What now?' but she hid her thoughts. Instead she asked Sophie, 'Where is he?'

'In the lounge. I've just seen him.' Sophie giggled.

Together they walked back to the house. Jessica was surprised when Sophie came into the lounge with her.

Jim Foster was talking to Neil. A half drunk cup of coffee rested on a table close by. Jim greeted Jessica as she appeared in the room.

'Good morning, Jessica. Come and sit down.'

Jessica returned his greeting and found a convenient chair. She was again surprised when Sophie, instead of leaving them alone, also sat down. Neil quickly excused himself.

Jim finished the last of his coffee and turned his attention to Jessica again. 'I hear you were sleepwalking again last night.'

'Yes, if that's what it was,' she replied.

'Why do you say that?'

Jessica had a ready answer. 'Apparently I got up out of bed, obtained a rope from somewhere, went outside and walked barefoot for about two hundred metres over pretty bad terrain full of sharp stones, put a noose around my neck and woke up hours later.'

He nodded. 'I see what you mean.'

Jessica expected another question on the subject, but he changed tack.

'Have you been taking the sleeping tablets I left with you?'

'No, I haven't.'

'That's a pity,' he remarked. 'They would have helped.' He paused for a second or two. 'In that case, if you're not going to take them I'll have them back.'

Sophie immediately jumped up. 'I'll get them. I know where they are,' she announced.

As Sophie left the room, Jim turned to Jessica again. He gave her a friendly smile.

'Have you given any more thought to spending a few days at the clinic I mentioned?' he asked. 'Neil is quite keen for you to go.'

'No. I'm going back to London in the next few days.'

'Oh, I see.'

At that moment Sophie returned with the box of tablets. She handed it to Jim. He shook it and then opened it to look inside.

He looked at Jessica. 'You said you hadn't taken any of them, but the box is nearly empty.' He clearly wanted an explanation.

Before Jessica could say anything Sophie piped up, 'It was me. I've been taking them. They help me sleep.'

The doctor looked gravely at her and tut-tutted. 'Sophie, you shouldn't take somebody else's prescription. In this case it doesn't matter. They were the same tablets I gave you, but don't do it in future.'

Sophie looked crestfallen. 'I'm sorry,' she whispered.

'As long as no harm is done.' He was smiling again. Suddenly he jumped up. 'Well, I'd better be getting on. Thank you for the coffee, Sophie.' He handed her the empty mug. He turned to Jessica. 'I hope everything goes well for you. If I can be of any assistance, you know where I am.' He added, 'I know Neil wants another word with me. I wonder where he is.'

'In the library,' Sophie replied immediately.

'I'll see him there.' With that, he left the room.

Once he was out of sight, Sophie turned to Jessica and giggled. 'I'm sorry I took your tablets, Jessica.'

Jessica laughed. 'It's fine with me. As long as they did you some good.'

'They're good for helping you sleep,' Sophie replied. Muttering another apology, she hurried away, leaving Jessica to return to her seat in the garden.

Over lunch most of the conversation was between Neil and Laura. At one point, Laura remarked to Jessica, 'Such a pity you didn't take up Dr Foster's offer of a few days in the clinic. It would have done you good.'

Jessica smiled and made a non-committal reply.

After lunch Neil claimed yet again to have some work to do, leaving her to her own devices. She had to admit now that this trip had been extremely disappointing regarding the company and attention she had received from him. It had begun to worry her, but she felt that while they were staying with his sisters there was no point in broaching the subject with him. She would wait until they were both back home in their own environment.

She decided to go to the beach again. She took a book with her, intending to spend some time reading. She had just settled herself down in the shade when she saw a dog approaching. It was Jojo, followed not long afterwards by Mrs Judd.

'Hello,' Jessica called out when they were within talking distance.

'Hello, dear.' Mrs Judd wiped her brow. 'It's so hot this afternoon.'

'Yes, it is.'

'It's all right for you, in your bikini.' Mrs Judd smiled. 'I wouldn't have come out, but Jojo wanted his walk.'

'Do you always come to the beach?'

'Nearly always. He likes to run on the sand and it's quite safe for him. He's getting a bit old now.'

Jessica was about to ask how old he was, but Mrs Judd spoke again. 'So, you're still here. I thought perhaps you'd have gone home by now.'

'In a few days' time,' Jessica explained. She was not expecting the next question.

'What's it like staying with Laura and Sophie?'

Jessica thought for a second. 'Oh, they're quite sweet really, but slightly old-fashioned in their ways.'

Mrs Judd nodded as if in agreement. Then she moved closer to Jessica and spoke in a hushed voice, as if she did not want to be overheard. 'How do you get on with Mags?'

'Well... ' Jessica found it a difficult question to answer. She need not have worried. Mrs Judd had more to say. Still talking in a hushed voice, she continued.

'In my opinion he should be in a home. Two years ago he was investigated by the police for allegedly molesting a girl in the village.'

Jessica was taken aback by the revelation. It explained quite a lot about the way Mags reacted to her. She made a simple answer. 'That's not good at all.'

'Don't tell anyone I told you,' Mrs Judd whispered.

Jessica smiled. 'I won't.'

They chatted for a few minutes more and then Jojo started to show signs of wanting to move on. Goodbyes were said, and Jessica watched the two of them leave the beach and start to climb the steps up the cliff. She stayed there for another half-hour, during which time the sky began to darken and rain to threaten, so she decided to hurry back to the house.

As she entered the hall she was met by Sophie.

'Neil's been looking for you,' Sophie announced. 'He's in the library.'

Neil jumped up to meet Jessica as she entered the room. 'Ah, there you are, poppet. Did you have a nice afternoon?' He kissed her.

'Of course,' Jessica replied, 'but it would have been nicer if you'd been with me.'

Neil sighed. 'Yes, I know. I feel I've been neglecting you.'

Jessica made no reply. This was a conversation for the future. Instead she referred to Sophie's greeting. 'Sophie says you were looking for me.'

Neil's face took on a grave expression. 'Ah, yes. Look, poppet, I know you won't like it, but I have to go to Birmingham urgently.'

Chapter 33

Jessica was aghast at Neil's announcement. She struggled to take it in. She was going to be left on her own again.

'But… but…' she stammered, 'you've only just come back.'

Neil took hold of her arms and looked at her. 'I know, poppet, but something urgent has come up.'

'But you said these trips were going to end, and now you're off again.'

He kissed her again. 'I'm dreadfully sorry, poppet. I didn't want this to happen, but I have to go.'

'How long will you be away?'

'A couple of days at most. I'll travel up tonight to save a day.'

'But you'll be tired out. You can't do that.'

'No, I won't. I'll get a couple of hours' sleep in before I leave.'

Jessica was quiet for a minute or so. She broke away from him, wandered to the window and looked out, deep in reflection. He followed her and put his arm round her.

'You're unhappy about it all,' he said softly.

Jessica turned sharply round to face him. 'My first marriage failed because my husband was never with me. He was always away somewhere. I don't want that to happen again.'

'I know exactly what you mean. I promise you these trips will end.'

Jessica nodded. 'Please,' she murmured.

He kissed her again. 'I promise,' he whispered. 'You won't be on your own long. Anyway, isn't Natalie coming to take you back to London?'

That's true, Jessica thought. It could be as soon as the following day. Then at last she would be back home. It was a lovely feeling.

'Yes,' she answered. 'That's what she said she'd do. She might even come tomorrow.'

They were interrupted by the arrival of Laura, who asked Neil what time he would be leaving that night.

'I'll have a couple of hours' sleep first. Two o'clock – something like that.'

'That's fine,' Laura replied. 'I was just wondering if you'd be here for dinner.'

Neil grinned. 'Absolutely.'

Laura fastened her steely gaze on him. 'Neil, you really are very unfair to Jessica. You're supposed to be on holiday. You work a great deal of the time, you leave her to amuse herself, and now you're going away again. You've not been back two days.'

Neil looked a bit embarrassed at being told off by his sister. 'Yes, I realise that. Jessica and I have talked about it. This is one of the last times.'

'I should think so. You're a married man now. You need to consider your wife.'

Neil did not reply. He clearly looked concerned at Laura's criticism. He was silent for a few seconds and then muttered something about needing to get some paperwork together for his trip. He quickly left the room.

As soon as he was out of sight, Laura turned to Jessica. 'Jessica, I'm sorry I said that to Neil, but I feel he is neglecting you. You need to become more forceful.'

Jessica gave a little laugh. 'I thought I was,' she replied.

Laura made a bit of a face. 'Not from what I've seen. Since you've been here, you appear to have had to spend a lot of time on your own.'

Jessica nodded. 'Yes, that's true. I suppose I'm used to being on my own, but I don't want the same thing to happen in my marriage to Neil as in my previous one.' She paused for a second.

'My first marriage failed mainly because my husband was always away somewhere.'

'Exactly. Don't let it happen this time. Put your foot down.'

Jessica smiled. 'I won't let it happen.'

Laura turned to leave. 'I'll make sure to keep an eye on you.' With that and a smile in Jessica's direction, she left the room.

Jessica quickly followed, making her way to their bedroom. As she climbed the stairs, she pondered over Laura's concern for her marriage to Neil. She had not imagined her taking such a motherly interest in her. Ever since their arrival at the house, she had thought her sister-in-law rather critical of her. She was also surprised at the relationship between Laura and Neil. Laura was still very much the big sister advising her younger brother what to do. This latest interest in Jessica was intriguing.

When Jessica reached the bedroom Neil was throwing a few clothes and other items into his case. She started to rummage in the clothes cupboard for something to change into for dinner, acutely aware that she was limited in choice. In the end she picked out the long skirt and blouse, old favourites that she already had worn to dinner on several occasions during her stay.

As she took the clothes and laid them on the bed, the room was suddenly lit up by a gigantic flash of lightning, followed shortly afterwards by a loud clap of thunder. The storm that had been threatening was making an appearance. Heavy rain started to fall.

'Gosh!' she exclaimed. 'Just look at that!'

'I hope it stops before I leave,' Neil remarked, glancing anxiously at the window. He went to the light switch and turned on the light. 'It'll probably pass over quickly.'

Just as Jessica was about to reply there was another flash of lightning. 'If it's still like this when you want to go, you can't drive in it. It won't be safe,' she insisted.

Neil just smiled. 'It'll be over by then.'

He was right. By the time they finished dinner, the thunder had faded into the distance. The rain at first settled into a steady downpour, and then very slowly it stopped to reveal a clear sky.

An hour or so later, Neil announced that he was going to try and get some sleep before his journey and would go to bed early. Jessica immediately made up her mind that she would join him. They left Laura and Sophie watching a play on television.

Once in the bedroom, Jessica put her plan into operation. She made sure she was the first to use the bathroom and then busied herself when she came back to the bedroom until Neil went in. Immediately after he disappeared she changed into her sexiest nightdress. Her idea was that perhaps they could make love before he set off for Birmingham. One of the things that had been a cause of concern for her on this trip had been their lack of intimacy. She had imagined that it would be the same as on their honeymoon, but things had not turned out that way. At first it had been the wrong time of the month for her, and then after that, despite her efforts, Neil did not seem to be interested in having sex with her. It worried her.

She did not get into bed until he returned, hoping that he would see her and get the message. Her strategy appeared to work. When he came back from the bathroom he looked at her for an instant and then came over to her. He started to kiss her passionately, his hands exploring her body. Slowly he moved her towards the bed and continued to kiss and caress her. Their intentions never materialised. Gradually he ceased to pay attention to her, and eventually Jessica realised that he had fallen asleep.

Disappointed and frustrated, she lay awake for what seemed to be a long time, with Neil sleeping peacefully beside her. She went over the events of the day, beginning with waking up cold and wet outside with a noose around her neck – a noose that was apparently made from Laura's new washing line. She almost chuckled to herself when she recalled Laura's indignation on finding the rope. The highlight of the day for her had been the telephone call from Natalie. With a bit of luck she might come to take her back to London tomorrow. Suddenly she remembered that because she had gone to bed early she had missed out on Sophie's ritual of making cocoa. There was also Laura's suggestion that she be locked in the bedroom. Clearly in the heat of their passion Neil had forgotten all about it. It made her wonder if she would hear the whispering again. While she was pondering the question, she fell asleep.

She woke with a start. There was movement in the room. She managed to get her fuddled brain into action. Neil was getting dressed,

'What time is it?' she whispered.

Neil glanced at his watch. 'Just coming up to two.'

As she made to get up, he interrupted her. 'Why don't you stay in bed?' he urged.

Jessica would have none of it. 'I'm going to see you off,' she insisted. 'And you need to have a cup of coffee or something before you go.'

Neil hesitated. 'That would be nice.' He grinned. 'Keep me awake.'

Jessica was out of bed in a flash. She grabbed her dressing gown and put it on.

Neil picked up his suitcase and coat and they crept downstairs. The house was silent except for the clock ticking in the hall. Neil whispered, 'I'm going to put my gear in the car.'

'I'll be in the kitchen,' Jessica whispered in return.

She had only been in the kitchen briefly a couple of times, either to see Mrs Benson or to return some dirty dishes. She had difficulty finding the light switch at first, but once the room was flooded in light she was able to concentrate on the task in hand. Filling the kettle with water was simple enough, but finding the coffee entailed opening several of the cupboard doors. Locating the milk was easy, as the fridge was clearly identifiable. By the time Neil reappeared she had a mug of coffee ready for him.

Neil took a seat at the kitchen table. Jessica sat down opposite him.

'At least the thunderstorm has gone,' she remarked, glancing out of the window. There were traces of moonlight.

He nodded. 'I knew it wouldn't last too long.'

They chatted in low voices while he drank his coffee. At last he finished and stood up. He made a face. 'Duty calls.'

He moved towards Jessica as if to take her in his arms. Jessica had other ideas. 'I'm coming out to see you off,' she insisted.

They made their way across the gravel to the car.

Neil put his arms around her. 'Sorry to run away and leave you again,' he said softly.

'Come back to me soon,' Jessica murmured.

'Sorry about last night,' he whispered. 'I was very tired.'

She smiled. 'We'll make up for it when you come back. But I might be back in London then.'

'I'll keep in touch.'

They lingered over their goodbye kiss, and then Neil got into the car.

He wound the window down. 'Behave yourself.' He was grinning.

'I'll try to.'

He started the car, blew her a kiss, and was off.

Jessica waved as she watched the car go down the drive, and waited as it turned onto the road. She stayed there until she could no longer hear it and then walked slowly back into the house.

The light was still on in the kitchen. She went in and washed up the mug. A few minutes later she turned off the light and made her way upstairs. She did not fancy sleeping in the room on her own. Instead of returning to their bed, she took her pillow and a blanket and crossed the corridor to the other bedroom. The key was in the lock, and she removed it. This time she would take the precaution of locking the door from the inside.

She put the pillow and blanket on the bed and then turned back to the door. Carefully and quietly she inserted the key in the lock. To her relief it turned smoothly. Feeling safe and secure, she put the key on the table, lay down on the bed and was soon asleep.

She woke several hours later from a disturbed night punctuated with strange dreams. The room was full of light. Had she overslept? She looked at her watch. The hands showed that it was just after half past seven. Later than she had intended to get up, but it would be all right. All she had to do was go back to her own bedroom, but first she wanted to check that all was quiet outside. She picked up the key and went over to the door. It only took a couple of seconds for her to unlock it. She slowly opened it and peered out into the corridor. Everything was quiet and peaceful. She reinserted the key in the lock on the outside of the door.

Leaving the door open, she returned to the bed. She gathered up the pillow and blanket and prepared to leave the room. As she reached the doorway, she suddenly came face to face with Mags.

Chapter 34

Jessica's reaction to seeing Mags standing in front of her was to let forth a scream of fright. She expected him to turn and hurry away, but instead he made a move to enter the room. She immediately retreated, intending to slam the door shut, but Mags was too quick for her. He almost knocked her over. She found herself shouting, 'Get out! Get out of here!'

Her words had the opposite effect. Muttering something, he pushed her towards the bed. She abandoned the pillow and blanket she had been carrying and tried to beat him off with both hands, but realised as she did so how futile her efforts were. He was much stronger than she was. She let out a single cry for help. The next instant Mags had clapped his hand over her mouth. She struggled violently as he tried to push her down onto the bed. What happened next she was never too sure about. She remembered the weight of his body holding her down on the bed and the next instant her nightdress being ripped with a penknife. She grabbed the knife and Mags let out a yell. He jumped up, holding his arm and wailing. Jessica sat up, shaken and distraught. Spots of blood were on her and the bed. She was still holding the knife.

'What on earth is going on?' Laura was standing in the doorway surveying the scene, a frightened Sophie behind her.

Laura was quick to sum up the situation and come to a conclusion. 'She's stabbed Mags!' she shouted.

Jessica struggled to respond. She shook her head. 'No… No, it was an accident.'

Laura took no notice. She turned to her sister. 'Sophie, go and telephone Dr Foster. Tell him it's urgent.'

Sophie disappeared. Laura turned to Mags next. 'Mags, you come with me,' she ordered.

Mags needed no urging. Still holding his arm and making odd complaining noises, he trotted out of the room. Jessica dropped the penknife, grabbed the blanket and pillow, and made to follow them, but Laura blocked her way.

'No, Jessica! You stay here!' Laura's voice was stern and commanding.

Still in a state of stress and shock, Jessica was about to protest, when Laura pushed her back into the bedroom. The next instant, the door was slammed shut, followed by the sound of the key turning in the lock.

The significance of this action hit Jessica hard. She was a prisoner. She beat on the door with both hands, shouting, 'Open this door!' There was no response.

She sat down on the bed. She was still shaky and close to tears. Why had Laura immediately assumed that she had attacked Mags? Had she accidentally hurt him badly? And why had Laura locked her in the room?

She sat there for a long time. She was being treated like a child, sent to the bedroom for some misdemeanour. After a while she went to the window and looked out. It was a long drop to the ground. There was no escape that way. She would just have to wait until someone came and unlocked the door.

After perhaps an hour she heard the sound of the key being turned. The door swung open to reveal Marie, who entered the room carrying a tray. Jessica's spirits rose. Perhaps she was going to be let out.

It was Marie who spoke first. 'Good morning, Jessica. I've brought you some breakfast.'

Jessica thanked her.

Marie put the tray down on the bed. She sat down on a nearby chair and looked at Jessica. 'Can you tell me what happened?' she asked.

Jessica was close to tears as she slowly recalled and related the events. 'I came in here to sleep last night. I was just about to leave this morning when Mags forced his way in.' She hesitated, remembering.

'What happened after that?'

Jessica wiped a tear away. 'He pushed me towards the bed. He was so strong…'

'And then?' Marie asked quietly.

Jessica found the next bit difficult to relate. 'He pushed me down onto the bed… He had a knife… He ripped my nightdress open. I struggled as hard as I could and somehow I managed to grab the knife and he got stabbed.'

As she finished, Jessica once again became concerned about Mags. She looked anxiously at Marie. 'I might have injured him badly.'

Marie smiled. 'I don't think so,' she replied. 'Dr Foster is with him now.'

'I don't know what to think. Everything happened so quickly. Laura thinks I stabbed Mags deliberately, and now I'm locked in here.'

Marie nodded sympathetically and then stood up to leave. 'Drink your tea before it gets cold,' she said.

At that point Jessica became aware of an urgent need. 'Please, I need a toilet.'

Marie hesitated. 'OK. You can go, but you must promise me you'll come back here. I'll have to lock you in again.'

'I promise.'

'All right, then.'

With that Jessica sped away. She returned several minutes later. On the way back she popped into the bedroom and collected her dressing gown. She slipped into it as she walked, glad of its power to cover her torn nightdress.

As soon as she was back in the room, Marie departed, locking the door behind her. Jessica was once again a prisoner. How long was she going to be kept like this? The whole situation was quite ridiculous. She sat down on the bed and turned her attention to the breakfast tray. Marie had brought her a bowl of muesli and a large mug of tea. Seeing the muesli made her realise that she was hungry, and she ate it gratefully.

She had just finished when there was the sound of the key turning in the lock again. The door opened and Laura entered, followed by Jim Foster.

Laura said nothing, but Jim greeted Jessica as he pulled up a chair and sat down facing her. She returned his greeting.

He looked at Laura, who was still standing there. 'Can you leave us alone, please?' he asked.

Laura made a face and quickly turned on her heel and walked out of the room, almost slamming the door behind her.

Jim turned to Jessica and smiled. 'Now, Jessica. Give me your side of events.'

Jessica was a bit surprised at the instruction, but she was calmer now, and slowly and carefully she related what had taken place. He listened, but made no comment. When she had finished talking about her experience, she again voiced her concern about her assailant.

'How is Mags? Is the wound serious?'

'On the contrary, it's only a minor cut.'

'It really was an accident,' Jessica stressed, still upset about the way things had turned out. She suddenly thought of something to reinforce her statement. 'It was Mags's penknife. It's here somewhere.' She picked it up from the floor.

'Shall I take that?' Jim suggested. Jessica handed it to him. He looked at it briefly and then carefully folded it and put it in his pocket.

Jessica began to feel alarmed at his reaction to her version of events. He had listened but had said little. She voiced her main concern. 'Laura thinks I did it on purpose. That's why I'm locked up in here.' She looked anxiously at him.

He nodded. 'Yes, I know. The thing is, though, what are we going to do about it?'

She looked at him in disbelief. She could tell that there was more to come.

He took his time to reply. 'I have to tell you that Laura was going to report the incident to the police.'

'The police?' Jessica was shocked. 'But… But why?' she stammered.

'Let's just say that she is perhaps over-protective of Mags.'

'Mags is her son, I was told.'

He looked surprised, but answered, 'Yes. That's correct.'

There was silence between them for an instant, Jim looking at Jessica, clearly wishing to continue his questioning about her future, and Jessica trying to comprehend why Laura found it necessary to involve the police, particularly as the wound Mags had received was apparently of a minor nature.

It was Jim who broke the silence. 'Getting back to you, I think we have to get you out of here.'

Jessica reacted quickly. 'Oh, but I am going. A friend is going to take me back to London.'

'When?'

'I'm not sure. It could be today, even. Certainly in the next few days.'

'That's fine. But I think we need to separate you and Laura immediately.'

'Why? Surely Laura must realise that it was an accident. And what about Mags? It all happened because he seemed to be intent on raping me.' She was beginning to realise the injustice of everything. Was she not the victim? Instead of that, everybody seemed to be on the side of Laura and Mags. She wished Neil was there.

Jim continued. 'I think it would be best if you went to the

Spicer Clinic for a few days. I've had a word with Dr Jackman, and he is willing to take you.'

Jessica was astonished at the suggestion, but he had not finished. 'I've gone over the situation with Neil, and he is in agreement.'

'What?' This was too much. Jessica was becoming agitated. 'You talked about me to Neil? Why didn't you talk to me?'

Jim smiled at her. 'If you remember, we did discuss you going there for a few days.'

Jessica did not answer immediately. She was still trying to make sense of the situation. When she did reply, it was with an abrupt and simple message. 'I'm not going.'

Jim sighed. 'I think you need to consider very carefully,' he said. 'It was difficult for me to persuade Laura not to call the police this morning. I cannot be sure that she won't change her mind. That risk is increased if you remain here.'

He paused for a second and looked straight at Jessica. He spoke softly. 'Which is better? A prolonged investigation by the police, or a few days away somewhere where you can relax and get rid of all the stress?'

Jessica said nothing. Thoughts were racing through her brain. If only Natalie would come quickly – today – everything would be all right.

Jim spoke again. 'You don't want to spend the next few days locked in here. That's what Laura will do, unless she contacts the police in the meantime.'

Jessica shook her head and sighed. 'I just can't believe what's happening,' she murmured, almost to herself.

'Unfortunately, it's a situation we have to deal with.'

'I just want to go home, away from all this,' Jessica said, almost to herself. She was staring at the ground as she spoke.

Jim stood up to go. He looked at her again. 'I think in the circumstances I have to use my professional power and recommend that you take a break as suggested,' he announced. 'I will arrange everything.' He made for the door.

Jessica jumped up. 'No, no! Please…'

He smiled at her. 'Don't worry. You'll find out that it was the best decision in the long run.' He opened the door to leave. 'Goodbye for now, Jessica. I'll see you later.'

Jessica darted to the door. 'Please listen to me,' she begged,

She was too late. The door closed and she heard the key turn in the lock.

It was all too much. She was close to tears. She staggered back to the bed and flung herself down on it. Was she really experiencing all this? Less than a month ago she had been an independent city worker, fully in control of her life. Now, in the space of a few days, her life had been turned upside down. Things had happened to her that a few weeks previously she would have thought impossible. Now she was a prisoner through no fault of her own.

Then there was Neil to think about. The fact that he had been making arrangements with Jim Foster behind her back concerned her deeply. It made her feel as if she was being treated like a child. This was something else she needed to discuss with him. On top of that, in the last few days he had not been as attentive as he had in the first few weeks of their marriage. Was it her fault? It was a question she could not deal with at present.

The big burning question was, when would Natalie come? She prayed that she would get there before something else happened. Suddenly a horrid thought struck her. How would she know when Natalie was coming? She had left her mobile on the table in her bedroom. Natalie would try to call her and not receive an answer. This provoked wild thinking. If she couldn't get an answer, perhaps she wouldn't come… If she arrived unexpectedly, would she be turned away by Laura and Sophie? Her fears went on and on. Only when she had calmed down a bit did rational thinking take over. There was a simple solution. She would involve Marie. When Marie next appeared, she would plead to be allowed to collect her mobile, or ask her to get it for her. It was a comforting thought.

Time dragged by. Every so often she looked at her watch. The hands seemed to move very slowly. Eventually she realised that she had been locked in the room for over three hours. Nobody had been near her since Jim had left. She felt badly in need of a shower and a change into more practical clothing.

Suddenly she heard footsteps outside in the corridor. The key turned in the lock, and the door began to open. Jessica perked up, thinking it might be Marie with her lunch. She was wrong. The door opened wide and a man and a woman, both dressed in white, entered the room.

Chapter 35

For a split second Jessica looked in disbelief at the two strangers entering the room. She sprang off the bed and faced them. 'Who are you?' she managed to croak.

It was the woman who answered. 'Hello, Jessica. I'm Annette and this is Robert. We've come to take you somewhere nice and quiet for a rest.' She spoke soothingly almost as if she were addressing a child.

'I'm not going anywhere,' Jessica replied calmly.

'Please do as we say. We don't want you to make this difficult for yourself.'

Jessica continued to protest, and when Annette took her arm and made to lead her out of the room, she resisted and tried to pull away.

She was not prepared for what happened next. Annette and Robert grabbed her firmly by the arms, one on each side of her, and walked her to the door.

She struggled in their grasp, but they were much stronger than she was. She found herself shouting, 'No! No! I'm not going with you!'

They took no notice and proceeded to lead her in the direction of the stairs and half carry her down. She was conscious of Laura and Sophie standing nearby. All the time, she was struggling and protesting at the top of her voice, at times even screaming. When they reached the bottom of the stairs, she saw to her embarrassment and horror that Marie and Mrs Benson were watching from the kitchen doorway.

Once outside, Annette and Robert led her to a white van with darkened windows. The next instant, Annette was pinning Jessica's arms by her sides while Robert opened the van doors and drew out a trolley.

Jessica realised what was about to happen. 'You can't do this!' she shouted. 'Leave me alone! You have no right to act in this way.'

The next instant she found herself being pushed firmly down onto the trolley. Straps were fastened across her body and her arms. She began to struggle again. 'Stop this!' she yelled. 'Release me at once!' It was a futile effort. She felt the trolley being manoeuvred back into the van and found herself looking up at the roof. Barely able to move, she continued to struggle and protest loudly.

'Shall we sedate her?' she heard Robert ask.

'No. Leave her to me,' replied Annette. She climbed into the van and sat beside Jessica. Robert closed the rear doors.

Annette touched Jessica's arm. 'I can see that you're upset, Jessica, but you really do need to try to calm down,' she said softly.

'I will not!' Jessica snapped.

Annette continued speaking calmly and quietly. 'Jessica, we're doing this to help you.'

'Even tying me down so that I can't move?' Jessica retorted.

'The straps are to keep you safe so that you don't hurt yourself.'

'But you're taking me away against my will,' Jessica insisted. 'I've done nothing wrong. I'm not ill, and you have no right to do this.'

'Jessica, please believe me. This is for the best. We'll look after you and keep you safe, but if you insist on shouting and struggling I shall have to sedate you.'

Annette's words had some effect. Jessica could see that it was useless to continue protesting, and after her recent experiences she had a horror of being drugged. She stopped struggling and gradually calmed down. She would just have to wait until she could talk to someone who would listen. Hopefully there would be someone in authority where they were taking her, wherever that was.

She was conscious of the van starting up and felt it moving off slowly along the gravel drive. Annette sat there quietly, keeping a close eye on her and occasionally glancing at her watch or making notes on a clipboard.

After a journey of perhaps twenty minutes, the van stopped. Robert opened the rear doors and wheeled the trolley out. Annette unbuckled the straps that held Jessica down and helped her to her feet.

They were standing in front of a large building that looked as if it might once have been a stately home. With a minder on either side of her, each firmly holding an arm, Jessica was led into the building, through a large reception area, along a short corridor and into a small room devoid of any furniture except for a couple of chairs. A large bath stood in the middle of the room. Robert disappeared and another woman came in. She was of the same build as Annette, muscular and strong.

'Hello, Jessica. Welcome to the Spicer Clinic. My name is Madge, and we're here to help you.' She paused. 'But you need to stay calm and cooperate with us.'

Jessica drew in a breath. 'I don't see why I should. I've been abducted and brought here against my will. I demand to see someone in authority.'

The two women exchanged a glance. Annette took charge. 'Of course you can see someone. But first you need to have a bath.'

'What?' Jessica was astounded. 'Go to hell.'

The two women looked shocked and surprised.

'Now, now. There's no need for that,' soothed Madge.

Jessica was about to say something else when the two women slipped her dressing gown off her shoulders to reveal her torn nightdress.

'Goodness! What have you been doing?' Annette asked.

'I was nearly raped at knifepoint,' Jessica replied icily.

She did not offer any resistance as they removed the remains of her nightdress. There seemed to be no point in protesting further for the time being. Better to wait until she could see somebody higher up the ladder. She felt embarrassed as she stood naked in front of the two women.

Madge pointed to Jessica's nightdress, which now lay in tatters at her feet. 'You won't be able to wear that again. It's completely ruined.'

Annette placed a finger on Jessica's chest. 'What happened here?'

Jessica glanced down at the area. A thin red line was visible, with a slight trace of blood. She knew all too well where it had come from. 'From the knife that was used on me, I assume,' she replied.

'We'll put something on it shortly,' Madge said. 'Now, Jessica, let's get you into the bath.'

Jessica allowed them to lead her to the bath and help her into the warm water. She was not prepared for the next part of the procedure. Both women had sponges and set about washing her from head to foot.

'I am quite capable of washing myself,' she protested.

'You must let us do it,' Madge said. 'Please just sit still.'

Jessica submitted without further protest. She was still wearing her watch, which she held up away from the water. When the two women had finished, they helped her out of the bath and rubbed her dry with a towel. Annette left the room and Madge produced a bottle of lotion and dabbed some on Jessica's wound. It stung a little. Jessica reached for her dressing gown, which was lying discarded on the floor.

'You won't be needing that while you're in here,' Madge said softly. 'We'll give you something else to wear.'

The next instant Annette reappeared. 'Now, Jessica, put this on for me, please,' she said.

Jessica glanced at the loose, shapeless garment Annette was holding. It had short sleeves and an open neck and looked as if it would reach below her knees.

'Surely you don't expect me to wear this thing!' she exclaimed.

'Please put it on. It's comfortable and practical,' Annette replied.

Jessica could tell that it was useless to try and change anything. Besides, she didn't intend to wear the gown for long. She grudgingly complied.

'I want to see whoever is in charge of this place,' she demanded.

'Yes, of course,' Annette soothed.

Expectantly, Jessica allowed Madge to lead her out of the room, preceded by Annette. They walked a little further along the corridor, and Annette threw open a door. 'Please wait in here,' she instructed.

Jessica stood in the doorway. The room was small and was painted a creamy-white colour. The floor was covered in what looked like cork, and the walls appeared to be lined with some kind of soft material. The only furniture consisted of a built-in bed. In an alcove were a toilet and washbasin. Light was coming in through a thick-glassed window.

Her first reaction was one of shock. She had assumed that she would be taken to see someone in authority. Instead she was being put in a padded cell.

'I'm not going in there,' she stated firmly.

'Come along, Jessica. It won't be for long,' Madge replied.

'I want to see somebody,' Jessica insisted.

'You'll be able to do that later,' said Annette, encouraging her into the room with a gentle push. Almost immediately the door was closed.

Jessica reacted quickly. She turned and banged on the door with both hands. 'Let me out of here!' she shouted.

It was to no avail. The door remained shut, and close examination revealed that it could only be opened from the outside. She was a prisoner in the tiny room until somebody freed her. She sat down on the bed. What was happening to her was unbelievable. Why was she being treated like this, and what was this place she had been brought to? It was supposed to be a clinic, but the room she was in looked more like a cell for a violent mental patient. Was that why she was here? Did they think she was unbalanced? And who had organised all this? Could it have been Jim Foster? Questions flooded her thoughts, but there were no answers.

She had hardly sat down when the door opened and a young man in a white coat entered, accompanied by Annette.

'Hello, Jessica,' he said breezily. 'I'm Dr Draper. I'd like to do one or two checks on you.'

Jessica had been harbouring the faint hope that he might be the person in charge she was waiting for. Clearly that was not so. She resigned herself to cooperating with him. For the next ten minutes she was obliged to undergo a medical examination and answer numerous questions about her health. Did she suffer from this or that? Had she had this disease or that? Forms were duly completed, and the doctor and Annette departed.

About an hour later the door opened and Annette reappeared carrying a tray. 'How are you getting along, Jessica? You must be hungry by now.'

'I am not hungry and I demand to see someone in authority,' Jessica snapped.

'Of course,' Annette replied. 'Dr Jackman is out at present, but he will see you as soon as he gets back. That's a promise.'

Jessica thought, I suppose I'll have to be content with that. I've got to see the man at the top.

'Now, do eat your lunch,' Annette urged. 'I'll take you to see Dr Jackman later.' With that she disappeared again.

Jessica turned her attention to the tray. There was some sort of stew, and some cut-up fruit, as well as a bottle of water and a plastic beaker. The smell and sight of the food made Jessica remember that she had not eaten since breakfast. Her appetite returned, and she ate every morsel. Afterwards she lay down on the bed, intending to rest there for ten minutes or so. Despite all she had been subjected to that day, she quickly fell asleep.

The sound of the door opening again woke her up with a start. A quick glance at her watch told her that she had slept for well over an hour. Annette entered the room.

'Dr Jackman will see you now,' she announced.

Jessica jumped up immediately.

Annette ushered her out of the room towards a short flight of stairs, which led to a bright corridor with sun streaming through the windows. A short distance along the corridor she opened a door, stood back to allow Jessica to pass, and followed her into the room. Jessica found herself in a light, airy office dominated by a large desk, from behind which a man rose to greet her.

He held out his hand. 'Mrs Atkins, please take a seat.' He spoke with a slight accent. He waved towards a chair in front of the desk, glancing at her bare feet as he did so. Annette sat down on a chair near the door.

Jessica shook his hand and sat down. She studied her host briefly. He was middle-aged, grey-haired and had a stubby beard.

'Mrs Atkins, you would like to talk to me, I think.'

Jessica took a deep breath and chose her words carefully. 'Yes, Dr Jackman, I do wish to talk to you.'

He gave her a smile of encouragement. 'Please proceed.'

Jessica needed little prompting. 'I would like to know why I am here. This morning I was abducted against my will. Strapped down on a trolley. Bathed like a baby and then put in a padded cell. I think I am due an explanation.'

Dr Jackman nodded. 'Of course. Of course.'

She waited as he glanced at some papers on his desk.

He cleared his throat. 'Dr Foster and your husband arranged for you to come here because they felt that you were suffering from stress and would benefit from some time to relax and get back to normal.'

Jessica felt obliged to respond to this. 'You say that Dr Foster and my husband arranged things, but why was I not informed of this decision?'

'I think they felt that you were under too much stress.' He added quickly, 'That sometimes happens.'

Jessica was outraged. Why had Neil and Jim Foster not said anything to her? Why had she been kept in the dark, and what was all this nonsense about being stressed? 'That may explain why I'm here,' she retorted, 'but it doesn't explain the treatment I have received from your staff this morning.'

Dr Jackman looked slightly embarrassed. 'Mrs Atkins, I feel I must apologise for what happened this morning. Unfortunately we were given incorrect information.'

'Incorrect? In what way?'

'We were advised that you had a violent disposition.'

'Violent? You can't be serious.'

'I'm afraid that was the information we received.'

Jessica could not believe what she was hearing. She spoke in a clear, calm voice. 'May I ask where you obtained the information that I was violent?'

'I'm afraid we cannot divulge the source.'

Jessica felt exasperated and angry, but she spoke calmly. 'Dr Jackman, are you aware that I was nearly raped at knifepoint this morning? I have a wound to prove it.'

The doctor looked concerned. 'I am not,' he replied.

Jessica was determined to take advantage of his apparent ignorance of the circumstances. 'I am here under false pretences and I intend to leave as soon as I can arrange for someone to collect me.'

Dr Jackman smiled. 'Mrs Atkins…' He hesitated. 'May I call you Jessica?'

'Yes, you may.'

'Jessica, you must admit that you have experienced a number of difficult incidents during the last few days—'

'Not incidents of my making,' she cut in.

'Nevertheless, that kind of thing can be very stressful.'

'I am not stressed,' she insisted.

He smiled again. 'Stress can manifest itself in many ways.'

'I am not stressed. And even if I were, I certainly should not have been brought here against my will.'

'Of course. I understand.'

Jessica was aware that he was looking at her intently. She returned to laying the groundwork for leaving the clinic. 'I have arrangements in place to return to London quite soon.'

'When will that be?'

'It could have been today,' she replied. 'Unfortunately, I was abducted by your staff before it could happen.'

Dr Jackman nodded briefly in acknowledgement and then sat silently looking elsewhere, gently tapping the desk with his fingers, clearly pondering something.

He turned to face her again. 'I would like to propose that you stay here until someone comes to collect you. We will move you to more comfortable accommodation for the duration of your stay and will ensure that you have complete rest.' He paused for a second and then added, 'A good rest will help disperse the stress you have been experiencing.'

Jessica had also been doing some thinking. Going back to Laura and Sophie's house did not appear to be a good option. She had not heard from Neil. She might as well stay at the clinic. The big problem was how to contact Natalie. She had no phone. Perhaps they would allow her to use one there.

Dr Jackman looked at her, waiting for an answer.

She had made up her mind. She gave him a smile of reassurance. 'In that case, I think I'd better be your guest for a little longer.'

'Excellent.' The doctor was visibly pleased with his efforts. 'Do you have any other questions?' he asked.

Jessica shook her head. 'Not really.'

It was the end of the consultation. Annette stood up and took her back to the room she had been in earlier. The door was locked again. Still a prisoner, Jessica thought.

She lay down on the bed and went over the conversation she had had with Dr Jackman. Her decision to remain at the clinic was made with the full intention of not being there long. She just had to get hold of Natalie.

She had been lying there for a while when the door was opened again and Annette appeared. She looked at Jessica briefly. 'You have a visitor, Jessica. Please come with me.'

Jessica stood up and silently followed her out of the room. She was intrigued about who the visitor might be. Perhaps it would be Neil. Annette led her along the corridor and eventually stopped in front of a door, which she threw open to reveal what looked like an interview room. Inside, holding a bag, stood a figure Jessica immediately recognised. It was Marie.

Chapter 36

Jessica could not contain her excitement. 'Marie!' she gasped. 'What are you doing here? It's wonderful to see you.'

Marie seemed to be a bit flustered. She dispensed with the formalities. 'I had to see you. I've brought some of your things.' She glanced down at the bag she was carrying.

'That's marvellous!' Jessica burst out in excitement. 'Thank you. You're an angel.'

Marie dropped into a convenient chair. 'I can't stop long. I had a job finding out where you were.'

'You saw what happened to me this morning?'

Marie nodded. 'Yes. I knew you had nothing with you, so I decided to bring you the basics. I thought you'd like your mobile as well.'

'Oh, that's fantastic! Thank you for thinking of that. I was wondering how I was going to communicate with anybody in this place.'

'How long are you going to stay here?'

'Until my friend from London can pick me up and take me back home.' Jessica grinned suddenly. 'Do you know they thought I was a violent and dangerous patient when they collected me?'

'What? Why?'

'I suppose somebody must have told them.'

Marie was silent for a second or two. When she spoke, it was almost to herself. 'I think I know who that was.'

Jessica was eager to relate more of the morning's events. 'The strange part of it all was that I was the one who was the victim.'

'What happened?'

'Mags tried to rape me in the bedroom. I struggled, but he's strong. He had a knife. He hurt me.'

She opened her dressing gown and pulled aside the gown underneath it to reveal the knife wound in her chest.

Marie was aghast. 'How did that happen?'

'It must have been while we were struggling. I tried to grab the knife.'

'Mrs Benson and I didn't know what was going on. We just saw them taking you away.'

Jessica made a face. 'That bit is best forgotten,' she remarked quietly.

Marie glanced at her watch. 'I'd better go. I'm on duty at half past five and it's five now.'

'Is it very far?' Jessica asked. 'It seemed a long way to me this morning.'

Marie shook her head. 'Not really. Five miles or so, but it was tricky to find.' She stood up to go.

'Thanks a million for bringing me my things,' Jessica said.

Marie hesitated for a second and then put her hand in her pocket. She pulled out a business card and handed it to Jessica. 'Here's my phone number. If you need anything, just give me a call.'

'Thank you for thinking of that.'

'No problem. Take care.' With that, Marie left the room.

'Thanks again,' Jessica called after her.

With a wave of her hand, Marie disappeared.

Jessica wondered if she should find her way back to the room she had spent the morning in, but in the end she decided to remain where she was. She glanced at the card Marie had given her. It bore the address and phone number of the village pub

Marie's father ran, but there was also a mobile number handwritten on it. It was comforting to have it.

She had been sitting alone for about ten minutes when the door opened and a young blonde woman entered. Like Annette, she wore a nurse's uniform.

She greeted Jessica with a smile. 'Hello, Mrs Atkins – or may I call you Jessica?'

'Yes, please do,' Jessica replied.

'My name is Melanie,' the newcomer announced.

Jessica was about to say something when Melanie spoke again.

'I'll be looking after you while you're here. Come with me and I'll show you to your room.'

Jessica wondered if it was going to be another 'cell', but she said nothing.

'Is this yours?' Before Jessica could answer, Melanie had picked up the bag Marie had brought.

Jessica followed her through a maze of corridors and stairs and eventually Melanie opened a door wide and stood back to let her pass.

Jessica's immediate reaction was one of surprise. She found herself in a pleasant, well-lit room. There was a carpet on the floor, and a bed with a bright cover stood against one wall. A desk, a comfortable armchair and a cupboard completed the furnishings. Even better, the room opened up onto a tiny balcony, complete with table and chairs. The early-evening sun was streaming through a window.

Melanie smiled. 'You had an unfortunate introduction to the Spicer Clinic. We want the rest of your stay to be as pleasant as possible.'

'Thank you,' Jessica managed to get out. Her interview with Dr Jackman seemed to have changed everything. She was no longer being treated as violent.

'You need some slippers,' Melanie said, glancing at Jessica's feet. 'What size do you take?'

'Five.'

'I'll get you a pair.'

Jessica thanked her and wondered where she was going to find any.

'I'll leave you to settle in now,' Melanie announced with a smile.

Jessica thanked her again and then turned her attention to the rest of her accommodation. A second door revealed a shower and toilet with towels and soaps. The balcony attracted her. Carefully she opened the door and ventured out. She was pleased to discover that there was a relaxing view of well-tended lawns and flowerbeds.

Back in the room, she turned her attention to the bag Marie had brought for her. The contents had been well thought-out. The bag contained a pair of slacks, a skirt, two blouses, a cardigan, a nightdress and two sets of underwear, as well as her old comfortable shoes. There was even her cosmetic bag. Most welcome of all, right at the bottom of the bag was her mobile phone, together with its charger. She quickly plugged it in to top up the battery.

She busied herself putting the items away. A surprise on opening the cupboard was to discover a warm dressing gown hanging there.

She had just about completed the task when Melanie appeared again with a pair of slippers.

'These are for you,' she said with a smile, putting them down on the floor in front of Jessica. 'Now, what would you like for dinner?' She handed her a piece of paper that turned out to be a menu.

Jessica studied it for a few seconds and then ordered a fish dish with some vegetables, some fruit and a pot of tea.

'Would you like it here in your room, or would you like to come down to the dining room?' Melanie asked.

Jessica opted to eat in her room. She did not feel like getting changed and meeting strangers. That could wait.

It seemed only about five minutes before Melanie returned with a tray. The food looked quite appetising and the sight of it made Jessica feel hungry all of a sudden.

'I'll collect the tray in about twenty minutes if that's all right,' Melanie said.

Jessica assured her that would be fine and turned her attention to the food.

She was anxious to try and contact Natalie. After several attempts she managed to get through.

Her friend sounded very concerned. 'Jessica, I've been trying to reach you all day. Every time I called, there was no answer on your mobile – just the message that you were unavailable.'

'I'm sorry, Natalie, but a lot has happened today. I haven't had access to a phone.'

'What's happened?'

'Well, you see, I'm not at the house.'

'Where are you, then?'

'I'm in a sort of clinic. I was brought here this morning.'

'What on earth are you doing there?'

'Well...' Jessica hesitated, trying to figure out the best way to explain what had happened.

Natalie was impatient. 'Come on,' she butted in. 'You're hiding something. I want to know what it is.'

'I'm not really hiding anything. You see, it all began early this morning...'

Slowly and methodically, so as to not leave anything out, Jessica went over the events of the day. When she had finished, she waited for Natalie's reaction. It was not long in coming.

'Let me get this straight. All this was arranged behind your back?'

'Well, sort of. I was asked several days ago if I'd like to come here for a rest, but I declined.'

'And this morning you had no choice?'

'They came and took me by force. Then they strapped me

down on a trolley and threatened to sedate me if I didn't keep quiet. It was horrible.'

'It doesn't sound an ideal place to be.'

'It's OK now. At first they thought I was violent, but I had a talk with the head person here and now everything has changed. The room I have now is quite pleasant.'

There was a bit of a laugh at the other end of the phone. 'You must have had some influence.'

'Not really.' Jessica was about to add something, but Natalie spoke again.

'Going back to what you've just told me, do you mean to say that you were the victim, and you were accused of being the aggressor?'

'Yes. Absolutely. In spite of being attacked with a knife and being injured in the process.'

'Sounds a bit odd to me.'

'It's called turning black into white.'

'Where was Neil when all this was going on?'

'He's in Birmingham.'

'Are you sure?'

'Of course I'm sure. Why do you ask?'

'Just curious.'

Jessica was about to respond with another question, but Natalie spoke first.

'Anyway, as I said, I've been trying to phone you all day.'

'Sorry about that. I was a bit concerned you might be trying to pick me up today.'

'That's why I wanted to get hold of you. This wretched car of mine broke down and it'll take a couple of days to repair.' There was a pause and then Natalie continued, almost as if she were talking to herself. 'They must have to get the parts from Timbuktu or somewhere like that.'

Jessica giggled. 'You're joking.'

'Well, you know what I mean. What it boils down to is that I don't have a car just when I need it.'

Jessica smiled to herself. Natalie seemed to have an endless battle with her car, which was some sort of fancy foreign-made sports model. She had purchased it during Jessica's marriage to Graham, despite Graham's advice not to do so.

'Why don't you change your car?' Jessica suggested, not for the first time.

'I suppose I'll have to one of these days.' Natalie did not sound enthusiastic. Suddenly she said, 'Darling, I've got to go. I'm going out to dinner this evening. Actually, it's with Graham.'

'Give him my regards.'

'I will. And I'll pick you up as soon as I have a car. I promise.'

'Super. But don't inconvenience yourself. I can wait.'

'Do take care, Jessica. And try not to worry.'

'I will. Bye for now.'

'Bye.'

Jessica had barely finished talking to Natalie when her phone rang. It was Neil.

'Neil! Where are you?'

'Birmingham. Where are you?'

'You know perfectly well where I am. You arranged it all and never said a word to me.'

'What do you mean?'

'You know exactly what I mean. I'm in the Spicer Clinic. I was dragged here this morning against my will.'

There was a brief pause.

'Look, poppet, it's not like that. You've got it all wrong.'

'I've got it all wrong? How?'

'It didn't happen as you think it did. I can explain everything.'

'I wish you would.'

Again there was a pause.

'I can explain, but here and now on the phone isn't the right time. When I come back we'll have a long talk.'

'I think we need to talk about several things.'

'As soon as I get back.'

'When will that be?'

'In the next day or two. I've still got a bit more to do.'

'Will you phone me and let me know when?'

'Of course I will.'

'You haven't forgotten that Natalie's going to come and take me back to London?'

'Of course not. When?'

'I'm not sure. Her car's broken down. A couple of days, perhaps.'

'I should be back before then. I'd better ring off now. My phone's running out of juice.'

'OK. I'll wait to hear from you, then.'

'Great. Bye for now. Love you.'

'Bye, darling. See you soon.'

Jessica clicked to end the call and sat thinking for a while. Things had changed between her and Neil. He was not as attentive as he had been in the early weeks of their marriage. Something had gone wrong. Was it her fault? Did he want something more than she could give? But then, taking a different view, everything had been fine until he had suggested that they visit his sisters. From day one strange things had started to happen to her. And now today she had been forced against her will to enter the clinic. For what? Nothing made sense.

It was late when she eventually went to bed. It had been quite a day. As she lay waiting for sleep to overtake her, once again her thoughts turned to recent events. A lot had happened in a short time. Perhaps things would get better once she was home in familiar surroundings. She hoped Natalie would phone her soon. With that thought she dropped off to sleep.

Jessica was mistaken in assuming that it would be Natalie or Neil she would see next. Unfortunately, it was to be neither of them. It was Laura.

Chapter 37

Jessica had now been in the Spicer Clinic for two days. After her difficult start, she had begun to relax and enjoy just sitting on the balcony in the sunshine. She had had relaxing massages and had spent hours in soothing baths. She had been looked after and pampered by Melanie and Amy. Gradually she began to think about life outside the clinic.

She was surprised that she had not heard from either Natalie or Neil. Natalie, she guessed, was still waiting for her car to be repaired. Neil she was more concerned about. She could not understand why he had not contacted her again. It was odd, and it worried her. Was their marriage going stale? She intended to get to grips with the situation once they were back at home, and talk things out with him. Then there was the question of getting another job. She wanted to secure a new position somewhere in spite of now being wealthy. Somehow, she hardly thought of her new status. It was something she would deal with in due course.

It was not until the afternoon of the third day, while Jessica was sitting on the balcony, that Natalie phoned.

'It's super to hear from you again,' Jessica said.

'How are you getting on?' Natalie asked.

'Fine. I'm relaxing and getting lazy.'

'Sounds great! Look, this is just a quickie. I've got a meeting in a few minutes, but I just wanted to let you know that I've got the car back and I'll come and pick you up on Thursday.'

'That sounds great. I'll be all ready.'

'I'm going to leave at the crack of dawn, so I should get to you quite early.'

'I'll look forward to that.'

'I've got to go now. See you on Thursday morning.'

'OK. I expect I'll still be here, but I'll let you know if I'm back at the house. Shall I give you the address of the clinic now?'

'Later. I'll call you again. Bye for now.'

'OK. Bye, Natalie. Thanks for ringing.'

Jessica was well pleased. At last she would be able to take up the pieces of her life again.

She had only just put the phone down when Melanie appeared. 'There's a woman named Laura Atkins asking if you'll see her. She says you know her. Shall I show her in?'

Jessica was surprised and shocked by Melanie's announcement. What could Laura want with her? The last time they had been in close contact was not pleasant to recall. The only way she could find out what it was all about was to see her.

'Yes. Please do,' she replied, her lack of enthusiasm reflected in her voice.

Melanie nodded and disappeared. Jessica went back into her room and sat down to wait. Melanie returned with Laura a few minutes later. Jessica rose from her chair to greet her sister-in-law.

Laura appeared to be a little flustered. 'Oh, Jessica, thank you for seeing me. I was afraid that after what happened you would refuse to.'

Jessica stifled a sigh. 'That's all right, Laura. Do sit down.'

'Thank you.'

Jessica was full of anxious anticipation.

'Would you like a cup of tea?' Melanie asked.

Laura's face brightened up a bit. 'Oh, thank you, dear. That would be lovely.'

Jessica smiled at Melanie. 'Yes, please,' she replied.

Melanie disappeared again.

Jessica turned to Laura. 'You came to see me for a reason?' she asked.

Laura looked stressed as she replied. 'Yes. It's about what happened the other day.' She hesitated before continuing. 'You see, I know a lot more about things now. I feel so bad about the way we treated you. How can you ever forgive me?' She looked as if she was about to burst into tears.

'You say you know more about things,' Jessica said. 'What things?'

Laura looked surprised. 'The…' she stammered. 'All the things that have been happening to you.'

Before Jessica could reply, Melanie reappeared carrying a tray, which she set on the table between them.

Laura looked at the tray and addressed Melanie. 'Thank you, dear. That's so nice.'

Jessica added her thanks. When Melanie had left she turned to Laura again. 'Shall I pour for us?'

'Thank you.' As Jessica handed her a cup of tea, she remarked, 'I don't really deserve your kindness.'

After pouring her own tea, Jessica returned to their previous conversation. 'You wanted to tell me something,' she urged.

Laura took a sip of her tea before answering. 'Yes. I know now what Mags has been doing to you.'

'Mags?'

Laura looked more miserable than before as she started to explain. 'I know why you were hearing all those voices at night. Mags had rigged up some sort of tape recorder in the loft above your bed and set it on a timer.'

Jessica was trying to make sense of what she had just heard. 'But there was a woman's voice at times as well,' she pointed out.

Laura gave a slight smile, the first since she had arrived. 'Oh, that would be Lisa, who sometimes spends time with Mags.'

Before Jessica could respond, Laura added some more details. 'It was Mags who locked you in the bedroom and carried you to the cellar.'

'But why?' Jessica asked, shocked at the revelations. 'Why would Mags do those things to me?'

'Sometimes he sees a woman and when he can't have her he acts funny.' Laura paused for a few seconds. 'You know that Mags is my son?' She scrutinised Jessica, waiting for a response.

'Jessica replied with a simple 'Yes.'

Laura appeared to want to relate more. 'Mags was born thirty-three years ago after a moment of madness on my part. Unfortunately, he was slightly brain-damaged.' She halted her explanation for a second or so, as if contemplating what to say next, and then continued. 'They wanted to put him in a home, but I thought it was best to keep him with me. He does a good job in the garden and he likes doing that.'

Jessica did not respond straight away. She was still trying to puzzle out what she had just heard regarding herself. Her thoughts provoked another question.

'What you've just told me answers some questions, but there have been other incidents that seemed to be a bit odd.'

'Tell me, dear,' Laura urged.

Jessica thought for a moment. 'I know now where the voices came from, but what about being locked in the cellar and being left under a tree with a noose around my neck? That was quite a distance from the house.'

'Mags carried you there.'

'Mags carried me there? But I was asleep. How come I didn't wake up?'

Laura took her time to answer. When she did there was a sadness in her voice. 'I was hoping I wouldn't have to tell you this, but you see Sophie was putting the sleeping tablets Dr Foster prescribed for you into the cocoa she prepared for you at night. I caught her doing it.'

Jessica was aghast. 'What on earth did she do that for?'

'The stupid woman thought she was helping you.'

'I see.' It was the only reply Jessica could summon up. What

Laura had been relating to her was almost unbelievable. It was like something out of a novel or a film. But something was still bothering her.

'What you've told me explains a lot, but there is one more thing that's puzzling me.'

'Oh? What's that?'

'What about my accident with the car? Did Mags have something to do with that as well?'

Laura responded quickly. 'No, dear. It happened to Neil as well a day or two ago. He had to have the car repaired. He told me so on the phone this morning.' She gave a little smile. 'He's going to see Mr Judd when he gets back tomorrow.'

Jessica reacted quickly to this latest remark. 'Tomorrow? Neil's coming back tomorrow?'

Laura seemed surprised. 'Hasn't he told you?'

'No,' Jessica replied. She thought, yet again I'm the last to know what's happening. It was something else to bring up with Neil later.

Laura broke the brief silence between them. She placed the cup on the table and dropped her hands onto her lap. She looked at Jessica. 'Now I've told you everything, I feel much better.' Almost as an afterthought she remarked again, 'I don't know how you'll ever be able to forgive me.'

'Thank you for telling me,' Jessica replied in a low voice.

After another few moments of silence Laura asked, 'Your friend is coming to take you home, isn't she?'

'Yes. The day after tomorrow.'

Laura looked at her sadly. Her voice was almost pleading. 'Jessica, I know how you must feel about what's happened, but I'm wondering...' She hesitated. 'I'm wondering if you'd consider coming back to stay with us until your friend comes to collect you. We'd love to have you.'

Before Jessica could say anything, she pleaded again. 'Please consider my suggestion.'

Jessica did consider the suggestion. She still did not know what to make of Laura's revelations, but the fact was that she knew that she could not stay forever where she was, not doing anything except being pampered. If she returned to the house tomorrow, Neil would be back, and the day after that Natalie would be coming to take her home to London. She thought she could probably survive the twenty-four hours she would be there.

After keeping Laura waiting for an answer for several seconds, she said, with a bit of a smile, 'As long as I can get a decent night's sleep.'

Laura's reaction was instant. She clasped her hands together and broke into a smile. 'Oh, thank you, Jessica. We'll look after you, I promise, and try to make up for everything.'

Jessica simply smiled back.

Laura suddenly looked at her watch. 'Goodness! I must be getting back. I've left Mr Judd outside waiting for me.'

'Why didn't you bring him in?' Jessica exclaimed. 'I'm sure they would have given him a cup of tea.'

'He didn't want to come in. He told me he was going to use the time to do some paperwork and make some telephone calls.'

Jessica was not expecting the next move. Laura stood up, moved over to her and put her arms around her. 'Thank you for being so understanding.'

Jessica smiled again but said nothing.

'Now I really must go. Thank you for seeing me.' Laura let go of her and headed for the door. Just as she was about to leave, she suddenly stopped and faced Jessica again. 'What about tomorrow, Jessica? Shall I ask Mr Judd to pick you up?'

'That would be very helpful. Perhaps about ten in the morning?'

'Ten it is.' Laura was already opening the door.

Jessica suddenly remembered something. 'Gosh, I need to pay for my stay here and I've got nothing with me to pay with. No credit card, no cheque book.'

Laura put up her hand as if to silence her. 'Think no more about it. Leave it to me. It's the least we can do, given the circumstances.'

'But… But…' Jessica stammered, but Laura was already gone with a wave and a smile.

Jessica leapt up and was going to rush after her, but she changed her mind. She would sort out the payment after she had spoken with Neil.

She sat back in the chair. Laura's visit had been both unexpected and enlightening, but she still found it difficult to relate to. While Laura's explanations appeared to be sincere and provided answers to the various incidents she had experienced over the last few days, in some ways they appeared to be too simplistic and did not account for everything. She guessed that she would never know any more. She felt that it was a good thing that her stay with the two sisters was coming to an end. One more day, and she would be able to put it all behind her.

She was also pleased that she would soon be leaving the clinic. She had enjoyed being able to relax and be cared for, but now it was time to pick up the threads of her life again. She wanted to return to being a working woman and to sort out what to do with her legacy. In the last few days she had hardly thought about either. Then there was her marriage to think about. She and Neil would have to sort out a number of problems.

Unfortunately, she was unaware of the changes in her life that were soon to take place and over which she would once again have no control.

Chapter 38

Jessica was up early the next morning. After collecting her few things together and packing them in the bag that Marie had brought, she went down to the dining room for breakfast, ate a bowl of muesli and some toast and made polite conversation with the two other patients there.

During her three days at the clinic she had got to know several of the other people who were staying there. She had also learnt more about the establishment. Apparently it was a private venture run by Dr Jackman that specialised in short periods of rest and recuperation. There was also a darker side to the clinic. According to one of the guests, a section of the building was devoted to the care of mentally disturbed patients, some of whom were predisposed to violence, sent there by caring relatives who had rejected a state-run asylum. When Jessica heard this, she was reminded of her own initial treatment at the clinic.

Mr Judd arrived on the stroke of ten. Melanie came to see Jessica off and seemed to be sad that she was leaving.

Jessica settled herself in the front passenger seat for the five-mile journey back to the house.

Mr Judd had greeted her on arrival but then appeared to be happy not talking. Jessica tried to make conversation but without a great deal of success. She was a bit surprised when he suddenly asked, 'What's the Spicer Clinic like, then?'

'It's OK,' she replied.

Mr Judd grunted. 'Got a bit of a mental asylum in there, haven't they?'

'Yes, I believe so.' Jessica did not want to go into detail.

Her reply was received with a further grunt from Mr Judd and another pointed remark. 'Folk round here don't think much of the place.'

'Really? I wonder why. I found it very pleasant there.' There was an element of surprise in Jessica's tone of voice.

Mr Judd seemed satisfied and made no further comment about the clinic. For the rest of the journey he just made the occasional remark here and there.

Jessica was surprised when they arrived at the house to find both Laura and Sophie waiting outside for her.

Laura immediately threw her arms around her and kissed her on the cheek. 'Welcome home, Jessica,' she greeted her.

Sophie's welcome was even more pronounced. She took Jessica's hand and whimpered, 'Oh, Jessica, how can you ever forgive us for what's happened?'

Jessica smiled. 'It's over now, Sophie.'

'But we feel so bad about everything,' Sophie sobbed.

Jessica put her arms round her. 'Let's forget about all that. It's in the past.'

'I wish I could,' Sophie replied, wiping away a tear.

Laura intervened. 'Stop it, Sophie!' she snapped. 'Let Jessica be.'

Her words had the desired effect. Sophie sniffed and made no reply.

Laura took control. 'Come on in, Jessica. I'll ask Mrs Benson to make you some coffee.'

Jessica turned to thank Mr Judd for the lift, but he had already driven off. She followed the two sisters into the house.

Once inside, Laura hurried away to the kitchen and Sophie made some excuse and disappeared. Jessica wandered into the library, grateful for its peace and solitude. The desk Neil used when he was working there was still full of paperwork and extremely untidy. Seeing it made her wonder when he would arrive. She would be glad of his company. The thought made her question yet again why he had not let her know himself that he would be back that day. It was something she knew they would have to talk about, and sooner rather than later.

She was interrupted by the appearance of Marie carrying a mug of coffee.

Jessica greeted her.

Marie looked puzzled. 'You've come back here?' she asked.

Jessica smiled. 'Yes. I'm here until tomorrow.'

Marie nodded, but as she turned to leave, she whispered, 'Please be careful, Jessica.'

Jessica smiled again. 'I will,' she asserted.

Marie made no further comment and hurried from the room.

Jessica was a little disconcerted by Marie's warning. It added to the feeling of anxiety she was already experiencing. Still, she was only going to be here for another twenty-four hours and in any case Neil would be back soon. What could possibly happen to her in that short time?

She finished her coffee and took her mug to the kitchen. Mrs Benson was alone there. She greeted Jessica and said it was nice to see that she was back.

Jessica returned the courtesies and left quickly. She made her way upstairs, carrying the bag that contained her things. She needed to empty it so that she could return it to Marie. As she approached the bedroom, she noticed that the door opposite was wide open. Seeing this brought back unhappy memories, and she hurried into her own room.

She took her time and it was almost an hour later that she ventured downstairs again. As she entered the library she was surprised to find Neil there.

'Neil, you're here! Why didn't you come and find me?' burst from her lips.

Neil came over to her, put his arms around her and kissed her. 'I wanted to surprise you,' he replied, grinning.

Jessica moved to sit in a chair. 'Well, you certainly did that. How was the trip?'

'Great.'

'But didn't the car break down?'

Neil looked puzzled.

'Yes,' she continued. 'Laura told me you'd had the same problem I had, with the brakes not working.'

'Oh, yes, of course. I'd almost forgotten.'

'Darling, do sit down,' Jessica begged. 'I want to talk to you.'

Neil took a seat opposite her. He grinned again. 'You have my undivided attention.'

Jessica chose her words carefully. 'Darling, why didn't you call me to let me know when you were coming back? Laura knew. She told me.'

Neil seemed to be in a playful mood. 'Tut, tut. Naughty Laura. It was supposed to be a surprise.'

'A surprise?'

Neil nodded. 'Absolutely. I intended to surprise you by picking you up at the clinic, but you had other arrangements in place.'

Jessica felt deflated. She had been upset when she learned that Neil had contacted his sister but ignored her. Now he had offered a plausible explanation and she felt rather silly. 'Oh, I see. I'm sorry,' was all she could manage.

Neil became more serious. 'I sense you want to talk to me about something,' he remarked.

'Yes. I'm unhappy about the way I ended up in the Spicer Clinic. It was all arranged behind my back.'

Neil shook his head. 'Not really...' he started to reply.

Jessica could not contain herself. She jumped in before he could continue. 'Do you know what happened to me?' she demanded. Without waiting for an answer, she continued. 'I was dragged from the house in my nightgown, strapped down on a trolley, carted off to the clinic and then bathed like a baby before being locked in a padded cell.'

She paused and waited for him to absorb her words.

He took his time to reply. 'Poppet, you've got it all wrong.'

'Wrong? How?' she retorted.

'Let me explain.'

She waited.

There was a pause before he continued. 'What happened to you was not arranged by me. It's quite true that earlier on I had a word with Jim Foster about you spending some time there, to get away from things and rest up a bit. I was worried about all the things that you were reporting were happening to you. But it was understood that the decision to go there had to be yours.'

Jessica felt a bit deflated. Neil's explanation appeared to be sound. She was still pondering his reply when he spoke again.

'As to all the things that were happening to you, I can only apologise that I didn't take as much action as I should have. I'm sorry you experienced all that from my own family. I never suspected that Mags was up to it.'

'But why was the Spicer Clinic told I was violent?'

'That was Laura's doing. She told the clinic you'd attacked Mags. I was angry with her for doing that.'

'It was the other way round. He was the one with a knife,' Jessica replied indignantly.

'Yes, and he injured you, I believe.'

'Yes, here.' Jessica pointed to her chest. She quickly added, 'But it's almost healed now.'

'That's good.'

'And it won't affect my sex life,' Jessica remarked flippantly.

'After your initial experience there, how was it in the clinic?' Neil asked.

'When I demanded to see Dr Jackman and told him how I felt, they put me in the pampering section.'

Neil nodded. 'I guessed that would happen. When Laura phoned me and told me what she'd done, I called Dr Jackman and put things straight.'

'Oh,' Jessica wailed. 'I thought it was my charm that changed things.'

Neil laughed. 'I guess it helped.'

Suddenly he stood up. He moved towards Jessica and put his arms around her. 'The main thing is that you're safe, poppet,' he whispered. The next instant they were kissing.

'So that's where you two lovebirds are.' Laura was entering the room.

Neil and Jessica sprang apart.

'Mrs Benson tells me that lunch is ready,' Laura announced.

The three of them made their way to the dining room.

As they walked, Laura pulled at Jessica's sleeve. 'You like sitting in the garden, don't you, Jessica?' she asked.

'Yes, I do,' Jessica replied.

'Feel free to do so. I've told Mags to keep away from there while you're here.' Laura almost whispered the information.

'Thank you,' Jessica replied in a low voice.

Lunch was quite a sociable event. Most of the conversation was between Neil and his sisters, but at one point Sophie asked Jessica what it was like in the clinic. Jessica replied as briefly as she could, saying just enough to satisfy her sister-in-law's curiosity.

After lunch Neil went back into the library. Jessica followed him. As they entered the room, he made for his desk.

Jessica took the opportunity. 'Your desk is a mess. It needs a good tidy up,' she remarked.

He gave a little laugh. 'I know. I'm not the tidiest of workers.'

'You spend a lot of time at that desk,' she pointed out. Then she felt she had to add, 'This was supposed to be a holiday.'

Neil looked at her enquiringly. Then he nodded. 'I know. You've had a rough deal this trip.'

'It's just that you also spend so much time away. You promised me that would change.'

He suddenly took her in his arms and kissed her. 'And it will change. I'll keep my promise. This last trip to Birmingham was to carry out my plan to cut out those trips.'

'Thank you,' she whispered.

They stood there embracing for a minute or two until Jessica broke free and announced, 'I'll let you get on with things. I think I'll go and sit in the garden.'

'Enjoy yourself,' he replied, blowing her a kiss.

Jessica wandered into the garden and sat down on her favourite seat. She felt better now that she had had the time with Neil talking and sorting out one or two things. He had been so open in his explanation of events and she felt sure he would keep his word.

She had been sitting there for about ten minutes when she heard a sound. She looked across the garden and the sight set her heart thumping. Mags was standing there looking at her. As their eyes met, he suddenly turned and hurried away muttering.

So Mags isn't obeying Laura, Jessica thought. Seeing him brought back the memory of the time he had attacked her. Shaken and in disbelief, she decided to go back into the house. If she met Laura, she would tell her what had just happened.

In the hall, she encountered not Laura, but Sophie, who seemed surprised to see her back indoors so soon.

'I thought you were in the garden,' she said, smiling.

'I was, but I think I'll go for a walk now and stretch my legs.'

'Oh. Where are you going?'

Jessica had only just made up her mind. 'Out on the road, just outside the entrance to the drive, there's a sign pointing to a cliff path. I thought I'd give it a try.'

'That's a lovely walk,' Sophie enthused. 'You'll enjoy it. There are some beautiful views. Take your camera.'

'Thank you. I will,' Jessica replied. She dashed upstairs and changed into a stronger pair of shoes, grabbed her mobile and hurried back to the library. She popped her head around the door and called out to Neil. 'Going for a walk.'

'Where?' he asked.

'The cliff path walk.'

'Enjoy it,' he replied, but Jessica barely heard him. She was already on her way.

She left the house, hurried down the drive and turned onto the road. Fifty yards away, she found what she remembered seeing from the car: a gap in the hedge, and a dilapidated sign reading 'TO THE CLIFF PATH'.

She turned off the road and started walking along the well-used path. There were trees and thick undergrowth on either side. After several minutes, it occurred to her that this was rather a lonely place to be walking, secluded as it was. She also realised that it was a much longer route to the sea than the one direct from the house. At one point she had the feeling that she was being followed, but when she turned around there was no one to be seen. 'You're imagining things again, Jessica,' she said to herself.

The trees ended abruptly and she found herself standing on a cliff overlooking the sea. The path stretched out on either side of her. She guessed that in one direction it would eventually lead to the beach where she had been swimming. The view was spectacular. She was standing very high above the water, and she could hear the waves pounding on the rocks far below.

For several minutes she stood there taking in the view. She attempted to take a photo with her mobile, but came to the realisation that although the view was pleasant to the eye, the camera would only produce an uninteresting picture of the sea.

She was about to replace her phone in her pocket when suddenly she was propelled forwards. She tried desperately to prevent herself from hurtling over the edge of the cliff, but the next instant she was falling. The phone flew out of her hand and a scream left her lips. She was briefly conscious of hitting something before blackness overtook her.

Chapter 39

Consciousness returned slowly to Jessica. Her eyes opened and focused on some curtains waving slowly in a breeze. She tried to puzzle out where she was, but weariness soon took over. She gave up the effort, and her eyes closed again.

The next time she woke up she was a little more alert. The room she was in was plain and white. She could see sunlight coming through a window and again the curtains moving gently. She was lying in bed, propped up with pillows. But why could she not move properly?

Slowly her memory came back. She could recall standing on top of the cliff, and her scream as she fell. She could remember hitting something, but nothing after that.

Her thoughts were interrupted by the opening of a door. A nurse entered the room. She came to Jessica's bedside and looked down at her.

'Oh, you're awake. Welcome back,' was her cheery greeting. 'How are you feeling?'

Jessica struggled to speak. Her mouth was dry and her throat felt rough. 'Where am I?' she managed to get out. Her voice was hoarse and unlike her normal one.

'You're in hospital. You've had an accident.'

Jessica took a few seconds to take in the information.

'Do you remember what happened to you?' asked the nurse in a quiet soothing voice.

'I fell off the cliff,' Jessica managed to croak.

'You've broken your arm and your ankle, and you've hit your head,' the nurse explained. 'But we'll look after you. You'll be as good as new in no time.'

Again Jessica took some time to register what the nurse had said.

'Would you like a drink?' The nurse was holding a glass of orange liquid. Orange? Whatever it was, Jessica wanted it. Her mouth and throat were so dry.

The nurse held the glass and helped her drink. Her mouth began to feel better.

'Now rest. I'll be back soon. If you want me, press this.' The nurse placed an emergency button close to Jessica's free hand.

Once the nurse had left the room, Jessica took stock of her situation. One arm lay across her chest in plaster. Her ankle was also in plaster, and when she lifted her hand to her head she could feel bandages.

She had no compulsion to move from the position she was in. She just lay there and dozed, and the hours slipped by. At one point a young doctor entered the room and stood beside her bed.

'How are you feeling?' he asked.

'A bit battered,' Jessica managed to reply.

'Do you know what happened to you?'

'I fell off a cliff and broke my arm and my ankle.'

'You also have a mild fracture of the skull. You were unconscious for three days.'

'Three days?' Jessica could not quite comprehend.

'Yes. You're very lucky. You must have a very thick skull.'

Jessica tried to adjust to what the doctor had said. Three days. She had been unconscious for three days.

The doctor did various tests and then departed. The nurse came by a little later and helped her eat some food, but otherwise the day slipped by with Jessica dozing most of the time.

The following day she woke up to find that she was much more alert. She managed to eat some breakfast and a nurse helped her have a wash. As the day passed she began to wonder why nobody was coming to see her. Where was Neil, or for that matter Laura? Did they even know where she was? Surely they would have been told about her accident? She felt lost without her mobile phone, which must have disappeared into the sea when she fell.

It was late in the afternoon when a nurse came into her room with some information.

'There's someone in reception asking to see you. Do you feel strong enough to have a visitor?'

'Yes, I think so.'

The nurse departed and Jessica waited anxiously. Who was coming to see her? Neil? Natalie? Or perhaps even Laura? She was wrong. When the nurse returned she was accompanied by a worried-looking Marie.

'Jessica, how are you? I just had to come and see you. They told me you'd regained consciousness.' She looked anxiously at her.

Jessica did her best to raise a smile. 'I'm still in one piece,' she replied.

'But you're injured.'

'Yes. I've got a broken arm and ankle and apparently I've also got a fractured skull.'

'Does it hurt?'

'A little. But it could be worse.'

'You're very lucky. The cliff is eighty feet high at that point, and there are rocks at the base that are covered by water at high tide.' She paused. 'The emergency services had a job to rescue you.'

'I'm very grateful they did,' Jessica replied softly.

'Does talking tire you?' Marie asked, concerned.

'Not really, but my voice is still not up to full strength.'

'I've brought you some goodies,' Marie announced, holding up a bag. Diving into it, she produced a bottle of juice and a huge bunch of grapes.

'I couldn't resist the grapes. They're delicious. Oh, and I thought you might find this useful.' She held up Jessica's toilet bag.

Jessica was ecstatic. 'Oh, Marie, you're an angel. Thank you.'

Marie sounded serious as she asked, 'Has Neil been to see you?'

Jessica wondered why she would ask that question. 'No,' she replied.

Marie did not respond immediately.

Her silence worried Jessica, whose fears were coming to the fore. 'What's happened? What's the matter?' she asked anxiously.

Marie hesitated. When she replied she was clearly concerned. 'I don't want to worry you Jessica, but Neil disappeared the morning after your accident.'

'The morning after?'

'Yes. I thought maybe he would have contacted the hospital.'

'Have you heard where he went?'

'No, but something's not right. Laura's in a foul mood and Sophie's dabbing her eyes every few minutes.'

Jessica was alarmed. 'Oh, no… Something must have happened to him!'

Marie shook her head. 'No, it's not like that. I heard Laura talking on the phone to him yesterday.'

Jessica was silent. One big question was on her mind. Why hadn't Neil come to see her or been in touch with her?

'Don't worry,' Marie said. 'I'll keep my ear to the ground, and if I hear anything I'll let you know.'

'Thank you,' Jessica replied.

Marie glanced at her watch and made a bit of a face. 'They told me I could only see you for a short time and I have to report for duty soon anyway, so I guess I'd better be going.'

'Thanks awfully for coming to see me,' Jessica replied 'and thank you for bringing everything.'

'A pleasure. Oh! I almost forgot. On the day after your accident, a friend of yours turned up at the house.' Marie looked at Jessica as if to make sure that she understood what she was saying. 'I don't think Laura gave her a very good reception.'

'I think I know who that would have been. Thank you for telling me.'

After Marie left, Jessica went over and over what she had said. It brought up questions for which she had no answers. Where was Neil, and why hadn't he been in contact with her? On top of that, what had Natalie – if it was Natalie – thought of the reception she had apparently had from Laura? She hoped the next day might produce some answers.

When the doctor came to see her the following morning, he announced after checking her over that the bandages could be removed from her head. She waited anxiously while the nurse carefully cut them off. The doctor scrutinised the wound and announced that it was healing well and that it did not need to be re-bandaged. He added that some tests would be required so that he could check on her progress.

Jessica waited patiently until the nurse and the doctor had left the room, and then, with the aid of a crutch she had been given, made her way slowly to the mirror. The first glance was one of shock and despair. One side of her head was completely devoid of hair. A red scar could clearly be seen.

Jessica stared at her image. 'Oh, no…' she let out. The sight of her half-bald head made her want to weep. She struggled back to the bed and lay down. Her beautiful hair had been ruined. She struggled with that thought for a little while and then logic crept in. 'Jessica, get a grip of yourself,' she said to herself firmly. 'It'll grow again, and you're lucky that's all that happened to you.'

Early that afternoon, following several hours of scans and tests, which the doctors seemed to be happy with, she was sitting in a chair, her leg stretched out on a support frame, when there was a tap at the door. It was one of the nurses.

'I've just had a call from reception. There's someone here

asking if she can see you. She says you know her and she told me to tell you that her name is Natalie.'

A wave of joy swept over Jessica. She could not keep the excitement out of her voice. 'Oh, yes, please! I'd love to see her.'

A few minutes later Natalie entered the room. Clearly full of concern, she looked at Jessica.

'Oh, darling, how are you? I was worried out of my life when I heard what had happened. Your poor head...'

Jessica did her best to smile. 'Well, as you can see, I'm a bit battered. I've got a broken arm, a broken ankle and a fractured skull, but I'm on the mend.'

Natalie still looked worried. 'The hospital wouldn't tell me much because I'm not a close relative.'

'I'm so glad to see you.'

'I wanted to come yesterday, but it was one of those days when I couldn't get away from work.'

'Did you go to the house?'

'Not today, but I went there on the day after your accident to pick you up as we'd arranged and got a bit of a cold shoulder from one of your sisters-in-law. Laura, is it?'

'Oh, how awful... Yes, that would have been Laura. I'm so sorry.'

'I came here, but they wouldn't let me see you. All they would tell me was that you were stable.'

'Well, I'm still in one piece, as you can see.' Jessica managed a little laugh.

'At least you're cheerful about it all.'

Jessica was not expecting Natalie's next question.

'Has Neil been to see you?'

'Not yet.'

Natalie was silent for a few seconds, as if deep in thought, and then she asked, 'How are things between you two?'

Jessica was surprised by the question, almost shocked. Her reply was short and sharp. 'Fine.'

Natalie scrutinised her for a few seconds, as if she was analysing the answer, and then she spoke again. 'Jessica, you know that you can always talk to me about anything. Remember, I'm on your side.'

'Yes. Thank you.'

'Did Neil say anything to you about his previous life? I mean, before he met you.'

'Not really, except that he was a bachelor.' Before Natalie could respond, Jessica asked, 'But why are you asking all these questions about Neil and me?'

Natalie looked at her sadly. 'I hate to have to tell you this, but Neil is already married.'

'What? You're not serious!' The suggestion was too ridiculous even to consider.

'It's true, Jessica,' Natalie said softly.

Jessica felt a mixture of shock and amusement. 'OK. Tell me more.'

'Neil goes to Paris quite a lot, doesn't he?'

'Yes. For his job.'

Natalie shook her head. 'Not for his job. To see his wife. She lives in Paris.'

'It's almost unbelievable!' Jessica could hardly comprehend what she was hearing. 'How did you find out?'

'From Graham. He suspected it from the start.'

'And how did he know?'

'Through his job. He has access to all kinds of information.'

'I wish he'd said something to me about it instead of allowing me to be taken in.'

Natalie rushed in. 'Don't be too hard on Graham. He cares about you a lot, and he wanted you to be happy with Neil. He only found out Neil was already married a few days ago.'

Jessica was silent for a while, doing her best to absorb what Natalie had revealed. In one respect it seemed all too fantastic to be credible, yet at the same time it did answer quite a lot of questions that had been bubbling around in her thoughts.

Suddenly she said, 'I guess I've committed bigamy or something. You can end up in prison for that, can't you?'

Natalie shook her head. 'No, Jessica. You're the innocent party.'

'What about Neil?'

'He'll be prosecuted for bigamy and if he's convicted he could receive a custodial sentence.'

Jessica was silent again.

After a minute or so Natalie said, 'I'm so sorry to bring you such awful news. I hope I haven't upset you too much, particularly when you're trying to recover.'

'It's a big shock, but I must confess that I was already beginning to think something was wrong.'

'You couldn't have known he was already married,' Natalie stressed.

'It was all too quick,' Jessica mused. She hurriedly added, 'Getting married to Neil, I mean.'

'You thought you were both in love and you did what you thought was right at the time.'

'I guess I'm just not the marrying kind,' Jessica observed wryly.

'Rubbish. You've just had bad luck, that's all,' Natalie declared firmly.

Jessica made no reply. She was still trying to come to terms with Natalie's revelation.

Natalie changed the subject. 'What's it like in here?'

The question jerked Jessica out of her thinking. 'It's fine,' she replied. 'The nurses are kind. I don't know how I came to have my own room, though.'

Natalie gave a little smile. 'Graham and I had you moved to the private wing of the hospital.'

Jessica was instantly fully alert. 'You mean you're paying for me?'

Natalie grinned and nodded.

Jessica felt embarrassed. 'I'll pay you back, I promise.'

Natalie grinned again. 'That can be sorted out later.'

'But—' Jessica protested.

Natalie cut her short. 'When do you think you'll be discharged?'

The question made Jessica change her focus. 'In a few days, I think. They're quite pleased with my progress.'

'Good. When you're ready, let me know, and I'll come and collect you. Will you be able to phone me?'

'Yes. I can ask the hospital to do that for me.'

'Good.' Natalie looked at her watch. She looked at Jessica enquiringly. 'Darling, I should really go soon. It's a long drive back. Would that be all right?'

'Yes, of course. I'm just happy that you came.'

'I'm so sorry about the news I brought. Will you be OK?'

'I'll be fine.'

Natalie stayed a little longer and then they said goodbye.

Left on her own, Jessica went over their conversation. It had been quite an afternoon. Prior to her friend's visit she had been a married woman. Now it seemed that she was the victim of a bigamist. She went over and over the period of her marriage, looking for incidents that could have alerted her to the reality of the situation. Had she been too complacent, too accepting of Neil's absences? What would happen now? The more she thought about things, the more questions came up. There were not many answers.

She had been quite shocked to learn that Natalie and Graham were paying for her private suite at the hospital. Good old Natalie, she thought. Just the sort of things she would do. As for Graham, it was very sweet of him to think of her, though no doubt Natalie had instigated everything. She would certainly pay both of them back.

There was not much she could do about anything for the time being except concentrate on getting better. She leaned back on the pillows and tried to rest, unaware that the next day would bring even more disturbing information.

Chapter 40

The following morning Jessica woke up early. She had managed to get up, have a wash and be ready and waiting for breakfast before a nurse appeared. She felt pleased with her efforts to look after herself and was getting used to the crutch, which was going to be part of her life for a while.

It was while she was in the bathroom looking at her reflection in the mirror and contemplating what remained of her hair that she made a decision. She waited until after breakfast, and when Jean, a particularly kind and friendly nurse, appeared, she made a request.

'Could you help me?' she asked.

Jean was immediately attentive. 'Of course, dear. What's the problem?'

Jessica grasped a fistful of her remaining hair. 'I want this off.'

Jean was horrified. 'But if that's removed, you'll be completely bald,' she stressed, looking quite concerned at Jessica's request.

Jessica was unperturbed. 'I know.'

'But what will your husband think?'

Jessica gave a hint of a smile. 'I don't think he'll be bothered,' she replied.

'Some men don't like a bald woman,' Jean countered.

Her efforts to dissuade Jessica had no effect.

'I still want it done,' Jessica said firmly. 'At the moment I look like a "before and after" advert for hair restorer or something.'

Jean shook her head. 'I really don't think I should do it,' she said doubtfully.

'Please do this for me. It looks ridiculous as it is.'

Seeing that she was fighting a losing battle, Jean reluctantly gave in. 'OK, but don't blame me if it goes wrong,' she said glumly.

'I'll make sure you're not held to blame in any way.'

'I'll go and get what I need,' Jean replied, with a bit of a sigh.

She disappeared for a few minutes, returning with the necessary tools. She pointed to a convenient chair. 'Sit here,' she instructed.

Jessica sat with her leg propped up and her eyes closed, listening to the snip-snip of the scissors, followed by the gentle rasping of a razor. She was surprised at how quick the operation was.

'That's it,' Jean announced, already starting to clear up the remains of Jessica's hair.

Jessica thanked her profusely.

As soon as the nurse had disappeared, she headed for the bathroom and looked in the mirror. A strange, bald woman looked back at her. Her head felt light and strangely cool. I've done it now, she thought. Now to deal with the consequences.

Not long afterwards the doctor came to see her. After doing the usual checks, he made the announcement she had been waiting for.

'I think we can discharge you now.' He suddenly smiled at her. 'That is, unless you want to stay with us a bit longer.'

Jessica shook her head. 'It's very nice here, but I really do need to go home and pick up the pieces.'

The doctor nodded in agreement. 'Don't try and do too much at first,' he warned.

'I won't.'

When he had departed, Jessica began to think of ways to contact Natalie. Perhaps the best solution would be to wait until the evening and ask reception to call Natalie at home.

Halfway through the morning, Marie appeared with Jessica's suitcase. Her first reaction at seeing Jessica's bald head was to let out a gasp. 'Jessica! What happened to you?'

Jessica smiled. 'I had it cut off so that it will grow again evenly.'

'Gosh! You're brave. I don't think I could do that.'

Jessica changed the subject. 'It's really nice of you to come and see me again.'

'I thought I'd better tell you my news,' Marie replied. 'I'm no longer working at the house. Laura told me they couldn't afford to employ me any longer.'

'You've been there quite a while, haven't you?'

'Two years. But I'm not bothered really. There's plenty of work for me at the pub, and at the end of this year we're moving to the coast. My father's bought a hotel and I'm going to help run it.'

Jessica was about to reply when Marie spoke again. 'Mrs Benson is going to leave as well.'

'Gosh! What will Laura and Sophie do without you two?'

Marie grinned. 'They'll have to do everything themselves, I guess.'

Jessica pointed to her suitcase. 'Why did you bring me this?' she asked.

'I thought you'd like some of your things here. I hope I did the right thing.'

'You did absolutely the right thing. I don't want to go back to that house again.' She hesitated and then continued. 'I found out only yesterday that Neil is already married.'

Marie looked aghast. 'But that's awful! Poor you!' she exclaimed.

Of course Marie wanted to know more details. Jessica told her enough to satisfy her curiosity, but limited things as much as she could. She guessed the story would soon be common knowledge anyway. Somehow it no longer mattered.

Marie's next question was easier to deal with. 'Any idea when you'll be leaving here?'

'They told me this morning I can go home, but I have to arrange transport back to London.'

'I don't think I'd be very good at driving in London…'

'There's no need. My friend Natalie will pick me up, but I have to try and contact her.'

'Let me do it.' Marie already had her mobile out. 'Give me the number.'

Jessica seized the opportunity, but there was no answer.

Marie offered to keep trying, but Jessica decided to leave it until the evening.

Marie stayed chatting with her for over an hour. Before she left, she asked Jessica to keep in touch. Jessica asked her to lift her suitcase onto the bed to make it easier to take things out, hampered as she was by her injuries.

Later that day, when Jessica was sitting quietly in a chair with her leg propped up, Jean came in looking worried.

'There are two police officers here asking to see you,' she announced anxiously.

'It's OK. Let them come in,' Jessica replied with a smile of reassurance.

The nurse disappeared and returned a couple of minutes later with two officers in plain clothes.

The older of the two introduced himself and his colleague. 'Good afternoon, Mrs Atkins. I'm Detective Sergeant Anderson and this is Detective Constable Baker. I hope you're well on the road to recovery and you feel strong enough to talk to us.'

'Yes, thank you,' Jessica replied. 'I'm feeling much better. The doctor says I've made good progress and can go home.'

Sergeant Anderson smiled. 'That's good to hear.' He returned to business. 'Mrs Atkins, we would like to ask you some questions about your accident and take a statement from you.'

'Yes, of course,' she replied, 'but there's not much to tell.'

He pulled up a chair and glanced at his notes, while his colleague sat down at the table, pen at the ready.

Sergeant Anderson began. 'Mrs Atkins—' He stopped abruptly. 'Is it all right if I call you Jessica?'

Jessica gave a little smile. 'Yes, of course.'

He gave a quick glance at his notes again. 'Jessica, it's been reported that you fell off a cliff. Can you enlarge on that?'

She thought for a few seconds. 'It was very odd. One minute I was looking at the sea, trying to take a photograph with my phone, and the next I seemed to be propelled forward off the cliff.'

'Do you have a history of vertigo?'

'No. Nothing like that.'

'Did you see anyone nearby?'

'No… That is, I had the feeling that somebody was following me on the way to the cliff, but I thought I was imagining things.'

'But you didn't see anyone.'

'No.'

Jessica was puzzled by the next question.

'How do you get on with your sisters-in-law?'

'Fine.'

'But recently they arranged for you to be taken to the Spicer Clinic.'

'Yes, but that was due to a misunderstanding.'

'Can you explain?'

'Mags, Laura Atkins' son, forced his way into my bedroom one morning and attacked me with a knife. Laura thought I'd attacked him. That's how I ended up in the clinic.'

'Did you get on well with Mags?'

'I had practically nothing to do with him. He always stared at me in an odd sort of way, but he never said anything. It was quite unnerving at times.'

Sergeant Anderson changed tack. 'Did anything else happen during your stay with your sisters-in-law?'

For a second Jessica was in a quandary. Should she tell him about the unsettling experiences she had had during her stay at the house? In the end she decided to. 'Well, some strange things did happen to me there,' she began. She hesitated.

The sergeant prompted her. 'What sort of things?'

Slowly and methodically Jessica related everything that had happened, beginning with the whispering and ending with the attack by Mags. She felt obliged to add, 'My understanding, from what my sister-in-law Laura told me, is that Mags was largely responsible for what happened to me.'

'You were told that by Laura Atkins?'

'Yes.'

'When?'

'A few days ago. She came to see me at the Spicer Clinic.'

The sergeant made no response to Jessica's revelations. The constable was busy taking down notes. The next question took Jessica unawares.

'I understand that you recently got married for the second time. Were you aware that Neil Atkins was already married?'

A feeling of gloom came over Jessica. She recovered quickly. 'Absolutely not! He told me he was a bachelor.'

'He has actually been married for five years. His wife lives in Paris most of the time.'

Jessica thought for a second. 'He used to go to Paris quite a lot. He told me it was for his work.' A horrible thought came to her. 'Will I face conviction for being an accessory to bigamy?' she asked.

'Not if you can prove that you were the innocent party.'

So it was as Natalie had told her. The detective's answer still left her concerned, but she brushed aside her worries on that point and asked another question. 'Do you know where my husband is? I haven't heard from him for several days.'

The police officer had a ready answer. 'Our understanding is that he is in London. He has been interviewed by our colleagues in the Metropolitan Police.'

'What will happen now?' Jessica asked.

'Further enquiries will be made, and if there is sufficient evidence against him, he will be charged with bigamy.'

'Will he go to prison?'

'If the accused is found guilty, the conviction for bigamy does carry a prison sentence.'

Jessica was silent. Wave after wave of misery swept over her. A few days ago she had been a wife looking forward to the future with her husband. Now she was the wife of a bigamist, with all the complications that involved. The seemingly indifferent attitude of the police officers only added to her feelings of wretchedness.

Perhaps her despondency was noticed, because the next comment from Sergeant Anderson showed some concern. 'I'm sorry if our questioning is upsetting you.'

Jessica did her best to force a smile. 'It's all right. It's just that the last few days have been a bit traumatic.'

'You've not been married to Neil Atkins very long, have you?'

'No. Only a few months.'

'And how was the marriage?'

This was a question Jessica dreaded having to answer. She thought for several seconds. She tried to be as honest as she could. 'We were very happy at first, but recently our relationship seemed to change. Neil became much more remote.'

'You mean he didn't give you as much attention as previously?'

'Yes, that's right.'

The sergeant cleared his throat as if to ensure he had Jessica's full attention. 'Is it correct that you have recently inherited a considerable sum of money?' he asked.

Jessica was surprised at the question, but she answered quickly, 'Yes, it is.'

'Was this before your marriage?'

'Yes.'

'How well do you know Gregory Patton?'

Jessica was completely thrown by this question. 'Gregory Patton?' she queried. Then she suddenly remembered. 'Oh, yes. I remember now. He was one of the witnesses at our wedding. He's a friend of Neil's. I only met him that one time.'

Sergeant Anderson nodded. The next instant he looked at Jessica intently. When he spoke, his voice was softer, more caring. 'Jessica, from the evidence we have gathered, I have to tell you that we are no longer treating your fall from the cliff as an accident. We believe it was a deliberate attempt to destroy you.'

Chapter 41

Jessica was stunned at what she had just heard. She struggled to make sense of what Sergeant Anderson had told her.

'You mean…' she started. 'You mean somebody wanted to murder me?'

'It looks that way.'

'But why? Why would anybody do that to me?'

The sergeant smiled at her kindly. 'Look at it this way, Jessica. You inherit a lot of money. Somebody who's a bit hard up finds out and decides to marry you. You meet with an unfortunate accident, and under your will that somebody gets all the money.'

Jessica was in a state of shock. She looked at the sergeant in amazement. The reality of the situation was beginning to sink in. After they married, Neil had insisted that they each make a will. She had left everything to him. Now what she had just been told started to make sense, unbelievable as it was.

At last she managed to speak. 'You mean Neil.'

'It looks as if that's a possibility.'

'I just can't believe it. I must have been so naive.'

'It's often the way in these cases,' Sergeant Anderson remarked gently.

'But it was all so cold and calculating.'

'I'm sorry I had to break it to you like this.' The sergeant's tone was quite caring.

Jessica did not respond immediately. She was still struggling to comprehend everything she had just been told. It all seemed to be so unreal, as if the conversation was about somebody else, but there the two police officers were in front of her, calmly suggesting that her husband had intended to murder her – the same husband who had been so kind and attentive when they first met.

After a few seconds she managed to find her voice. 'It's all right. It's just been such a shock to find out that my husband wants to kill me.'

The sergeant nodded. 'Yes, of course. I understand.'

One thing was still perplexing Jessica. She chose her words carefully. 'Can I ask how you found out that my fall wasn't an accident?'

The sergeant glanced at his paperwork again and then looked directly at her. 'We believe we have two witnesses. Two local men were in a boat out at sea, fishing, within sight of the cliff. They saw you standing there and then somebody pushing you over the edge.'

'Did they see who it was?' Jessica cut in.

'Unfortunately not. They were unable to give us an accurate description from that distance.'

Jessica was trying to work out who it might have been. 'It couldn't have been Neil. He was in the house,' she remarked, almost to herself.

Sergeant Anderson had an immediately reply. 'We believe there were other people involved in the plot.'

This was another shock for Jessica. 'You mean Laura, Sophie and Mags?' she asked.

The policeman nodded. 'It's quite possible,' he replied. 'Unfortunately, at the present there is insufficient evidence to bring charges against any of those under suspicion.'

Jessica made no reply. It all seemed to be so complicated.

Sergeant Anderson began to bring the interview to a close. 'That's all we need from you for now, Jessica. We would like you to sign a statement, and we will advise you about any further developments arising from our investigation. How long do you think you will be here?'

Jessica had almost forgotten she was due to leave the hospital. 'I'm hoping to return home to London tomorrow,' she replied.

'We'll need your address and contact number.'

Jessica gave the required details. The constable read the statement out to her, she signed it, and the two men prepared to leave.

Suddenly the sergeant reached in his pocket and pulled out a plastic pouch, which he handed to Jessica. 'I believe this is your property,' he said. 'It was found at the scene of the crime.'

Jessica let out a gasp of delight. 'My phone! I'm lost without it. Thank you so much.'

'I don't know if it'll work.' The sergeant grinned at her.

As soon as the two men had left, Jessica tried out her phone. To her relief it worked, but it needed charging. Fortunately the cable was among the items Marie had brought her.

It was early evening before Jessica managed to get through to Natalie.

'Jessica,' her friend greeted her, 'how are you?'

'I'm OK. I had the police interviewing me today.'

'Oh! What about?'

Jessica took a deep breath. 'Well, it seems my fall wasn't an accident. Somebody was trying to bump me off.'

'What? Do the police know who it was?'

'Well, suspicion appears to fall on the Atkins family, but at present there is insufficient evidence to make any arrests.'

'But that's awful. How do you feel about it?'

'I don't really know. It all seems so unreal. I guess I must still be in shock.'

Natalie snapped into action. 'We've got to get you home. Any news about when you'll be discharged?'

'I've been told I'm well enough to leave.'

'Great! When?'

'As soon as I like. Tomorrow?'

'Fine. I'll come and pick you up. Oh, hang on... I don't think I can make tomorrow... I need to check something. Can I come back to you?'

'We can make it another day.'

'No. Leave it with me. I'll give you a ring back.'

It was almost two hours before Jessica heard from her.

Natalie came straight to the point. 'Darling, I can't make tomorrow. I've got an appointment I just can't cancel or alter.'

'Please don't worry. I can wait another day.'

'No. I've got another idea.'

There was a bit of a pause. Jessica waited to hear what her friend had in mind.

When Natalie spoke next, her voice had a degree of uncertainty to it. 'Look, there's another way.' There was another pause before she continued. 'How would you feel about Graham picking you up?'

'Graham?' Jessica had not imagined that alternative.

'He's quite happy to do it. In fact, he'd love to do it.'

Jessica took her time to answer. Natalie's suggestion was gradually sinking in. The idea slowly caught on. Why not? she thought. It would be nice to see Graham again.

'OK, if he's willing,' she answered.

Natalie's pleasure at Jessica's agreement could be heard over the telephone. 'I'll ring him right away,' she almost squealed. Then the practical side of things took over. 'What time shall we say? Eleven tomorrow morning?'

'That would be fine,' Jessica replied. Since she only had the good use of one arm, that would give her plenty of time to pack her things.

'Eleven it is, then. Leave it with me. I'll catch up with you soon. Bye for now.'

With that, Natalie was gone.

Jessica put her mobile down. She went over the conversation again. She had sensed Natalie's anxiety at suggesting that Graham pick her up. On reflection, she didn't mind at all. After all, they hadn't parted on bad terms. In fact, she realised that she was quite looking forward to seeing him again.

Now that she had her mobile phone back, she took the opportunity to make several other calls. She remembered that Marie would want to know when she was leaving the hospital. Otherwise she might visit again and find her gone. Fortunately, she managed to catch her.

Gwen, her neighbour, would want to know that she was returning to the apartment. She thought she would probably be able to talk to her that evening, and she was proved correct.

Gwen seemed pleased to hear from her. 'Oh, I've been wondering how you're getting on. I didn't think you'd be away for so long,' was her opening remark.

'I thought the same when we left, but things got a bit complicated. I had an accident and broke an arm and my ankle. I've been in hospital.'

'Goodness, how awful! How did that happen?'

'I'll tell you all about it when I get home. I'll be coming back tomorrow.'

'You are brave. Can I get you anything? You'll need some milk – and what about bread?'

Jessica thought quickly. 'Milk and bread would be lovely, if it's not too much trouble. I've got most other things.'

'Leave it to me,' Gwen replied. After a pause, she added, 'It will be so nice to have you back. The house has seemed so quiet with just me in it and not seeing you or Neil regularly.'

Jessica was about to explain something about Neil, but Gwen beat her to it.

'I don't know if I should mention this, but I was really puzzled and worried about something that happened the other day.' Gwen stopped short, as if wondering whether she should say any more. Then she spoke again. 'I hate to ask you this, Jessica, but is everything all right between you and Neil?'

Jessica took a deep breath. This was the kind of question she knew people would be asking. She was trying to come up with a suitable answer, but Gwen continued speaking.

'You see, Neil came here on his own and it looked as if he was taking away all his things. I spoke to him and he said he was moving out. I didn't like to ask questions.'

Jessica thought for a second before answering. How best could she satisfy Gwen's curiosity? Her answer was short and evasive. 'It's true, Gwen. Neil and I have parted. The whole thing is quite complicated. I'll explain in detail when I get back.'

'Oh, I'm so sorry…' Gwen's voice trailed off.

Jessica chipped in. 'Don't worry. I'm still around. I'll tell you all about it over a cup of coffee.'

Gwen appeared to be reassured. Jessica wound down the conversation and said goodbye.

She put her phone down, leaned back in the chair and went over the day's events. It had been quite an ordeal, particularly the visit of the police and their disturbing revelations. The highlight of the day, her forthcoming discharge from hospital, had almost been masked by everything else. And then there had been the call from Natalie and her concern about whether Jessica would allow Graham to pick her up. She had felt unable to tell Natalie that in fact she was delighted with the arrangement. She was looking forward to seeing him again.

Chapter 42

Graham Scott brought his car neatly to a stop in the hospital car park. He glanced at his watch. There were ten minutes to go before the arranged pick-up time. It would be better to wait a short while before going in. He didn't want to arrive before Jessica was ready.

At the start of the journey he had been on top of the world, keen to meet her again. Now he was actually at the point of seeing her, doubts and anxiety were beginning to creep in. Suppose she wasn't all that happy to see him? It was a possibility. By now she must know that her ill-fated marriage to Neil Atkins was over. She might think that he was trying the same tactic to get his hands on her money. The guilt of how his obsession with his job had caused the end of their marriage still preyed on his mind. If only he had not been so insensitive, they would no doubt still be married, and Jessica would not have had to suffer her recent terrible ordeal.

He had been pleased when Natalie asked him to pick Jessica up, but now he was apprehensive. All he could do was hope for Jessica to receive him cordially.

He waited until there were two or three minutes to go and then made his way into the hospital. After making the mistake of using the main entrance, he was redirected to the private wing.

A friendly woman at the reception desk checked his credentials and told him the number of Jessica's room. He tapped at the door, and a familiar voice bade him enter.

Jessica had been ready and waiting for him for almost an hour. She had managed to dress in a summer frock, which was easy to put on and did not interfere with her injured arm in its sling. She had a sandal on her good foot, had managed to apply her makeup, and for good measure had included a touch of lipstick. She had intended to wear her sun hat to cover her shaved head, but at the last minute she changed her mind and kept it near her.

She had been wondering whether Graham had changed since she had last seen him, but she need not have worried. He looked just the same as she remembered, with his crop of sandy hair.

He looked at her and smiled as he closed the door. 'Hello, Jessica.'

'Hello, Graham. Thanks for coming.'

'I wanted to.' Might as well be honest, he thought.

'You must have left at the crack of dawn. Would you like a cup of tea or coffee?' Jessica asked, an element of concern in her voice.

Graham shook his head. 'I stopped on the way and had a coffee.'

'Well, at least have a rest for a few minutes,' she urged, indicating a nearby chair.

Graham sat down and looked at her. 'How are you feeling now?' he asked.

She grinned. 'Well, I'm still in one piece, but several bits of me are not functioning too well at present.'

'What's happened to your hair?' Graham had always liked her flowing locks.

Jessica put on a bit of flippancy. 'Oh, that. They had to shave half of it because of my head injury.' She turned her head so that Graham could see the scars. 'I had the rest cut off to match.'

'But—' Graham started to say something, but Jessica had thought of something else to say.

She made a face. 'It's my new image. It should put off any more men who want to marry me for my money. I'm told nine out of ten men don't like bald women.'

Graham grinned. 'And what happens when you meet the tenth man – the one who likes them?'

Jessica gave a little laugh. 'When I meet him, I'll let you know.'

Graham smiled but said nothing. He recognised the signs. He knew that the light-heartedness Jessica was adopting was to cover up the misery and uncertainty she felt. He waited a second or two and then, adopting a softer voice, he asked, 'So, how are you really feeling?'

Jessica was silent for a few seconds. The misery flooded over her. 'I don't really know. Everything has happened so quickly. It was only yesterday that the police told me someone had been trying to kill me…' She paused as the emotions poured in. When she continued, it was almost as if she were talking to herself. 'I feel so stupid. How could I have got myself into this situation? I must have been so incredibly naive.' There were tears in her eyes as she spoke.

Graham had the urge to hug her and calm her, but he was afraid it might do more harm than good. Instead he replied softly, 'You acted in good faith. You couldn't have known what the outcome would be.'

'But Neil's sisters were so nice to me. They treated me like one of the family – yet all the same time they were planning to murder me.' She stopped talking for a moment, deep in thought, remembering. She continued in a low voice. 'And Neil planned it all from the start, yet he pretended to be so loving to begin with.'

'All thanks to Greg Patton.'

'Greg Patton? Oh, yes. I remember. He was the guy at our wedding.'

'And a close friend of Neil's.'

Jessica looked at him questioningly.

'He works for Dinton, Walley & Dinton.'

She understood immediately. She took a deep breath and started to sum up her thinking. 'Now I see. Greg Patton finds out about my legacy and tells Neil. Neil decides to marry me, gets rid of me somehow, and he's a rich man.'

'Graham nodded. 'You've got it. Two nasty characters. Greg Patton would certainly have been in for a handout.'

'After I had been disposed of,' Jessica observed grimly. She suddenly thought of something else. 'Neil's sisters – Laura and Sophie – they were part of the plot as well.'

Graham nodded again. 'Probably.'

Jessica shuddered. 'It's horrible to think of.'

'You were lucky.'

'More than lucky. The cliff I went over is very high. I'm told I hit some vegetation, which broke my fall. If I hadn't, I'd have crashed onto rocks nearly eighty feet below.'

Graham spoke softly. 'I'm very glad that didn't happen.'

Jessica suddenly thought of something that had been on her mind ever since Natalie had told her about Neil already having a wife. 'There's one thing that's still puzzling me,' she began.

'What's that?'

'How was Neil found out? How did it suddenly come to light that he was already married?'

Graham smiled at her. 'You have friends who care about you. They did a little bit of research and put in a word in the right place.'

Jessica now realised what had happened. Graham and Natalie. She owed them a lot. Eventually she would get the full story. She had sufficient information on that point for now.

She looked at Graham and simply said, 'Thank you.'

He grinned in return.

Suddenly Jessica thought of something else. 'There is just one more thing.' She paused for a second, and then continued. 'I met Neil at a party given by Natalie. How did she know him?'

Graham gave a brief smile. 'Natalie, Neil, Greg and I all use the same gym.'

'Oh! I understand now.'

Graham just smiled again. Then he asked, 'Where's Neil now?'

'I don't know. Gwen – you know, my neighbour – told me yesterday that he'd cleared all his things out of the flat.'

'Clearly wants to avoid a face-to-face meeting with you.'

'I don't ever want to see him again after all this.' She paused. 'I must have been such a fool to be taken in by him.'

'Thank goodness he didn't manage to carry out his plan successfully.'

Jessica decided to change the subject completely. She tried to brighten up her voice a little. 'Here we are, you've driven all this way to pick me up and I've hardly even thanked you for coming, to say little of you and Natalie paying for me to have treatment here. On top of that, all we've talked about is me. So how are YOU?'

Graham grinned at her. 'I'm just happy to see you again,' he replied.

Jessica had more questions to satisfy her curiosity. 'What are you up to these days?'

He smiled. 'Not a lot. Still working in the same place. I lead a very quiet life.'

Jessica was still curious. 'What? Do you mean to say you have no women chasing you?'

'No, though there is one I'd like to have chasing me.'

'Why don't you pursue her?'

'I'm not sure if she's still interested in me, and on top of that until quite recently she was tied up with somebody else.'

'Oh, I see. Forbidden fruit,' Jessica teased. She knew now that Graham was referring to her.

Graham laughed. 'Something like that.'

She still had one big burning question. 'Are you still tearing around the world for your job?'

Graham shook his head. 'Not any more. I was promoted last year. I'm in the office most of the time, sending somebody else on the trips I used to make.'

'Good for you.' Jessica could not have had better news.

She was tempted to ask more questions, but she did not want to appear too curious. Instead she changed the subject completely again. 'I'm ready to leave when you are,' she said casually, making a move to stand up.

'Good,' he replied. 'The sooner we start, the better. It's quite a long drive.' He suddenly thought of something. 'I stopped for coffee in a rather pleasant pub on my way here. I thought perhaps we could have lunch there on the way back.'

'That sounds like a good idea,' Jessica responded. 'There's just one thing, though. You'll have to cut it up for me. It's a bit awkward one-handed.'

Graham had already jumped up from his chair. He moved to help her as she struggled to manoeuvre her crutch into a comfortable position. He placed his arm around her for support. 'That's the least I can do for you,' he replied with a grin.

'Thank you,' she murmured. She turned to face him and kissed him softly on the cheek.

The next instant their lips met.

'Let's go home,' she whispered.